What Readers Are Saying About
The Legacy!

"This is an awesome novel. I laughed, I cried and cried some more. I couldn't put this book down. Mrs. Adams did a wonderful job of expressing true and unconditional love!"

"All I have to say is that this book was a great read. It made me cry, it made me think, and made me love romance. Please buy this book. You would not regret it."

"This a wonderful book. I thought it would be your average quick story, but it is actually a beautiful story of belief in self, God, transitions, love, jealousy, and forgiveness. It will make you laugh and cry and be thankful for the blessings you take for granted. This is a story of a full lifetime of commitment and it was very refreshing. It is very true to what we live through in this real game called life. I hope you will take time to explore a really unique and different approach to an interracial relationship."

"This is the most captivating story I have read for a good while. I couldn't put it down."

"Jewel Adams has written a wonderful book that has intertwined many story lines. Just when you think you know where she is going with a story line, she fools you and the story takes an unexpected turn. You had better have a tissue box next to you also. There are several times in the story that you will cry. It has touched my heart in several places by hitting very close to home. She has shown us how through trials and tribulations that we can come to learn unconditional love and learn to forgive, not only ourselves, but others as well, bringing us joy, peace of mind, and helping us find our own true self-worth."

"This is one of the most amazing stories I have ever read. I've never been filled with so much emotion from a book. I'm glad I got a chance to read it. Jewel Adams is an amazing author, who knows exactly how to reach our minds and hearts. I laughed and cried. And I enjoyed every second."

"I could die happy now. This is just the best story I've read in my life!"

"This story is absolutely beautiful. It constantly tugged at my heart, and brought me to tears on numerous occasions. I could not stop reading it. Reading this book helped me understand and appreciate my own life, and helped bring me closer to God."

"I couldn't stop reading! It is truly the best love story I have EVER read. I laughed, I cried, I felt as though their lives was unfolding before me. The writer is so talented. I definitely will recommend this book to everyone."

The Legacy

J. Adams

The Legacy
Fourth Edition Copyright © 2019
Copyright © 2010, 2011, 2013, 2015, J. Adams
Jewel of the West Publishing
All Rights Reserved
ISBN-13: 978-0615502588
ISBN-10: 061550258X

Library of Congress Control Number: 2011910410

For all who were once victims,
But are now survivors.
May you all be blessed.

A higher power has charted the course for my life,
and my feet are set on that path.
Now, I will just be still.
Adagio St. John's journal.

Asheville, North Carolina

I am so tired, I can't move!

Dropping into a chair at one of the restaurant tables, I count the tips I've made for the night. Using a linen napkin, I wipe the remaining beads of perspiration from my forehead, grateful that my workday is over. It had been a very busy shift and I am pretty sure I have done well. After counting my cash and the tips left on credit card receipts, I smile. I have indeed done well, and just as I normally do after every shift, I silently thank the good Lord for blessing me with the money I need. Somehow, I am always able to reach my nightly goal.

After I pay my rent and buy some groceries, I will have a little money left to buy a new pair of shoes, which I desperately need. I need other things as well, but they will just have to wait.

One of my coworkers calls from behind the bar, "Cisely, you need a ride home?" I gratefully accept the offer. It saves me the taxi fare I would have to pay because there are no buses running late at night.

By the time I get to the small apartment I call home, I am so exhausted, I can barely get changed into my pajamas.

Slipping into bed, I turn out the light, hoping my tiredness is a good sign. Maybe I will be able to forgo the usual thoughts that haunt me, no matter how hard I try to keep them away. Maybe tonight I will have some peace. But as soon as I close my eyes, the familiar feelings of loneliness and doubt of my worth fill my heart once more.

Not tonight. I won't feel this way tonight.

Instead, I try to focus my final thoughts on a dream I had a week ago today. In the dream, I sat next a little boy on the bank of a beautiful river. He was young, but his emerald eyes were full of wisdom. He told me that because I have changed my life, new changes will soon come, and I will be blessed with great and marvelous things.

He said that God has a wonderful life prepared for me. And though I will still go through sorrow and great trials, I will one day come to experience joy unlike any I have ever known. He told me these things were promised to me before this life and will only be mine if I remain strong.

I have no idea what those changes will be. I only hope I will be ready for the future and everything that will come with it. I also hope I will be worthy of these wondrous gifts when they do come.

One

Having stuffed my last pair of jeans into a large suitcase, I zip it shut and hope the seams won't burst. It was given to me by a friend because I've never had one of my own. I've never traveled anywhere before to need one, and until now, I never thought I would. After filling the carry-on bag with the few cosmetics and toiletries I possess, I take in my reflection in the large mirror hanging above an old, cracked dresser that until today, held all of my clothes. It has to be the oldest piece of furniture in the apartment.

Studying the brown-skinned woman looking back at me, I smile, but my honey-colored eyes hold a sadness I have never been able to rid them of. People have always told me I have sad eyes. I know it is true, yet they aren't privy the pain behind my eyes. I have never let anyone get close enough. I don't know if I ever will.

Running a brush through the dark auburn hair hanging down past my shoulders, I push it back with a brown headband.

3

I ponder adding a few curls but decide against it. Straightening the collar of the yellow blouse I purchased for this trip, I apply some clear gloss to my full lips, a coat of mascara to my lashes, and a touch of blush to my cheeks. Studying my reflection once more, I decide this is as good as it's going to get.

I have always considered myself average looking, and hard as I try, I just can't see what others say they see when they looked at me. I have been told by the people around me that I am beautiful—that my skin is satiny smooth, my voluptuous figure very trim, and my voice is like silk to the ears. Truthfully, I have never seen any of these things and I can't help but wonder how and why others see them. Pondering this a moment, I deduct that my mind has somehow been trained to think there isn't anything about me that is worth much, and no matter how hard I try to tell myself otherwise, all I ever see are flaws.

Sighing, I sit on the edge of the bed and look around the almost bare studio apartment I've lived in for the past year and a half. A bout of sadness envelops me as I think about my life up to this point, and once again, I begin to doubt my worth.

In my twenty-two years of life, I have seen and suffered things no one should have to. Having been raised by an alcoholic mother and an abusive father, childhood was nothing but miserable for me. From the age of six to twelve years old, when other children were laughing and playing and sharing secrets with their friends, I was a woman-child, barely surviving and telling my secrets to no one. In the afternoons after school when I should have been busy being a child, I was subjected to the screams of my mother as my father beat her. And at night while other children were safely tucked in their beds and sleeping, I was forced to endure the sickening presence of my father in my room as he abused and defiled me.

4

One day my mother finally found the courage to leave her husband. She packed our things while he was working and moved us from Charlotte back to her hometown of Asheville. Unfortunately, the move was too little, too late, for my life had been permanently scarred. And it didn't help that every man my mother moved into our home seemed to think I should be part of the deal.

In the past, I had felt dirty and cheap, but more than anything, I felt alone. There was no one I could turn to and share my painful burdens. Later in life, that loneliness guided me to make decisions that only added to my misery, bringing even more shame upon me.

A single tear slips down my cheek as I remember the days and nights of endless partying, each manic episode filled with drugs, alcohol, and many times, immoral conduct. When I was younger, my father made it his solemn duty to tell me repeatedly that I was worthless and only good for one thing in life. It seemed his comments found a permanent place in my mind and heart. My father had foreseen my future and had helped as much as he could to make that future happen. But I know in the end the choices had been my own, just as the choice to finally change had been.

A heavy melancholy encompasses me as I think back to the day I made the decision to abandon the self-destructive lifestyle. It was a little over a year ago. I had just gotten home from work. I was tired, my feet were sore after working all day waiting tables, and I was looking forward to a tall can of beer and some rest. I had just sat down when there was a knock at the door.

When I opened the door to a braid-wearing teenage girl donning heavy makeup, a dirty mini skirt, and scuffed up high heels—one of them broken—my first words were, "Sorry, no customers at this house."

She gave me a teary smile and replied, "I'm not looking for a customer . . . I'm looking for a way out." She hesitated and then added, "You may not believe this, but I was praying earlier, asking the Lord for help, and a voice guided me to your door."

Warm tears stream down my face as I ponder how my heart had instantly gone out to her. I knew the life she'd lived and what she'd suffered before reaching this point. No, I didn't know *her*; I had never seen her before. But I *knew*, because I had been there, myself.

Stepping aside, I invited her in and listened as she talked, my suspicions about her abusive childhood confirmed. I fed her a meal, invited her to use my shower, and gave her some clean clothes to change into. Taking the tips that I'd made that day from my purse, I called a cab, took her to the bus station, and put her on a bus to Raleigh to go and live with her aunt. When I got back home, I sat on the sofa, closed my eyes and cried. Nothing I had ever done in my life left me feeling as much peace as that one act had.

I immediately threw away every bit of alcohol in the apartment, vowing to never take another drink, pop another pill, or smoke another joint for the rest of my life. I stopped partying and made a commitment to change my life. I was determined to do this, despite family members and friends telling me I would never change. Sadly, there was no support from anyone except the counselor assigned to me when I enrolled in a free substance abuse program. No one in my family, nor the people I associated with would let go of the past. So how was I supposed to? I couldn't escape it because it surrounded me and was constantly being thrown back in my face.

Even now, I still struggle with doubts. I've listened to several motivational talks on learning to forgive oneself, letting go of past mistakes and moving on, but the messages never seem to stick, and in my heart I continue to feel too unworthy to deserve more in life. We reap what we sow, as they say. Apparently, I haven't sowed enough good.

Opening my purse, I pull out a letter that came in the mail three weeks ago. It is from an older woman named Jessica who lives in Salt Lake City, Utah.

I met Jessica Kelly at a motivational conference for women that was held downtown. We sat next to each other and were instantly taken with one another. At the close of the conference, Jessica told me she wanted to get to know me better. Reflex prompted me to ask why—there had to be a hidden reason, of course—but I bit my tongue.

We had lunch together the next day. And throughout that week when I wasn't working, I spent a great deal of time with her and we did many things together, seeing and visiting places in the city that I never thought I would.

Jessica managed to get me to open up a little about my life, something I had never done before. I don't know how she did it. Maybe a deeper part of me *needed* to share, if only to relieve a little pressure. Though I didn't give many details, the little I shared with her brought the poor woman to tears. I hated making her cry, but I appreciated that she cared.

In that week, I grew to care about Jessica a great deal, and I found myself wishing my own mother could be more like her.

How sad that in just one week I developed more of a relationship with the older woman than I ever had with my own mother.

Jessica told me she has always been alone. She never married and it saddens her that she was never blessed with children of her own. And except for the times her nephew comes to visit from Australia, her life is basically a solitary one.

I read the letter again in renewed awe. Jessica invited me to come and stay with her for a while in Salt Lake City. She even sent a plane ticket with the letter, making it harder for me to say no, just as she had known it would. She knows me well. I've never dreamed of going so far away, and to say I am nervous is an understatement. But the excitement of starting over somewhere where no one knows me or anything about my past overrides my nervousness. I re-read the last part of the letter.

Now I know you don't like to feel like you're not pulling your own weight, so before you say no, I just want to tell you I own a women's clothing boutique downtown. One of my sales ladies had to quit suddenly. The position is yours if you want it. It is only three days a week, so we will still have plenty of time to visit and sight see, and of course, shop. We're going to have the time of our lives! It will mean so much to me to have you here, Cisely. More than you could ever know. Call me soon.

Much love,

Jessica.

Hearing the taxi honking outside, I refold the letter and slip it back into my purse. After touching up my makeup, I place the key to the apartment on the counter for the landlord. Sadly, there are no more goodbyes to be said. My mother doesn't seem to care that I'm leaving. Neither does anyone else for that matter, but I have received various opinions on how they think my life will turn out. *"You'll be back,"* my so-called friends told me.

"You're going to be right back here partying with the rest of us. You can never escape where you've been or who you are."

Squeezing my eyes shut, I shake my head to dislodge the negative thoughts. Looking around the half empty room one last time, I grab my bags and leave.

Two

Salt Lake City, Utah

Cutting up the last of the fruit, I put it in a small serving bowl. I have been in Salt Lake for two weeks now, and I finally feel comfortable and settled in Jessica's large and stately home. It reminds me of one of the mansions in Biltmore Forrest, an old and very prominent section of Asheville.

Jessica's home is beautiful. It boasts a large wraparound porch with a swing. There are three levels with hardwood floors and cherry wood doors and molding throughout the house. The kitchen is large and airy with windows stretching to the ceiling.

I love the kitchen. It is one of my favorite places in the house, next to the bedroom I sleep in. If I didn't know any better, I would swear Jessica gave me the largest room in the house. My whole apartment could easily fit into the one room, and that's not including the connecting bathroom.

But the place I love best in the house is the living room, because in its center sits a beautiful, black baby grand piano. I

11

learned to play the piano in the first grade and had stuck with it through the years. Having developed my singing voice in high school, I fell in love with playing and singing. Later in life, the talent lay dormant for a long time, and now that I have access to a piano, I've picked it up again. It is like reconnecting with a lost love, and I am giddy every time I play.

Everything in Jessica's home is so elegant, it's like I am living in a palace. I have never stayed in a place so lovely, not even close. Still, with all the material things Jessica possesses, she is the kindest, most loving and down to earth person I have ever known, and I feel blessed to be in her home.

"I think that's it," Jessica says, taking the plate of muffins over to the small breakfast nook by the corner windows.

"I think you're spoiling me too much," I tell her as we sit down to eat. Since the day I arrived, Jessica has made every meal special. In the mornings the table is set with everything from fruit, cheeses and muffins, to bacon and Belgium waffles. Lunches are finger sandwiches, meats, cheeses, and luscious pastries. And dinner is always so full of variety, three meals can easily be made from the one. Having grown up poor and standing in government food lines with my mother, and then always having to budget for even cookies as an adult, I am continually overwhelmed with the wealth of food I am now receiving.

"You deserve to be spoiled, my dear."

My smile is guarded. If only I could see the facade of myself no one seems to be able to look past. And I can't stop the negative thoughts from intruding.

If you really knew me and everything I've done, you wouldn't feel that way about me.

12

As if Jessica can read my thoughts, she places a hand over mine. "You deserve everything that's good in this life, Cisely. Truly you do." She pauses, her voice growing softer. "I don't know the full extent of what you have lived through, but you are truly more special than you could possibly know, and I know with all my heart that there are some marvelous things in store for you."

I smile, refusing to let the tears come. I have never felt so much love from someone. I can't count the many hours and agonizing moments I spent as a child, wishing for and needing a mother's love—for someone to hug me and tell me everything would be okay. I squeeze Jessica's hand.

"Thank you for being so good to me," I say softly, swallowing hard at the lump pressing in my throat.

"No need to thank me, dear. That is what this life is all about."

We enjoy a leisurely breakfast, talking about various things. I love the time I've spent with Jessica and have come to learn so much more about her life.

Jessica was born and raised in Melbourne, Australia. When she turned twenty-five, she moved to Salt Lake City to attend college. Her younger sister and two brothers still live in Australia with their families. Though her family comes to the United States every now and then to visit her, the visits she enjoys most are the ones from her favorite nephew, Ingo. At least three or four times a year he pops in for a week-long visit. She cherishes those times.

I noticed several pictures of him in Jessica's bedroom when I first arrived and was surprised by how handsome he is. To Jessica, Ingo is the son she never had, and she loves him very much. I can't help thinking of how fortunate he is to have Jessica as an aunt. However, I am also reaping the blessings of having this loving woman as my friend.

Having finished eating, we clean up and put everything away. Then I quickly touch up my makeup and check my outfit once more before leaving to catch the bus to work. Taking in my reflection, a shy smile curves my lips. A couple of days after I arrived, Jessica took me to the boutique and introduced me to two of the women I would be working with. They were friendly and very welcoming. They gave me a tour of the shop, helped me to get familiar with the place, and went over what my job would entail.

While we were there, Jessica had me try on about a dozen of the outfits she sold there and bought them all for me despite my strong protest. I told her they were too expensive and I didn't want her to spend money on me. I have never been accustomed to people giving me things and didn't know how to accept Jessica's gifts. She simply replied, "My dear, I have more money than I could possibly spend in this lifetime and it makes me very happy to spend it on the people I care about." Then she promptly ended the discussion.

So, whenever I go to work, I'm a walking billboard for Jessica's boutique, but the clothes are so beautiful, I don't mind one bit. Today the springtime weather is comfortably warm, so I've chosen to wear a tan, knee-length, crocheted sundress with a matching shrug and gladiator sandals. The outfit actually looks nice on me. My hair is pulled up in a bun and wispy bangs lay lightly against my forehead. The sunlight always brings out the highlights in my auburn hair, and each time I leave the house, Jessica calls out after me, "You look just like a fashion model, only healthier." I always laugh and wave, figuring I will humor her. I am nowhere near being model material.

14

Jessica continually urges me to drive her car to work, but I insist on taking the bus, just in case something should come up and she needs the car. I have a North Carolina driver license, but I have never owned a car and am used to taking the bus. And the part of the Avenues in which we live isn't too far from downtown, so sometimes I even walk part of the way. Gazing up at the beautiful, elegant old homes is one of my favorite past-times because they remind me of Asheville. Only now I am actually living in one instead of dreaming about it. The fact that I am living in Utah is a dream in itself and I still pinch myself sometimes.

Today I am the first to arrive at the shop. Lifting my eyes to the clear blue sky, I silently thank God for blessing me with this new job and life. I absolutely love working at the boutique. Fashion is still kind of new to me, but it truly feels good to not only sell beautiful clothes, but to wear them as well. I have never owned so many lovely things or worked in a nicer place.

Pulling the key from my purse, I quickly unlock the door. Having opened the store for business before, I know what to do to prepare for the day. I still can't believe Jessica put so much trust in me. When I talked to one of my co-workers about it a few days before, she told me that Jessica is just that way. She loves and trusts many people. To be included in that group is an honor, and I am determined to never let her down.

About an hour after opening the shop, the phone rings. I am always hesitant about answering the phone, but it is an unavoidable part of the job.

"Jessica's Boutique. This is Cisely."

"Hi, it's Wendy."

"Hey. You don't sound good."

15

"I know. I think I've caught the flu. I was going to try and come in, but I can't even stand up."

She really does sound miserable, and having had the flu myself a couple of times, I can definitely empathize. "You just rest and don't worry. I can handle things here."

"Are you sure? You won't even be able to take a lunch break if you're there alone."

"Don't worry about me. I can always have something delivered and eat when I get a chance. You just get some rest and get better. Okay?"

"Okay. I'm really sorry about this."

"It's totally fine. I'll be okay."

"Thanks, Cisely."

"You're welcome." Hanging up the phone, I sigh deeply and gear up to go solo. I actually do feel pretty confident about handling things. Wednesdays are usually slow and I've only had a couple of customers since opening anyway. Besides, if it gets too busy, I can always call Jessica.

I have a sandwich and a drink delivered from the deli down the street and I am able to take a bite or two in between customers. It feels great being responsible for the boutique. And after finishing the final paperwork this evening, I am truly happy about the way the day went.

I call Jessica to let her know how business was and tell her when I will be leaving. She always makes me promise to do this so she will know when to expect me. It helps her to not worry, though I actually love the fact that for the first time in my life, someone cares enough about me to worry. It's nice to know I matter to someone.

"Wendy called in sick today," I tell her. "She has the flu."

"Yes, I know."

"She called you?"

"Yes. She called me this morning after talking with you because she worried about you being there alone. But I knew you could handle it."

Her confident words make me smile. "Well I appreciate your faith in me. I would have been worried if I were you." I almost laugh at the thought of actually owning a business.

Jessica chuckles. "I knew you would do well, my dear. I have complete faith in you."

"I'll be home in a bit."

"You have your cell with you?"

"I do."

"Remember to call me when you are on your way."

"Yes, Mother."

I can hear her laughing as I hang up the phone.

A short while after ending the call, my jolt of confidence slowly fades as the haunting feelings that have become my unwanted companion begin to resurface. I hate not being able to keep my thoughts in the present, and I wish I could leave the negativity behind.

If I could only forget the past and move on.

If I could truly believe it doesn't matter, that none of it matters. Hanging my head, I squeeze my eyes shut.

I have to get over my past. Otherwise, how can I ever look to the future?

Three

Ingo smiles contentedly as he parks the rented gray BMW in front of his aunt's home. He hasn't seen Jessica in about five months and has missed her terribly. He didn't call to tell her he was coming because he loves surprising her, and she is always overjoyed to see him. Turning off the engine, he gets out and hauls his luggage up the front steps.

When Jessica opens the door, she releases a delighted squeal.

"Ingo, my boy! It's so good to see you!" She immediately throws her arms around him and he leans down to accommodate her short frame, soaking in her warm embrace.

"It's good to see you too, Aunt Jessica. I've missed you."

"I've missed you, too," she says, patting his face. "Well, come on in. Let's get you settled. Then you can fill me in on what's been going on with you and the family."

Ingo follows his aunt up to the top floor, then back to the bedroom that has become his second home. Looking around the

19

cozy room, he smiles. *Nothing has changed. It's still home sweet home.* Deciding to wait and unpack later, he places his luggage on the bed, anxious to visit with his favorite aunt. He has always felt a special closeness to Jessica. Not only is she the most down to earth person he knows, she is also one of the few people who never judges him or tries to interfere in his life in any way.

Being thirty years old, a successful photographer and very wealthy, Ingo's family has determined it is time for him to settle down. Everyone he knows seems to be in cahoots with his family in search of a bride for him, with the exception of his best friend who lives in Italy, and they have all done their fair share of matchmaking.

But not Jessica. She understands him better than anyone. She truly knows his heart and the kind of woman it will take to claim it. Sometimes he thinks Jessica knows him better than he knows himself. Still, she never interferes or tries to push her opinion on him, and because of this, Ingo respects her tremendously.

Jessica carries two glasses of lemonade over to the table. "Now, tell me what's been going on with you."

Ingo smiles. "Oh, nothing new really. Same old things. I'm still peddling my photos and dodging matchmakers."

"I don't doubt you are doing wonderfully with your photography. You do well at everything you set out to do, and I'm sure the family wouldn't know what to do if they couldn't play multiple Yentas."

He laughs. "Aunt Jessica, I don't know what would I do without you. You always know exactly what to say to make me feel better about life."

She pats his hand gently. "That's what I'm here for. Now, I noticed you brought an extra bag with you this time. Does that mean I'm going to have a longer visit with you?"

"That's kind of what I wanted to talk to you about." He pauses, pushing a hand back through his wavy hair. "I guess I'm in need of a change."

There is no way Ingo can explain the restlessness he is feeling, and has been feeling for some time now. He needs to do something, but he has no clue what exactly. He has a beautiful home in Australia and life is good, but for some reason, he still doesn't feel settled. "I was wondering if I could stay with you for a while, just until I decide what I want to do."

Jessica smiles but doesn't answer right away. Ingo watches her close her eyes, remaining quiet for a few seconds, and wonders if there is going to be a problem with him staying. Then she opens them and again smiles at him, and he wonders at the sudden twinkle in them.

"I think you staying is a marvelous idea. It would make me very happy."

He heaves a small sigh of relief. At the moment, there truly is no place else he would rather be. Jessica's home *is* home to him, even more so than his own. "Thank you, Aunt Jessica. I'll keep from under foot and try not to be too much of an inconvenience."

"Nonsense," she says, waving a hand. Walking over to the cupboard, she takes down some dishes to set the table for dinner. "You could never be an inconvenience, love. I'm just glad you're staying."

"So am I. It will just be until . . ." Ingo stops speaking as his attention shifts to the woman entering the kitchen.

Jessica turns, a wide smile lighting her face. "Hello, my dear. Come and sit with us." She places a casserole, several side dishes, and a basket of rolls on the table, continuing to smile as the woman approaches.

"Hello," Cisely says, taking a seat at the table, her eyes never breaking contact with Ingo's.

Ingo is motionless, unable to tear his gaze away from her. She is absolutely the most beautiful thing he has ever seen and his hands suddenly itch to hold his camera and capture her on film. He is gawking like an idiot and he knows it, but he can't help it. Continuing to stare, he takes in her every feature. During his years as a photographer, he has taken his share of photos of beautiful women. But none of them hold a candle to the one before him now, even with the slight sadness in her eyes. None have ever come close. And the silky tone of her greeting only adds to her allure.

It is obvious to Ingo that she is surprised by his presence, but he also sees recognition in her eyes. Maybe she has seen one of Jessica's photos of him. Watching her studying him, he wonders what she is thinking and takes a mental account of his features. His hair is a wavy, light brown with blond highlights, and his eyes are a steel gray. Women find him handsome, but this is the first time a woman's thoughts really mattered. He watches her pull her eyes away and quickly glance at Jessica.

Jessica clears her throat. "Cisely, I would like you to meet my nephew, Ingo. Ingo, this is my dear friend, Cisely Matthews."

"It's a pleasure to meet you," he says, standing and extending his hand, smiling as she shakes it timidly. She is tall, he

22

had noticed, maybe five-foot-nine or ten. At six-foot-four, he still towers over her.

"It's a pleasure to meet you, too."

Sighing inwardly and allowing the tone of her silky voice to wash over him, he reluctantly releases her hand and sits back down across from her.

After Jessica pronounces a blessing on the food and they have begun to eat, Ingo asks his aunt, "How do you two know each other?"

"I met Cisely when I visited North Carolina in January." The two women exchange smiles. "We hit it off immediately and spent some time together while I was there. I invited her to come and stay for a while, hoping that she would come to love it here so much, she'd want to stay. She has only been here for a couple of weeks and we've had a splendid time. I feel like I've known her forever."

Ingo turns his gaze back to Cisely. "And how *do* you like Salt Lake so far?"

"I love it," she answers, again meeting his eyes. "Utah is very beautiful, and Jessica has been wonderful, almost like a mother to me. I feel very welcome and fortunate to be here."

"It is I who am fortunate," Jessica says. "I only hope you will choose to make this your home."

Ingo watches the change in Cisely's expression and can almost sense her discomfort at being the center of attention. He wonders if she has always been this way or if it is just his presence. She looks like she is ready to escape, and she has hardly eaten. This is not good. Not good at all. She stands and picks up her plate, her food barely touched.

"Well, I guess I'll leave you two alone to visit."

"Oh, please don't go," Ingo says standing quickly, trying not to sound desperate to keep here there but failing miserably. "Stay and talk with us for a while." There is indecision in her eyes. He doesn't try at all to hide the hopeful look in his, and he senses her warming slightly.

"I don't want to intrude on your visit together."

"You're not intruding," Jessica says.

Ingo again notices the twinkle in his aunt's blue eyes, and for the first time ever, he sees her in matchmaker mode. He almost laughs because it is so unlike her.

When Cisely sits down again, Ingo begins asking her questions about herself. Her answers are brief and he gains no insight into her life at all. Glancing at his aunt, it is obvious she has picked up on Cisely's evasiveness as well. He wishes she would open up more and hopes in time she will.

Ingo tells her about his job as a freelance photographer and talks with them about his two older brothers and the sheep station they own and run together. And once again, he has Jessica in stitches as he talks about his parents', as well as his aunt and uncles' matchmaking escapades.

Ingo loves the way Cisely listens to him intently and hopes his own carefree nature won't overwhelm her. He has always been one to embrace life with both hands and she seems more reserved than any woman he's ever met before. But when she smiles, it lights up his whole world and fills him with warmth.

Covering her mouth, Cisely finally muffles a yawn and he accepts that their evening is drawing to a close.

"I think I'll turn in now," she says, standing. She takes her plate over to the sink.

He takes his over as well. "It has been a pleasure visiting with you."

"It's been fun," she tells him. "I'll see you both in the morning." She turns to leave.

"Hey, Cisely." He stops her with a light touch on her arm. "Are you busy tomorrow? I mean . . . if you aren't, I would really like to take you out. That is, if you don't have any plans."

She stares at him blankly. He has caught her off guard again in a major way. "Uh, I have to work. I'm—"

"That won't be a problem," Jessica cuts in quickly. "I was thinking about going into the shop tomorrow for a while anyway. So why don't you two go out and have some fun?"

Ingo watches Cisely's eyes widen and almost feels guilty for putting her on the spot. Almost.

"But . . ." she sputters.

"No buts," Jessica says. "You should get out for a bit. It will be good for both of you."

Cisely finally turns to Ingo and pauses before saying, "Sure. I would be happy to go out with you."

"Great," he says with an easy smile, attempting to keep his excitement level down. Inside he is almost flying apart. "Then I will see you in the morning."

"Okay." She smiles slightly. "Goodnight, Ingo."

"Goodnight, Cisely."

She stares at him a moment longer before finally turning away. "Goodnight, Jessica."

"Goodnight, dear. Sleep well."

Jessica watches Ingo's eyes following Cisely as she leaves the kitchen, warmed by the way things are going between the two. If ever two people produced fireworks, it was those two.

Ingo releases a sigh as he sits down at the table again. "I don't know how it happened, Aunt Jessica, but I'm pretty sure she just took my heart upstairs with her."

"I think I knew that," she agrees, unable to mask the sadness in her voice.

"What is it, Auntie?"

"I have grown very fond of Cisely, and I've been so happy having her here, but she seems to be surrounded by a wall I can't break through no matter how hard I try."

"What do you mean?"

Jessica sighs deeply. "She is such a wonderful person, but I think she's carrying around a lot of unnecessary guilt." She pauses, rubbing her eyes. "From what Cisely has told me, and you as well, she had a pretty hard life being raised by an alcoholic mother and all, but I think there is more to it than she will say. I don't know the full extent of what she has gone through, but I do know this: for some reason she can't seem to let go of her past. She seems to handle her childhood okay, but I think it's the choices she made later in life that she is having problems with.

"She feels unworthy of anything good happening to her, even though that part of her life no longer matters. I think she feels that she will never be good enough." Jessica wipes her eyes again as more tears fill them. "She has never said it, but I can sense her feelings of worthlessness, and at times I can see it in her eyes. That is part of the reason I offered her the job at the boutique while she's here. I told her it was because I knew she wanted to pay her own way, which was true, but I also did it to help her somehow feel better about herself."

Ingo's eyes drift to the kitchen doorway, his thoughts following Cisely upstairs. "How could someone so beautiful and incredible . . . how can she feel that way about herself?"

"I don't know. But I do know she couldn't be more wrong. I've witnessed first-hand how marvelous she is. She just needs to learn to see the good in herself and not dwell on the past."

Ingo silently contemplates his decision to stay with Jessica. At first, he couldn't understand why he had felt such a strong need to be there. He'd even thought about staying with his best friend Adagio in Italy, but it just didn't feel right. Adagio had been disappointed when he decided not to come to Italy but said he understood. He told Ingo he needed to do what he felt was best. At that time, Ingo didn't know *what* was best.

For the next couple of weeks, he still couldn't dismiss the urgent need to stay with Jessica.

Now he understands why.

Pondering this a moment, a slow smile spreads across his face. "I don't know when or how, Aunt Jessica, but I know I am supposed to be here for Cisely. It might sound crazy, but I feel we are meant to be together . . . that I am meant to be here for her."

"I feel it too," Jessica replies, her voice soft. "I feel it too."

Unable to sleep, I stare up into the darkness, still unable to believe I agreed to go out with Ingo. Of course, Jessica hadn't given me much of a choice. I had to accept, and as much as I try to deny it, deep down I wanted to. I haven't dated anyone since leaving the party life, and even before then, it wasn't what you could really call dating because it never went beyond a night. I shudder as the terrible memories come back, and I wonder if I can go through with this.

Ingo is so good–everything I am not–and the last thing I need is to fall in love with him and risk being hurt, or hurting *him*. If I'm not careful, that's exactly what will happen, and the falling part won't be very hard. Already, he has found a place in my heart I didn't want found.

Closing my eyes, I picture his handsome face, hear his thick Australian accent singing in my ears, and see his kind eyes. Taking in the wonder of our visit for a moment, I finally sigh, shaking my head.

He's too good for me anyway, I decide. *Or rather, I'm not good enough for him. He needs someone good and wholesome, and clean. He needs someone pure.*

Someone that is all the things I'm not.

Still, even with all the negative thoughts running through my head, deep within the secret reaches of my heart, love is the one thing I want more than anything–to be loved by someone so deeply and completely that none of the things in my past will matter. I just don't know if it is even possible for me to open up and trust someone enough.

Giving in to the urge to do something I haven't done as often as I should, I get up, slip to my knees by the bed, and silently pour my heart out to God, because I desperately need comfort.

Ending my prayer, I stay on my knees a moment longer before climbing back into bed. Oh, how I long for some peace in my heart concerning the past. Sighing, I make a final request before closing my eyes.

Please help me to get through tomorrow.

Four

My hand is tucked in Ingo's as we enjoy a carriage ride through downtown Salt Lake City. I've always watched couples riding by when walking through town on my way from work and thought how fun it must be, but I never imagined I would actually have the chance to ride in one of the lovely carriages, much less have a man sitting next to me in one. I smile contentedly, relishing the feel of my hand nestled in his, silently musing that my life is starting to be filled with surprises. This one was definitely unexpected.

"Are you enjoying yourself?" Ingo asks.

"I am, very much. Thank for bringing me."

"You're very welcome. And thank *you* for coming out with me today. When I first asked you, I was terribly afraid you would say no. I don't think I've ever been as grateful to my aunt as I was at that moment."

His words fill me with an unexpected emotion that I can't explain. Just the thought of a man actually wanting to spend time with me and nothing else is something I will have to get used to.

"I was grateful for her, too," I say softly, meeting his eyes.

He squeezes my hand gently, holding it between his. Then he presses his arm against mine and I watch him studying the contrast of our skin tones.

"Your skin is very beautiful."

"Thank you." I smile. "My father is dark and my mother is very light. I came out somewhere in between, I guess."

"Well, I think you're perfect."

I look into his eyes, not liking the direction my thoughts are traveling but unable to stop them. "You don't know me well enough to say that." Judging from the seriousness of his expression, he knows I am not referring to the tone of my skin. *Why do I do this?*

"I know. But I would like to know you well enough." His tone is fervent and unyielding.

Looking away, I fix my gaze on a homeless man standing in front of Main Street Plaza, holding a sign asking for help. A few people stop and give him money while others pass him by. I try to focus on something else, anything to divert my attention and keep from looking at Ingo.

I don't know if I can do this. I've never formed an attachment in my life, except for Jessica, but that is different. Emotionally, I don't think I am strong enough to handle *this* kind of attachment. This is unfamiliar territory for me, and I don't know how to let anyone get close.

But I desperately want to.

Ingo must sense my guard going up again. He places a gentle hand on my cheek, urging me to look at him. "Please, Cisely. All I ask is that you give me a chance."

Closing my eyes at his touch and struggling to hold back the tears blurring my vision, one manages to escape and roll down my cheek. "I want to," I confess, my voice a whisper. "But . . ."

"But what?" he presses, caressing my cheek with his thumb. When I don't answer, he finishes the sentence for me. "You are afraid." Sighing, I try to turn away, but he gently catches my chin. "Please tell me what you're feeling."

Returning my eyes to his, I cover the hand he holds to my cheek. "I'm not good at this kind of thing, and I don't want to hurt you."

"You won't, love. I'm going to be living with Aunt Jessica for a long while, so we will have plenty of time to get to know each other more. I promise to take things slow and try not to push you. Just open up to me a little. Let me be part of your life."

"But . . . this is . . ."

"This is what?" I hesitate and he presses. "It's what?"

"This is just too easy."

"What do you mean?"

"I mean *this. Us.*"

A deep furrow creases Ingo's brow. "I don't understand, love."

I sigh, frustrated that my thoughts aren't coming out as clearly as I want them to. They never seem to pass my lips. "I know you don't understand. It's just that nothing has ever been easy for me, and this seems so . . . well, effortless. I just don't know if it can work."

He smiles and I glimpse understanding is in his eyes. "I am not going to give up, Cisely." He caresses my cheek softly. "It will be all right. Just keep your heart open. Try to stay open to me. Can you do that?"

Exhaling deeply, I slowly smile. "I'll try," I answer, marveling at how open he is with his own feelings. I am fast discovering that he is a person who seizes every moment and makes the most of them, and I really like that about him. I also come to the conclusion that trying to fight my growing feelings for him is useless.

As he draws me closer, I rest my head against his shoulder. It is the first time I've ever felt completely safe with a man–the first time I have ever experienced such innocence. And for this moment, I am happy.

Five

We pick a quiet spot at Liberty Park and share a pizza for lunch. Handing me a can of pop, Ingo laughs as I try to shoo away a group of seagulls slowly closing in around us.

"We're not even half done and here they are, ready and waiting for a feast," he says.

"Well, I know these guys eat scraps for a living, but they will just have to wait."

As if they understand my words, the seagulls do indeed back up and wait, drawing a chuckle from Ingo. "Well, I guess they know who's in charge of this party."

"I guess so," I agree, laughing with him.

The weather is amazing today, or maybe it is just me feeling unusually giddy. I won't analyze it, I'm just happy to be outdoors. Having finished eating, I stretch out my legs, lean back on my hands and close my eyes, soaking in the sun's warmth. I smile slightly, sensing Ingo's gaze on me. He seems to enjoy watching me, and my face warms even more because of it.

"You're beautiful," he says softly.

Opening my eyes, I search his face for sincerity and find it immediately. Needless to say, I am not used to this kind of attention, but he seems determined to *get* me used to it.

"Thank you," I finally say.

He moves the pizza box from between us, then scoots closer to me and folds his legs Indian style and I do the same, our knees touching. "Okay. Tell me more about your life. I want to know everything about you."

"No," I mumble, "you don't want to know everything."

"Oh, but I do."

He isn't letting me off that easily. Heaving a resigned sigh, I decide to just get it over with.

Ingo listens as I tell him about the job I left in North Carolina and the people there. I also tell him a little about my dysfunctional family. Going a little deeper, I share with him what it was like being an only child and growing up in a home where my mother was never sober. I tell him of the beatings my mother suffered at the hands of my father and how I witnessed most of them. When I share how I prayed endlessly that God would take us away from all of it, emotion fills his expression. Tears rise in his eyes, causing my own to burn. I blink the moisture away.

"I'm sorry your childhood was so hard," he says.

The snort that escapes me is devoid of humor or amusement. "Watching my mother be abused was hard, but there were other things . . . there were other things that were just as hard."

Ingo keeps my hand between his. "What other things?" he presses gently.

Releasing a slow breath, I allow my gaze to drift away from his. "My father molested me from the age of six until I turned twelve." At my words, pain and anger dominate his handsome features–pain on my behalf. There are no words to describe what his response means to me. He squeezes my hand and my heart accepts his offering of comfort.

"You know," I continue, "about a week after my twelfth birthday, my mother finally took me and moved back to our hometown."

"Too little, too late," Ingo says, his voice hard.

"My thoughts exactly," I mumble.

I know he is waiting for me to say more, but I don't. For a few moments we sit in contemplative silence. He continues to hold my hand, silently absorbing the things I have shared with him. As we watch one another, I marvel that we are together like this. I timidly reach up and touch the soft lock of hair resting against his forehead and smooth it back. Ingo closes his eyes, leaning into my touch.

"Thank you," he finally says, breaking the silence. "Thank you for sharing such a painful part of your life with me." I can tell he knows there is more that I don't say, but he will not ask. Instead he says, "You know you can tell me anything, Cisely."

I nod, grateful for his kindness. "Thanks for listening."

"You're welcome." Raising my hand to his lips, he kisses it softly.

We spend the rest of the afternoon just talking and enjoying our time together. Later on, Ingo takes me out to dinner and we go dancing, which has always been one of my favorite things to do.

I have never enjoyed dancing so much. Going to a place where there is no alcohol or cigarette smoke permeating the air is a new experience for me. I actually come away feeling clean. Ingo promises to take me dancing whenever I want and I assure him I will hold him to it.

By the time we arrive home, Jessica has already gone to bed, much to Ingo's dismay. He'd wanted me to play the piano for him, but he doesn't want to wake Jessica, so we agree to wait. I'd told him earlier about learning to play when I was younger, and how I sometimes used playing as a means of escaping the emotional pain I went through. Jessica had mentioned to him how much she enjoyed my singing and he was looking forward to hearing me. Seeing his disappointment, I promise I will play for him tomorrow when I have some time.

We stay up and talk for a while longer. The day has gone so fast. It feels amazing being with Ingo, to know that he wants to just *be* with me and isn't expecting anything immoral in return. In the past, that was the only thing I knew. Of course, I was different then. I am living a new life now—a clean life—the kind of life I was meant to live all along.

By midnight, I reluctantly decide to go to bed or I won't be able to function at work. The night is ending, and though I love my job, I can't help wishing I didn't have to go in tomorrow.

Ingo walks me to the foot of the stairs. "I've had a wonderful time today, Cisely."

"So have I. Thank you for everything."

"You're welcome." He squeezes my hand. "How long do you have to work . . ." he pauses, looking at his watch, "today?"

36

I laugh softly. "I work until five."

He groans. "I don't know if I can wait that long to see you."

Pressing my hand against his cheek, I smile, warmed by his growing affections. "I'm sure you will be able to find something to do to occupy your time."

"Besides visiting with Aunt Jessica, I can't think of a thing, except . . . maybe swinging by the boutique to see you."

"I would like that."

"Good. It's a date."

He pulls me into his arms and I go willingly, practically melting in his embrace. Drawing back slightly, he slowly lowers his head and timidly presses his lips to mine.

My head is swimming from the warmth of his kiss, my arms automatically moving around his waist as the intensity increases.

Tightening his embrace, he holds me so close, I can feel his heart pounding. I have never experienced anything so wonderful.

Parting his lips from mine and pressing them to my brow, he says, "Cisely, I'm so into you I can't think straight." His voice is husky.

I gaze up into his handsome face. "I feel the same about you." And I truly do. His kiss is the most wondrous and innocent I have ever known. That I am even with someone like him is amazing. I can't deny it. I have fallen and fallen hard.

"So, I'll see you later," he murmurs, pressing his lips to my temple.

"Definitely."

He brushes my lips with another lingering kiss before drawing back. "Goodnight, love. Sleep well."

"Goodnight," I say, not wanting to leave the warmth of his arms. As I turn to go, Ingo's hand tightens around mine. Pulling me back to him, we stand a few moments longer, simply holding each other.

"I never thought this day would come," he whispers. "I never thought this would ever happen to me."

"I know what you mean," I whisper.

We finally part and I slowly climb the stairs, leaving him staring longingly after me.

Six

Ingo spends a few hours at the boutique with Cisely, talking with her when she isn't busy, and just watching her when she is. He loves watching her interact with the customers because she is such a natural, and they absolutely adore her. The more time he spends with Cisely, the more he knows she is meant to share his life someday. Even now, he wants that more than anything. However, they have only known each other for a couple of days and he doesn't want to scare her, so he will continue to take things slow.

At least he will *try* to.

Later in the evening, Ingo takes me out to dinner, then to a show at the Capitol Theater. Afterward, we go for a short walk through downtown. Every moment I spend with Ingo is wonderful and exciting. He is introducing me to a whole new world and I am now doing things I've only dreamed about. To many people, these things may not seem like much, but for me, these activities are everything.

When we finally arrive home, Ingo asks me to sing something for him, and I am flattered and nervous at the same time. Other than in a high school program, I have never performed for anyone, but I did promise him last night that I would. I often think about the music teachers I had through the years in school, and each time I sing or play now, my gratitude for them is renewed.

Sitting at the piano, I am a bit nervous, but as I warm up my fingers and the notes begin to fill the room, I am carried away, my nervousness fleeing. I play an old Natalie Cole tune, my voice soon joining the music.

Discreetly glancing over at Ingo, I find him listening intently, his eyes closed. At the song's end, he opens his eyes and I am warmed by the emotion in them.

"That was beautiful, Cisely!"

"Thank you." Despite being nervous about performing for him, I really did enjoy it, and I am happy he liked it.

"Promise me you will sing for me again."

Smiling warmly, I say, "I promise."

Seven

The following Saturday, Ingo and I go for a long drive up Millcreek Canyon and have a picnic. I love the beauty of the canyon. Some spots remind me of the Smoky Mountains in North Carolina because they are so green. The trees are lush, and a continuous breeze gently stirs the warm air. The temperature is comfortable, the weather perfect.

We have a wonderful time exploring and just being together. I have never been the adventurous type, but Ingo makes every experience exciting. With him, I feel like I can do anything. Since this is my first real picnic, he promises we will make a habit of it.

Later, with a big bowl of popcorn between us, we watch a movie with Jessica.

Contentment washes over me as I rest my head against Ingo's shoulder, his hand firmly clasping mine. The sadness I have felt for so long is slowly fading, and I am beginning to hope. Maybe I can finally let the past go. Each moment I spend with Ingo loosens another brick in the wall of self-preservation I have kept in place for so long.

Jessica glances over at me and smiles. She sees the changes taking place in me, and I feel how much she cares. She has wanted nothing but happiness for me, and I now realize why the desire she'd felt to have me come to Utah had been so strong. Like a butterfly spreading its wings for the first time, I am beginning to fly. And though I have no idea what is in my future, I am certain moving to Utah and meeting Ingo was a major part of it.

It has been weeks since Ingo arrived, and we have become so close, it is hard for us to be apart when I have to work. The only thing that keeps us going is the anticipation of spending our evenings together. I have never enjoyed being with someone so much, and I continually savor the innocence of it all.

Having slept in this morning, I awaken to find a large bouquet of red and white roses in a crystal vase on my bedside table. It is the first time I have ever received flowers. I inhale their sweet fragrance then read the card.

Good morning, love. I missed you while I slept,

and I long to spend another amazing day with you.

Ingo

After gazing dreamily at the flowers another moment, I quickly shower and change and do my hair, finishing the look with some light makeup. I am about to head down to the kitchen when Ingo appears at the door, carrying a breakfast tray.

"You are supposed to still be in bed," he says, his eyes stern, but his voice is playful. I can tell he really is a little disappointed I am already up. "I guess I'll have to be a little faster next time."

"I'm sorry," I say, raising on my tip-toes to kiss him. "I didn't mean to spoil your surprise. Would you like me to change and get back in bed?" I smile sweetly, trying to make him laugh and succeed.

"No, that's okay, but I would like you to get back *on* the bed so I can at least serve you your breakfast."

I grin, immediately complying. When I am settled, Ingo places the tray over my lap.

"Thank you," I say, marveling at his thoughtfulness. Just when I think there is nothing he can do to make me feel any more special, he surprises me by showering me with even more attention. "I've never had breakfast in bed before."

"Well, then this will be the first of many times." He presses a hand to my cheek. "I'm glad that I can be the one you experience so many firsts with. But before you start eating . . . there's something I want to tell you."

"Now wait just a minute. You bring me this amazing breakfast," I say, gesturing to the tray, "and now you're telling me I have to wait to eat it? You're talking to the woman with the mega appetite, remember? I can smell sizzling bacon a mile away. You're seriously telling me I have to wait?"

He laughs. "Just for a minute, if you don't mind."

"Oh, I mind, but I guess I'll wait."

"I promise it will be worth it." His smile fades slightly. "At least I think so. I hope so."

"Okay." Setting the tray aside, I give him my full attention. All playfulness is gone. This seems serious and I hope there isn't anything wrong.

"I need to say something to you. But I don't want to frighten you. That is the very last thing I want to do."

"Okay," I repeat, trying to keep my voice neutral and not let my imagination run wild.

He watches me looking at him expectantly, emotion filling his expression.

"I love you, Cisely. So very much. I need you in my life, more than I have ever needed anything."

I have never heard anything as beautiful as Ingo's declaration of love and it leaves me in awe. Placing my hand against his cheek, a tears slips unchecked down my own.

"I love you, too, Ingo. You're the best thing that has ever happened to me."

He kisses my palm. Pulling a small red box from his pocket, he places it in the same hand. "Will you marry me?"

44

My heartbeat speeds up a notch. Over the past weeks I have let myself dream of this moment, and now that it is here, I am speechless. I continue to stare at him, marveling at his proposal. Yet doubt immediately intrudes.

"Are you sure you want to marry me? I come with a lot of very heavy baggage. I know you are aware of that, but are you really sure?"

"I've never been surer of anything in my life, love." He moves closer, taking my face in his hands. "I know many people would consider a single month of dating moving too fast, but you mean more to me than anything in this world. And as for the baggage, we can carry it together."

Releasing a deep sigh, I allow happiness to move through me, warming me to the very core. Though I still feel unworthy of him, I can't doubt his feelings. Love shines through his eyes, making me feel like Cinderella about to become a princess. "Nothing would make me happier than being your wife, Ingo."

"Is that a yes?"

"It is."

His eyes shine even brighter and a grin splits his handsome face like he has just been handed the world's greatest treasure, which astounds me a little—no, not just a little, a lot!

When did I become such a prize? How is it possible? Interrupting my mental musings, he presses his lips to mine, kissing me slowly. Drawing back, he takes the ring from the box and places it on my finger.

"It's beautiful," I say, admiring the heart shaped solitaire.

"Just like you."

Kissing him again, I touch my forehead to his. "I love you."

"And I love you," he whispers. "More than you could ever know. And Aunt Jessica will be very happy for us. I think she has wanted this all along."

That's an understatement. "I'm sure you're right," I agree, remembering how Jessica practically pushed me into spending that first day with Ingo. How grateful I am now that she did. "I guess it wouldn't do to disappoint her."

"No, I guess it wouldn't." He places the breakfast tray back over my lap. "All right, now you can eat. But hurry so we can share our news with Aunt Jessica."

"No need to tell me twice." I take a bite of the bacon, unable to stop smiling.

I can't believe this is happening—he just asked me to be his wife! I am going to be Mrs. Ingo Kelly! How did I win a man so amazing? What did I do to deserve such a blessing?

I don't know the answer to either question, but I intend to do everything I can to be worthy of him.

Eight

Jessica is about to leave for work when the phone rings.

"Hello, I'm sorry to bother you, but I am trying to get in touch with Cisely Matthews."

"Yes. Hold on just a minute and I'll get her."

Jessica appears in Cisely's bedroom doorway and points to the phone. "It's for you, dear." Noticing wariness in Cisely's eyes as she turns to get the phone, Jessica leaves to give her some privacy, though she can't help being curious. The female caller has a prominent southern accent. Jessica can't recall Cisely ever receiving a phone call from home, and she silently prays everything is okay with her family.

"Cis, girl, this is your cousin, Velma."

At the sound of my cousin's voice, I suddenly feel the need to sit down. I move over to the bed, lowering myself on the edge. In all the time I have been in Utah, no one in the family has ever called me, nor have I expected them to. Even when I was in Asheville I received no contact from relatives unless I initiated it, which leads me to believe something is definitely wrong.

"How are you, Velma?" My cordial tone is forced.

"I'm doing okay, girl, but I have some bad news. Your mama died last night."

It takes a moment before the statement registers in my head. In stunned silence, I press a hand to my mouth as my cousin's words take hold in my mind.

Mama is gone! I can't believe it!

"Cisely, are you okay?"

"I'm fine," I finally answer. "How did it happen?"

"The paramedics said she had a heart attack. Kenneth–a guy she started hanging out with last week–called them. By the time they got there it was too late. She was already gone. I found your number in her purse."

Heaving a weary sigh, I stare at a hummingbird hovering just outside the window. So many thoughts drift through my mind concerning my mother's life and what she went through, but none of them produce the tears I would expect to come. I briefly wonder if something is wrong with me. This was my mother, the woman I spent over half my life with, and right now I can't even cry for her. We have never been close, but I should feel a little more grief. Surprisingly, there isn't even a desire to cry.

Maybe I'm in shock.

Velma's voice breaks through my thoughts. "Well, Mama told me to call you so you could take care of the funeral arrangements. You're the only one who can since you are named the beneficiary on her life insurance policy."

I realize it is my responsibility to take care of the arrangements, regardless of whether there is insurance or not, because I am Geneva's only child, and I know from experience I can't count on my mother's family for anything.

"I'll be there by tomorrow evening."

"Okay, girl, I'll tell Mama you're coming."

Hanging up, I numbly return my gaze to the window, staring at nothing in particular; the hummingbird is nowhere in sight.

I can't believe Mama is gone. We haven't really been a part of each other's lives for years, but it is still hard to imagine her not being in the world.

I guess all those years of drinking finally caught up with her. But she's better off now. A soft knock draws my gaze to the door.

Ingo and Jessica enter. He sits down next to me and takes my hand. "What is it, love?"

"My mother passed away last night."

Jessica gasps softly. "Oh, no! I'm so sorry."

Ingo pulls me close. "So am I."

"Thank you."

"What can we do?" he asks.

"I need to go back and take care of the funeral arrangements. I guess I'm the beneficiary of her insurance policy."

"Thank heavens she had insurance," Jessica says, patting my free hand.

"I would like to try and get there by tomorrow evening. I have some money–"

"Don't worry about that," Ingo interrupts. "I'll take care of everything."

"I can't let you do that."

He puts up a hand, halting my protests. "Listen, love, you're going to be my wife, which means everything I have is yours. Please let me do this."

I am deeply touched by his need to take care of me, and I can't imagine loving him more than I do at this moment. "Thank you."

"You're very welcome."

Hesitance fills me, producing nervous knots in my stomach. Ingo squeezes my hand, sensing there is something more.

"What is it?"

Slow to answer, I look away as tears press. "Well, I know it's a lot to ask, but . . ."

"But," Ingo urges. When I don't continue, he somehow guesses what I need but can't bring myself to ask. "Would you like me to come with you?"

Relieved that he has picked up on my feelings, I exhale deeply. I have always considered myself independent, never really needing anyone, but that isn't true anymore. I need Ingo. I truly need him. I'm not strong enough to do this alone.

"Yes," I finally answer.

Kissing my brow, he holds me close. "Nothing you ever ask could be too much. I want to be there for you, always."

"And I'll take care of your shifts at work," Jessica adds.

I smile at the woman I have come to look to as a mother, as well as a dear friend. "You have both been so good to me. I don't know what I would do without you."

She squeezes my hand. "You'll never have to find out."

Ingo quickly makes all the travel arrangements. Using his laptop, he purchases our tickets, reserves the hotel rooms and a rental car. I am grateful to him for taking care of all the details. He has thought of everything and I love being taken care of for the first time in my life.

I take a moment to remind him about how distant my family will be to me, but he assures me everything will be okay.

Ingo is so optimistic about life, and I wish some of his optimism would rub off on me, especially when it comes to my family. I need to be strong, and I pray that he will really be okay. I am used my family's ways, but I don't want him hurt. That would make me feel worse than anything they could ever say to me.

Later in the evening as I sit nestled in Ingo's arms, my gratitude for the privilege of having him in my life is increased. I know we will have trials and life won't be perfect, but I'm determined to be the best wife I can possibly be and try to make our life together a happy one.

Nine

My Aunt Gladys lives in a historic part of town. Though many homes have been renovated, most of the houses in her neighborhood are old. Some of them have windows missing, while others look like a good stiff wind would knock them right over. Even when I lived in Asheville, I never ventured to this part of the city. Maybe if my aunt had been willing to have some kind of relationship with me, I might have braved it and gone. But just like everyone else, Gladys holds the mistakes of the past against me. Sure, I made a lot of choices that I will regret for the rest of my life, and I'm not perfect. But then neither is Gladys.

A sense of dread enters me as we pull up in front of my aunt's home, and I can't help wishing we were back at the hotel.

Ingo senses my feelings. "Hey," he says, raising my hand to his lips. "I love you, and it's going to be all right."

Nodding, I close my eyes and take a deep breath, grateful he is with me. I couldn't do this without him. "I love you, too." We share a brief kiss. Drawing back, I smile nervously and get

53

out of the car. Unfortunately, my panic only increases as we head up the walk. My grip on Ingo's hand tightens.

"I'm right here, love. It will be okay."

"Please keep telling me that."

He presses a kiss to my brow before knocking. "Are you ready?"

"As ready as I'll ever be." I lock a smile in place.

I watch the amused twitch of Ingo's jaw when Velma opens the door. The girl is completely flabbergasted upon seeing him with me and it definitely shows. If my nerves were a little steadier, I really *would* laugh.

"Hey, Cis," she finally says. "Ya'll come on in."

"Thank you." I enter with Ingo close behind me.

Gladys is sitting in an old over-sized green chair smoking a cigarette. She almost chokes on it upon seeing Ingo. I am used to the smoke, having been raised around it, as well as having done my fair share of smoking in the past, but I hope it won't be too much for Ingo. At the rate my aunt is puffing and exhaling, we will probably need to shower and make a trip to the laundromat after we leave.

"Ya'll have a seat," Gladys says, waving a hand in the direction of the plastic-covered sofa. Growing up, I found plastic-covered furniture to be common in the homes of many people I knew. I never understood the concept or reasoning behind it, but I figured there must have been some hidden method behind the madness.

Once we sit down, I make the introductions. "Aunt Gladys, Velma, I would like you to meet my fiancée, Ingo."

"It's truly a pleasure to meet you," Ingo says, standing with his hand outstretched.

What happens next is both expected and amusing. Gladys' eyes literally bulge from her wide, round face and Velma's mouth drops open. Shocked isn't strong enough to describe their reactions, but I had expected as much. When it comes to showing tact, however, my family has definitely been left out of the loop.

Gladys doesn't shake his hand but gives a small grunt, acknowledging him.

"O . . . kay," Ingo mumbles under his breath. He extends his hand in Velma's direction and she shakes it eagerly.

"Where are you from?" Gladys asks as he sits down again.

"I'm from Melbourne, Australia."

She again grunts in acknowledgment.

"Okay," comes his repeated mumble and I fight the laugh bubbling to the surface.

"How have you two been?" I ask, attempting to lighten the moment and hold some sort of conversation.

Velma glances to her mother, as if waiting for a response. "We're doing fine," she answers instead.

I wince inwardly as Gladys flings a disgusted look in her daughter's direction. Mashing her cigarette in a small ashtray on the arm of the chair, she hefts her large body up and pulls a key from her pocket.

"Here's your mama's extra key. You can go on over there now if you want. The insurance papers are on the table in the kitchen."

Leaning forward, I take the key from her, not missing the greed in her voice. I know Gladys doesn't think I should have the money and would like to lay claim on it herself. It seems all my family thinks about is what they can get. If you don't have anything they want, you are of no use. If you can't do for or give them anything that they deem valuable, they don't want anything to do with you. And I am sure after I go back to Utah, Gladys will descend on my mother's apartment like a vulture, taking everything that she can get her hands on. Sadly, I have seen it happen before in my family. It is always expected with the death of a family member.

I shake my head sadly at her abrupt dismissal. *So, I guess this is it, then. No, "How have you been?" No, "It's good to see you." Just here's your mama's key and you can go now.* I glance at Ingo to gauge his reaction, but his face is unreadable. He squeezes my hand, though, and I know he understands my frustration. He shakes his head slightly at the situation and I draw comfort from that. I have traveled all this way, have been in my aunt's home for exactly two minutes, and she has barely spoken to me. These people are supposed to be my family, but they don't seem to care about me at all, or at least Gladys doesn't. I sense Velma warming slightly, which helps a little.

I finally stand and Ingo quickly follows suit. The sooner we leave, the better as far as I am concerned. Pressing his lips to my temple, Ingo whispers, "Let's get out of here."

I nod. "Well, I guess we should head over to Mama's place. I'd like to get things taken care of as soon as possible." I turn to Velma. "Thank you for calling me. I really appreciate it."

Velma opens her mouth to respond, but Gladys cuts her off. Though Velma and I have never been close, we have always been civil toward one another. In some ways I feel sorry for Velma. It must be hard having such an overbearing mother.

"We didn't have no choice but to call you," Gladys booms. "We sure can't afford to bury her. She was my sister and I loved her, but this is your responsibility." The last words reek of accusation.

Ingo again squeezes my hand. "It was good to meet you both," he says and guides me toward the door, anger furrowing his brow.

"It was good to see you, Aunt Gladys," I say, making one last attempt to elicit a positive response. When there isn't one, I smile at Velma and again turn to leave.

"I want to talk to you for a moment." The softness of Gladys' voice startles us both.

"Okay." I am wary, but I genuinely want to make some sort of peace with my aunt. However, one look at her face tells me that hope is also futile.

"I want to talk to you *alone*, if you don't mind."

Ingo's grip on my hand tightens as he leads me toward the door. "I'll bet she does," he murmurs. "I'm not leaving you alone with her."

Stopping, I press my lips to his ear. "Will you wait outside for me?"

He clearly wants to say no, and is about to, but the pleading in my eyes stops him. I want him with me, more than he knows, but I have to do this alone. I pray for strength enough to handle whatever my aunt dishes out at me.

"I'll be right outside," he says softly.

Taking in his expression, my heart aches, because this is equally hard for him. He has become so protective of me and I love him for it. No one has ever made my heart feel so safe. As he glances back at me, I give him a reassuring smile. He smiles back and leaves to wait at the car.

Closing the door, I face my aunt, fully aware of what is coming. Despite having little contact with them, I have always been able to read Gladys and her brother Pete like a couple of books. The two are exactly the same and I dread having to see him just as much.

Gladys leans back in the chair and lights another cigarette, and I take this moment to study her. She has always been a heavy woman, but now her arms and legs are so swollen, she looks ill. Her graying hair is a disheveled mess and her clothes looks as if they haven't seen soap and water in a while. She truly looks unhappy, and for a moment I almost feel sorry for her.

Almost.

My aunt takes a long drag of the cigarette, blowing the smoke upward. "Girl, when you up and moved to that white state I thought you were crazy, but now I know you are. What do think you're doing marrying that white man?"

"I'm marrying that *man* because he loves me and makes me happy." I am unruffled by her bluntness. I am used to it and well aware of her feelings of racial superiority. Her opinion has always been that people should stay with their own kind.

Gladys laughs. "No, I don't buy that, Cis. I can tell you the real reason you're with him."

"Oh, really?" My attempt to sound amused is failing.

"Really," she continues as if ours is the most natural conversation in the world. "See, I think you're with him because you're trying to make people think you're better than you are. You brought him here to show us that you're moving up in the world. You think being with him is gonna make you look good."

I had known it was coming, but I am still appalled that she could think such a thing. I could never use someone like that no matter how down I feel on myself.

Straightening my shoulders, I look at her intently. "Well, Aunt Gladys, if that's what you want to think, then feel free. I know the truth. For the first time in my life I have someone who truly loves and cares for me. I have a good life in Utah and I'm happier than I've ever been. Just because I want a better life doesn't mean I think I'm better. Anyone who wants something bad enough and goes after it can be blessed with it."

Velma is leaning against the wall, listening intently, never uttering a word. She never does when her mother is speaking, but this time she has no interest in her mother's words. Not that she ever has, anyway. She is only interested in what Cisely is saying. She has never been close to Cisely, but she truly admires the way her cousin changed her life. Velma has made mistakes as well, and just like Cisely, Gladys never lets her forget them.

She truly envies her cousin.

"Good speech," Gladys says, clapping her hands. "That was a good speech, but let me ask you something. How much does that man really know about you?" Wincing, I look away, which gives her the added fuel she needs to keep going. "Does he know you're used merchandise, probably fifty times over?"

Struggling not to cry, the tears escape anyway. "That is all in the past. I am not—"

Gladys rides over my weak defense. "Does he know about your druggie days? What about your drunkard days? And how would he react if he knew about your nights of sleeping in houses other than your own, waking up next to men you didn't even know?" She punches up the spite level with each word.

I remain quiet as my heart revisits the despair I thought I'd left behind. It seems my emotional relief was only temporary. I should have known better.

Watching the triumphant smile spread across Gladys' face, I wait for her closing remarks.

"So, you see, Cisely, you can never escape who you are. You can never escape your life. You are what you are, and you, Miss High and Mighty, are nothing more than a tramp trying to change something that can't be changed."

I hastily brush the tears from my cheeks. "I'm not a tramp, and I'm not that kind of person anymore." But even as I utter the statement, I don't truly believe it. Surrendering to my belief that it is useless to deny it any longer, I quietly leave.

Ten

Ingo takes one look at Cisely's face as she emerges from the house and knows she has been broken. He'd spent the entire time hoping she would be strong, that Gladys would not be able to hurt her more or break her spirit. She has done both, and those familiar sad eyes that had once broken his heart are back, only worse. Wordlessly, he pulls her close, pressing a comforting kiss to her brow.

After a minute, she draws away, leaving his arms empty. He knows she needs his comfort, but she won't allow him to touch her, and he can only imagine what she'd gone through with her aunt.

Ingo opens her door. When he gets in, he puts the key in the ignition but doesn't start it. "Talk to me, love," he says softly, taking in her pain-filled expression.

"I can't right now."

"Cisely, I'm here for you. You know that, right?"

"Yes," she whispers. "Please, just drive."

Starting the car, Ingo blinks back tears. Swallowing his anger, he pulls away from the curb, silently praying he will be able to reach her somehow.

The only words spoken between us are my directions to Mama's apartment.

As we pull up in front of the old building, dozens of memories flood my mind. I lived in this building with my mother until I turned sixteen. Then I left and stayed with friends until I turned twenty and could afford a place of my own. Until today, the pain of those memories had faded, but now it is as fresh as ever.

As I move to get out of the car. Ingo places a gentle hand on my arm.

"I love you, Cisely." There is so much emotion in his eyes and voice, I want to weep. "No matter what, I love you."

"And I love you," I say back, longing to have him hold me, but feeling so unworthy of him. I know I need to get past these feelings and let them go, but right now everything is too fresh, the pain too intense. I just need some time to sort things out.

When we enter the apartment, I push everything down inside me and concentrate on what I need to do. Looking around the place a bit, everything is just as it was before I left, only cleaner. The insurance policy is on the kitchen table, just as Gladys said. I sift through the papers, surprised at the amount of coverage my mother had. I wonder how she had even been able to afford a policy this size when she had no income—at least, not that I know of.

Three hundred thousand dollars! No wonder Aunt Gladys was so upset. This would keep her supplied in cigarettes and booze for a long time. Showing the amount to Ingo, he whistles and looks over the papers. I know it isn't a lot of money to him, but he understands why it is to me.

Refolding the policy, I take a moment to look around the room a final time, memorizing little details I'd long since forgotten. Then realizing there is no comfort to be gained here, I slip the policy into my purse and we leave.

At the hotel, Ingo sits next to Cisely on the sofa while she calls the funeral home and makes an appointment. He admires the way she is able to take care of the arrangements, and if he didn't already know her age, he would never guess she is only twenty-two. All the trials she's faced in her young life have matured her fast.

Later, as he sits with Cisely in the funeral director's office listening to them discuss the arrangements, he can't help watching her, and he allows his gaze to travel over her beautiful features. She seems like a different person since leaving her aunt's house, but he knows the real Cisely is still in there somewhere. He just needs to help her remember how special she is. To him, she is the most amazing person in the world and their marriage can't happen soon enough.

As he continues to watch her, longing flows through him. He aches to be alone with her, to feel her in his arms, her body molded against his, her breath on his face, and her lips pressed against his own. Never before has he ever needed the touch of a woman. Before meeting Cisely he'd never really given marital intimacy a thought. He had never been close enough to anyone to think that far ahead. But now things are different, and he is anxious to be married and share that intimacy with Cisely. They just need to get past this trial and get on with their plans.

After the final arrangements are made, Ingo takes Cisely out to dinner. She says very little and he doesn't push her to talk. He's determined to be there for her and assure her of his unconditional love. She will open up when she is ready. Until then, he will wait.

Eleven

I absently gaze through the balcony doors and take in downtown Asheville. The city lights are beautiful and blend into the gray darkening skyline.

No matter how hard I try, the clutter of negative feelings will not leave my head or my heart. I've been trying nonstop all afternoon to let them go, but they have only become stronger. The conversation with my aunt did a number on me, and her hateful words have renewed the torment I thought I'd conquered. My new-found self-confidence is gone now, and in its place is the all too familiar self-doubt. Maybe the feelings hadn't gone away after all but had only lay dormant for a short season.

Hearing a soft knock on the connecting room door, I turn. Ingo is standing in the doorway, his features expressing as much pain as my own. I hate what this is doing to him, what *I* am doing to him. But I don't know how to deal with this fear of not being good enough for him. I turn back to the city lights.

I sense his nearness before he even touches me. His arms circle my waist, and he draws me to him, the pounding of his heart against my back causing my own heart to race. Trying to fight the desire growing inside me is useless. Closing my eyes, I tip my head back against his shoulder, shuddering as the warmth of his breath fans the side of my face.

"I love you, Cisely," he whispers, brushing his lips against my ear. "Please say you love me."

Turning in his arms, I draw his head down, slowly brushing my lips against his. "I do love you."

As the passion of our kiss grows, his embrace tightens and I melt against him. My fingers are buried in his hair as his lips trail over my face, making a path back to my own.

Lifting his head, he looks into my eyes, tears brimming his.

"You are my whole life, love, my whole world. And we can't be married soon enough."

Dropping my eyes, I slowly turn away. I can't think about marriage right now when my yesterdays are still taking over my life.

"What is it?" His voice is pleading. "Please talk to me. Tell me what's going on inside you."

Keeping my back to him, the wild thumping of my heart takes away my breath and I don't respond. I can't.

He tugs at my arm gently. "Please, Cisely, talk to me. I can't read your mind, though I really wish I could sometimes."

Latching on to a small thread of anger, I whirl on him. "No, you don't! If you could, you wouldn't like what you saw there and you would leave me as quick as you could!"

"First, you can't tell me how I would react because you won't even give me a chance! And second!" He takes my arms in his hands. His voice softens, but his grip tightens gently. "I

66

would never leave you, Cisely. Never. There is nothing you could say to make me want to leave. There is nothing in this world that could take me away from you except death, and I don't plan on going anytime soon. I love you. Can't you understand that? I'm in this for the long haul." Releasing my arms, he takes my hands, pressing them against his chest. "You are a part of me. If I ever left you it would be like leaving a part of myself behind, and I just can't do that."

A painful moan escapes me as emotion bubbles to the surface, and the tears come hard and fast. Ingo pulls me into his arms, rocking me slowly back and forth, crying with me. After a few moments, I move back. Taking a deep breath, I decide to just get it over with. My confessions will decide my fate with him. I am risking everything, but it is a risk I know I have to take.

Here goes nothing.

Tentatively, I force the first words from my lips.

"My father used to tell me I would only be good for one thing in this life. Each and every time he entered my room and had his way with me, afterward he would say the very same thing. *"You are only going to be good for one thing in this world, girl."* And . . . he was right." I pause. If I am going to tell him everything, I can't look at him. I don't want to see the pain my words bring etched in his handsome features. Fixing my gaze on a painting hanging on the wall over the sofa, I continue.

"When I moved out of my mother's apartment, I moved in with people I thought were my friends. They made me feel welcome and were willing to share all they had with me." I release a humorless chuckle. "Well, all they had was a fridge full of beer instead of food, cupboards full of liquor instead of food, and last but not least, a medicine cabinet full of every drug known to man." I shake my head at the visual. "At least the drugs were where they were supposed to be in the house."

Pausing, I glance at Ingo. He is listening quietly, his expression unreadable.

"It wasn't hard to get hooked you know? It was like an all you can take and drink buffet. After a year it became my breakfast, lunch and dinner. I soon discovered the more I drank, the more I could numb the pain of the past. The more pills I popped, the more marijuana I smoked, the less pain I felt. And even though I had found a way to medicate myself, it still wasn't enough. It was never enough. Pretty soon I was so far gone, I completely stopped caring about anything. I mean . . . my father always said I was only good for one thing." I stop, coming to the worst of it, and I don't know if I can admit it out loud.

Placing a finger beneath my chin, he softly says, "Tell me."

Taking a deep breath, I release it slowly as another wave of tears trickle down my face. *I guess we are at the make or break point, huh?* "I proved my father right. It turned out I *was* only good for one thing." Wiping the tears away, I force myself to look into his eyes. "You're getting used merchandise as my aunt so bluntly put it. I'm not pure. For that matter I don't think I ever was. I've slept around, Ingo. A *lot*." I release an inward sigh. *There. I've said it. It's all out in the open now.*

Ingo presses a hand to my cheek, wiping my tears. "I know, love." His words stun me and I stare at him, disbelieving. "I've known from the first. But I needed to let you tell me yourself. I wanted to hear it from you."

"And now?" I am afraid to hear the answer, but I need to know where things stand between us.

"Nothing has changed, except my love for you. I didn't think I could love you more, but I was wrong." He wipes at his own tears. "And by the way, you are very pure and I don't ever want to hear you refer to yourself as used merchandise again. Ever."

"But . . . how can you say that? How can you still love me knowing what you know now?"

"How could you think I would stop loving you? It's all in the past. It doesn't matter."

"But it does matter!" I cry, frustrated, mainly with myself.

"Can you tell me why?"

Closing my eyes, I rub my aching temples. My soul is weary and I long to explain what I feel inside, but I don't know how. I have lived with the secret of my dirty past for so long, it is hard to just let it go. My choices were terrible and unforgivable, and ever since then, my mind has been conditioned to think it can't be that easy to let go.

Ingo sighs. "Let me ask you something. Do you want to do those things anymore?"

Of course not. "No."

"Are you sorry about those choices?"

"Yes."

"Do you ever want to repeat them?"

Sniffling, I wipe my face. "Never. I have too much respect for myself now and . . ."

"And?" he presses.

"I have you." *Don't I? Please say I still do.*

69

"You will always have me. But you have to let the past go, love. Until you do, we can't move forward. *You* can't move forward."

I nod, closing my eyes. He's right, but it is still so hard.

"Cisely, look at me." As I open my eyes, he gently wipes my fresh tears away. "You are an amazing person. You are beautiful, strong, talented, caring, giving, and kind. But until you leave the past behind, you will never see what I and everyone else sees in you." Drawing me close, he whispers against my ear, "Let it go, love. Just let it all go."

As if I had only needed his permission, a dam breaks inside me and I press my face against his chest, my shoulders trembling in agony as all the sorrow I've carried for so long rises to the surface and finds release. The pain that has crushed my spirit for all these years brings me to my knees.

Ingo sinks to the floor and just holds me, sharing my heartache, as well as my sweet release.

"You are a wonderful person, Cisely," he continues to whisper, holding me tighter. "You are stronger and more loved than you can possibly know, and I will never let you forget that."

Holding to his words, I continue to cling to him, my sobs soon lessening as the peace I have needed for long enters me. He moves back a little, gazing at me and I smile. I know my eyes are red and swollen and I must look a sight, but I am happy—truly happy.

"I love you, Mrs. Kelly, almost."

I laugh. "And I love you, Mr. Kelly. More than I can say."

Smiling, he lowers his head. As he kisses me this time, I hold nothing back. For the first time in my life I feel free, and the kiss we share is glorious. It is filled with love, passion and healing. The new tears that slip down my cheeks are no longer from pain, but from the pleasure of knowing I can now be his completely—my heart, my mind, and my very being.

And I know he will keep them all safe.

J. Adams

Twelve

We hold a simple graveside service for my mother. Though I want to introduce Ingo to my uncle and his wife, they stay so far away from me, I don't really get the chance. I am used to the way things are between us, but this is my mother's funeral, for heaven's sake! I can't believe they are being so cold to me on a day like today. We should be sharing some kind of connection and the past shouldn't matter. But it still matters to them. Why, I don't know. Except for my cousin Velma, they are all as rude as they can be. And all because I did the unforgivable in their eyes; I changed my life and moved away to have a better one. Glancing at Ingo, I squeeze his hand. He gives me a sad smile and I know he understands what I feel.

The attendance is small, which is fine with me. It seems all of Mama's drinking buddies and ex-boyfriends are otherwise occupied.

I had asked the reverend of the church my mother attended as a teenager to officiate and he'd happily agreed. As he says the final words and her casket is lowered into the ground, I am regretful that Mama didn't get to see how I changed my life. Not that it would have mattered much. I only wish I could have made peace with her. I guess she has a better view of me now, and hopefully she is happy for me.

We shake hands with the reverend and thank him for the service. Ingo gives him an envelope and he smiles, slipping it into his suit coat pocket.

Walking to the car, I glimpse a lone figure standing in the distance and my heart lurches. The person quickly turns and walks away. I can't be sure, but it almost looks like . . . No, it can't be him. I am certain it's not.

My face is expressionless, but I am sick inside. Tightening my grip on Ingo's hand, I take a deep breath and keep walking, never slowing my step. I don't want Ingo to worry, nor do I want to think about who the person could have been. I'm not up to it, and I never will be. So, I put it out of my mind.

Following the service, Ingo treats me to lunch and we do a little sightseeing. We take a quick tour through *Biltmore House and Gardens* and visit the Thomas Moore house.

We spend the rest of the evening repacking and getting ready for our trip back.

And as we board the plane the following day, I realize that for the first time in my life, I have no regrets. Sure, it would have been nice to make peace with my family, but I did all I could and I have to let it go now.

Ingo keeps my hand between his as the plane takes off. Fingering my engagement ring, he tells me how blessed he feels that I am still wearing it after all that has happened. He had been afraid of losing me, to which I reply, "You will never again have to worry about that. It's not an option."

I have enjoyed the time I've spent with Ingo in North Carolina and will treasure it always. Because it is there that a miracle occurred. He helped me understand that my past doesn't determine the rest of my life, and that overcoming the trials I've faced so far has made me stronger and shaped who I am now—the person he loves.

Now when I think of home, I will remember it as the place where I truly became whole.

I am happy, life is good and I look forward to the future.

So why does a small part of me still feel unsettled?

Thirteen

We set our wedding date for the end of July and it is already the middle of June. Time is passing fast and I am so grateful for Jessica. With her help, we are able to put the wedding together quickly. Most of the people we're inviting–besides Ingo's family–are the ladies I work with at the boutique and a few of the regular customers I have gotten to know. I am a little sad that there will be no family of my own at the wedding, but it can't be helped, and I frequently remind myself that Ingo and Jessica are my family now.

Ingo
Ingo is excited to call his parents and tell them about Cisely, as well as invite them to the wedding. And as he'd

expected, they are blown away by the news. They will all be flying in for the event. He can't wait for them to officially meet Cisely.

When he makes his monthly call to his best friend Adagio, he tells him about Cisely and invites him to the wedding.

"Congratulations, my friend!" Adagio says heartily. "I am so happy for you! Of course, I was beginning to wonder if, like me, you were going to be a confirmed bachelor for the rest of your life."

Ingo laughs. "Yeah, you and everybody else, but when you meet Cisely, you will understand why she's the only woman for me. She was worth the wait. No one else has even come close."

"She must be amazing to have pinned you down. And just wait until I tell the guys at the restaurant. Sam will probably call you right back to make sure I am not making this up."

"I can believe that. Those guys have always considered me a lost cause anyway, especially Mr. Happily-Married-For-Fifteen-Years Sam."

Adagio laughs. "You were not lost, just wandering, same as me."

"Well, I'm no longer wandering, my friend. I've found my destination and she is amazing. I love her so much."

"I can tell."

"So, what's happening with you and Maria?"

"Actually . . . nothing is happening."

"What do you mean? I thought things were moving along between you two."

"Sadly, she turned out to be like the other two before her. My money and my restaurant were my biggest draw."

"I'm sorry, man. I can definitely empathize, as you well know. Been there, done that."

"I do know. I guess it comes with the territory when you are single *and* wealthy. But I am sure God has a plan and I still have hope. I am also still waiting for that plan to emerge."

Ingo chuckles. "Well, while you're waiting, get your travel plans made, because you're my best man."

"It's about time you admitted I am the best."

"But of course," Ingo agrees with a snort.

They talk a little longer and Ingo shares more about Cisely, wanting Adagio to understand just how special she is. Before hanging up, he gives Adagio the date of the wedding and Adagio assures him he will be there.

Adagio

Treviso, Italy

Hanging up the phone, Adagio rakes his fingers through his tousled hair and smiles. He can't believe his friend is finally getting married! Ingo is never far from his thoughts, and he is happy the man he has come to think of as a brother has finally found someone to share his life with. At times it still amazes him that he and Ingo are so close, and the connection between them is unexplainable. It is as if they have known each other all their lives. Having grown up an only child, Adagio treasures the close relationship he shares with Ingo. True, he has other friends, coworkers and acquaintances, but Ingo is definitely a kindred spirit.

Adagio lost his mother when he was sixteen. His father had died before Adagio was born and there were no other relatives to speak of. When his mother died, she left him money she had saved through the years from cleaning houses, and he used the money to fulfill his dream of becoming a chef and opening his own restaurant.

Five years ago, Adagio traveled to America and opened an Italian restaurant in Salt Lake City. It became a very popular place and business was excellent. A couple of years later, an arsonist burned the place to the ground. He had suspected it was a disgruntled employee he'd fired, but he couldn't prove it. In any case, the person was never found. Disappointed and saddened, Adagio moved back to Treviso, the place of his birth, which is only twenty minutes away from Venice. He bought a villa, opened a restaurant in the right wing of the home, and invested in stocks. The years have been very good to him as far as finances go.

He smiles once more as his thoughts return to Ingo's good fortune. Chuckling, he heads over to tell the guys at the restaurant. They are not going to believe it!

Fourteen

During the week of the wedding, Ingo and I help Jessica prepare the extra five bedrooms for our expected guests. I have never seen Jessica so excited. She hasn't seen her family for almost a year and is eagerly looking forward to their reunion.

Taking a break to sit and visit for a bit, Jessica and Ingo talk about the family and speculate about what they are up to, but my own longing for family brings an unexpected sadness. I continue to smile, attempting to blink away the tears that have come unbidden, but Ingo notices and immediately moves to the sofa and sits next to me. Jessica joins us.

"I'm sorry, love," he says, squeezing my hand. "I know this is hard for you."

"I'll be okay," I assure him with my brightest smile. "After all, I have you and Jessica now."

"And you always will," Jessica says, then moves back to the chair across from us. "Since we have a few moments, this is the perfect opportunity to discuss something very important with you. I was wondering, have you two discussed where you will live after you are married?"

Ingo and I glance at each other. "Well, we kind of wanted to wait until we got back from our honeymoon before we make any decisions," he says.

"I'm glad, because that is what I wanted to talk to you about." She looks from Ingo to me. "You know, since I was never blessed with children of my own, both of you have been like my children. Ingo, you come to see me regularly and I don't need to tell you how much I enjoy our visits."

Ingo smiles. "You know you've always been my favorite aunt."

"I know. I love the fact that you come here to escape the rest of the family." He grins sheepishly and Jessica and I laugh.

"And then there's you, dear," she says to me. "The day I met you was the most fortunate day of my life. You have become the daughter I've always dreamed of having, and I have grown to love you very much."

"I love you too." Her unexpected outpouring of feelings is just what I need right now. "You've also been like a mother to me. You have been there for me when I've really needed one."

"Thank you." Wiping a tear away, she goes on. "Well, the reason I'm glad you're waiting is because a couple of weeks ago, I had some things changed in my will. Now mind you, I've put a lot of thought and prayer into these changes and I feel very good about my decision." She pauses, her eyes intent. "Cisely, when I die, this house and everything else I own will be yours."

The word stunned doesn't come close to describing what I feel. It takes me a moment to really grasp what she just said, and then another before I can speak. "But . . . why?"

"Because I love you. You've brought joy and sunshine into my life. And now that you are marrying my favorite nephew, it will belong to both of you. So, if it's okay with you both, I would like you to stay here, because if you leave, I will be lonelier than I've ever been. I bought this place thinking I would one day marry and fill it with children of my own, but that never happened. One old woman in a house this size makes for a very lonely life."

"You really want us to stay with you?" Ingo finally asks, his expression mirroring mine. I know how much he loves this house and I don't want to leave any more than he does. When his eyes meet mine, they affirm that our feelings are the same. "Aunt Jessica, we would love to live here with you."

Sighing, Jessica smiles, drying her eyes. "You have made this old woman very happy."

We stand and embrace. The wealth of love present flows through me, warming my entire being. I finally draw back and kiss Jessica's cheek. "Thank you for loving me so much."

"Thank you for giving me the chance to love you."

"I have to second that," Ingo says, kissing his aunt as well.

As I stand in the loving embraces of these amazing people, I know that no matter what happened in the past or will happen in the future, mine is a blessed life.

At moments like this, the slight uneasiness that tugs at me from time to time simply disappears.

Fifteen

It is three days before the wedding and Ingo's family arrives in a caravan of rental cars. His parents, Gloria and Patrick, are amazing and immediately take me into their family. His brothers, Michael and Luke, and their wives, his uncle, Bill, and his wife, as well as his aunt, Sarah, and her husband are all equally welcoming. Ingo's nieces and nephews are a jumble of names, but one day I will finally remember them all.

As Ingo had warned me, Patrick and the rest of the men immediately break me in. They tell Ingo what a babe I am and joke with him about holding out on them, making me extremely grateful for my brown skin, because I would definitely be two shades of red by now.

I love watching Ingo interact with his family throughout the day, and I am grateful they embraced me so readily. Understanding the emotional baggage their son is willingly tying himself to, his parents accepted me with no judgments. The day Ingo called to tell them about the wedding, I had given him permission to share the details of my life. They in turn have shown me nothing but love and support.

Gloria follows me to the kitchen to grab more sandwiches and lemonade for everyone.

Placing her arm around my shoulders she says, "Jessica has told me over and over how special you are and how fortunate Ingo is to have you. I agree with her. I couldn't understand why he never liked anyone enough to even attempt a relationship. I guess he was saving himself for you and didn't know it." She smiles, squeezing my shoulder. "I'm so happy to be acquiring such a beautiful daughter-in-law."

I'm not going to cry! I'm not going to cry! I'm not . . . "Thank you," I manage to say as disobedient tears brim my eyes. "I'm happy to be part of your family."

She wipes her own face and we embrace.

"Hey, what are all these tears about?" Patrick says, entering the kitchen.

Gloria laughs. "Oh, you know I get emotional a lot. Probably my hormones."

"Yeah, probably," he agrees, dodging his wife's attempt to swat him with the dish towel. I laugh as he ducks behind me. They are a total riot and I love them already!

Patrick smiles, placing a fatherly arm around me. "I know it's not official yet, but welcome to the family."

"Thank you." I briefly take in his handsome features, marveling at how much Ingo looks like him.

After talking another moment, we take the sandwiches and lemonade to the family room and rejoin the others. A while later, Ingo discreetly pulls me into the hallway. Wrapping his arms around my waist, he presses me against the wall and whispers, "Have I told you today how much I love you?"

"Yes, but it *is* okay if you want to tell me again."

"I love you." He kisses me tenderly.

"I love you, too," I murmur.

"So . . . you wanna get married?"

"Married?"

"Yeah, you know, married? Get hitched, tie the knot, jump the broom, live together, sleep together, and make babies. Married."

"Sounds like a good idea to me. Maybe we should."

Grinning, he kisses me again. "We probably should head to the airport to pick up Adagio."

"I can't wait to meet him."

Ingo sticks his head in the family room and tells the family we're leaving and won't be too long.

"Shall we take your car or mine?" he asks as we head to the garage.

I smirk. "I guess we should take yours. It's roomier."

"Well, my SUV *is* a lot roomier than your Jag."

"Ya think?"

Laughing, he kisses me quickly, bringing back to mind the day he gave me the beautiful car. After returning from North Carolina, Ingo had decided he needed to get himself some permanent transportation. He also decided I needed a car of my own. I couldn't believe it when he pulled up in the shiny, metallic, gray Jaguar and presented it to me as a wedding present. I laughed and cried for almost an hour as I drove it around the city. I'd never dreamed of owning something so extravagant. I immediately traded my North Carolina license for a Utah one.

Smiling at the memory, I pull him close for another kiss before getting in the car.

On our way to the airport, Ingo tells me more about meeting Adagio in Italy when he was there doing a photo shoot. He was renting a room near Adagio's villa and dined in his restaurant one afternoon. The two began talking, and when Ingo mentioned he would be heading to Utah to see his aunt after his job was finished, Adagio told him about once living in Salt Lake City himself and Ingo knew he'd found a friend. Adagio introduced Ingo to his kitchen staff, and then had him over for dinner the following evening and shared more about his own life. They have been best friends ever since.

Ingo shares what Adagio told him about losing his parents when he was young, and about his move to the U.S. over five years ago to open *Little Venice*.

"I love the name," I say. Of course, I love Italian food, period—no, I love *everything* Italian. In fact, I sometimes think I was born on the wrong continent.

"It was a pretty catchy name," he agrees.

He talks about a disgruntled employee setting fire to Adagio's restaurant, destroying the place. "It's pretty sad that they never caught the guy. Adagio worked so hard for that place, and to lose it like that was terrible. Fortunately, he had good insurance and was able to start over. And I have to say I really like his restaurant in Treviso. It's in a wing of his home and it's beautiful."

"What is his new place called?"

"*St. John's Place*. Has a nice ring to it, don't you think?"

"It does," I agree. "It's awful that a person can be vindictive enough to destroy lives that way."

"I can't understand it, but it happens."

Sadly, I do understand all too well the cruelty of others. And after hearing all that Adagio has been through, I am even more excited to meet him.

Ingo pulls into the airport parking garage and finds a spot near the terminal entrance. We quickly go in and check the arrival manifest, then stand near the security gate and wait for Adagio. Twenty minutes later Ingo spots him exiting the security area. "There he is," he says as his friend moves through the large crowd. Adagio waves when he sees Ingo.

Smiling, I watch Adagio's eyes light up when he sees Ingo. Though I have never seen him before, there is something familiar about him. I could almost believe I've met him before, but I know that's impossible. I would definitely remember if I had.

I notice several women gawking at Adagio as he passes through the crowd and I can understand. Simply put, he is a very attractive guy. A couple of inches shorter than Ingo, his build is lean and very muscular. Black, wavy hair, striking emerald eyes, gleaming white teeth, and a wide smile give him that movie star quality people work so hard to achieve. Surprisingly, he seems completely oblivious to all of it.

The two men hug, slapping each other's back heartily.

"It is so good to see you, my friend!" Adagio says.

"It's good to see you too! I'm glad you could come."

"Like I would have missed this. It is definitely going to be the event of the century."

Laughing, Ingo pulls me close. "Adagio, this is Cisely, my wife-to-be. Cisely, meet Adagio."

"It's good to finally meet you," Adagio says, embracing me.

"I'm happy to meet you too. Ingo has told me so much about you."

"He has told me much about you as well. I hope you don't mind."

"I don't mind at all. I'm glad he did."

"Well, just let me say that any woman that can capture this beast deserves my deepest honor and respect."

"He's that bad, huh?"

"Oh, look who's talking," Ingo interjects. "You're going to be next, buddy."

"Definitely," I agree, smiling at Ingo. "You can count on my help in finding a mate for your mate." Looking at Adagio, I give him my best angelic smile and he laughs.

"I do believe your wife-to-be is another kindred spirit."

"I think so, too." Ingo points to some empty chairs. "Honey, why don't you wait over there while we go and grab Adagio's suitcase. Looks like it will be coming in on the last carousel."

"Okay."

While I wait, I watch other passengers come through the gate into the baggage claim area. Some have friends and loved ones waiting, some passengers head straight over to retrieve their luggage, and a few are standing and looking around like they are lost. How well I remember the day I arrived in Salt Lake City. Entering the terminal, I had been afraid, nervous and excited. Then I walked through the security gate and saw Jessica, and I felt like I had come home. Now here I am, living a new life and about to marry an amazing man. I can't ask for anything more.

Watching a young woman come through the gate and embrace another woman who looks like an older version of her, I experience a brief sadness. Turning in time to see Ingo and Adagio approaching with his luggage, I quickly smile, pushing all unhappy thoughts from my mind.

When we arrive at the house, Ingo introduces Adagio to his family. The women swoon, the young girls giggle, and the men wonder what all the fuss is about. I mentally lay ten-to-one odds that the men will eventually hit Adagio up for a few romantic Italian phrases to use on their wives. I mention this to Ingo and Adagio and they both laugh heartily.

After we've all visited for a while, Ingo shows Adagio to his room, leaving him to unpack and rest. Later, when everyone else has gone to bed, the three of us sit at the kitchen table and enjoy some lemonade.

Adagio retells me the story of meeting Ingo. Listening to their friendly banter, it is easy to see how close they are.

Prompted by Ingo, I share with Adagio the story of my life-changing experience with the young girl, as well as my meeting Jessica earlier in the year. I could never have guessed our meeting would lead to me falling in love and becoming engaged.

"Despite the trials, I've been very blessed."

"I don't doubt that," Adagio agrees. "It seems you have some marvelous things heading your way. I mean, you have a great guy here, and this is only the beginning."

"He *is* a pretty amazing guy, huh?"

"I am, aren't I?" Ingo agrees.

Adagio smirks. "And your humility is astounding, is it not?"

"Indeed."

"Then since I am your best mate, that means I share your amiable qualities, true?"

"Oh, good grief!" I mutter. "You guys are too much."

"Too much what?" Ingo asks, his expression one of mock contrition.

"Too much everything."

"But you love us anyway."

"This is true."

I talk with them a few minutes more before saying goodnight, leaving them to visit a little longer.

Adagio lifts his glass and Ingo refills it with more lemonade. "So, how are you feeling? Are you ready for this?"

"Oh, yeah," Ingo answers, wearing a lazy smile. "I've never been more ready for anything in my life. I keep wondering what I did to deserve her. I mean, with everything she has been through in her life, she is simply amazing."

"She is pretty special. And the love you share is obvious. I have never seen you so happy."

"I've never *been* so happy."

"Man, I never thought it would happen, at least, not until you were fifty or so."

Ingo snorts. "Tell me about it."

"In a way, it feels like I have always known her, just like when I met you."

"I felt that, too, from the very first. It's like she has always been a part of my life. She makes me so happy."

"No need to tell me that, my friend. You have completely changed her life. And if anyone deserves happiness, it is Cisely."

"Truer words have never been spoken."

Staring out my bedroom window into the darkness, I am lost in thought when Jessica knocks.

"Come in."

She sticks her head in. "Am I disturbing you?"

"Not at all, come on in." Entering, she comes and sits next to me on the bed.

"I was just contemplating my life and thinking about Ingo and how grateful I am for him."

"He's a good man."

"He is." Standing, I move to the window and lean against the frame, my thoughts settling on my mother. "I'm grateful for you and for my life here, but I still . . . and don't take this the wrong way, but I think about my mother, and I wish I could have talked to her before she died and settled things better between us. I've tried to make peace with her in my heart, but I wonder if it will ever be enough."

Jessica's eyes are thoughtful. "Cisely, I can't even begin to comprehend what life was like for you, but I have to believe your mother did love you in her own way. How could she not?"

"I don't know. I want to believe she did."

"Then hold on to that belief, Cisely. Don't ever let it go."

"I'll try," I say, sitting down beside her again. "How do you always know just what to say?"

Instead of answering, she simply hugs me. "We are all living amazing lives, Cisely, and we need to recognize and enjoy each and every blessing that comes, because we never know what the future holds. We are continuously being prepared for something greater. Each and every trial we face in this life makes us stronger, if we allow them to. We just need to persevere and live the best we can."

"I do believe that now. Thank you, Jessica." She hugs me once more and leaves me to my thoughts.

Pondering a little longer, I send up a prayer of gratitude for Jessica and Ingo. I am also thankful for Adagio, and for the special friendship he and Ingo share that has expanded to include me.

Sixteen

The day before the wedding, there is a flurry of excitement throughout the house. Everyone is busy preparing for the big day. While I help the women do the baking for the wedding breakfast, the men wash and wax the cars and take care of the children. Everything seems to be going smoothly.

Occasionally, Ingo seeks me out and we disappear for a few moments alone. Each time we return, we are kidded by everyone about not being able to survive for five minutes without seeing each other. I'm completely all right with that and I am sure Ingo is too.

Jessica throws a surprise bridal shower for me. She planned it a couple of weeks ago and managed to keep it secret.

I am overwhelmed by the love and kindness of the women attending. I receive so many beautiful things, it is like Christmas, or at least how I imagine Christmas is for some people. Smiling shyly, I consider how a few of the gifts will please Ingo more than others.

I thank everyone for their thoughtfulness. After the shower, Jessica helps me take all the presents up to my room. We pile them in the corner until I can put them away. Ingo and I have decided to use my room as our permanent bedroom, and now most of his personal belongings are in the closet with mine, as well as on the dresser. I briefly look around the room and imagine sharing it with him. My eyes move to the bed and my face warms.

"A dollar for your thoughts," Jessica says, a knowing smile curving her lips. Though she has never married, I'm sure she isn't ignorant of things pertaining to the wedding night.

"Is it that obvious?"

"It is quite obvious, my dear. And I'm sure it is perfectly normal."

Sighing, I sit on the bed. "I know it was never right in the past, but this is different, very different. I've never longed to share this kind of closeness with anyone." I silently mull over that fact for a moment. "It was never love before. It was always induced by drugs and alcohol, and it was dirty and cheap."

Jessica sits next to me. "But it's not this time."

"No," I say. "Not this time."

"You deserve the best life has to offer, Cisely. And Ingo is definitely one of the best men to ever walk the face of the earth."

"I know," I agree softly. "I know."

At midnight Ingo softly knocks on my door and quietly opens it. He tiptoes over and kneels by my bed. Feeling his caress on my cheek, I smile.

"Were you awake, love?" he whispers.

"Yes. I can't sleep either. I don't think I've ever been so excited or nervous in my life."

"Neither have I. I just had to see you."

"I'm glad you came. I hope no one saw you, though. I would hate to create a scandal the night before our wedding."

Thanks to the moonlight shining through the curtains, I can clearly make out the wide grin splitting his face. He leans over and kisses me. "I can't wait until you are totally mine," he whispers.

"And I can't wait to be yours."

Kissing me a moment longer, he clears his throat abruptly before pulling away. "I guess I had better get back to my room before I really do cause a scandal."

I chuckle. "I guess you'd better."

"I love you, Cisely."

"I love you too. And I'm looking forward to beginning our new life together."

"So am I, and it will be a wonderful life."

"I think that's the name of a movie."

"I think you're right. Look at me turning cheesy all of a sudden. Don't tell anyone, okay?"

"Your secret is safe with me."

Kissing my brow, he finally stands. "So, I guess I'll see you in about seven hours."

"You mean six hours, forty-five minutes," I correct him, smiling dreamily.

"Good night, love. Sleep well."

"You, too."

Seventeen

The tears in Jessica's eyes mirror mine as we stand in the spacious dressing room of the church, gazing at my reflection in the large mirror. My beaded white gown is beautiful and I feel radiant.

"I think you are without a doubt the most beautiful bride I have ever seen."

"Thank you." Fingering the lovely strand of pearls Jessica gave me yesterday, I continue to examine my reflection, and for the first time in my life, I really do feel beautiful.

"I can't believe I'm about to be married."

"Believe it," Jessica says, wiping a tear away. "Oh, just look at me, starting with the waterworks already."

I chuckle, wiping my own cheek. "I'm so glad you're here with me. I can't think of anyone else I would rather have standing in my mother's place."

Jessica's smile fades slightly. She pulls an envelope from her pocket, holding it out to me. "This came for you yesterday."

Taking the envelope, I read the front, raising my eyes in surprise. "It's from my cousin, Velma."

"I would have given it to you yesterday, but for some reason it slipped my mind until this morning. I think you were supposed to have it today."

I open it. Along with the letter from Velma is a smaller envelope addressed to me. Stunned, I look up at Jessica. "It's from my mother."

"Would you like me to leave and let you read it in private?"

"No, please stay."

"Are you sure?"

"Yes. You are my family and I want to share this with you." It is hard for me to believe that I am actually holding a letter from my mother. I gaze at her handwriting on the front of the envelope. Mama always had beautiful handwriting. First, I read the letter from Velma.

Dear Cisely,

I just wanted to say how sorry I am for the way things were when you came back. Our family could never win a prize for niceness, but they were just plain cruel to you and I am truly sorry for that.

I admire you very much for the way you have changed your life. You are such a good person and I am trying to be just as brave. After you left, I made the decision to move out. I have been sharing an apartment for the past few weeks with two other roommates. It feels so good to be on my own.

Thank you for setting the example for me to follow. Enclosed is a letter from your mother. I found it while I was helping Mama clean out her apartment and thought you should have it. I guess she never got the chance to mail it.

Thank you again for the example you have set. Maybe one day I too, might finally get away from this place. I will write you again soon. Take care.

Velma

Blinking tears onto my cheeks, I refold the letter. How amazing is that? It is unbelievable that I have actually been a good example for someone, especially someone in my own family. My heart swells with joy at the thought of my cousin finally breaking free and choosing a new course for her life. I will keep in touch with her from now on.

"I've always known you were pretty special," Jessica says.

"That's because you are completely biased."

"Of course, I am, but it's still true."

Refolding the letter, I take a deep breath and open the one from my mother, and struggle to contain my emotions as I read her final words to me.

Dearest Cisely,

I know you're probably shocked to be receiving a letter from me, and I must admit that I don't blame you. I was never there for you when you needed me in the past. For that, I am truly sorry.

I guess the first thing I should tell you, which I'm sure you already know, is that I am an alcoholic. Can you believe it? I'm finally admitting it. It has taken me far too long to realize this fact. I've been sober now for a month, which isn't long, but for me it's a good start. It's been very hard to stay that way, but I'm not about to give in if I can help it. I'm only sorry it has taken me so long to get to this point.

Cisely, more than anything I just want to let you know how proud I am of you for getting away from here and making a better life for yourself. I know life has never been easy for you, and again I am sorry for my part in all of it. I wish I could change the past, but I can't. Anyway, I just wanted you to know these things.

Have a good life, Cisely. You deserve all the good this old world has to offer. I only hope you can forgive me for the past and let me be a part of your life now. Thank you for being such a wonderful daughter, despite my poor parenting.

I love you very much,
Mama

Pressing a hand to my mouth, I futilely fight a growing sob. Wrapping her arms around me, Jessica cries with me. I cannot believe I have finally been given the peace I have prayed so hard for. To know my mother really did love me, that she really cared, and my life truly did matter to her is all I could have hoped for and more. And to read her final words on my wedding day! It is definitely the best wedding gift I could ever receive.

"Are you going to be all right?" Jessica asks, pressing a hand to my cheek.

I nod, still too emotional to speak. She dries my tears with a tissue. "Well, you had better fix your makeup."

"I do look a sight, don't I? Studying my reflection, I dry my face.

"You always look beautiful no matter what. As for me, I don't have anyone to impress, but you do."

"Oh, I wouldn't be too sure. I've noticed Seth Walker checking you out lately. He's quite a catch, you know."

Jessica laughs softly. "I'm too old to go fishing now. I'm not sure I even have the bait anymore."

I giggle, feeling giddy. "You've still got it. If you don't believe me, just ask Seth."

"I just might do that. We do still have an afternoon of dancing ahead of us." When I arch an eyebrow brow, she laughs. We quickly touch up our makeup, finishing just as the reverend's wife tells us it is time.

The wedding ceremony is more wonderful than mere words can express. As Ingo takes my hand and we face one another, the reality of our union takes my breath away. We speak our vows, exchange rings and are pronounced husband and wife.

Ingo reverently places a hand on my cheek and I touch his in return. My happiness is indescribable. When we share our first kiss as husband and wife, there isn't a dry eye in the chapel.

After endless hugs and picture taking, we head to the reception hall.

As things get underway, I notice Ingo checking his watch every few minutes. I understand the reason perfectly. Smiling knowingly, my heart races at the thought of giving myself to him fully. Heat rushes to my cheeks as his eyes hold mine, making me again grateful for my brown skin. Taking my hand, he leads me out onto the floor for a dance, holding me close as we sway to the soft ballad.

"I love you, Mrs. Kelly," he whispers in my ear.

"I love you," Mr. Kelly." And did I tell you I love my new name?"

"You did. I love it too."

When our dance ends, we join Jessica at the table.

"Where's Adagio?" Ingo asks.

"He's out in the hall on the phone," Jessica says. "One of the chefs from his restaurant called."

"Is everything all right?" I ask.

"I don't think anything was wrong." She looks at us and smiles. "You two are absolutely glowing."

I squeeze Ingo's hand. "It's because I'm so happy."

He raises my hand to his lips. "So am I."

"Yes, it's quite obvious. This is the first time I've ever seen my nephew grin for two consecutive hours without stopping. I think his face is stuck."

We laugh. "I think you're right," Ingo says, massaging his cheeks. He points a finger at his aunt. "But just remember, this is all *your* doing."

"I admit it. I wanted my two favorite people together. Is that so terrible?"

Taking in her exaggerated expression of innocence, he chuckles. "It's not terrible at all." Scanning the room for a moment, he looks toward the hall. "Hmmm, I think Adagio is hiding. He's had single women trying to attach themselves to him all morning."

"Poor Adagio," Jessica says with a chuckle. "He hasn't had a moment's peace since he got here."

"Did I hear my name?" Adagio sits down, looking at us expectantly. I release an unladylike snort and Ingo and Jessica snicker.

"What?" he asks, looking at us.

"Oh, nothing," Jessica says, patting his face in a motherly gesture. "Ingo was just talking about how much your animal magnetism is driving the single women wild and obliterating their self-control."

"Uh huh. What is that American phrase you use? Oh, yes. Whatever." Ingo chuckles, patting his shoulder.

The music soon changes and an upbeat Motown tune by Gladys Knight and the Pips fills the hall. It is one of my favorite songs and I automatically start snapping my fingers and moving to the beat. Adagio is also snapping and grins at me. I guess he knows the song as well.

"Ingo, I am going to take your wife for a spin on the dance floor, okay?"

"Sure, but I think it will be the other way around." Ingo grins, winking at me. "Cisely, honey, try not to school the old man too much. Let him keep up a little."

"Who are you calling old? I am only a couple of years older than you."

"And in my book, that's old." Cutting his eyes to his aunt, he smiles contritely. "No offense, Aunt Jessica."

She laughs. "None taken, my boy."

Adagio shakes his head. "I *have* danced a little, you know."

Listening to them banter back and forth, I realize the old saying, '*Boys will be boys*' fits them perfectly. Ingo gives him a humoring nod to go ahead and Adagio rolls his eyes.

"Come on, Mrs. Kelly," he says, taking my hand. "Let us teach this husband of yours a lesson." Chuckling, I let him lead me out onto the floor.

"Hey, he really is pretty good!" Ingo says.

"I must say I agree," Jessica says as Adagio and Cisely dance circles around everyone on the floor. "And how in the world does she move like that in that dress?"

"I don't know. She's pretty amazing."

Jessica shakes her head, smiling. She squeezes Ingo's hand. "Do you have any idea how much you have changed her life?"

"Probably as much as she has changed mine." Sighing deeply, he gazes out at Cisely for a moment. "I am the luckiest man in the world to have her, Aunt Jessica. And seeing her change has been amazing. But you have watched those changes, too."

"Indeed, I have."

"When we first met, she was a beautiful lost soul." He swallows, emotion welling inside him. "Being able to love her and help her understand her worth has been the most meaningful experience of my life. And to actually have her as my wife just . . . it just blows me away."

"I am sure she feels the same. How could she not?"

He kisses Jessica's cheek. "Thank you for inviting her to come and stay with you."

"You're very welcome."

As the song ends and we stop to catch our breath, Adagio squeezes my hands. "You are a special lady, Cisely, and I am glad you and Ingo found each other. You two deserve all the happiness in the world."

"Thank you."

He hugs me, adding, "Thank you for letting me share this special day with you."

"I'm happy you were able to be here. You just promise to stay in touch. After all, you are family to me now."

He smiles, hugging me again. "I promise."

Ingo and I catch a flight to Long Beach, California, then board a Mexican cruise ship. I have always dreamed of going on a cruise but never thought I would.

Our wedding night is magical. I never knew the sacred act of making love could be so emotionally consuming. Sharing that kind of intimacy is a powerful thing, one that I will never take for granted. As Ingo holds me in his arms afterward, I marvel at the feeling of oneness between us.

We savor every moment of our honeymoon, spending our days going ashore in Catalina and Ensenada, shopping for souvenirs for family and friends.

On Sea Day, I treat myself to an afternoon in the ship's spa and enjoy being pampered. We dine a couple of nights in the formal restaurant on board the ship, but most of the time, we order in room service and treasure our time alone.

When we finally return, Jessica greets us with a delicious welcome home dinner. We tell her about our trip and show her our photos. After dinner we unpack and give Jessica the gifts that we purchased for her. I make a mental note to send Adagio's gifts off to him the following day. He will definitely find the ones Ingo picked for him amusing.

The last few months have been the best of my life, and I know this is only beginning. I am truly happy. I cannot imagine things ever being any different.

Eighteen

The months have passed quickly and Thanksgiving is fast approaching. I cannot remember ever being more grateful at this time of year. Marriage to Ingo has been amazing, and as Jessica fondly says, "We are as happy as clams."

Since we have no money worries—a fact I still find hard to grasp sometimes—I quit my job at the boutique. I am able to travel with Ingo to out of state photo shoots. There is nothing we enjoy more than being together.

Awakening one particular morning, I peel my eyes open, encountering a bedroom full of sunlight, and I realize I have slept in a little later than normal. When I sit up, I am hit by a wave of nausea. Lying back against the pillows, I close my eyes and swallow hard, telling myself I cannot be sick now. Ingo and I plan to take a trip down to Southern Utah in two days and I'm really looking forward to it.

I make another attempt to get up when the phone rings. Grateful for a reason to stay in bed for another moment, I answer it and smile when I hear Adagio's voice, despite feeling sick. He is calling to say hello and catch up on what has been going on with us. We have only talked a couple of times since the wedding and both conversations were brief because he has been so busy with the restaurant.

"So, how are things?" I ask.

"Things are good, just trying to keep up with the increasing traffic and keep the kitchen guys in line. They are pretty crazy in there."

"It sounds like you're having fun."

"I am. They are great to work with."

"Well, I'm sure you are a pretty great boss." I again close my eyes and swallow against the queasiness.

"So, how's marriage treating you guys?"

"Ahhh, sigh. We love it!"

He laughs. "I can hear it in your voice. You two are great together. Now all you need is a little one of your own to make it complete. Uncle Adagio has a nice ring to it, do you not agree?"

"I agree completely," I say, chuckling. "I looking forward to being a mom . . ."

Wait . . . My period is late. As my hazy brain clears, I quickly calculate the days. *I'm two weeks late . . . and I'm sick.* My mind is reeling at the possibility. I have been so busy preparing for our trip and doing other things, I hadn't noticed.

"Hey, Cisely, are you still there?"

"I'm here," I answer, embarrassed to have let my thoughts drift so far.

"Are you all right?"

"Yes, I'm okay." *I'm better than okay!*

"I should probably let you go, and I had better get back over to the restaurant."

"It must be nice to work from home, so to speak."

"It is convenient and I do enjoy it."

"I'm glad. Hey, I'll tell Ingo you called, but only if you promise to call him later. You know how much he looks forward to your calls."

"I know. He needs to hear my voice once in a while."

"It's the accent," I say and he laughs. "Promise you'll call him."

"I will. *Ciao*, Cisely."

"*Ciao*."

Hanging up the phone, I stay in bed a little longer, waiting for my stomach to calm some. Deciding it is pointless, I drag myself out of bed and make my way to the kitchen. After searching the cupboards for crackers to no avail, I settle on a piece of toast and a glass of juice. Within a few minutes I am a little better and am able to take a shower. Then I make a quick trip to the neighborhood pharmacy for a pregnancy test.

I quickly take the test, grinning as I examine the positive result.

"I'm pregnant!"

J. Adams

Nineteen

Even the slight nausea doesn't dampen my spirits as I wait for Ingo to return from an all-day photo shoot. I am glad Jessica is at the boutique today. She is usually so observant she would have easily seen behind my smile and guessed my news before I could share it with Ingo.

Ingo arrives home a little after four and I meet him at the door. "I missed you," he says, pulling me close for a kiss.

"I missed you, too. I'm glad you're home." Drawing back, I look into his eyes, feeling positively giddy.

"Either you're extra glad to see me or something good has happened. So, which is it?"

"Both."

"Both? Do I need to sit down before you tell me?"

"Maybe." I smile at his arched brow.

"Okay." Taking my hand, he leads me into the living room, then promptly pulls me onto his lap. "Okay, let's have it."

"Well, I just found out that someone I know is going to be a daddy."

"Really? Who . . ." Pausing, Ingo grins, then he releases a delighted chuckle. "Really? Are you sure?"

"I am."

He hugs me. "I can't believe it! I'm going to be a father." He caresses my cheek. "You've made me so happy." Pressing his hand against my flat stomach, he draws me against him and kisses me slowly. Stirred by my breathless response, he quickly leads me up to our room, and there we stay until darkness falls.

When we finally head back downstairs to get something to eat, Jessica is sitting at the table enjoying a cup of hot chocolate.

"Well, good evening, you two," she says with that knowing smile I recognize all too well. "Dinner is in the fridge if you're hungry."

"I'm sorry about dinner," I say. It had been my turn to cook.

"I'm sorry, too, Aunt Jessica. It was my fault she forgot." Of course, he smiles as he says this. I slug him playfully, embarrassed.

Jessica chuckles. "It's okay, dear. You can take my turn tomorrow."

I take a seat at the table while Ingo heats some dinner for us. Watching him pull several things from the fridge, I muse that I will soon be taking full advantage of the large meals Jessica always prepares.

While the food is heating in the microwave, Ingo places his hands on my shoulders. "Sweetheart, we should tell Aunt Jessica the good news."

"What good news?" Jessica asks, her eyes bright.

"I don't know," I tease. "Are you sure we should tell her?"

"Hmmm, maybe we shouldn't just yet."

"Tell me what?"

"You know," Ingo says, "just forget we said anything."

"Ingo and Cisely Kelly! You stop messing around and tell me this instant or I'll . . ."

"Okay, okay," I give in, laughing. "We're going to have a baby."

"Really?" she squeals. "Oh, my goodness, how wonderful! Congratulations!"

"Thank you," Ingo says. "We're pretty excited."

Jessica claps her hands jubilantly. "Your parents are going to be thrilled to hear this."

"I think thrilled is an understatement. Unless one of my brothers' wives has made an announcement recently, this will be their first grandchild. I'll call them tomorrow. I'm sure they will let everyone else know pretty quickly."

"Oh, you should call Adagio back and tell him he's going to be an uncle," I add. "He called this morning and mentioned that Uncle Adagio has a nice ring to it before I even realized I was pregnant."

"That's Adagio for you. I'll call him in the morning, too."

Adagio whoops loudly when we tell him the news.

"Congratulations! I'm so happy for you!"

"Thank you," Ingo says. "We're pretty excited."

"We will be officially calling you Uncle Adagio soon," I say on the other extension, swallowing against the underlying nausea.

"And I will be ready for it! As a matter of fact, I think I will plan another visit soon."

"We would love that," Ingo assures him. "You know you're welcome anytime."

"I know."

"We'll let you know the due date as soon as we find out," I say.

"I will be waiting to hear. I have been told there is nothing as wonderful as bringing a child into the world. And Ingo, my friend, I know you will be a great father. Cisely, you being a good mother is a given."

"Thanks, Adagio. That means a lot."

"I only speak the truth."

"Well, you just get ready for your uncle duties," Ingo tells him.

"I am looking forward to it."

After talking a few minutes more, we give him our love and say goodbye. Lying on the bed and taking me in his arms, Ingo holds me close, kissing my brow.

"I'm sorry about having to postpone the trip, Ingo."

"Don't be sorry, love. We can go another time. Besides, it wouldn't do for you to be sick all the way down."

"This is true," I agree.

"I guess we should call my parents now. Only I'm sure we'll be on the phone a lot longer."

"You're probably right." I know how much his parents enjoy talking to us. They will be so excited to hear about the baby, we will indeed be on the phone for a while.

Twenty

On Friday morning, Ingo comes with me to my appointment. My midwife, Judy March, is a good friend of Jessica's. A kind and pleasant woman, she is a lot like Jessica as far as personality, and I can see why they are friends. She gives me a full checkup and pronounces me healthy. The baby will be due in July and I am grateful I won't have to go through the complete summer pregnant.

The following morning after we finish breakfast (when I could finally fight off the nausea enough to get up and get ready,) Ingo suggests that we go window shopping for baby things and I eagerly agree. We spend the morning roaming in and out of various stores and see so many cute things, Ingo insists on purchasing a few. Shaking my head, I laugh as we walk out of store after store carrying full shopping bags.

"Just a few things, huh?" I say.

"I can't help myself. I'm in a spoiling mood already."

"I can see that."

We put everything in the trunk. As he closes it, I give into the urge to wrap my arms around his waist. "Thank you for this morning, and for being so wonderful."

"You're welcome, love. Thank you for giving me a reason to smile each day."

We have lunch at my favorite Italian restaurant, and now that I am expecting, I don't feel as guilty about stuffing myself. Not that I've had to worry much about my weight in the past. So far, I have been one of those lucky people who can eat basically anything and not worry about my figure. But I'm sure that will change after I have the baby.

We enjoy a leisurely lunch and talk of our plans for the future. Afterward, we stop by the boutique and visit with Jessica for a few minutes before heading home.

We carry the bags up to our room. Sensing how tired I am, Ingo insists that I take a nap, and I am so worn out, I don't protest.

"I don't remember shopping ever being this exhausting," I say, resting my head on the pillow."

He covers me with a fleece blanket and kneels beside the bed. "I'm sorry I wore you out today."

"No, don't be sorry," I say, pressing a hand to his cheek. "It was a lot of fun. And I really enjoyed watching you. You can out-shop me any day."

He smiles, kissing my palm. "We're just going to have to make sure you take it a little easier for a while. You relax and get some rest. I'll take care of dinner this evening."

"You don't have to do that." After eating such a big lunch, at the moment, the very thought of cooking makes me a little queasy, but I am willing to deal with it and take my turn.

"I know, but I want to."

"You're just too good to me."

"I could never be too good to you, love." He kisses me and leaves me to sleep.

A while later Ingo wakes me.

"I'm sorry to wake you, love, but your cousin Velma is on the phone. I thought you would want to talk to her."

This is a pleasant surprise. "Yes, I would." I pick up the phone, and Ingo leaves me to talk.

"Hello, Velma."

"Hi, Cisely. I was just calling to see how you were doing."

I smile, happy to actually have someone in my family thinking of me. "I'm glad you called. How have you been?"

"I've been great. I'm enjoying being out on my own. I love the freedom. How are you?"

"I am doing well. I have an amazing husband and . . . I'm pregnant."

"Really?"

"Really."

"Girl, I'm so happy for you and Ingo!"

"Thanks. We're pretty happy, too."

"Have you found out when you are due?"

"Yes, we're having a July baby."

"That's good. I am so excited for you guys."

"So are we. In fact, Ingo is so excited, he nearly bought out a few department stores today. We were only supposed to be window shopping."

Velma laughs. "I can only hope to find a guy like that one day."

"You will. I am sure of it."

"From your lips to God's ears."

"It's only a matter of time."

For a long moment, Velma is silent and I wonder if everything is all right. Just I start to ask, she finally speaks again.

"Cisely, I just wanted to tell you how amazing I think you are. Because of you, I know anything is possible. I often think about your life and the things you went through. I know it wasn't easy growing up in a family like ours, but you completely turned your life around. You're an inspiration to me, and I'm glad you found Ingo. I'm grateful to be able to call you both my family."

Darn these tears! "Thanks so much, Velma. We're grateful for you, too."

"You've had so many awesome things happen to you, Cisely, and I'm sure there is even more to come. I hope for me as well." She laughs. "Listen to me. I sound like a fortune cookie."

I chuckle. "You sound great."

"Well, I'll stop rambling now. Basically, I just wanted to say I love you and I am one family member who will be here for you whenever you need me."

"Thank you, Velma." I am deeply touched by her outpouring of feelings. "That means so much to me. You are an inspiration to me as well. I've never had a sister, but if I did, I would want her to be just like you. I love you, too. Thanks for calling me."

"You're welcome. Well, I'll let you go now. But remember to call me if you ever need to talk or anything and I'll do the same."

"I will. And Velma, thanks."

Hanging up the phone, I lean back against the pillows and allow my thoughts to linger on Velma. I have truly grown to love her and I wish we lived a little closer to each other.

Phone calls are good, though.

Reflecting on the changes in my life, I think of Jessica and her capacity to love everyone. I am grateful for the close relationship we share. I think of the women at the boutique and the friendships I have formed with them. It's sad that in all the time I worked at the restaurant in North Carolina, there wasn't one person there I could truly consider a friend.

I think about Adagio, and I am deeply grateful for his friendship and the close relationship he shares with Ingo. There is nothing the two would not do for each other and that means a lot.

Finally, I think of Ingo. He means the world to me and I cannot imagine where I would be without him.

With this final thought, I drift to sleep. However, a few minutes later I am confronted by the vision of a face that again enters my dreams unbidden. I awaken with a gasp.

It was just a dream. Just a dream, just a dream . . .

Squeezing my eyes shut, it takes a lot of effort, but I force the visual from my mind.

The frequent invader of my sleep is a part of my past, and I pray that he will not keep intruding upon my future.

Twenty-one

It is still early when we wake to the ringing of the telephone.

"That's probably John calling about shooting the house photos," Ingo says sleepily. "He was going to call if he couldn't make the appointment this morning."

"How is he doing anyway?" I am now fully awake.

"He's okay. The divorce has been hard on him and he really needs to get the house sold. The payments are pretty hefty and too much to handle with just his income. That's–" There is a knock on our door. "Come in."

Jessica sticks her head in. "I'm sorry, but it's for you . . . It's your friend, Adagio. He said it was really important."

Ingo quickly picks up the cordless and Jessica hands me the other one, so I can listen in.

"Adagio, what is it?" Ingo asks.

"I am sorry to call you so early, but I am about to board a flight to Salt Lake and I was wondering if it would be all right if I stayed with you and Cisely for a few days."

"Sure, you don't even need to ask. What's going on? Wait, Cisely is listening in too." I turn the other phone on.

"*Ciao*, Cisely."

"Hi, Adagio. What has happened?"

"I got a call from a good friend in Salt Lake. He and his wife just lost their little boy. He was killed by a drunk driver."

"Oh, no!" I gasp. "That's terrible!"

"I know. After he hit the boy, the young man ran into a tree a little farther down the road. Otherwise, he would have gotten away."

"How is the poor family holding up?" Ingo asks.

"They are pretty broken up. Tara, the mother, is not well at all. He was eight years old and their only child. She can't have any more children."

I tearfully try to imagine what the couple must be going through. It brings back a few memories of being in cars with drunk drivers myself—that is, when I was sober enough to notice. It is not a pretty picture and I quickly put it out of my mind. "Can we do anything to help?"

"I don't know at the moment. Gary, the boy's father, asked me if I would help them with the arrangements. Neither are close to their families through no fault of their own. I will let you know if I need any help once I get there and can talk with them about what they want."

"When does your flight get in?" Ingo asks.

"My plane was delayed for a couple of hours, but we are almost ready to take off. I will be there at midnight. I have already reserved a car, so you won't need to pick me up. I'm sorry to be coming in so late."

"Don't worry about it," I say. "We will just be glad to see you."

"I look forward to seeing you as well."

After the call, we get up and begin making preparations, readying a room for Adagio. We look forward to seeing him again. We only wish it were under happier circumstances.

Twenty-two

Adagio

It is just after one in the morning when Adagio parks his rented Mazda in front of Ingo and Cisely's home and hauls his luggage up the steps. The living room light is on, so he knows someone is waiting up for him. Ingo opens the door before he even knocks and the two men embrace.

"I appreciate you letting me stay with you."

"You never have to ask. You're always welcome."

"Thank you."

He follows Ingo up to the same guest room he stayed in when he came for the wedding.

"Cisely said she'll see you bright and early in the morning." Looking at his watch, he grins. "I guess that would be today."

Adagio chuckles. "It is always so strange to lose half your day and not even know it."

"I know what you mean. Can I get you anything?"

"No, I am okay."

"Well, make yourself at home"
"Thanks. I will see you later."

Adagio

Adagio closes the door and places his suitcase on the bed. Taking out a pair of pajama bottoms, a t-shirt and his toiletry bag, he quickly changes and gets into bed, deciding to leave the unpacking until after he's had some sleep.

But as tired as he is, he can't sleep. His thoughts are on Gary and Tara and their loss. Brian was only six years old the last time Adagio saw him. At that time the little boy followed him around like a shadow most of the time, and Adagio loved it. Smiling, Adagio ponders the times he shared with the family, going to ball games and out for pizza. He had even baby-sat for Gary and Tara a few times so they could get out for a bit. He remembers how he envied their happiness and contentment in life. Gary and Tara had each other, they had their faith, and they had Brian. They had needed nothing else. Now Brian is gone and a gaping hole is left in their life.

Adagio's thoughts shift to his mother. Even after all these years he still misses her. He misses her laughter, her beautiful smile, her unwavering faith.

He thinks back, as he has so many times before, to the last conversation he had with his mother before she died. She told him he would one day face a trial that would shake his faith to the very core before receiving blessings beyond measure. At first, he'd thought it was when the restaurant burned down. He had put so much work into the place and suddenly it was taken away.

It had all been for nothing, or so he had thought. He has learned much since then about business and is grateful for the lessons.

Still, he wonders about the trial he is facing now, because it seems to be growing harder with each day that passes.

It is the trial of loneliness.

Some days he is okay because he knows God has a plan, though he has no idea what that plan is. But during moments like this, it is hard to see past the pain enough to think about future blessings.

He misses his mother and he is lonely.

However, he does have friends and a good life.

He has much to be grateful for.

Adagio is sitting at the kitchen table enjoying a cup of hot chocolate, hoping the big dose of sugar will give him a needed energy boost when Jessica enters.

"Hello," he says, standing.

"Adagio, my boy!" Jessica reaches up to hug him and he leaned down, accepting her embrace. "How are you?" she asks, releasing him.

"I am well."

"Ingo told me about your friends' loss. I am so sorry."

"Thank you. I can't imagine what they are going through. I am heading over to their place in a few minutes."

"Well, though I don't know them, please give them my condolences."

"I will." He smiles. "I guess you are pretty excited about Cisely and Ingo's little one. Since you have adopted the role of Cisely's mother, you really will be like a grandmother."

"I'm very excited. Since I never had little ones of my own, I welcome babies anytime. I hope the house will be full one day."

"I hope you are right," Adagio agrees. "I can picture Ingo chasing them up and down the stairs now."

"Now that would indeed be a sight."

Adagio looks up as Ingo and Cisely entered the kitchen. He grins. "Hello, *bella.*"

"Hey, you," Cisely says, grinning back as he hugs her. "I'm so sorry about your friends."

"Thank you. I am heading over now, but I couldn't leave without saying hello and thanking you for letting me stay."

Cisely waves the comment aside. "You are family, so you're always welcome."

Adagio visits with them another few moments before heading out.

Adagio puts his arms around Gary and Tara and they cry against his shoulders. For a few moments he saying nothing, just offers what comfort he can. There is nothing else he can say, no new words to offer, and definitely no advice since he's never been in their position or even close. Losing a parent is one thing, but losing a child is something he's never had to comprehend.

"Let's go into the kitchen," Tara finally suggests. "We have a counter full of cookies and pastries that some of the neighbors dropped off last night."

"Sounds good," Adagio says.

They sit at the table for a while, talking about Brian and what a special boy he was. Adagio sheds a few more tears thinking about how much he will miss him.

"We had so many plans for the future." Tara says, fresh tears brimming her eyes. "We were going to enroll Brian in a karate class in a couple of weeks. He was so excited about that. He wanted to be able to defend himself should he ever run into bullies in school." Closing her eyes, she heaves a sad sigh. "There is just never enough time."

Gary wipes his eyes. "There's so much I wish we had done with him, so much I wish I had said."

Adagio places a hand on Gary's shoulder. "You were the best parents a kid could ever ask for, and you will always have your memories of him and the life you all had together. Nothing can ever take that away. In the short time you had together, you probably gave him a lifetime of love."

"We tried to," Gary says. "We'd like to think we did."

"Trust me, you did."

Adagio accompanies Gary and Tara to the funeral home and helps with the service arrangements. He finally says good night, embracing them both, assuring them he will always be there for them. They thank him and write down the address of the church.

They tell Adagio how grateful they are for his friendship, and he assures them it is the other way around; they had shared their son with him. That meant more than he can ever say.

Twenty-three

It seems that every person the Flynn family has ever known is in attendance for their son's funeral and they receive much support. The church is filled to capacity and I'm sure it comforts the grieving parents to know their son had touched so many lives. Many wonderful and kind things are said about Brian during the service. He had touched countless people during his short life and was truly loved by everyone he came in contact with. Glancing around the packed building, it is obvious Gary and Tara have touched many lives as well.

The day before, Adagio asked a favor of me when he returned from the Flynn's. They wanted a musical number and he remembered Ingo telling him I sing and play the piano. He asked if I would sing one of Brian's favorite songs during the service. Though I have never performed in front of a large crowd before, I said yes. I spent half the day practicing, wanting to get it just right.

Walking up on the stand and taking a seat at the piano, I am not nervous, but I do say a silent prayer that I will be able to get through the song. I want to comfort the couple in any way I can, which is why I had agreed so readily to do it. I can't imagine losing a child, or anyone close to me for that matter. I absently touch my flat stomach. Contemplating our unborn child renews my gratitude for the gift of motherhood.

The Flynns had requested that I sing a song by a popular Christian group, which I do with all my heart. I tearfully imagine the little boy smiling down on the congregation, completely at peace.

The service concludes and Brian is soon laid to rest. Gary and Tara thank me for singing, saying it made them feel closer to their son. I assure them I was happy to do it.

Gary squeezes Adagio's shoulder. "It has meant the world to us to have you here. Thanks so much for all your help and support. I know it made Brian happy you were here."

"I'm glad I could be here. I had planned to visit you in January when I come back to see Ingo and Cisely. I wanted to bring something special for Brian. I am sorry I will not have the opportunity to give it to him."

Tara wipes her eyes. "He knew you loved him, and he probably knows that even more now."

"I think so too," Adagio agrees.

Ingo and I leave the three alone to talk for a few minutes more. They soon say goodbye to one another and Adagio heads back home with us.

Relaxing in the living room, we spend some more time visiting. Adagio fills us in on what he's been up to since his last visit.

"So, how is the love life coming along, my friend?" Ingo asks. "Anyone new we should know about?"

Adagio laughs. "Sorry, but not even close."

"What are we going to do with you?" I ask, shaking my head.

"I don't know. I ask myself that very question from time to time, with no answers."

"Hey, I know," I say brightly. "We could put an ad in the paper. You know, post your picture in the "Lonely Hearts" section along with your stats? Beneath the photo we could specify your requirements in a mate. What do you think?"

Book men look at me with straight faces, but it isn't long before the room is ringing with their boisterous laughter.

"Hey, I was serious, guys," I pout and they laugh even harder. "Fine, I know when my help is not appreciated."

Ingo wipes his eyes, drawing me close. "I'm sure Adagio appreciates your help. Don't you?"

"Definitely," he agrees, wiping his own eyes. "Thank you, Cisely. I needed a good laugh today."

"You're very welcome."

"What are your plans now?" Ingo asks. "Will you stay for a while?"

"Probably just through Thanksgiving. Then I will need to get back to the restaurant. I left it in good hands and I'm sure everything is okay, but we've been pretty busy lately and I should probably be there."

"I can understand," Ingo agrees.

"You two will have to come and visit me before Cisely is too far along to travel. She would love Treviso and Venice."

Yawning, I lean my head against Ingo's shoulder. "We will. I would love to see it. Actually, I would love to tour the whole country." Covering my mouth, I yawn again. By this time of the evening, I am always exhausted.

"Maybe you should go on to bed, love. I'll be up in a bit."

"Maybe you're right," I agree. "I'm sorry, guys. It's getting harder for me to keep my eyes open these days."

"I understand completely," Adagio says. "I really appreciate your help today. It meant so much to the Flynns, and to me."

"I was glad to do it, really." Smiling sleepily, I head up to bed.

Adagio

In his dark bedroom, Adagio stands at the window, staring out at the night sky.

What is wrong with me?

The question runs through his head over and over, and the answer is always the same.

He needs something more.

He doesn't need material things. He is not after fame, glory, power or prestige. He has no need of such things and he recognizes the many gifts in his life. Each new *day* is a gift to him.

No, what he seeks goes far deeper than any material or worldly idea. His quest is a quest of the heart. His need is an emotional one.

This experience with Gary and Tara has taken a bigger toll on Adagio's emotions than he realized, and he sees so much that he is missing out on. Love and laughter. A family to call his own. He craves those things like a man in a desert craves water.

His gaze moves to an object lying on the dresser with his rental car key, the sparkling stones reflecting the moonlight. It is his mother's ring. He always carries it with him, and he has no idea why. Maybe to feel closer to her. Maybe it is for luck. Maybe it is an unspoken dream of finally meeting and placing it on the finger of the woman he loves.

A dream it pains him to think about at the moment.

I don't know what to do with this, Lord. It hurts.

He pulls back the covers on the bed, but he can't force himself to lie down. He is so lonely that the pain is threatening to tear him apart. Slipping to his knees by the bed, he closes his eyes.

Please help me to be patient, God. I know you have a plan for me. I just need to be patient. Please help me. Burying his face in the covers, he lets the tears come, losing track of time as the emotion he has been holding back for so long finds its blessed release.

Adagio's next awareness is sunlight filtering through the blinds. He doesn't remember crawling into bed, but he feels better, calmer, like everything will be okay.

Now he will wait patiently and continue to take life one day at a time.

Twenty-four

We hear from Adagio once or twice a week. When he left after the funeral, he seemed more somber and we were worried about him. We still worry. He constantly assures us that he is okay and tells us *not* to worry, which is easier said than done.

I visit Tara Flynn once a week and I have gotten to know her better. During our visits, we talk about Brian. Tara shares stories with me of her son's childhood and things they did together. Her grief is still deep and I am glad to be a listening ear. She even shares her pregnancy experiences with me, which I enjoy a great deal. I ask questions about labor and delivery and Tara freely answers them. Though I know every woman's pregnancy is different, it is still helpful to know a little more about what to expect. I appreciate her very much and we have become great friends.

Adagio comes back to spend Christmas with us. He is doing well but couldn't stand the thought of spending Christmas alone.

On Christmas Eve, we celebrate with eggnog and the cookies and cakes Jessica and I baked all day. Adagio had even made cannoli and chocolate biscotti, both of which are the most heavenly treats I've ever eaten. Sitting near the tree, we listen to Ingo read the nativity story from the Bible, then we sing Christmas carols with me accompanying on the piano.

On Christmas Day, Gary and Tara Flynn join us for dinner. It is a tender day for all of us as we remember Brian and other loved ones near and far away.

I have never enjoyed the holidays more. It is the first time I have truly felt the spirit of the season. Surrounded by family and good friends, I cannot ask for a better Christmas.

Twenty-five

It snows frequently in January and February, but I absolutely love Utah in the winter time. Even though the temperatures are sometimes freezing, it still feels warmer than the coldest winter in humid North Carolina. I am feeling pretty good and am no longer experiencing debilitating morning sickness, or as I like to call it, 'anytime sickness.' The fatigue has eased up as well. And with each week that passes, I am more content, and I eagerly anticipate the birth of our child.

February is almost over, and being almost halfway through my pregnancy, I am now wearing maternity clothes. Ingo often tells me I'm beautiful and never fails to show me how he feels.

I notice that Ingo has become more protective of me—so much so that he puts off doing things he normally enjoys, preferring to stay home with me. And while I appreciate his concern and enjoy having him home, I feel guilty that he never takes any time for himself. Whenever I suggest that he get out for a bit, he makes an excuse to stay. Though I am grateful for his determination to be here, he needs something to take his mind off me. He needs to do something fun.

March has breezed in and Ingo has yet to indulge in one of his favorite sports–skiing. Concerned about his vitamin-D exposure, as well as his low total on the winter fun-o-meter, I call a couple of his friends, who in turn call Ingo and invite him to go skiing. And as expected, he doesn't want to leave me alone.

"Maybe this isn't such a good idea, love," he says, pulling on a flannel shirt. Watching me where I am resting on the bed, he buttons his shirt and tucks it into his jeans. "I need to be here in case something should happen."

Shaking my head, I get up. "Nothing is going to happen, Ingo. Stop worrying so much."

"I can't help it." When I arch a brow, he holds his hands up, already guessing what I'm about to say because he has heard me say it many times. "I know, I know, women have babies all the time, but if something happened while I was gone, I could never forgive myself."

"I'll be fine. Honest. It's just for the afternoon and you really need this time. Besides, I can always call you on your cell if there is an emergency, which I'm sure there won't be. And if I can't get you, I can call Wendy at the boutique, or Tara."

He heaves a resigned sigh. "Are you sure? Because I can always–"

I silence him with a kiss.

"Hmmm," he growls. "I *know* I don't I want to go now."

144

"I'll be here when you get back."

"Then I'll have to hurry back."

"You do that."

He is set to leave after lunch. I am in the kitchen packing a bag of snacks for him to take when he pulls me into his arms. "You know, you could go with me. We could purposely get lost in the woods somewhere and try to find ways to keep each other warm until help arrives."

"We could, but I don't know if I would want to be found."

"Me either. But then again, that *is* the plan."

I laugh, handing him the bag. "Hold that thought until you get back."

"Don't worry, love. I will."

I kiss him and walk him to the door. "Have a good time."

"Thanks. I'll try."

"And don't worry about me, okay?"

"You're asking the impossible. But I'll do my best."

Kissing him again, I close the door behind him and move to the family room window, watching him get in his car.

He really needs this time.

As Ingo backs out of the driveway, he looks up as Cisely waves through the side window. At the same moment, an acute ache fills his chest. The pain startles him so, he immediately puts the car in park. Pressing a hand to his chest, he closes his eyes, and takes a deep breath, briefly wondering if he is experiencing a heart attack. But when the pain quickly subsides, he figures it must have been some sort of panic attack, probably stemming from worry over Cisely.

"Look at me," he mutters. "A grown man and I can't even spend one afternoon away from my wife. Get a grip, Kelly!"

Opening his eyes and looking up at Cisely again, he pulls back into the driveway, then gets out and trots back into the house. Pulling her to him, he holds her close.

"Are you sure you're going to be all right?"

"I will be fine. I promise. Just go and have a good time."

"Okay." He kisses her, holding her another moment. "I love you, Cisely."

"I know," she says, cupping his cheek. "I love you, too."

He finally forces himself out the door.

"Are we ready, gentlemen?" Ingo asks, getting off the ski lift. He takes in the vast surroundings. The blanket of white is almost blinding but beautiful. Thankfully his goggles are tinted.

"I'm definitely ready," Ben says. "What do you say, Tim?"

"I say the need for speed is about to be satisfied!"

Ingo grins at the excited men. They are like eager little boys let loose in a candy store. He really is glad to have come, despite worrying about Cisely. But she is right. She will be okay until he gets back. Shaking his head, he muses that even though he has tried not to, he really has become a worrier. He can't understand why. Maybe it is because he'd never loved anyone until Cisely. She is constantly on his mind, and just the thought of her warms his entire being.

Cisely had been through so much in her life, and everything inside Ingo yearns to keep her heart safe, to never let her be hurt again. Even still, thinking about how far she has come, Ingo knows that even if he never had another day with her, his love helped to produce a great work. She knows who she is now, and she knows her worth.

He had smiled as he'd watched couples coming and going earlier while he sat putting on his skis, and remembered how he had joked with Cisely about coming with him. Now as he stands in the frigid weather, those thoughts heat him to the core and he doesn't feel the cold. Looking down at the lodge, a dot in the distance, he contemplates bringing Cisely up for a few days in the fall, and he makes a mental note to make reservations before leaving.

Ingo, Ben and Tim get into position, calling from one to the other, "See you at the bottom!" Then they are off.

Ingo experiences heightened exhilaration with each slice of his skis in the snow. It is a rush he hasn't experienced in a long time and he is enjoying every second of it. He has always loved skiing and the feeling of freedom it brings. He'd learned to ski as a teenager during their family vacations in Utah and quickly took to it. He smiles as those memories come to mind. His form is perfect and he is feeling pretty confident, his concentration level high.

Then, out of nowhere, the pain he had felt earlier returns. When it does, his concentration flees.

Sitting on the living room sofa, I study the movements of the little boy inside me. We'd found out the sex of the baby as soon as we could, and though we would have been just as happy with a girl, we are excited to be having a son first. Ingo says every little girl needs a big brother, so he is sure we will have a girl next time.

Up until now, I have only felt slight flutters here and there, but today I can actually feel him moving around, and it is unlike anything I ever imagined. To feel this life growing inside gives me the ultimate feeling of peace and makes me marvel anew at how truly miraculous and sacred procreation is.

I spend some time reading a maternity magazine and a few pamphlets on childbirth. Some things I have already learned from Tara, but as I read about the phases of labor and delivery, as well as the options available, I decide to take a natural childbirth class and prepare as much as I can. I will discuss it with Ingo when he gets back.

Pulling a folded piece of paper from the desk, I again look over my list of things we will need for the baby's nursery. We still need to buy a crib and get the bedding. There are already lots of clothes, blankets and diapers, thanks to Ingo's window-shopping sprees and Jessica's surprise purchases.

My thoughts roam to Jessica. She is in Australia for the month visiting her family. Though she has only been gone for a week, I miss her a great deal. She calls each day to check on me and make sure I'm okay. Between Jessica and Ingo, and even Tara checking on me from time to time, I am covered.

The growl of my stomach reminds me that it is time to eat something. Even though I'm a fairly decent cook, I still miss Jessica's delicious meals. She usually cooks so much, there are leftovers for days. I wonder if her family is taking advantage of her culinary skills.

Probably.

As I am heading to the kitchen, the doorbell rings. Answering it, I squeal.

"Hello, *bella!*"

"I can't believe you're here!" I cry, throwing my arms around Adagio's neck.

He laughs and embraces me. "Look at you! You look so beautiful!"

"I look big."

"You are not big, just pregnant. And you still look beautiful."

"Thank you. Come on in."

Adagio picks up his suitcase, setting it in the hallway by the stairs.

"So why didn't you tell us you were coming? I could have gone shopping and prepared something special for dinner."

"I told Ingo I would be coming one day this week," he says, squeezing my hand. "He wanted you to be surprised."

"Well, you both succeeded."

He grins. "It is so good to see you," he says, hugging me again. "I have missed you."

"I've missed you, too. I just wish we could see more of you. I wish you didn't live so far away."

"I do, too. But I am on no time table right now, so I can stay until I wear out my welcome."

"Oh, you could never wear out your welcome."

"I was hoping you would say that."

"Ingo went skiing today. He left a couple of hours ago so he might be a while."

"That's okay. You can keep me company until he gets here."

I make a couple of mugs of hot chocolate and bring them to the living room where we sit and visit.

"Tara tells me you have dubbed her your personal pregnancy guru."

"I guess I have," I confess with a chuckle. "She's fun to talk to. I really enjoy our visits."

"She does as well. Your friendship means so much to her."

"She and Gary are pretty amazing people."

"They are."

"So, how are things with you?"

"Good. Business is great and the guys in the kitchen tell me I do nothing but take up space."

"Ha! You see what happens? You teach them your secrets, show them how to cook your coveted dishes and suddenly they can do without you. Good thing you own the place."

"I know, otherwise I wouldn't be allowed in the kitchen."

"Probably not. In any case, I'm so glad you're here."

"So am I. Besides, you know me. I never pass up an opportunity for free room and board."

"Well, if there's one thing we do have plenty of, it's room and board. We just need more people to fill them."

"That's what I am here for. But I do plan to earn my keep, so feel free to put me to work at any time."

"Oh, don't worry. My request is a pretty simple one."

"And just what would that request be?"

When I smile, he grins. "Aha. I will do my best to take care of your Italian food cravings. Your every wish is my command." He finishes with a dramatic flourish.

"Thank you. One meal a week should do it. After all, I do have to keep up my domestic duties in the kitchen, or look like I am anyway."

"I am sure carrying a child is a major domestic duty in itself, but I do want to help out in any way I can. You just say the word and it's as good as done."

"Well, I can't let you do too much or there won't be anything for Ingo to do."

"And we would not want that, would we?"

"No, we wouldn't, but *he* might not agree." I glance at my watch. "You know, I think I'll call his cell and leave a message telling him you're here. And when he gets here, I'll give him a sound talking to for not letting me know you were coming."

"Well, don't be too hard on him. It was partly my fault."

"But you're going to make it up to me with your culinary skills."

"True," he agrees.

Just as I reach for the phone the doorbell rings.

"I'll be right back."

Looking through the small window on the door, my breath catches. It's Ben Gaylord, and a police officer.

What's going . . . I don't finish the thought. Opening the door, I take in Ben's red eyes and tear streaked face, and my heart lurches.

Twenty-six

"Where is Ingo?"

Ben opens his mouth but doesn't say anything. He won't even look at me.

Panic growing, I grab the front of his coat. "Where is Ingo?" I repeat, my voice raising a pitch. I sense Adagio's quiet approach.

It is the policeman who finally speaks. "Mrs. Kelly, I'm sorry to have to inform you that your husband was in a terrible skiing accident a while ago. He didn't make it."

"What?" I whisper, staring at the two men. "I don't believe you! It's not true!"

"It is, Ma'am. I'm so sorry."

No! This can't be happening! It cannot be happening!

Adagio gently pulls my hands from Ben's coat, putting his arm around me. "How?" he asks in a broken voice.

"No one knows what caused it, but he lost control, snowballed, and crashed into a tree coming down a steep slope. He died instantly."

"No!" he whispers. "Oh, please no."

The officer holds Ingo's personal belongings out to me, but I don't move to take them. I can't. I can't move or even think. Time has stopped and I'm trapped in a single moment.

As my weight shifts, Adagio adjusts his arm around me. It is the only thing keeping me from falling. I watch him take the bag from the officer. "Thank you," he says.

"Mr. Kelly has been taken to Cottonwood Hospital. An autopsy will be done as soon as possible." He hands Ingo's SUV keys to Adagio. Apparently, Ben drove it here. "Again, I am truly sorry."

Ben finally raises his eyes to mine. "I'm so sorry, Cisely," he sobs. "I'm so sorry." Then he and the officer leave.

Taking my hand, Adagio gently draws me back into the house and shuts the door. I think he says he is sorry, I am not sure, but that is the last thing I hear before the world around me starts spinning and everything goes dark.

"Cisely!" Tears spill down Adagio's face as he quickly lifts her and carries her up to her room. Though his own heart is ripping in two, he needs to take care of her. With Jessica gone, there is no one else. Reaching her room, he places her on the bed and covers her with a light blanket.

Noticing a list of numbers on the dresser, he scans it for Ingo's parents. Finding the number, he takes a deep breath and quickly dials, praying he will get through.

"Hello."

"Hello. Is this the Kelly residence?"

"Yes, this is Patrick Kelly."

"This is Adagio St. John, Ingo and Cisely's friend."

"Yes, I remember you. Has something happened?"

"Yes. . . It is about Ingo."

Keeping his emotions in check, Adagio tells Patrick about Ingo's death, and then listens quietly as Ingo's father weeps softly. He attempts to offer his condolences, but the words sound trite even to his own ears. He hears Patrick's wife crying in the background and his heart goes out to them both.

Patrick tells Adagio they will be there the day after tomorrow. He says to tell Cisely they love her.

Ending the call, Adagio moves back to Cisely. He presses a hand to her cheek and tucks the blanket around her. Then he wearily sits in the chair across from the bed and silently cries.

He can't believe it. His best friend is gone. How can Ingo be gone? Heart aching, Adagio rocks back and forth, missing him more than mere words could express. Dropping his face in his hands, he thinks back on the conversation he'd had with Ingo last week.

Ingo had been so excited when Adagio told him he was coming for a visit. They discussed how fun it would be to surprise Cisely. They hadn't decided on a specific day, but the day of his arrival was supposed to be a happy one.

Adagio futilely wipes at his tears. Losing Ingo is like living a nightmare, only this nightmare is more Cisely's than his. Squeezing his eyes shut, he rubs his temples as the pressure builds in his head.

Why?

He knows better than to ask such a pointless question. But just as he wasn't able to stop himself from asking it when Brian died, he can't help it now.

He looks up as Cisely slowly comes to and moves to the edge of the bed, wanting to be there for her.

Emerging from a heavy fog, I open my eyes and sit up, thinking I have awakened from a bad dream until I look into Adagio's red eyes. It all comes rushing back, the policeman's words again echoing in my head.

"Your husband was in a terrible skiing accident. He didn't make it."

Shaking my head in denial, I grip the front of Adagio's shirt. "It's not true, is it? Please tell me it isn't true!"

"I wish I could," he answers, emotion cracking his voice. "But I can't." Wiping his face, he takes my shoulders in his hands. "He is gone, Cisely."

His words are a blow to my heart and I immediately crumble. Adagio draws me to him, holding me as I cry, rocking me as my sobs grow. The pain is unbearable. I've lost everything and right now I want to die, too. My world has been turned upside down and there is no way to right it. Clinging to each other, I feel more than hear the sobs ripping through him, blending with my agony, making it hard to even breathe.

What am I going to do without Ingo? I can't go on. He is the only man I have ever loved. We were supposed to grow old together and watch our children grow to raise children of their own. How can those dreams be gone?

What am I going to do? Oh, God, it hurts! It hurts so much!

Adagio tightens his arms around me. "Shhh," he whispers against my ear. "I am here, angel. I am here."

My sobs lessen and I finally draw back, taking in his soaked shirt through swollen eyes. "I'm sorry."

He gives me a teary smile. "Don't be sorry. I have plenty of shirts. You can cry on them all if you need to." He hands me a box of tissues from the bedside table.

I have to admit, I am glad Adagio is here, because I need him. I can't do this alone and I'm grateful for his presence. Blowing my nose, I let my gaze slowly move around the room, taking in all of Ingo's things. Emotion wells again. "He's gone. Everything is gone."

"Listen to me, Cisely." He dries my tears with his fingers. "Ingo will always be with you because you will keep his memory alive in your heart."

I try to latch on to his comforting words, but it is too hard. Grief blinds me to everything except Ingo's absence. My husband is never coming back through our door. This is all I know. It's I can think about. This is my reality.

"It hurts so much. I can't stop crying."

"Don't stop. Just let go and cry."

And I continue to do so as I press my face against his shoulder, sobbing like a lost child. A large chunk has been cut out of my heart, leaving a gaping hole with no way to heal itself. The pain clenching my insides is beyond description.

Minutes go by before I can speak again.

"It was my fault. He didn't want to go skiing because he didn't want to leave me here alone, but I practically forced him to go. . . I should have let him stay home. If I hadn't made him go, maybe . . . he would still be here."

Drawing back, Adagio presses a gentle hand to my face. "Don't do this to yourself, Cisely. No one is to blame. It was simply his time to go. It is hard for me to say it, to accept it, but I know it is true. It was his time, Cisely." He closes his eyes, fresh tears falling down his face, his voice growing softer. "It was not your fault. Ingo would not want you to blame yourself."

"We didn't have enough time," I whisper. "We didn't have enough time together. He was supposed to always be with me, to help me raise our baby."

"I know," he soothes. "No matter how much time we have with someone, it is never enough. But as I reminded Gary and Tara when they lost Brian, you will always have your memories of him and your life together."

My heart begrudgingly validates the truth of his words. I will always have treasured memories. But right now, this knowledge isn't helping much. I need my husband with me *now*.

"I should call Ingo's parents," I say with my head against his shoulder. I dread this task. I don't know how to tell them their son, my husband, is gone. I never imagined having to make such a call.

"I already called them."

I draw back in surprise. "You did?"

"I didn't want you to have to worry about it. You have so much to handle already."

Tears of gratitude clog my throat. "Thank you." I ache even more thinking about Patrick and Gloria and what they must be going through having lost their oldest son.

Adagio wipes my tears once more. "You should lie down and rest."

I shake my head. "I need to make other phone calls. Then there are arrangements to be made. I have to . . ."

"The arrangements can wait until morning, and if you will give me your list, I will make the calls."

"I can't let you do all that."

"I am your friend, Cisely. That is what I am here for, to help. And I want to do everything I can to take as much of the burden off of you as possible. I worry for you and the baby. You don't want anything to happen to Ingo's child. This baby is a gift from him."

I realize the importance of his words, but instead of feeling comforted, a fresh batch of pain surfaces. "Oh, Adagio, I love him so much. It hurts . . ."

"I know," he soothes. "I don't know how to be without my best friend, either. But you will eventually be okay. We both will, I promise." He urges me to lie back down, spreading the blanket back over me. "Try to rest. I will call everyone. Where do I find your address book?"

"In the drawer," I say, pointing to the bedside table.

"I will take care of everything."

I reach for his hand. "Thank you."

Brushing a wisp of hair from my face, he presses a kiss to my brow. "You are welcome."

Closing my eyes, I imagine Ingo lying next to me. I need to feel him near, and I ache for another chance to tell him I love him. One afternoon has completely changed my world. In an instant I have lost everything. I didn't even get to say goodbye to him. I never got to tell him how much joy he brought into my life, how happy he made me.

"Oh, Ingo, please know how much I love you."

Turning over, I bury my face in Ingo's pillow, breathing in the scent of his after shave and sob until I am exhausted. I drift to sleep, still holding on to his pillow, longing for the comfort of his arms.

Grabbing the phone, Adagio sits at the desk in the family room, unable to staunch the flow of tears. He misses Ingo desperately and the pain is excruciating. To know he will never see his friend again in this life is tearing him up inside, but he needs to be strong for Cisely. Swallowing his emotions, he makes the calls.

Ending his final call with Gary and Tara, he glances out the window. It has grown dark, and realizing it is well past dinner time, his thoughts shift to Cisely. She needs to eat something to keep up her strength for herself and her baby.

Looking through the refrigerator, he pulls out an assortment of meats and cheeses, as well as some leftover cheese and broccoli soup. While the soup is reheating, he makes a sandwich. After pouring a little of the soup into a mug and putting the sandwich on a plate, he mixes a can of frozen orange juice and pours a small glass. Placing it all on a tray, he takes it up to Cisely.

Adagio quietly opens the bedroom door. Cisely is lying on her back, clutching a pillow, staring up at the ceiling as tears trickle back into her hair. The sight affects him deeply, causing his own eyes to burn again. Clearing his throat, he enters.

"I brought you something to eat. You need to keep up your strength."

She sits up and wipes her eyes. Adagio places the tray over her lap and sits down. She looks down at the food, then at him. "Thank you." Her voice is hoarse from crying. She probably has no appetite, but even a few bites will be better than nothing.

"You are welcome." Watching her take a small bite of the sandwich, he wishes he could say or do something to take away the pain, but only time can do that. The bottom has just dropped out of her world and her pain is too fresh. He will do everything in his power to help her through the times ahead.

The Flynns and a couple of ladies from the boutique stop by and offer their condolences. They tell me they will coordinate and bring in meals for the entire family for as long as they are here. There are no words to describe how grateful I am for their friendship. It is a comfort to know they care and that those things will be taken care of. Right now, I can't handle much more.

After they leave, Adagio holds me for a while in the living room. We talk of Ingo and our love for him and how much we already miss him. It is hard to believe how much my life has changed in a single afternoon. If only I could go back . . .

Lost in thought, I adjust my head on his shoulder, my mind going back over the day. "Earlier today before you came, I was thinking about Gary and Tara and the pain they faced losing their son. I tried to imagine how I would deal with that kind of loss and I couldn't comprehend it at all. I felt there would be no way I could handle that kind of grief . . . and I prayed that I would never have to deal with it." Shuddering, emotion bubbles to the

surface, making it hard to talk. "How *can* I deal with this? I don't
... I don't know how to cope. Oh, Adagio, it's ... just too hard."
Burying my face in the folds of his shirt, I absorb his comfort.

"I know, angel. I can't comprehend how hard this is for
you. I only know how much my heart aches, for you and for my
friend. He was my brother in spirit and I feel like I *have* literally
lost a brother. But I promise, Cisely, you will make it by taking it
one day at a time. We both will."

"I miss him so much."

"I know," he croons softly. "I know."

Pulling me further into himself, he holds me and dries my
tears until I am too tired to cry anymore. I finally head up to bed
to get some rest, though I know sleep will not come easy.
Locking the doors and turning off the lights, Adagio follows me
up, making sure I am okay.

Waking up alone—after knowing the bliss of sheltering
arms and a familiar warm body—is hard, and it takes everything
to make myself get out of bed. I'm not ready to face the day, but
there is too much to do.

Adagio agrees to come with me to make the funeral
arrangements. I want to get it over with as quickly as possible.
Searching through our personal files, I locate our insurance
policies. Looking over Ingo's, I gasp at the amount. When added
to the fortune we already have, I can take care of our child and
myself for the rest of our lives. Though I am grateful, it does
nothing to dull the ache in my heart. I would give it all and more
to have my husband back. Given the choice, I would live in a
shack with a dirt floor if it meant I could be with Ingo again.

Sitting in the funeral director's office, I find it ironic that I am again making arrangements to bury someone. I loved my mother, despite our strained relationship at the time, and I was saddened by her death. But this is different. This time I am literally burying a part of myself.

A chill in the room causes me to shudder. Adagio takes my hand, warming it between his. Smiling sadly, I lay my head against his shoulder, finding comfort in the feel of his cheek resting against my hair. Closing my eyes, I struggle against the threatening onslaught of tears. I know how much Adagio loved Ingo and I am glad he agreed to come with me. I don't think I could have handled it alone and I silently absorb the comfort he gives.

At one point, I am too emotional to answer the director's questions so Adagio speaks for me, making me again grateful for his presence.

When Ingo's family arrives, I am showered with hugs, and endless tears are shed. How he will be missed! The world is an emptier place without him, and it is like I was given a priceless gift and told to treasure it above all else, just to have it taken away. I will never get over the loss.

We spend the day remembering Ingo and the great man he was. Gloria and Patrick are especially grateful to have a grandchild from him.

The funeral will be held tomorrow. Lying in bed, I ponder the service, hoping I can make it through it. My strength is all but depleted. After hours of staring into the darkness, I am finally able to fall into an exhausted sleep.

I numbly shake hands and accept hugs from faceless people as they walk by to view Ingo's body before the service. Each time I gaze down at his handsome face, I wonder how I will ever make it through this life without him. He had been everything to me, making me feel valued and treasured for the first time in my life, and his love had healed my battered heart. For a moment, I'd had it all.

Now here I am, alone again, gazing down into the still face of the man who gave me the world.

Oh, God, why did you have to take him? We didn't even have a whole year together. Why? And what do I do now? I don't know what to do without him.

With a great deal of effort, I am able to shut my emotions down long enough to get through the services and the rest of the afternoon. But tonight, as I lay in bed in our dark room, emotion floods through me with force, and I again curl myself into a ball and weep, desperately longing for the comfort of my husband's arms.

Twenty-seven

When Ingo's family finally leaves, it is hard for Cisely to say goodbye because their presence helps her feel closer to Ingo.

Jessica cuts her vacation with the family short to stay home with Cisely. She too, is still deep in grief. Losing Ingo was like losing her own child and the pain is sometimes more than she can bear.

Through the week, Jessica manages to be strong for Cisely most of the time, but sometimes her emotions get the better of her, making her grateful for Adagio's presence. His being there for Cisely allows Jessica the opportunity to retreat and deal with her sorrow.

Adagio takes an extended leave from his restaurant. There are enough chefs on the payroll to cover the few shifts he works and he has complete faith in his management staff. Adagio gives

Sam Cisely's number just in case he can't reach him on his cell. Sam and the rest of the staff are deeply saddened by the news of Ingo's death, and they send Cisely their condolences along with a large flower arrangement.

Adagio moves into a vacation rental downtown so Cisely can adjust to life without her husband. He knows it will be hard for her being alone, but with time it will get easier. However, he is always there whenever she needs him. His apartment is only a few minutes away. All she has to do is call and he is there.

Twenty-eight

April brings longed-for sun and warmth. As the weeks pass, Adagio coaxes me out of the house a little, even if just for walks around the block. The past month has been one of the hardest times I've ever faced in my life, including the painful years as a child. This time the pain hasn't been brought on by the cruel choices of others, but by life; this pain is far worse.

Taking life one day at a time, I manage my grief. Some days I don't know if I will make it to the next one, or if I even *want* to. I have never felt so alone. Sometimes the grief makes it hard to function when it comes to even the most basic things. But somehow, I make it through these times. I have no choice. It is either endure or die, so I endure.

Occasionally I enter my bedroom and take in the spaces where Ingo's personal things had been. At these times I miss him more than I can say, and the absence of his personal belongings hurts deeply. But it is becoming a little more bearable.

I frequently sit on the bed, wrapped in one of the few shirts I kept of Ingo's, and remember the love we shared here. My mind wanders to the little things Ingo did for me each day. From serving me breakfast in bed to bringing me flowers, to just simply sitting with me, holding me or rubbing my back. I miss these things more than I believed possible. I just miss *him*. But through it all, I endure.

There are also times when I still need to cry on Adagio's shoulder. When the pain becomes too much to bear, he is always more than willing to let me, and he comforts me in any way he can. He understands better than anyone what I am going through and is always able to reach me somehow. I know he is putting his life on hold for me, but I couldn't get through this without him.

I depend on Adagio for his strength, and words could never describe how grateful I am that he came when he did. I often think of that fateful day and marvel that he was here when I received the most painful news of my life. Had I been alone, I honestly don't think I could have handled it.

Thinking on these things often, I consider them tender mercies.

Adagio

One day Adagio arrives at Cisely's around noon to find she hasn't come down from her room all morning. Jessica tells him Cisely hasn't eaten and she is worried about her. Adagio's concern for her overrides everything else. Immediately heading to the kitchen, he puts together a sandwich and a salad and takes it up to her. Knocking softly, he opens the door a little.

Cisely is dressed and sitting on the bed, her back against the pillows. She turns as he enters.

"I brought you something to eat."

"I'm not really hungry." Her voice is flat, devoid of emotion.

"But the baby probably is. You need to eat for him. He depends on you." Sitting on the edge of the bed, he places the tray over her lap. "Please, Cisely."

Her mouth curves in a sad smile, her eyes tearing up. "I'm sorry, Adagio. I don't mean to worry you and I appreciate you thinking of me. I guess I'm just having a hard time today . . . again."

He takes the tray, placing it on the floor. Reaching for her hand, he wipes her tears. "I'm sorry."

"Thanks. Some days I think I'm doing okay. Other days . . ."

"Other days, you need a little help."

"Truthfully, some days I feel like a basket case and you and Jessica are my only link to sanity."

Pressing a hand to her cheek, he brushes a tear away with his thumb. "You are not a basket case. You are a woman who lost her husband a month and a half ago and you are still grieving. And that's okay. It is normal. If you were not still struggling, then I would worry."

She smiles again, placing her hand over his. "I'm really glad you're here, and I'm grateful for all you have done for me, but I can't help feeling a little guilty and selfish. I worry about you putting your life on hold for me."

"You are definitely *not* selfish, and my life is not on hold, it is just a different life for now. Everything is fine at home with

169

the restaurant and I really don't worry about it. I am happy here because I know this is where I need to be right now. I wouldn't want to be anywhere else. So please don't worry about that."

Leaning forward, Cisely rests her cheek against his shoulder and he wraps an arm around her.

"You know," she says, her voice somber, "sometimes I imagine I hear Ingo's voice inside my mind. I hear him saying, *"Count your blessings, love. Just keep counting your blessings and you will be fine.""*

"That does sound like something Ingo would say."

She nods, adjusting her head on his shoulder. "I'm going to try harder to do that."

"I think that is a good idea."

She is quiet for a moment, then surprises him by saying, "I count you as one of my blessings."

"I am glad to be someone's blessing," he says, kissing her forehead. He is both humbled and grateful she feels that way.

"Thank you for being so good to me," she says after a moment.

Drawing back slightly, he looks into her eyes. "You are easy to be good to. And I meant what I said. Don't worry about me. I am happy to be here. All right?"

"Okay. And I promise I'll force myself to eat from now on, even when I don't feel like it."

"That's my girl." He places the tray back over her lap. "Maybe when you are finished, we could take a walk and get out for a bit today. We could even go sit in the park."

"I would like that. Jessica told me the gardens are beautiful right now. I've always loved looking at the flowers there."

"Then we will go."

Cisely takes a bite of the sandwich and smiles. He smiles back, happy to be with her. It feels nice to be needed by someone. His eyes brighten. "Oh, I have a surprise for you."

"Really? I love surprises."

"I know. You keep eating and I will be back." Running out to his car, he returns a minute later with a wrapped package and promptly places it on the bed.

"Adagio, what did you do?"

"I just saw this the other day and wanted to get it for you."

"But it's not my birthday or anything."

"Who says you need a reason to receive a gift?"

"I think you're spoiling me too much."

His expression grows serious because she could not be more wrong. "That is not possible, Cisely. You deserve to be spoiled." Moving the tray from her lap, he places the gift in its place. "Open it."

When an anxious grin practically splits his face, she laughs. "Oh, all right." He watches her carefully remove the wrapping paper.

"Oh, Adagio, it's beautiful!" The porcelain doll looks angelic dressed in white velvet. "I've only had one other doll in my life, and that was when I was five." Holding the doll up, she takes in the delicate features. "I absolutely love it." She kisses his cheek. "Thank you."

"You're welcome," he says, pleased she likes it. Cisely is constantly in his thoughts, and anything he can do to bring a smile to her face is worth it. It seems that making her smile is his mission these days, and each time he succeeds, it pleases him immensely.

"Thank you so much for everything."

171

"You are welcome. I would do anything for you."

Twenty-nine

Adagio

Adagio and Cisely relax on a wooden bench beneath a large walnut tree and watch some children playing in the distance. A soft breeze rustles the leaves on the trees and pigeons coo to one another as they snatch up the bread crumbs Cisely tosses their way. Even with the distant sounds of downtown in the background, their surroundings are peaceful.

"You've been away from home so long," Cisely comments. "Do you have someone looking after your house for you?"

"I have a cleaning lady named Anna who comes in twice a week. She has a key and keeps an eye on things for me. Her son is one of my chefs, so she is very trustworthy."

"It's good your work is at home. You have lots of eyes watching out for you that way."

Smiling, Adagio turns his emerald gaze to her, taking in the highlights of her dark auburn hair. He understands why she is making these comments and can almost read her thoughts. "Ingo used to say you are too noble for your own good sometimes."

She smiles. "He said that to me, too."

"He was right. I see that now." He catches her chin in his hand. "Cisely, look at me." When her eyes meet his, he says, "Please stop worrying. Everything is fine at home."

"I can't help it."

He takes her hand and squeezes. "You are going to have to help it, because you are not getting rid of me."

She gives him a slow grin. "Is that a threat?"

"Definitely."

"Okay, then."

That is the last she says on the subject and he hopes she truly understands. He isn't going anywhere. He is where he's supposed to be.

Adagio helps out by cooking dinner for us a couple of extra days a week. I have grown to love his cooking, even crave it. A popular Italian restaurant downtown has always been my favorite place to eat because I love good Italian food, but now my favorite meals are the ones Adagio cooks. His meals are amazing. He believes in variety and hardly ever cooks a dish the same way twice, and I love each and every meal.

Adagio usually gives us a mini Italian lesson, pretending to be an eccentric cooking instructor, and by the time he is finished, Jessica and I are holding our sides from laughing so hard. Whenever I improvise my speaking of the language and try to match his Italian accent, it sends him into fits of laughter as well.

Because of these times, we are slowly building some joyful memories.

I also cook some Italian meals, with Adagio's assistance, of course. When a dish turns out well, he praises me. When it turns out not so good, he still gives me an A for effort, and he and Jessica eat it anyway. This is definitely the sign of a good friend—to eat a terrible meal without complaint.

At night Jessica and Adagio visit while I play the piano softly. I had all but stopped playing when Ingo died, but Adagio coaxed me into playing again. He knows how much I love playing and I'm grateful for the extra push.

During our visits, Adagio and I grow to learn more about each other's lives as we open up and share experiences from our pasts, as well as our hopes and fears for the future. In the process, our mutual admiration grows, as well as the bond we share. We talk of Ingo often and the impact he had on our lives. We share our own private stories of him, some of them producing bouts of laughter, and others bringing bittersweet tears. But even the tearful moments are a little easier because we have each other to lean on. I am really grateful for that.

Jessica is also glad Adagio is here and appreciates the support he gives her. His strength is a boon and his presence brings great comfort. She will miss him when he finally returns to Italy.

And I will too.

Thirty

Having cleaned up after another sumptuous meal prepared by Adagio, we relax in the family room. Adagio is in a spontaneous mood and says some fun time is in order. Pulling a Latin music CD from the shelf, he puts it in the player.

As the music fills the room, I start snapping my fingers, the beat moving through me. If there is one thing I love, it's dancing. Adagio grins, holding his hands out to both Jessica and me.

"Come. Let me teach you ladies how to salsa."

Jessica claps her hands and quickly stands. "I'm game!"

I laugh. "I'm a little too big to salsa. I would be a terrible student right now."

"Nonsense," he says, not about to let me off the hook. "I told you, you are *not* big, just pregnant. You will do great." He takes my hand, gently pulling me up.

"Okay," I concede with a sigh. "They're your toes on the line. Pregnancy has given me two left feet."

He laughs and stands between us, teaching us the basic steps. He is very good. In fact, I'm surprised by how good he really is. I knew he was a great dancer, but his salsa is amazing. I quickly catch on, surprising myself, and soon Adagio and I are dancing like a couple in a club. Jessica is a little slower catching on, but she eventually gets it and is thoroughly enjoying herself.

"Very good!" Adagio says to me. He teaches me a couple of other Latin dances and I pick the steps up quickly.

"You're a natural," he says, turning me around and back. He praises Jessica as well.

I am completely enjoying myself. I love the exercise and dancing always makes my spirits soar. I haven't enjoyed dancing so much since . . .

My thoughts immediately shift to the last time I danced with Ingo. It was on New Year's Eve, and we danced in this very room. Suddenly the memory is vivid, as if it just happened yesterday.

"I think I'm done," I say, backing away from him. I quickly smile to hide my sudden shift of emotions and feign exhaustion.

He looks at me intently, his eyes full of understanding. I cannot hide anything from him. He knows me well and I am sure he glimpsed the pain.

"You rest," he says, gently letting me off the hook. "I will keep my other lovely partner up here a little longer." He grins at Jessica and she laughs, still moving a little to the beat.

At the song's end Jessica declares she has had enough and heads to the kitchen for a drink of water. Adagio congratulates her on a job well done. Turning the stereo off, he sits on the sofa next to me.

I want to apologize to him for letting my emotions get in the way. I open my mouth to do that when he squeezes my hand and says, "One day at a time, angel. Just take it one day at a time."

Awakening in a cold sweat, I sit up, glancing at the clock. It is just after one in the morning, and I am trembling.

The nightmares have started again. The haunting dreams of my childhood are back, though not as frequent as they were before. Still, the fact that I am having them again is disturbing, and I wish I knew why the memories continue to plague me. I let my head fall back against the damp pillow and wipe a hand across my forehead. Night time is still hard for me because it is when I feel most alone, and on these nights, it is even worse. The bed feels cold and empty, no matter how much I snuggle into the covers.

I miss having warm arms to curl into, a strong heartbeat against my ear to lull me to sleep. I miss whispered conversations in the dark and the security of muscular limbs draped possessively around me. I miss waking and not being alone.

I stare up into the darkness, feeling exactly that–alone.

I'm so lonely. "Ingo, I am lonely and you're not here, but . . ." *I need . . . I need . . .*

Fingering my wedding rings, I close my eyes and pray for comfort. Eventually comfort does come and I drift back to sleep, praying that the dreams will leave me again and never come back. My final thought is an echo of the same two words.

I need.

Adagio decides that I need an evening out. When he arrives at my house, he asks to treat me to dinner and I accept. Other than going for walks around the neighborhood and to the park, I really haven't gone anywhere, and instead of eating out, I usually order take-out and have it delivered. It will be nice to go somewhere else for a while.

As he pulls out of the driveway, he tells me the restaurant is my choice. He hadn't made any definite plans, deciding to play it by ear.

"You really don't care where we eat?" I ask.

"Not at all. We can go wherever you want."

"Well, in that case, I would like a burger. The biggest, sloppiest burger we can find."

Adagio glances at me. "Really?" he says, grinning. "You want a burger?"

I nod, laughing at the incredulous look on his face. "The bigger and messier, the better."

"Hmmm. All right, if a burger is what you want, a burger is what you shall have. You just point the way."

A little while later, we are sitting in one of my favorite pubs with two double burgers in front of us along with a basket of beer-battered onion rings. While Adagio studies his burger, I dig right in.

"Mmmm, this is so good. Thank you for bringing me here."

It takes him a moment to chew the large bite before he can respond. "You are very welcome. And you were right, this is pretty good. I must say, I have never had a burger that forced me to stretch my mouth so wide."

I laugh. "Neither have I. The last time I came here, the most I could eat was a regular burger."

"Well, you are eating for two now. I guess the baby will digest half of it."

"I think you're right. And I know I'll probably pay for this later on tonight when heartburn sets in."

"But right now, it is worth it to you, right?"

"Exactly."

"So, tell me, what other secret cravings have you been experiencing?" His tone is teasing.

"Well, now that you asked, I could really go for a hot fudge sundae with lots of nuts and pineapple."

He shakes his head, laughing softly. "Well, I did say your every wish is my command. When we are done here, I will search the city until we acquire a hot fudge sundae for you. How does that sound?"

"Mmmm, sounds wonderful. I think you're spoiling me. If you keep this up, I won't ever let you go back home."

Looking into my eyes, he gives me a slow smile that makes my face warm. "Then maybe I will stay."

Shyly returning his smile, I blame the familiar skip of my heart on the baby's movements. It can't be anything else.

Adagio

Turning his attention back to his meal, Adagio tries to ignore the jolt of emotion Cisely's innocent comment stirred. *And why did I just say that?*

They continue to eat, filling the silence between them every now and then with comfortable conversation about life in general, as well as the various things she still needs to do to prepare for the baby.

"What else do you need to get?" he asks.

"Not too much more. I just need to pick up more disposable and cloth diapers, a baby monitor, bath products. Just small things like that. I can get the crib and other furniture next month."

"Well, maybe we can stop by the *Target* we passed and pick up some things."

"You don't mind baby shopping?"

"Not at all. I am actually a fabulous shopper. Been doing it for years." He grins and winks, making her laugh, which is what he'd intended.

"You do seem capable," she says.

"I have yet to meet a cashier who doesn't want to take my money, no matter how horrible the tie is I'm buying or how atrocious the china pattern I've picked out is."

She snorts. "Are you sure I should be taking you with me?"

"Of course. I am very good at picking out things." He feigns confusion. "Checks do go with stripes, right?" he asks, winking again.

"This will be very interesting." Having finished her meal, Cisely leans back in the chair, rubbing her stomach. "I can't believe I really ate it all."

"I can't either," he says, popping the last of the burger into his mouth.

"I still say it was worth the coming heartburn."

"In this instance, I agree." Wiping his mouth with a napkin, he leans back in his chair, studying her contented smile. "So, do you still have room for a sundae?"

"Definitely. There's always room for anything with chocolate." She massages her stomach a bit, causing the baby to shift. "See? Instant room."

He chuckles. "Well, I guess that's one way to make room." After sitting and talking for a few more minutes, he stands, holding a hand out to help her up. "Shall we go?"

"Yes, I think I'm ready." She takes his hand.

Looking down at her slender hand in his, he again does his best to ignore the skip of his heart and the new warmth filling him. "I am so glad you are doing better, Cisely. It is good to see you smiling again."

"Thanks." For a moment their eyes lock, and then she shyly lowers her gaze. Squeezing his hand, she says, "Thank you for being here for me. You have helped me more than you know. I don't think I could have made it through if you hadn't been here."

Her words stir him in a way he can't explain. He smiles, pressing his free hand against her cheek. "You will never have to worry about that. I will always be here for you, Cisely. Always."

Adagio takes me to *Dairy Queen* for a sundae. Since I don't think I can eat the whole thing, we ask for two spoons and share. He laughs as I take a bite and close my eyes, moaning softly. For a moment he simply watches me, and the look in his eyes brings back the warmth I experienced earlier. Smiling slightly, I look away, focusing on a young mother at the next table with twin toddler girls. She has them both in booster seats, trying to keep them from making a complete mess. Just watching them increases my anticipation of my son's birth.

Adagio turns to see what has me so enraptured. When he turns back to me, his eyes are gentle.

"You are going to be an amazing mother, Cisely. No child will be more blessed."

I nod, swallowing hard. "Thanks. I just didn't expect to be doing it alone."

He reaches across the table, taking my hand. "None of us ever get what we expect. But you will never be alone. You have Jessica, and you have me."

There is truth in his words, but I can't contemplate it too much right now. Smiling, I squeeze his hand and we finish our sundae.

We are loaded down with shopping bags when we arrive home. Jessica has gone to bed, so Adagio helps me haul everything up to the baby's nursery, which is next to my room. Just as with Ingo, with Adagio, there is no such thing as buying just a few things. And I never took my wallet from my purse. Adagio wouldn't let me, insisting on paying for everything himself. He said to think of it as an investment in his nephew, and he turned a deaf ear to my protests. I finally stopped complaining and just went along, and I had a blast.

We place the bags in a corner on the floor. The room is dark, but the moon shines through the open blinds. Adagio walks over to the window and stares out into the night. "Beautiful view," he says, looking at the city lights.

I join him. "It is." He turns to me but says nothing. I keep my focus on the distant lights, very aware of his gaze. "Thank you for dinner and shopping. It was really nice of you. What am I saying? You practically forced me to keep my purse closed, you brute."

"I had to be. I was only exercising my prerogative to try and spoil you more. I had not done a sufficient job because you never let me, so tonight I took matters into my own hands." He pauses, nudging me. "Are you mad at me?"

"Maybe," I answer, nudging him back. "Of course, I'm not mad at you. I could never be."

"So, does that mean I can do this again should I choose to without you making a scene in public?"

"I did not make a scene," I say in a huff, poking his chest. "You did."

"Just because I tell the woman not to take your money doesn't mean I am making a scene." He grins. "Besides, it made her like me."

"Oh, really?"

"Uh huh." He sobers a bit. "But seriously, Cisely, please let me do these things. I've never had anyone to spend money on before. I want to and it makes me happy. All right?" When I don't answer, he repeats, "All right?"

"Okay," I finally agree, reaching for his hand. "Thank you, for everything."

"You're very welcome."

Squeezing my hand, he pulls me closer to his side, pressing a kiss to my brow. With my head resting against his shoulder and his hand firmly clasping mine, we continue to stare out into the night. Part of me wants to analyze this night, but I don't.

    I can't.

Thirty-one

As June rushes in and the weather goes through its changes, so do I, in more ways than one. With less than a month until my due date, I am doing better emotionally and eagerly anticipating the birth of my son.

Jessica and Adagio are excited as well. They help me decorate the nursery and get everything ready. They shop with me for baby furniture and accessories, making sure I have everything I need. Adagio even assembles the crib and rocker, and I am grateful that I don't have to tackle the job. I am not handy with tools in the least and probably would have put everything together backwards.

My heart full of gratitude for both these amazing people. Jessica has truly been a mother to me, showing me all the love and support I could ever need. Sometimes I muse that I was probably sent to the wrong family and should have been hers. But deep down, I know it isn't true. I needed to go through the trials I'd been given, and Jessica is in my life now. I often think back to the day I met her at the motivational seminar and the instant friendship that formed between us. At the time, I could never have guessed how much meeting her would affect my future. I don't know where I would be without her.

Then there is Adagio. He is my lifeline, and there is nothing he doesn't or won't do for me. Even though he lives downtown, he always manages to be here and see to my every need, and I never have to ask for anything. He gives so much of his time and sacrifices so much of himself. He has helped me to know I'm not alone, that I will never be alone. He is an amazing friend, and I thank God every day for sending him right when I needed him. We are now connected in a way that can't be defined.

My thoughts never stray far from Ingo, but the memories are not as painful, and the bittersweet moments have lessened. I still miss him and I know a part of me always will. He taught me so much about life and love. He also helped me to grow and become the kind of person I've always wanted to be. I will forever treasure his love, as well as my memories of him and our life together.

It has been hard, but I have been able to go on after all.

Adagio

Adagio observes the changes in Cisely, and as happy as he is about the strength she has gained, there are also changes that have taken place in his own heart–changes he never expected to experience, and they have happened slowly.

Adagio spends more and more time with Cisely and longs to be with her whenever he is away. He thinks of her constantly and even tried staying away a couple of times, just to see if these feelings would leave him if he didn't spend so much time around her. But he couldn't go a whole day before giving in to his need to be near her.

Every moment he is in her home, Adagio watches Cisely's every move. He takes in her every expression and wonders what she is thinking at a particular moment. When she leaves the room, he counts the minutes until she returns, and when she does his heart always skips a beat. Just a look from her or the feel of her hand in his sends a warmth through him that is almost overwhelming at times. He now craves her touch, and just holding her is no longer enough.

He loves feeling her softness against him, loves the fragrance that radiates from her hair when he presses his face into it. He has grown accustomed to the way her body fits against his side and his arms often feel empty when she isn't in them. He loves the way her eyes sparkle whenever he comes through the door and the silkiness of her voice when she says his name. It is like a caress, so warm, so familiar. Being with her is like coming home. He has never felt anything like this before. It is a need that both thrills and scares him.

He remembers the moment he truly accepted that things had changed. It is a moment he will never forget, and because of it, his world is no longer the same.

One week ago.

Adagio looked for Cisely to tell her lunch was ready. Approaching the doorway of the living room, he found her standing in front of the large window staring out at the city. She was wearing a knee-length, form-fitting yellow sundress. The silky material hugged the curve of her abdomen, the color of the outfit enhancing the tone of her beautiful brown skin perfectly.

Her hair, which had grown even longer during her pregnancy, was swept up and away from her face and hung down her back in loose curls. Barefoot, her toes donned red nail polish.

He memorized her every detail, and hard as he tried, he couldn't pull his eyes away. Gazing at her profile, he was unable to move, like some unseen force was keeping him bound to that spot.

She's so beautiful! *he breathed inwardly.* Oh, angel, you're so beautiful!

And at that moment, he wanted nothing more than to take her in his arms, kiss her irresistible mouth and never let her go. He couldn't believe the thoughts that were swirling in his head or the intensity of his feelings. He had felt the emotional changes for a while now and had fought them as best he could, but in that moment, he was overwhelmed. Suddenly the words from the ballad playing softly in the living room leaped from the speakers, echoing through his mind.

You smile at me and my heart is no longer empty,
You touch me and everything becomes clear.
As long as you're near me, I'll never be alone,
In your arms I've found my home.

The lyrics pierced Adagio's heart, stirring his emotions so, he found it hard to breathe. He continued to gaze at her as a terrible longing filled him, making him oblivious to everything but her presence. The emotional pull was more powerful than anything he had ever felt in his life. Oh, how he wanted her for his own at that moment! How he needed her!

Adagio didn't know how long he had been watching Cisely and didn't realize he was holding his breath until she turned and smiled at him. He released it slowly as her eyes held his.

Oh, *amore.* Can you not see what you are doing to my heart?

Cisely had suffered and endured much in her life. And now here she was, smiling at him, a new light present in her beautiful eyes, her very gaze intoxicating him.

"Lunch is ready."

Jessica's voice startled him and heat rose to his face. "That is what I came to tell you," he said to Cisely after finding his voice. He wondered how long Jessica had been there. When he glanced at her, she gave him a knowing smile and headed back to the kitchen.

"Are you coming?" Cisely asked, brushing by him and giving him a smile that again made his heartbeat skip.

"Yes, I will be in right after I make a phone call." It was just an excuse and he knew it. Watching her walk away, he closed his eyes as guilt quickly assaulted him. He headed upstairs to the guest room that he had used whenever he visited. Sitting on the edge of the bed, he dropped his head in his hands.

What am I doing? I am losing it, that's what I'm doing! She was my best friend's wife.

The feeling of betrayal was brutal. How in the world had he allowed himself to fall in love with his best friend's wife? Yes, Ingo was gone, but still . . . He rubbed a hand over his face, tugging it back through his hair and closed his eyes.

I don't know how this happened. I didn't plan it, but I can't help it. What should I do?

What should I do?

Even now, as he stands in front of his living room window looking out across downtown, Adagio still ponders the question, and he is no closer to an answer than he was on that day. That he loves Cisely is without question. He couldn't deny it if he tried. He just doesn't know if it is right to act on it, and he can't be certain Cisely feels anything other than friendship for him. He had caught something in her eyes that day when she looked at him, and he had sensed a change in her as well, but he doesn't know if any of it is real or just wishful thinking on his part. Being near her affects him in ways he can't begin to describe, and at times the longing is physically painful. Even now he aches to be with her, to hold her, to touch her and claim her for his own.

But in his mind, she is still off limits. And he is afraid.

He is afraid to cross the line that has always been there. Maybe after a little more time has passed, he will consider it. Maybe. For now, he will leave things as they are. It will be safer this way.

As will his heart.

Thirty-two

Jessica washes the last of the breakfast dishes and hands them to me. I dry them and place them in the cupboard, then I wipe off the kitchen table, humming softly.

"You must be feeling pretty good this morning," Jessica says.

"I do feel good, actually," I reply, looking up.

When Jessica smiles, I notice something I haven't seen in a long while. The twinkle is back in her eyes. "You must be feeling pretty good yourself, today," I say, returning my attention to the table.

"I am. So, did Adagio happen to mention when he would be over today?"

"No, but I never expect him until ten or so." Trying to ignore the way my heart skips a beat at the mention of Adagio's name, a smile curves my lips before I can stop it. Having finished, I look up and Jessica is staring at me, and that familiar twinkle is definitely there. "What?"

"Oh, nothing. It's just that you smile whenever Adagio's name comes up these days."

"He's my friend. Of course, I smile." My attempt to sound casual belies what I feel inside.

"You don't smile like that when the names of other friends are mentioned. Just Adagio's."

Startled by her comment, my mouth opens in automatic response, but there is nothing. My brain clocks out on me.

"Cisely, it's okay."

"What's okay?" *Don't go there, Jessica.*

She sighs. "It's okay to care for Adagio."

"I know it's okay. He's my best friend and I do care about him, very much." *Please don't go there, Jessica.*

"You know what I mean, Cisely. It's okay to care for him in other ways."

I really do not want to have this discussion because it is a truth that I am not ready to face. Though I have felt the stirrings in my heart for a while now, I have fought them every step of the way, but they have only become stronger. I try to blame it on loneliness, but in my heart, I know it isn't true, and I feel all the more guilty.

I don't want to think about Adagio, but to my dismay, sometimes—all right, most of the time—I cannot think about anything else but him. It has only been three months since Ingo died, but his best friend consumes my thoughts more and more, and I can't seem to stop it.

I look forward to seeing Adagio every day, and when he is here, just being near him brings butterflies to my stomach. I have even begun to dream about him. Sometimes the dreams are so vivid and real, I can barely breathe around him. Even now, thinking about him calls forth a familiar warmth and I again experience that tangible ache. But I cannot go there. I won't let myself.

"He was my husband's best friend," I finally say. "It would be wrong."

"And just what makes you think that?" Jessica dries her hands and takes a seat at the table across from me. "I want you to listen to me, Cisely. Now, I've never had the opportunity to marry, but I do know a little something about life, and love. And the one thing I know for sure is that man cares for you more than he will admit. He is in love with you, Cisely. I have watched him fall in love with you. It's in his eyes every time he looks at you, and in his voice when he talks to you. There are times that I have caught him watching you with eyes so full of longing, I almost weep. He wears his heart on his sleeve. He tries to hide his feelings, but I can see them. I can tell you have feelings for him, too, and I think those feelings are deeper than you realize."

Guiltily, I look away, pushing my ever-intruding feelings aside. I can't do this now. "He's been very good to me, but all we could ever be is friends."

Jessica makes a contemplative noise and is thoughtful for a moment. "You know, I knew you and Ingo were meant to be together when I introduced you two. And that night after you went to bed, he told me he knew it as well."

What? "You both felt that?"

"Yes, we did. And neither of us knew the future any more than we knew he would be taken away so quickly. But I did know you and Ingo would eventually be married. Now I'm sure when Adagio met Ingo in Italy, he didn't know how their meeting would affect one another either. But there is a reason for everything. We are all given gifts and blessings in life. And sometimes we don't realize what they are until they are staring us right in the face. And even then, they are sometimes easy to miss."

Contemplating her words, I realize how right she is. "I have been told by a few people, yourself included, that there are many gifts and blessings in store for me in the future. A couple of days before Ingo died, he told me that as well. It was almost like he knew something I didn't. We talked about our baby being one of the gifts." I blink back the tears that come with the memory.

"You know, sometimes during quiet moments when I am feeling a little down, Ingo's words suddenly come from nowhere, like he knows what I am feeling and he is right there beside me." I don't bother commenting about the guilt I experience at those times as well.

"Really?"

"Yes. Many times, I have felt him comforting me, but now that I think about it, I haven't felt that in a while."

Jessica slowly smiles. "Maybe because you no longer need it. You may not want to hear this, but I think you and Adagio really need each other."

Closing my eyes, I shake my head. "What are you saying, Jessica?"

"What do you think I'm saying?"

"I don't know." She looks at me skeptically. Truthfully, I *do* know what she means, I just don't want to say it. I can't allow the words to pass my lips.

"Well?" Jessica prods softly, meeting my eyes. "Tell me you haven't thought about it. Can you honestly tell me it hasn't crossed your mind?"

If I answer her truthfully, I will have to admit what my heart has fought against for a while now. Deep down, I know there is truth to Jessica's unspoken words. I can feel it even now, but I can't admit it. Adagio has been a tremendous comfort to me during the past months and the most devoted friend I could ever ask for, but he has also become more important to me than I dare say.

"Cisely," Jessica says, interrupting my thoughts, almost reading them, "you still have a very long life ahead of you, too long a life to spend alone. And I don't think Ingo would want that for you. You aren't meant to be alone. I know it has only been a short while since Ingo died and you need to do what is best for you, but you also need to remember time is irrelevant when the feelings are there. You thought you could never be happy again, that you would never find love again, but it's right in front of you, Cisely. You are being given a second chance."

"But what if I don't want a second chance?" I blurt out. "What if . . . Jessica, what if I took it and ended up loving Adagio more?"

"What if you *do* grow to love him more? Is that so wrong?" She sighs. "Cisely, I loved my nephew more than I could ever tell you, and I'm grateful for the happiness you brought to him, but he is gone now and your life is still going on. Don't turn your back on this chance because of fear. If you search your heart, you will see I am right."

Rubbing my temples, I take a moment to digest what Jessica is saying. I am so torn. And confused. *And* guilt-riddled. I've been fighting this so hard that I am almost afraid to stop because if I do, I will completely lose my heart. Truthfully, I already have, but I don't know if I am ready for the next step, whatever it might be.

We talk for a few minutes more, or rather Jessica talks and I listen. She looks at her watch.

"I'm going up to get ready, but if you need to talk some more, I can go in a little later."

I shake my head, my mind going in a thousand different directions. "You have given me a lot to think about. Thank you."

"You're welcome, dear, anytime."

Transferring a load of laundry to the dryer, I put another batch in the washer. Adagio is late and I am glad. I need time to adjust my thoughts and get a handle on my feelings. He has not called and I am glad for this as well, because right now, even hearing his voice would be too much. The whole conversation with Jessica has left me unsettled and confused.

Stretching, I rub the dull ache in my back and stomach. I climb the stairs to my room and spend some time on my knees, praying and pondering what I should do about my feelings for Adagio. I can't help thinking it is somehow wrong for me to care for him romantically, or anyone else for that matter. But each time I try to come up with excuses, Jessica's words reenter my mind and hammer away at my heart. After an hour, I am still confused and don't know what to do about it.

I finally head back downstairs. Standing in front of the large living room window, I gaze out over the city. It is one of my favorite past-times because the view is so pretty and it's easy to think here, which is something I have been doing a lot of lately. Focusing on a small group of pigeons congregating on the front lawn, I try to clear my mind in the hope of gaining some clarity, but almost immediately, thoughts of Adagio rush in with such force, I don't try to fight them this time. I do not have the strength to anymore.

I have studied him so much when he isn't looking, his face and features are etched in my memory. Without a doubt, he is a very beautiful man, both inside and out. Taking a long moment, I allow my thoughts to run free.

Heat slowly fills me as I think of the warmth of his muscular embrace. I have begun to crave his arms around me. Whenever he is near, I fight the urge to run my fingers through that dark wavy hair of his. It looks perfectly tousled and neat at the same time. He is definitely male model material, and that he is so oblivious to it makes him even more beautiful. There is nothing shallow about him, and no matter how many women gawk at him when we are out and about, his attention is always centered on me.

There is a soothing tone to his heavily accented voice, and I especially love hearing him call me 'angel.' I love the scent of his cologne, the way it mixes with his body chemistry. He smells so good, I want to curl up into him sometimes and never move. The deep dimples that appear on his cheeks when he smiles make me long to reach out and touch his face. And when he looks at me with those emerald eyes, it's as if he can see through to my very soul and I long to lose myself in his gaze.

Closing my own eyes, I see his mouth. His lips are full and look as if they are begging to be kissed. Thinking about them now makes my mouth suddenly ache with longing for the touch of his.

Everything about him is familiar to me now—the warmth of his smile, the openness of his gaze. I love the way his handsome brow furrows when he is deep in thought, the way he pushes a hand through his hair and stands with a look of puzzlement on his face when he is looking for something he has misplaced, then mumbles in Italian while he searches. Everything about him is alluring. He has a magnetism that emanates and stirs my entire being. My emotions go into overload when he is near. Sometimes all he has to do is look at me and I have to leave the room to calm my racing heart. I wonder if he has any idea how his mere presence affects me. I can't believe how much I have come to care for him.

Each and every day, my mind reasons that it should not be this way, that it isn't right for me to feel this way so soon, if ever. But to my heart, it is almost natural, and that alone is confusing.

He was my husband's best friend, for heaven's sake! How can this be happening? How have I allowed my emotions to go this far?

Deep down, I know the answer to these questions. It is because Adagio has been here. He has always been here. How can I *not* have feelings for him? It should all feel so wrong.

But it doesn't.

Pressing my forehead against the window, I continue to ponder my feelings when sudden recollection dawns on me. Turning toward the doorway of the living room, my mind shoots back to the day Adagio stood staring at me while I was in this very spot. I did not allow myself to admit it then, but the look in his eyes stirred me so, it nearly took my breath away. Not until Jessica approached was I able to pull my eyes away from his, and even then, I still felt his gaze on me. I had tried to tell myself the way he looked at me had not meant anything, that what I saw in his eyes was . . .

I can't even think of an excuse because I know what I saw in his eyes that day. They held a look of longing, a look of . . .

Wow! Jessica was right. It really has been there the entire time, clearly exposed for the world to see.

My resistance fading, I allow my heart to open, tears stinging my eyes as another simple truth dawns on me; and that truth is I had felt the same emotions I saw in his eyes that day, and I have every day since.

I do love him. Pressing my face in my hands, I sigh deeply, finally accepting what my heart has been trying to tell me.

I can't believe this is happening to me.

"Oh, Ingo," I whisper brokenly, "I'm in love with him. I didn't mean for it to happen. I tried not to love him, but I can't help it." *Now what do I do? Where do I go from here?*

Standing a while longer contemplating my feelings, my breath catches. Like a movie screen appearing before my eyes, I see the dream I had before leaving North Carolina. The memory of the little boy's words brings a startling realization to light.

"*This is what you meant, isn't it?*"

As a rich warmth fills my entire being, I know it is true. There is not a doubt in my mind and I am amazed. My attempts to close myself to love have all been futile. I can no longer deny what I feel, nor will I even try. And now that I have finally accepted my love for Adagio, I can only hope he truly shares my feelings. This whole thing scares me to death, and I don't think my heart can handle being alone in this.

Adagio

Adagio's step is a little lighter as he exits his apartment. It is well past noon and he is late going to Cisely's, but it couldn't be helped. He had needed this time away from her. He had spent most of the morning, as well as last night going over his feelings. He has tried for weeks to fight them, but he can't anymore because it has become impossible.

He is deeply in love with Cisely.

He loves her like he never thought he would be able to love anyone. It is the desperate kind of love that he had heard others talk about but had never experienced himself.

Adagio knows Cisely will always love Ingo and a part of her will miss him, but surely, she can make room in her heart for someone else—that someone being himself. Surely, he has a chance. What he feels for her completely fills the emptiness in him. He will forever think of Ingo and treasure the friendship they shared, but he knows Ingo would never deny him this chance at happiness.

Warmth flows over him, through him, validating that his love for Cisely *is* right. It came to him only moments ago that Cisely is the gift his mother had spoken of. Even as he ponders it now, the warmth only increases, again telling him this is the way things are meant to be.

He needs to tell Cisely how he feels, and he hopes that wherever Ingo is, he really understands. Somewhere in his heart, Adagio is sure he does, and maybe even wants this.

J. Adams

Thirty-three

Adagio stops by Gary and Tara's to drop off his cannelloni recipe. Tara is planning to make the dish for her husband. He finds her in the backyard, wearing a wide brimmed straw hat and gloves, trimming a large rose bush.

"I really appreciate this, Adagio," she says, taking the card from him. Looking over the ingredients a moment, she slips it into her shirt pocket.

"It is no trouble at all. I hope Gary likes it."

"Well, since it's your recipe, I know he will, providing I get it right."

"I am sure it will turn out great."

Tara takes in Adagio's countenance, noticing the brightness in his eyes.

"You've decided, haven't you? About Cisely, I mean."

Adagio is taken aback by her perceptiveness. "Yes, I have. But how did you know?"

She chuckles. "It's not very hard to figure out. I only have to look at your face and it's obvious. I can tell Cisely cares a great deal for you, too. I can see it in her eyes every time you two are together. It's in her voice whenever we talk about you during our visits. I think she holds back a lot because she is afraid, but it's there in her every action." She pauses, smiling. "Gary and I talk about you a lot, and we've prayed that you would find the person you are meant to be with. And personally, I think Ingo would be happy to know his best friend has found happiness with the woman he loved so much. You two already spend so much time together, Cisely has probably come to depend on the comfort and security she gets from you. If you left, it would break her heart. You need each other."

Adagio smiles, thinking about Cisely being a permanent part of his life. It is soon and the emotions churning inside him are still fairly new, but his love for her runs deep, and right now he wants that permanence more than anything. It will bring him the happiness he has longed for.

"I hope you are right. I don't think I realized just how much I love her until now. Maybe it's because I have tried so hard not to, for fear of hurting my relationship with her and betraying Ingo. As a matter of fact, it has taken so much out of me, I am exhausted."

"Then it's time to stop fighting and just accept that it's meant to be."

"It *is* time," he agrees, and now that he has accepted it, he can't get to Cisely fast enough. He kisses Tara's cheek. "Thank you for listening, and for your insight."

She chuckles. "You're welcome."

"I had better get going. I have a stop to make on the way to Cisely's."

"Good luck," she calls after him.

J. Adams

Thirty-four

I am so nervous that I can hardly breathe. I usually anticipate Adagio's arrival, but today is different because I am finally admitting what I feel.

I am in love with Adagio St. John.

I did not think I would ever fall in love again. I didn't want to, but I have. And now that I have accepted it, the feelings have only increased. The thought of opening up to him scares me a little–okay, a lot, but I will no longer deny my heart what it wants–what it needs. I won't try to compare my feelings for him to what I felt for Ingo because my heart only knows one way to love, and that is fully. I pray that Adagio feels the same, and right now I am in agony waiting for him.

I could call him . . . but what would I say? I release a nervous laugh. *I've seen him every day for the past three and a half months and suddenly I can't come up with anything to say. Get a grip, girl!* Standing by the living room window, I wait anxiously.

When Adagio finally pulls up, my heart starts pounding so hard, I grow light-headed. It is another moment before he gets out. Moving away from the window, I take a calming breath, my fear growing the closer he gets to the door.

Breathe. Just breathe.

Adagio

Sitting in the car for another moment, Adagio tries to calm his racing heart and get a grip on his emotions. For years, he has wondered if he would ever feel this way about a woman. He hadn't known if it would ever happen, or that he would ever experience emotions so strong.

Adagio wants this to work out so badly, and it hurts to think of Cisely rejecting his affections. He needs her with an intensity he never thought possible. Closing his eyes, he takes a deep breath and gets out of the car.

When Adagio knocks, I take a moment to compose myself. I am about to cross a line that both excites and frightens me. Once I take that step, I can never go back. Nor do I want to.

Breathe, breathe, breathe.

"Please don't let me ruin this," I whisper before opening the door. "Hi."

"Hello."

He looks amazing in a beige polo and jeans, his hair tousled, muscular arms lightly tanned. But then again, he always does. And I look . . . I look big.

Shyly dropping my gaze, I move aside, letting him in. "You must have been pretty busy this morning," I comment in a steady voice, wondering what took him so long, yet glad that it had.

He closes the door. "I had some things I needed to take care of. I wanted to spend the whole day with you, and I didn't want anything to interrupt. I hope that is all right."

His words catch me by joyful surprise. "It's more than all right." My gaze locks intently with his, and I don't try to disguise the longing anymore, but I still have to remind myself to breathe because my heart is racing like crazy.

Moving closer, he presses a hand to my cheek, caressing it softly. He has touched me many times, but never like this.

Keeping my gaze riveted to his, I soak in the warmth of his hand. His face is so close to mine, I can smell his cologne, and the warmth of his breath on my skin is indescribably intoxicating. I shiver as a heady wave of emotion surges through me.

His eyes roam over my face for a moment and I imagine him taking in my every feature—my brown skin, my full mouth, and my emotion-filled eyes. I hope he can read in them what I have yet to say. What a curiously-vulnerable situation I find myself in—longing to know how he really feels, but too afraid to reveal my own heart. His next words change all that.

"Cisely, your friendship is the most important thing in the world to me." Moving back a little, he takes my hands, lacing his fingers between mine. "I never expected this to happen. This is probably too soon, and out of respect for Ingo, I have tried to wait, but I can no longer keep my feelings hidden." Tightening his fingers slightly, he draws me closer until our bodies are almost touching. "I am in love with you, Cisely."

Fully absorbing his words, I release a shaky breath, ready to bare my soul.

"And I am in love with you."

Smiling with wonder in his expression, he gently captures my face in his hands, brushing his thumbs over my skin. I marvel at the words and feelings that have just passed between us. Reverently caressing my face, he softly brushes a thumb across my lips before lowering his head and pressing his mouth to mine.

Adagio

Adagio's insides quiver at the softness of her lips and the sweetness of her kiss. It is new, yet familiar somehow. As her warm mouth softens under his, anxiously answering his heated affections, he finds that kissing her is so perfect, he wants to cry. He has never experienced so much from a single kiss, and he never will again with anyone but her.

Tears slip down my cheeks as I relish the feel of his moist mouth plying mine. His kiss is warm and demanding, producing emotions that stir my very soul. I never imagined feeling so much from a kiss. Moaning softly at the feel of his tongue grazing mine over and over, I circle my arms around his waist, pulling him closer, needing to be wrapped in his warmth. The emotional rush is staggering, and in this moment, I know I belong in his arms. The haven of his love is now all that exists.

Adagio parts his lips from mine and I press my face in the hollow of his neck. Sighing contentedly, he holds me close, and I lose myself in his warmth. For a while now, we have denied ourselves emotions that can't be helped by either of us. We've spent so much time together during the past three and a half months, the feelings that have grown between us were inevitable. Now there is no more denial, only acceptance.

Adagio draws back slightly, lifting my chin with his finger. "Do you really love me?"

"I really do."

"You do?"

Smiling, I nudge him playfully. "I do."

"Slow down, we haven't even gotten to that part yet."

"Adagio!"

Laughing, he touches his lip to mine whispering, "I have something to ask you, *amore*."

"Okay."

"Would you mind if we sat out on the porch swing?"

"Not at all."

There is a mild breeze as we step outside. It tousles his already tousled hair, making it look wildly perfect. Taking my hand, he rocks the swing gently. "I don't want to be alone anymore, Cisely."

"Neither do I."

"I need you in my life, more than I have ever needed anything. I want you by my side always." Taking a small, black velvet box from his pocket, he places it in my hand.

"We will have a good life together," he says, opening it. "Will you have me, Mrs. Kelly? Will you take my name and share my life?"

I nod. "Yes."

With a teary smile, he takes the oval solitaire from the box. The stone is surrounded by tiny emeralds. "This was my mother's ring. My father gave it to her and before she died, she gave it to me, probably hoping I would give it to my future wife. I've never had a desire to give it to anyone until now. Don't ask me why I have it with me because there really is no answer. I have always taken it with me wherever I've gone. I suppose for luck. Call me crazy."

"I would call it fate," I whisper.

"I agree," he says, touching my face.

"It's very beautiful."

"I stopped on the way here to get it cleaned and polished a bit. If it doesn't fit, we can have it sized."

I gaze momentarily at the ring with its glittering white gold setting. Removing my wedding rings, I put them in the box, staring at them another moment before closing it. I am trading one ring for another—trading the symbol of one man's love for the other. It is odd that it should feel so right.

Adagio places the ring on my finger. It is a perfect fit, as if it was made for me. He brings my hand to his lips, and then gently draws me against him, wrapping his arms around me.

"I love you, Cisely."

"And I love you."

As he presses his mouth to mine again, I literally feel his love through his kiss. A familiar warmth flows through me and I draw back a little. Looking into his eyes, I see that he feels it too.

"This is right, isn't it?" I ask in awe.

"It is, *amore.*"

"Would it be terrible of me to say I'm a little afraid?"

"No, because I am, too." Pressing a kiss to my forehead, he whispers, "God is in control, and we are very blessed to have each other."

"We are," I agree.

"Everything will be different now," he breathes. "Think we are ready for the change?"

"I'm definitely ready."

"So am I." He brushes a few flyaway strands of hair back from my face. "I have needed you in my life longer than I wanted to admit. It has been hard being so close to you every day, unable to share my true feelings. Some moments have been agony because of wanting to tell you so badly, but I was afraid of scaring you away. And I worried about betraying Ingo. But no matter how I tried, the longing was always there."

"I have needed you too, though I didn't want to admit it either. It frightened me to need you so much."

"There is no need to be afraid anymore."

"No," I agree. "There isn't."

"So, what should we do now?" he asks.

"It doesn't matter. As long as we're together, anything is fine."

He smiles, kissing me lightly. "Well, whatever we decide, I think we should at least share our news with Jessica. Where is she, anyway?"

"She went down to the boutique. She wasn't really scheduled to go in. I think she just wanted to give us some time alone. She talked to me this morning about not fighting my feelings anymore."

"She did, huh? Well, remind me to thank her when we see her."

"I already did, but I'm sure she wouldn't mind hearing it from you." Reaching up, I bury my fingers in his hair the way I've wanted to for a long time. "It was the best advice she could have given me."

"I agree," he says closing his eyes, leaning into my touch.

We keep our arms wrapped around each other. With my head resting against his shoulder, I silently revel in our closeness. Now that I am wearing his ring, I never want to let him go.

"Cisely?"

'Mmmm?"

"Ingo told me about Jessica leaving you the house in her will, and I know how much you love it here. That being the case, once we are married, if you want us to stay here it will be all right."

I am warmed by his concern for my feelings. "I do love it here and I always will, but Italy is your home, so it will be my home, too. I'll admit it makes me a little nervous to think about moving away, but I will follow you anywhere, Adagio, and wherever we are will be home."

He rests his forehead against mine. "You mean everything to me, Cisely," he whispers. "Everything."

"And you mean everything to me."

His hand slides down to my stomach, pressing gently. "And I promise to love this little one like he is my own."

Covering his hand with mine, I lightly trace the masculine veins beneath his skin. "I know you will. You will be a great dad."

"Thank you," he says humbly. "I will do my best. I owe it to Ingo."

A melancholic sadness briefly touches me. "Ingo would have been a great dad. He was a great man." Gazing into Adagio's eyes, I touch his face. "Now you can do what he can't."

"It will be a privilege."

Falling into a comfortable silence, he continues to caress my stomach, causing the baby to move. "Wow!" he says, feeling a firm kick. "He is a strong one. Maybe he will be a soccer player."

"He's really active and gives me some pretty hard ones. Maybe he will be. Will you teach him?"

"It will be one of the first things on my list to do with him when he is old enough." He lets his hand follow the baby's strong movements for a while longer before finally lacing his fingers between mine.

"When do you think you would like to be married?" he asks.

Longing to start a life with him, I would marry him *today* if I could and it still would not be soon enough, but I have to be reasonable and plan. "How about a month after the baby is born? It will give us time to prepare and get mine and the baby's things sent ahead of time. And maybe my figure will be half way back to normal by then."

He gives me a warm smile. "It will be difficult, but I guess I can hold out that long." His thoughts are transparent, his gaze causing warmth to spread through me because my thoughts are the same.

"Besides," he adds, "it will be enough just to be with you and know you will be completely and legally mine soon."

"I feel the same." I caress his face, not able to resist touching him. I love touching him, and having him touch me. Looking at me intently, he opens his mouth to stay something, then stops.

"What is it?" I ask.

"Well . . . I don't how to say this except to just say it." He twists a lock of my hair around his finger. "Cisely, I have never . . . you will be the first for me . . . the first and only."

I am touched by his need to share this with me. Of course, that fact would have eventually been known, but I am still amazed and grateful for his moral principles–principles that I once lacked. "And you will be my last." I silently study his handsome face for a moment. "You know, I keep mentally asking the same questions. Why am I so lucky? What have I done to deserve this? To deserve you?"

He pulls me against him, tightening his embrace, pressing his lips against my brow. "I ask myself those same things. "What have I done to deserve *you*? I have no answer. But I know we are meant to be together now."

"I feel the same."

Adagio says nothing more. He doesn't need to because I know his heart and he knows mine. We are beginning a new chapter in our lives. I can't believe how much everything has changed in a matter of months. The changes have been painful, but the tender mercies have been wondrous.

"Well," Adagio says, "shall we go and share our news with Jessica?"

"Sure. I'm ready whenever you are."

He helps me up, immediately pulling me into his arms. Holding his face between my hands, I am freshly amazed at the love I see in his eyes. I am tempted to feel guilty for loving him, but a deeper part of me knows Ingo would not begrudge us the happiness we've found in each other.

Adagio presses his mouth to mine, kissing me passionately. And as the passion of our kiss grows, so does my longing for him.

He draws back slowly. "I promise to never hurt you, Cisely. I will try to be a good husband. I know I can never take Ingo's place in your heart, nor would I even try, but I do promise to love and cherish you always."

"And I promise you the same." My thoughts drift as I contemplate the fact that I am not alone anymore. I will be sharing my life and raising my child with the last person I ever expected to be with this way. And he is perfect for me in every way.

When I am silent a little too long, Adagio asks, "Are you really all right with this, Cisely? Do you think we are moving too fast?"

I smile, shaking my head. "No. I want to be your wife. I was just thinking about how much you have filled the space in my heart . . . and I hope Ingo truly understands."

"He does, angel." he says, brushing a hand against my cheek. "This is right. A week ago, I was not sure about anything. Today I am sure about *everything*."

Wrapping my arms around his neck, I kiss him again. A sudden kick from the baby interrupts the moment.

"Okay, little one," he says, rubbing my stomach. "I will stop for now, but we are going to pick this up later." As if the baby understands, he makes another small movement and I chuckle, grimacing slightly.

"I think he got that."

Entering the house to grab my purse, I stop for a moment and rub the ache in my stomach. It soon fades and I can't stop the grin from spreading across my face. I am happy and in love, and nothing will be the same again.

Adagio

Adagio meets Cisely at the bottom of the stairs, taking her hand. Walking out onto the porch, her step slows. She suddenly presses a hand to her stomach, grabbing Adagio's arm with the other.

"What is it, *amore?*"

It takes her a few seconds to answer. "It was a contraction. I've been having them on and off for a couple of days now, but . . . not like this one."

Adagio puts his arm around her and waits for the pain to pass. "Come. Let's go and sit." He walks her into the living room and eases her onto the couch. Sitting down next to her, he lifts her legs, placing them across his lap.

Leaning back against the pillows, she releases a deep sigh. "Thank you. I think if I sit here for a moment, I'll be . . ."

Before she can finish, another contraction hits and it is much sharper than the first. Looking at his watch, Adagio starts timing them, just in case it is actual labor. When she has another contraction a few of minutes later, he says they should head to the hospital.

"Where is your bag?"

"It's in my bedroom closet on the floor."

Locating the small suitcase that she packed a couple of weeks ago, he hurries down and sets it by the door, and then goes back to Cisely.

"Can you walk?"

"I think so." As she stands, another contraction hits, and she moans, gripping his arm.

When the pain passes, he lifts her in his arms and carries her out to the car. Leaning the seat back, he makes her as comfortable as possible. Putting the suitcase in the back seat, he quickly gets in and heads up to the hospital.

J. Adams

Thirty-five

Adagio reaches for my hand and I squeeze as another pain comes.

"It's going to be okay, baby." His voice is soft.

Nodding, I concentrate on breathing deeply and it helps to make the pain a little more bearable. Beads of perspiration cover my forehead. At the squeeze of my hand, I open my eyes, taking in the worried look on his face. "I'm okay, my love."

He smiles a little, kissing my hand. "I love you."

"I love you, too, and I'm so glad you're here with me."

Adagio's relief is audible as we approach the hospital a few minutes later. He pulls up to the emergency entrance and parks the car. Running in and grabbing a wheelchair, he is soon back and wheels me inside where they direct us to labor and delivery.

The pain is so intense, I can hardly think. My water breaks, and the nurse calls my midwife. When Judy arrives, Adagio waits in the hall while she checks me. When he returns, she tells us it won't be long. She is also surprised at how fast my labor is progressing with it being my first baby. Adagio sits on the edge of the bed, holding my hand. With each contraction, I grip his hand so hard, I am sure there will be bruises. He kisses me, brushing the hair from my face. Another contraction comes and I breathe through it, never taking my eyes from his. His presence sustains me and his comforting strength makes me love him even more.

When Judy tells us it is time, Adagio moves to leave and I tighten my grip on his hand.

"Don't go. Stay with me . . . please."

"Are you sure?"

I nod, breathing through another contraction. He stays at the head of the bed with me, whispering words of comfort against my ear as I begin the stage of pushing. I latch on to his added strength with each breath I take and each contraction I push through.

Then our son is born and neither of us can hold back the tears.

Relaxing against the inclined bed with my face pressed against Adagio's, my thoughts shift to Ingo and I try to imagine his joy at the moment, wondering if it is anything close to mine. I will forever be grateful for the part of himself he left behind.

"You did it, Cisely!" Judy says, squeezing my hand.

I smile, relief flowing through me. "Is he okay?"

"He's absolutely beautiful and perfect." The nurse wraps the baby in a blanket and places him in my arms. "Without even weighing him, I can tell he's eight pounds. Not bad for being a week early."

"He's so beautiful!" Adagio says, caressing his soft cheek.

"He is," I tearfully agree.

"So, what's the little guy's name going to be?"

Meeting Adagio's loving gaze, I smile. "Ingo Kelly St. John." Adagio and I made the decision on the way to the hospital. In our hearts we know there can be no other name.

"St. John?" Judy questions.

"Adagio and I are getting married. He will be Ingo's father."

"Congratulations to you both!" There are tears in Judy's eyes.

"Thank you," Adagio says, kissing my lips softly. "I am a very blessed man."

"Amen to that," Judy says with a smile.

Adagio

While Cisely is changed and settled, Judy sends Adagio down to the nursery to bathe Ingo. He then takes a moment to call Jessica at the boutique. He tells her about their engagement, and when he announces they now have a son, he has to hold the phone away from his ear as Jessica shares the news with the women in the shop and they all cheer.

Entering Cisely's room, he pushes a small bed with the sleeping baby inside, taking a moment to silently gaze at the beautiful face of the woman he loves. Lifting little Ingo from the bed, he cradles him, marveling at the miracle of his new life.

"*Amore*," he says softly.

Cisely opens her eyes. Her smile is serene.

"Our son wants to be with his mama." He places the sleeping infant in her arms. She slides over on the bed and Adagio gently lay back beside her.

Cisely presses her nose against Ingo's cheek, inhaling the scent of his soft skin. "He is so perfect."

"He is." Adagio caresses the tiny fingers. "He is a miracle. *Life* is a miracle."

"I am so happy, Adagio. And having you with me means so much."

"I will always be here for you." Touching her face, he marvels anew that she is really going to be his.

"The only thing that will make everything complete is becoming your wife."

His smile is warm. "I look forward to that day more than anything." Kissing her tenderly, he silently thanks God for helping Cisely get through the delivery and blessing them both with this precious gift.

Thirty-six

I gain my strength back quickly after the birth of Ingo, and I am filled with a joy that cannot be put into words. Having a child of my own is a fulfilling responsibility, one that I eagerly look forward to each morning. I cherish every moment with our son, celebrating each waking cry and savoring each feeding.

Adagio is an amazing father already, the role seeming as natural to him as breathing. He now spends most of his time with me, helping out with the baby whenever he can so I can rest. Now that we are engaged, our need to be near each other is even stronger and we desperately long for our wedding day. It can't come fast enough.

I receive a large package from Ingo's family containing gifts for the baby. I call Gloria and Patrick to thank them. I am a little nervous about telling them of my engagement to Adagio, but it has to be done. Ingo is their grandson and they should know he will have a new father. I am both surprised and touched by their support. Patrick says Adagio is a great guy and will make

227

a good father for Ingo. And because Adagio was such a good friend to his son and has been here for me, he cannot think of a better man for me to marry. I promise to keep in touch, as well as keep them updated on their grandchild. And at Adagio's insistence, I invite them to come and see little Ingo whenever they want.

We stay busy packing and preparing for the wedding, our excitement and longing for each other growing by the minute. There is much to do, which helps to pass the time. Adagio buys a stroller for Ingo, and in the evenings, we take walks through the neighborhood. It gives me the exercise I need and helps me get back in shape.

I also spend a lot of time pondering my future. Though I will miss my home in Utah, I am looking forward to my new life with Adagio. Italy will definitely be a big change, but it is a change I am ready for.

The summer night before our wedding is pleasant after a scorching afternoon. At 101 degrees, the air conditioner has been running all day and staying outdoors for any length of time was misery, so the cool breeze is appreciated and savored.

Sitting on the front porch swing, Adagio tells me more about Treviso, our home and the restaurant, which lays a lot of my fears to rest. Tackling the language is going to be a big job, but being married to a man who speaks the language fluently will make the transition much smoother. I am actually looked forward to learning Italian. I have always thought it a beautiful language.

Adagio's arms are around me, his embrace comfortable and secure. "I hope you don't mind, but I had Anna purchase some nursery furniture for Ingo. I also had her redecorate the master bedroom a little for us."

"You did?" I am surprised and touched.

"Yes. I told her to add a few feminine things, you know, brighter bedding and curtains and things, just to add a woman's touch. Of course, if you don't like it, you can change it."

"I'm sure I will love it. You really didn't need to change anything, but thank you for being so thoughtful."

"I just want you to be happy there. It means everything to me."

"I am happy, Adagio, completely happy. I have everything." Waving at a passing neighbor, I am thoughtful a moment. "I have lost much, I've been given much, too. I have little Ingo to always remind me of Ingo, and I have you. I can't ask for anything more."

Smiling warmly, he touches his forehead to mine. "You are amazing."

"So are you," I say, kissing him. "I love you," I whisper, longing for tomorrow.

"I love you. And I am counting the minutes until I am your husband." Tightening his embrace, he brushes the hair from my face and slowly lowers his head until his mouth hovers just above mine, his voice a husky whisper. "And I can't wait to make love to you, angel."

My breath quickens as his mouth claims mine, heat rushing through my entire body, and I melt against him. Pressing my hands into his hair, I draw him closer still. The low moan that escapes him ignites an inferno of desire inside me, and as the urgency of our kiss grows, we begin to lose ourselves in our need for one another. Adagio finally parts his lips from mine and we simply gaze at each other for a moment, our breath mingling, hearts pounding, and adoration burning in our eyes.

Sighing, I caress the shadow of soft stubble on his cheek and rest my head against his shoulder. He rocks the swing gently, and there we stay until late, anticipating our wedding day.

Before going to bed, I open my dresser drawer and take out the black ring box. Flipping it open, tears slowly blur my vision as I gaze at my old wedding rings. They are still shiny and look almost new. I hadn't worn them long enough to show more signs of wear, a fact that is no one's fault.

But the thought still hurts. I am about to marry again and tie myself to my best friend, a man I love very much. However, at the moment, the ache for the other man who held my heart before him is present.

For this small increment of time, I let the ache have its moment. I let the tears come. Hanging my head, I clutch the rings to me and whisper, "I still love you, Ingo, and I miss you. I don't mean to hurt you, but . . . I . . . I love Adagio. I love him so much. I'm not sorry for that. I can't be." *Please understand.*

Closing my eyes and crying silently, a subtle war of emotions rages inside me, then a feeling of warmth slowly begins to surround me and I gasp as Ingo's voice softly whispers to my mind, *"I love you, Cisely. But this is the way it was meant to be from the beginning. This is God's plan for you, and for Adagio. Live the plan and be happy."*

Drying my tears in amazement, I smile. "Thank you," I whisper.

Looking at the rings a final time, I close the box and place it back in the drawer, allowing the tears to wash the last of the hurt away.

Now my heart can belong to Adagio completely.

Thirty-seven

We marry in the backyard beneath an arched, rose-covered trellis. Because I am nursing and have been exercising regularly, I do regain my figure. The slim fitting, ivory silk and lace dress fits well, falling just above my ankles. My hair is styled by Tara Flynn in an intricate up-do that is truly a work of art. From the moment Adagio sees me, he tells me repeatedly that I am beautiful and never takes his eyes off me.

And I had not thought Adagio could be any more handsome, but the dark blue Armani suit he wears looks like it was made just for him, and there isn't a more perfect looking man on the face of the earth. I know he is breaking hearts everywhere by marrying me, and I'm okay with that.

Our only guests besides Jessica are Gary and Tara, and the women from the boutique. We felt a small wedding was best.

Vows and rings are exchanged and we are pronounced husband and wife.

When it is time for us to share our first kiss, Adagio softly caresses my cheek, the tears in his eyes mirroring my own. Taking me in his arms, he kisses me and I sense his restrained passion. The yearning in his gaze as he parts his lips from mine warms me to the core.

"I love you, Mrs. St. John," he whispers.

"I love you, Mr. St. John."

After receiving hugs and heart-felt wishes, we have a few light refreshments. We thank the reverend for performing the ceremony, as well as everyone else for coming and supporting us.

Since I am nursing Ingo, I can't leave him with Jessica, but I wouldn't anyway because he is so young, and I cannot bear the thought of being separated from him even for two days.

Adagio puts our bag in the trunk while I say goodbye again to Jessica. Giving her one last hug, we leave for the hotel.

We check into an executive suite at *The Grand America.*

While Adagio puts our things away in the bedroom, I nurse Ingo before placing him, now-sleeping, in the portable crib, and then head to the bathroom to change. Taking a little extra time, I contemplate that I am now Mrs. Adagio St. John. I whisper my new title and sigh. It is hard to believe we are really married.

Having finished changing into a peach lacy chemise, I check my reflection once more, pressing a hand against my stomach, a rush of butterflies surging within me. Taking a deep breath, I open the door.

Adagio

Sitting on the side of the bed, Adagio stares out at the vast city, marveling that Cisely is now his wife. After being alone for so many years, he had wondered if he would ever find love. He had searched, pondered, prayed, and waited. Then he decided to just be still and trust God.

When Ingo died, it nearly crushed Adagio. Losing his friend was one of the hardest things he'd ever had to face. It was also hard to see Cisely alone again and his heart had gone out to her. Supporting her through her grief, he sometimes wondered if she would ever truly be okay again. He had also wondered if his own wants and desires even mattered anymore.

He had been wrong to doubt.

Because a miracle happened. Without even realizing it, the desires of his heart were being granted. Cisely had healed his heart and claimed it as her own.

His insides swell with love and longing as he thinks of Cisely. His feelings for her are so strong, he can't imagine not being with her now. He loves her with every fiber of his being, and now that she is his wife, he can fully share that love with her.

As I enter the room, Adagio stands, letting his eyes roam over me. "Beautiful," he says softly. I swallow hard, my pulse quickening at the sight of him standing before me shirtless, his arms, chest and torso looking like they were chiseled from marble. His hungry gaze sends a rush of heat through me.

"I love you," he says softly before drawing me into his arms and kissing me.

"I love you," I murmur against his mouth. Drawing back, I leisurely take in his perfect form, awe filling me. "Do you have any idea how beautiful you are?"

Looking into my eyes a moment, he replies, "Not until you looked at me. What you see is the only thing that matters."

"I feel the same." I stare into his eyes a long moment, sharing my thoughts and feelings without words. Tightening his embrace, he pressed me against him and I surrender my heart and body to the warmth of his arms and the safety of his love.

Lying in Adagio's arms, I bask in the intimacy we have just shared. We talk quietly as little Ingo sleeps.

"Are you okay?" I ask softly.

He sighs, pressing his face into my hair. "There are no words. I have never experienced anything so incredible in my life."

I smile. "Thank you, for saving yourself for me."

"Thank you for making me so grateful that I did." Burying his fingers in my hair, he whispers against my lips, "And I know I could never tire of making love to you."

"The feeling is definitely mutual." I kiss him and glance toward the bedroom door. "And I can't believe Ingo didn't make a sound."

"I can't believe it, either. Maybe he knew we needed this time."

"Maybe you're . . . right." Ingo lets out a loud cry and we laugh.

"Let me get him," Adagio says, immediately getting up. I watch him walk over to the door and can't help likening his body to a Greek statue. He is so masculine, so perfect.

Adagio coos as he picks Ingo up and brings him to me, placing him in my arms. Changing him quickly, I begin to nurse him. Adagio slips back under the covers next to me and watches. "He is growing more handsome every day."

"He is. He's such a miracle. All babies are."

"Does that mean you are willing to go through this again?"

"I am definitely willing, as many times as I am blessed with the opportunity."

He kisses me. "I was hoping you felt that way. I didn't bring it up before because you just had Ingo and I thought it might be a while before you would even want to think about it, but I am glad you do."

"Well, truthfully, I want as many children as God cares to send us. And I know you love Ingo like he is your own flesh and blood, but I do look forward to the day that I can have your child."

"I do as well," he says with a smile.

When Ingo drifts to sleep again, I place him back in his bed and stand for a moment, watching him sleep, marveling at how blessed I am. I have a new life with a wonderful man and a beautiful child. After suffering such loss, I never dreamed I could be this happy again, that I could be so content.

I sigh as Adagio moves behind me, circling his arms around my waist. Leaning back against him, we stand for a moment longer, watching Ingo sleep. Turning in his arms, I glimpse the renewed desire burning in his emerald eyes. Smiling lovingly, he lifts me and carries me back to bed.

Adagio

Adagio watches as moonlight sifts softly through the drapes, falling on Cisely's sleeping form nestled in his arms. He can't sleep because he doesn't want to close his eyes–not yet. Drawing back a little, he gazes at her face through the dim light. He cannot help himself; he just has to look at her. Feeling her soft breath against his skin, he listens to her even breathing. His gaze roams over her slender curves. If ever there was a body made for his, it is hers.

And she *is* his! This beautiful, amazing and incredible woman is his wife, his best friend, and the love of his life. He is no longer alone. For the first time ever, he is lying in bed next to a woman, and his life is completely and irrevocably connected to another. It is a wonderful feeling.

Heaving a deep sigh of contentment, he draws her closer, tightening his embrace, soaking in the warmth of her body. Then he finally closes his eyes and begins to drifts with her name on his lips.

Awakening with a sigh, Cisely slides a hand caressingly up his arm and lays her warm palm against his whiskery cheek. "I love you, Adagio, she whispers, raising her lips to his, her voice raspy with sleep.

On the edge of sleep, he murmurs against her mouth, "*Ti amo, cara mia,*" before waking fully to drink in her kiss.

Thirty-eight

I am going to miss you so much," Jessica says as she tearfully hugs me, then Adagio.

"I'm going to miss you, too. Thank you for everything."

"Thank you for letting me be a part of your life. And never forget you have a home here, both of you. After all, when I'm gone the house will still be yours."

"I love you, Mama," I whisper.

With that one spoken phrase, a river of tears splashes down Jessica's face. "And I love you, my daughter." She hugs me again for a long moment, then kisses little Ingo goodbye.

"Take care of her," she says emotionally to Adagio.

He hugs her again. "I will. I promise."

I wave at Jessica as we pass through the security gate and head up the escalator to our terminal. Adagio and I take turns holding Ingo and rocking him while we wait for boarding time, which helps to keep my emotions at bay, if only for a small time.

When we finally board and are settled in our seats, a mental picture of Jessica again living alone in that large house causes my heart to ache. With Ingo and I there, she'd finally had the family she always wanted, but Ingo is gone now and I am leaving to start a new life. Turning my face toward the window, I try to discreetly wipe away my tears, but Adagio sees them. I can't hide anything from him.

"It will be all right, baby," he says softly. I know he understands how hard this is for me and I am grateful for his comfort.

"I know." I say, squeezing his hand. "I'll be okay." Drying my tears, I smile. "I'll be okay because I am going home with my husband and little boy today."

Smiling, he lifts my hand to his lips. "And I am taking my wife and son home. I could not be happier."

Tilting my head against the seat slightly, I silently look into his eyes for a moment, my thoughts turning melancholy. "I'll bet you never guessed on your way here you would be bringing a wife and child home, did you?"

Holding my hand between his, he brushes his thumb across the back of it, meeting my unwavering gaze. "It was a most unexpected blessing."

"It was for me too."

We continue to stare at one another, silently conveying our thoughts. The changes in our lives have taken us both by surprise and sometimes it is still hard to believe all that has happened. Ingo will always have a place in my heart, and though I harbor moments of unspoken confusion, I cannot deny how right my love for Adagio feels. I know everything is as it should be. Moving forward, our lips meet in a warm kiss, a kiss born of sweetness and dreams for the future.

During the times of the trip when we are awake and Ingo is settled, I spend a little time studying a book on Italian, and with Adagio's help, I pick up quite a bit. I am grateful for the words and phrases he has taught me over the past months, but I had no idea I would really come to need the language one day.

It's true what they say. Life is full of surprises.

Awestruck doesn't begin to describe my feelings as we turn onto the cobblestone driveway and pull up in front of the large villa.

It is absolutely breathtaking! The building is covered in peach-colored stucco with white trim. The main entrance boasts two white columns with a large potted plant in front of each. The lower window terraces are lined with beautiful flower boxes and the landscaping is amazing. The right wing of the home is *St. John's Place*. The left wing and main part of the building are the living quarters.

"Welcome home, *amore*," Adagio says as we get out of the taxi. The driver unloads our luggage and Adagio pays him.

I give him a look of astonishment. "This is incredible!" It's like at a scene from a European travel show.

He smiles and kisses me. "This is your home now, Mrs. St. John."

I again stare up at the large building. *My home! I can't believe it!*

Once Adagio sets our luggage on the porch, he takes Ingo from me and leads me inside.

"Wow!" I whisper as we enter the grand entryway. Above us hangs an antique crystal and brass chandelier. Casting my eyes down, I take in the beautiful mosaic tile.

"Come." Adagio loops my arm through his and gives me a tour of the place. Most everything is updated, but the home still has a lot of the original decor, giving it a vintage feel, and I fall in love with it completely. I lose track of time admiring the paintings, antique fixtures and elegant Baroque decor. I still can't believe this is really my home.

While Adagio checks on things at the restaurant, I put Ingo down to sleep in the nursery and unpack my clothes and a few boxes we had sent ahead of time. Stacking the empty boxes in the corner, I begin unpacking Adagio's clothes.

Closing my eyes, I press one of his oxford shirts against my cheek, breathing in the faint lingering scent of his cologne, and marvel at the rush of emotion it brings. Hugging the shirt to me, I cast my eyes around the room for a moment. It is not quite as large as the room at Jessica's, but it is cozier and the elegance matches that of the finest hotels.

Adagio's maid did redecorate the room and I am pleased with the results. The high, black four-poster wooden canopy bed is draped in sheer ivory netting and covered in burgundy and ivory-colored bedding. There are multi-color striped square accent pillows on an ivory sofa in a corner of the room that is designed as a sitting area. A vase of summer flowers sits on a small bistro table near a corner window and Venetian landscape paintings hang on the walls. Taking in my surroundings, I look forward with anticipation to the nights I will share with Adagio in this room and the memories we will make here.

Walking over to the large window, I gaze out at the city and the River Sile in the distance, and try to picture Adagio standing alone looking at this same view. I take comfort in the knowledge that I will be here to share it with him now. It is all so incredible, I can scarcely take it in. This is now my home and where my life will be.

Adagio's strong arms come around me and he presses a soft kiss to the side of my neck. His warm lips against my skin sends shivers of pleasure through me.

"I absolutely love it here."

"It makes me happy to know that. I felt guilty thinking I was taking you away from everything and everyone you loved. I never want you to be unhappy, *amore*. I give you all that I have and will do everything in my power to give you a happy life."

Turning, I wrap my arms around his neck. "I am the happiest woman in the world, and as long as I am with you, I will always be, no matter where we are. This is home now."

"Even with the language challenges?"

"Well, what better way for me to learn Italian than marry an Italian man?"

"I agree completely. Especially," he says, kissing the corner of my mouth, "since it's me you married."

"Oh, definitely," I agree, chuckling at his handsome smirk and the amused twinkle lighting his green eyes. I return my gaze to the river and he enfolds me snugly against his chest.

Tightening his embrace, Adagio rests his head against mine, taking in the panoramic picture with me. "You don't know how good it feels to share this view with you. I have always found some pleasure in it, but it was not the same. To have you here makes everything so different. I feel as though I am seeing it for the first time. Nothing will ever be the same for me again."

"You know," I say, turning back to face him, "even when Ingo was alive, it saddened me to think of you feeling so alone here." I press a hand to his face, touching my fingers to his lips. "But I am grateful it was me you waited for, though I still find this all hard to believe sometimes." I pause, silently staring into his eyes. "So many changes."

Growing quiet a moment, Adagio meets my gaze, his own unwavering. "I am not sorry to have you," he says softly, yet I hear the conviction in his voice. "I will always treasure the friendship I shared with Ingo, but I am not sorry to have you now. I could never be ungrateful for the blessing of loving you." Sighing, he rests his brow against mine. "I can't."

Blinking back tears, I take in the poignancy of the moment. "I am not sorry, either. I will always treasure my marriage to Ingo, but I am not sorry for loving you." I touch his face. "You believe me, don't you?"

His eyes roam over my expression, not missing the bittersweet irony there. "I believe you, angel."

"This is where I am supposed to be—right here." I wrap my arms around his neck. "Right here in your arms. And this is where I will always stay."

Adagio smiles and kisses me, and kisses me. Then he carries me to the bed and makes love to me, and we relish the happiness we feel as we begin our new life in the country of his birth, and the home we will fill with love.

Thirty-nine

Settling into my new life is even easier than I thought it would be. My heart overflows daily with the joy of motherhood, and being Adagio's wife brings me a happiness I never thought I would have again, only in ways I cannot begin to define.

Each day I watch Adagio revel in his role of being a husband and father. Hiring another chef, he moves Sam, his most experienced chef, up to his position, which enables him to spend most of his time with us. Being together is our favorite past-time.

My love for Adagio has grown in intensity over the weeks and I treasure each moment we spend together. We are seldom apart from one another, and if we are, it usually isn't for very long. Our need to be close is very strong.

I have a new friend in Anna, our housekeeper. We get along well and she frequently expresses her happiness that Adagio isn't alone anymore. Anna only speaks a little English, but it is enough for us to understand one another. I also get to know Sam and the other chefs, as well as the rest of the staff at the restaurant, and it is easy to see how much they love Adagio. It seems everyone who knows him feels this way, and I am proud to be his wife.

Treviso is beautiful with a very tranquil and peaceful elegance. Boasting canals with backdrops of the Sile and Dolomite Mountains, it is unlike any place I have ever been. Many days find us packing Ingo in the stroller and touring the old churches stretching from piazza to piazza. I enjoy walking down the cobblestone streets and alleyways, having relaxing lunches at the pizzerias and trattorias. Sometimes we head out into the countryside, taking scenic drives among the rolling hills with their beautiful vineyards, olive groves and orchards.

Adagio often takes us into Venice. We ride the train across the ocean to the beautiful city. Walking around St Mark's Square, we shop at the small stands, straying off the beaten path every now and then. My favorite spot is the Rialto Bridge, where we stand watching the gondoliers steer their vessels through the canal. We've visited museums and toured the palaces along the Grand Canal, which are now mostly hotels, restaurants, and shops. I am convinced Venice is the most beautiful and romantic place in the world. A day trip to Verona and Milan are next on our list.

Adagio promises to take me on a longer trip through the country and show me more of Italy when Ingo is older. Since we never really had a honeymoon, I am looking forward to it.

Forty

Ingo releases a happy gurgling sound as I change him in the nursery. Our little bundle of joy is now three months old and definitely growing. His dark brown hair is wavy with a few blond highlights, and unusually thick dark lashes frame his honey-colored eyes. His complexion now has an olive tone.

Smiling up at me, Ingo coos softly and I begin singing a lullaby. The sound of my voice seems to have a calming effect and I definitely love singing to him.

Adagio

Adagio walks down the hall and is about to enter the nursery but stops when he hears Cisely's silky, soulful voice. How he loves hearing her sing! It's as if angels are singing each time a song escapes her, and to him there isn't a more beautiful voice in the world. He often thinks back to the first time he heard her sing. It was at Brian's funeral. As he listened to her that day, her voice took his breath away, and he was sure everyone there felt the same. She has an extraordinary gift. He listens for a moment longer before going in, wanting to be near her.

"That was beautiful, *amore*," he says moving behind her, kissing her cheek.

"Thank you."

Wrapping his arms around her, he asks, "How old were you when you started singing?"

She is thoughtful for a moment. "You know, this may sound funny–or even strange, but I remember being five and singing to the animals through the fence bordering the backyard of the housing project we lived in. The owner had a couple of horses grazing out back. Whenever I started singing, they would come over and press their noses to the fence and let me pet them. It happened every time. I guess that was when it started. After that, my voice just kind of took off on its own." She smiles at the memory.

"I feel very blessed to be married to such a gifted woman– a woman who possesses much integral strength, especially having been placed in a life with so many trials for one so young."

"I don't feel integrally strong, especially with all the terrible choices I've made in the past."

"Ah, *bella*, but look at the choices you are making now. That is what matters, not the past."

"I know. That's why I was so grateful for the chance to leave the old life behind."

"And I am grateful for you." He pauses, lightly touching his mouth to hers. "You are my life, Cisely." he whispers against her lips. "You know that, don't you?"

"Yes," she whispers back. "And you are mine."

When her lips part with a breathy sigh, he deepens the kiss, warmth spreading through his whole being.

"I should go and check on the quiche," he breathes, parting his mouth from hers slightly.

"If you have to," she says with a coy smile, pulling his head down again, drawing a low growl from him.

"I guess a few more minutes won't matter," he murmurs.

We spend the afternoon stretched out on the family room floor, playing with Ingo and taking pictures. Wanting to capture as many moments of his childhood as I can, snapping photos of our son is now a habit for me. I've also started doing more scrapbooking. I learned to like the hobby while living in Utah, and since having Ingo, my love for it has grown. I already have one book full of photos of him, both alone and with Adagio and me. I also created a small album to give to little Ingo when he is older; it contains a collection of photos of Ingo, Jessica, and me, so little Ingo will know his biological father as well.

When Ingo falls asleep in Adagio's arms, he takes him up to the nursery while I pick up the scattered toys and place them back in the basket. Adagio finds me in the kitchen, washing the last of the lunch dishes.

"I can't believe he's really three months old now," I say as I wash the plates.

Adagio grabs a towel and dries them. "I can't either. Time is passing so quickly. It seems like just yesterday that we brought him home from the hospital."

"I know. I was so glad to finally be able to hold him in my arms, but I also miss carrying him in a way. While he was still inside me he was sheltered. I didn't have to worry about him being hurt or suffering in any way. You know what I mean?"

"I know exactly what you mean. This world can be a scary place."

"Exactly," I agree. "But I wouldn't trade bringing children into the world for anything."

"Neither would I." He pulls me close. "You are a wonderful mother, Cisely."

"Thank you. And you are a wonderful father. I wouldn't be able to do it without you."

He smiles and kisses me.

After we've finished cleaning, I call Jessica to thank her for the package of new baby cloths we received from her last week. Hearing her motherly voice always lifts my spirits. I miss her so much and it's hard to say goodbye whenever we talk. Our conversations are pretty lengthy and I'm grateful to be able to talk for as long as I want and not have to worry about the cost. It makes being so far apart a lot easier.

Adagio surprises me by bringing in dinner from the restaurant. We dine on ziti with roasted eggplant and ricotta cheese, Caesar salad, and stuffed mushrooms. He even prepared orange creme brulee, which is now my new favorite dessert.

"So, did you cook *all* of this yourself?"

"I did," he answers, smiling. His chefs are used to him wandering in every now and then to prepare himself a meal, and they are really happy to see him preparing meals for two for a change. His employees are very loyal to him and love him because he is so easy to work for. He appreciates them just as much for being such good workers and often rewards them for their loyalty.

"Well, I guess it *is* your kitchen." I take a bite of the eggplant. "And you are definitely the most amazing cook in the world."

"*Grazie, amore.* I am sure there are better ones, but I feel pretty good when my dishes turn out well."

After dinner we are both so stuffed, we decide to take a walk around the grounds. I grab the baby monitor to listen for Ingo. We hold hands and casually stroll around the grounds.

"I will never get tired of gazing up at this place," I say, again taking in the large home, it's shadow looming over us, providing cooling shade from the sun.

"You know, I actually got a good deal on it. It didn't take much to get it cleaned up and updated."

"It's beautiful and the view is perfect. I feel very blessed to be here living here." Warmed by his gaze–an effect that I am sure will never fade–I smile shyly. "I feel like a princess."

"You are not just a princess, angel. You are a queen. And the home is blessed because you are here. Your presence has made everything complete, including me."

"The feeling is very mutual." He draws me close, kissing me warmly, and we cling to each other for another moment before continuing our walk.

Coming around the side of the house, we stop and sit for a bit on the veranda. Lightly running my fingers across the surface of the glass-topped, wrought iron table, I think about how romantic it would be to have lunch or dinner here sometime, and I decide to surprise Adagio one day this week with a meal here. Of course, to me, any meal I share with him is romantic.

Gazing out at the old buildings within our view with their various shades of stucco and stone, I find myself imagining what life was like here when they were new. I will have to read a little more about Italy's history when I have some time.

Taking my hand, Adagio presses a kiss to my palm and I marvel at the sweet sensation it brings. His touch in any way always has that effect on me.

"Thank you for dinner. You are so good to me."

"You are welcome. I will always be good to you."

"Then I'm sure if our sons follow your example when they are married, their wives will be the happiest and most content women in the world."

He smiles and kisses me. "Then I will have to make sure I train them well."

As I again scan the land surrounding us, I begin to picture future generations of our family. I can't help thinking of the unique heritage they will claim from us, and I am determined to make sure they know where they come from on both sides. Little Ingo will also know his biological heritage in addition to ours.

"Our children will have good lives here," Adagio says, seeming to read my thoughts. "And they will know they are loved."

I look at him in amazement, unable to believe how perceptive he has become to my feelings. Sometimes it is as if he knows me better than I know myself. "They will."

We sit for a few more moments, watching the sunset before going back into the house through the veranda entrance to take care of Ingo before getting settled for the night.

Securely wrapped in Adagio's arms, I ponder his birthday coming up in October and wonder what I can give him. He has given me so much happiness, I want the gift to be something special, something that will let him know just how much he means to me.

Inevitably, Adagio has become everything to me, and the love we share sometimes overwhelms me to tears. After Ingo, I never imagined I could love someone so much, but I do. As I lay contemplating my dilemma, the words of a song by one of my favorite recording artists comes to mind. Letting the soft ballad flow through my head, I realize it describes my feelings for Adagio perfectly. No other song even comes close. Making a final decision of what I will give him, my fingers suddenly itch to touch the piano keys.

Before we married, Adagio purchased a black grand piano for me as a wedding present and had it delivered a week after we arrived. I cried the first time I sat down to play it, and at Adagio's insistence I play a little each day.

Smiling, I contemplate learning the love song for him. I snuggle closer and send up a silent prayer of thanks for the contentment I feel in my life. I am so happy.

That final thought drifts through my mind as I fall asleep. But in the next moment, the peaceful picture of my life changes, the places and faces altering to one I recognize and instantly recoil from.

I am back in my old childhood bedroom. My father's form is hovering over me in the dark, forcing himself upon me. I try to awaken, but I am trapped in the nightmare. I continue to struggle, trying to fight him off, but he is too strong. I scream, but his hand is covering my mouth, making it hard to breathe. I hear him saying, "*Stop it, girl. You know you ain't good for anything else. You never will be.*"

"Nooo!" I mumble. "Stop it! Please stop. It hurts!"

Adagio

"Cisely," Adagio whispers, touching her and she jerks awake. He sits up and turns on the lamp.

Her eyes are wild, her expression disoriented. When Adagio reaches for her, she cringes, jerking back.

"Cisely, it is okay. It is just me, *amore*." He keeps his voice soft, reaching for her a second time, and again she moves back.

"Cisely, please. I won't hurt you." There are tears in his eyes, and in his voice. He has never seen her this way before. "I would never hurt you." Doing his best not to frighten her, he slowly leans closer, whispering again, "I won't hurt you, baby. I promise."

Adagio's emotional pleas slowly cut through the shadows of the nightmare, reaching through the darkness, providing a guiding light for my broken spirit–a light that draws me safely back to him. My emotions finally cave and I crumble.

Hesitantly, Adagio reaches for me and as he does, I fight the urge to flinch. Then he takes me in his arms. Leaning back against the pillow, he pulls the covers over us. My whole body is trembling and I can't seem to stop.

"It is all right, baby," he whispers, pressing his lips to my forehead, rocking me gently.

Clinging to him tightly, I begin to sob. This dream seemed so real that I feel like I've just relived the abuse. Every second of it came back to me in that single dream.

Needing to get control of my emotions, I chant inwardly over and over, "It wasn't real. I am safe. It wasn't real. It's over. It's over . . ." That part of my childhood is gone, never to return. I try to soak in Adagio's warmth and comfort.

Adagio

Cisely's trembling eases, her sobs lessening, but Adagio's tears continue to fall, and he now clings to her as desperately as she holds onto him. His next whispered words of comfort are not in English but Italian.

There is no need for him to ask about the nightmare. He already knows. This is not the first time he has awakened to her tortured pleas for her father to stop the sickening act. The pleas usually fade after a few seconds, but this is the worst it has ever been. This is the first time she has awakened completely terrified.

He continues to whisper in Italian of his love, and he vows to never let anyone hurt her again. He promises that she will always be safe with him.

I feel, more than understand his soft croons. Burrowing deeper in his embrace, I fuse against him, absorbing all he gives of himself. I don't know why the dreams come. They had started again before I married Ingo. Afterward, the dreams eased up a bit because I had felt safe, like nothing could ever harm me. Then Ingo was gone, and after a while they became frequent again.

Maybe they are the result of a fear seated deep within me, a fear of being left alone, of being a victim again. I feel so secure with Adagio now, safer and more secure than I've felt in a long time. Maybe some part of me is afraid of losing him, too, of being left alone yet again.

Maybe I love him too much.

Adagio

"Please don't ever leave me, Adagio" she whispers against his chest, holding him tighter. "I couldn't bear it if I ever lost you. I would die too." She presses her face into the hollow of his throat. "Please don't ever let me go."

Renewed emotion washes over Adagio as her desperate pleas tear at his heart. Burying his face in her hair, he whispers fervently, "I will never leave you, baby." He lifts her face, whispering against her mouth, "And I will never let you go." Her response is immediate and he deepens the kiss, wishing he could pull her into himself and absorb all her pain. As the passion rises between them, he realizes he is doing just that, and she takes everything he gives.

With the subsiding of passion comes the quiet calm at the end of the storm. Adagio waits until Cisely's breathing has become deep again before drifting to sleep himself, still clinging to her, praying that God would give her peace, and keeping his promise to never let her go.

He will never mention this night to her.

J. Adams

Forty-one

I practice the song for Adagio using the hour he spends at the restaurant each day. I have the sheet music, but I hardly use it. I am able to play by ear and I learn the music quickly. Though my voice will never compare to Minnie Riperton's, the lyrics stir my feelings for Adagio so much, I hope I can sing it well enough.

When the day finally arrives, Anna agrees to watch Ingo at her home for a while to allow us some time alone. I had wanted the night to be slightly formal, and since Adagio is getting dressed in the bedroom, I change in the bathroom, taking a little more time than normal, wanting to look as close to perfect as I can. I don't ever want him to forget this day.

A few minutes later, I exit the bathroom wearing a slim-fitting red dress with matching strappy high heel sandals. My hair hangs in loose spiraled curls, giving me a sultry look that even surprises *me*.

Adagio's smiles and whistles. "Wow, *bella!*" he says, looking up at me from where he sits on the bed. "Beautiful is not a strong enough word."

"Really?" I say, smiling coyly. "Then what would be a strong enough word?"

"Well, let me see. You are a wondrously beautiful, breathtaking goddess! How is that?"

I laugh. "Thank you. You look very handsome yourself."

"*Grazie.*"

"You're welcome."

Taking his hand, I lead him downstairs. The living room is lit by a dozen votive candles in crystal holders and a table covered in lace is set for two near the piano.

"Happy Birthday, Adagio."

"Thank you!"

He takes a seat at the table. Standing next to the piano, my stomach is quickly consumed with butterflies. His smile is loving, his warmth leaving me freshly amazed that just a look from him affects me so.

"I love you very much," I tell him.

"I love you too, angel."

"I wanted to give you something special for your birthday and I hope you like my choice. I've been working on this for a while now and I hope that through this song, you will know how much you mean to me."

Adagio turns his chair, his face full of anticipation.

Taking a deep breath, I begin Minnie Riperton's *Loving You*. As my fingers begin caressing the keys, my voice softly rises. Closing my eyes, I sing from my heart. Other than singing to our son, I've never felt as much emotion as I do at this moment singing to Adagio. Oddly, my mind drifts back for a moment to the few times that I sang for Ingo when he was alive. Though I enjoyed it immensely, the difference is I always sang *for* him, never *to* him. I don't know why that is, and it is a pointless thing to ponder now.

Adagio

As Adagio listens to the words of the song, they stir his very soul. To have her singing to him is indescribable, and it touches him deeply. He can hear her love in every word and feels blessed to have her as his wife.

When Cisely is finished, she moves into Adagio's waiting arms. "Happy Birthday," she says once more before pressing a kiss to his lips.

"Thank you, *amore*," he breathes. Holding her tightly, he passionately ravages her mouth for another moment before drawing back slightly and pressing a hand to her cheek. "I have never received such a wonderful present. And nothing makes me happier than listening to you sing."

"I love singing for you." She picks up the small wrapped box sitting on the piano and hands it to him.

"Another present?"

"It goes with the song."

Opening the box, he looks at her in wonder. "Is this what I think it is?" She nods and he hugs her. "I cannot believe it!" he says, taking the mini compact disc from the box.

Cisely had asked one of their friends to come over one day when she knew Adagio would be gone for a while and had him record her singing the song that she'd just performed for him, as well as a few others to listen to whenever he wanted.

"I will treasure this always."

They enjoy the meal Cisely spent the afternoon preparing. To Adagio, she has always been a pretty good cook, but since moving to Italy, her skills are even better. He spends a great deal of time teaching her how to prepare Italian meals, including helping her brush up on what he'd taught her in Utah, and she has managed to master quite a few Italian dishes.

Later, Anna drops Ingo off and I thank her for helping out. She wishes Adagio a happy birthday and gives him a present before leaving. He laughs as he opens the box, pulling out a colorful chef's apron that is perfect for him.

After I nurse Ingo and get him settled, Adagio blows out the candles in the living room and helps me take the leftover food to the kitchen.

"Thank you for a wonderful birthday." He pulls me close. "I will never forget it."

"You're welcome. I wanted to make it memorable for you."

"Well, you definitely did. And I can't believe you recorded a CD. How did you manage it?

I grin slyly. "Oh, I have my ways."

"Since when did you become so sneaky?"

"Mmmm, it's a recent development." I kiss the corner of his mouth. "But it was worth it. You deserve this and much more."

Closing his eyes, he touches his forehead to mine. "I have everything I could ever want. Thank you, Cisely."

We spend the rest of the evening wrapped up in one another while the disc I recorded plays softly in the background.

I lay awake for a while, pondering the evening. My plan had been a success and I am grateful. Anything I can do for Adagio is worth it, especially since he has to deal with so much of my emotional baggage. He is always a comfort to me and never complains when my nightmares interrupt his sleep. He simply holds me and tells me everything will be all right. He is a patient man and nothing I ever do for him would be enough.

Asheville, North Carolina

Across the ocean in a government housing complex, Alton Matthews sits at an old, wooden kitchen table in the one-bedroom apartment he moved into last week, taking the pills prescribed by a doctor at the health department. He grimaces, but not because the pills are hard to swallow. His painful expression is the product of a sudden long reflection on his life and the choices that find him in this situation.

During his adult years, he has hurt many, many people, causing irreparable damage that he can never take back. He has done things in his life that will surely see him in hell, the worst of his acts being so unspeakable, he can barely think about it. It was horrid and unforgivable.

And now he is suffering for all of it.

Leaning back in the chair, he closes his eyes. He had known he was sick for some time—for years, actually. He'd tried to ignore it and numb himself by drinking more, but it finally became too much, and he found himself waking up in the emergency room one night. Hearing the prognosis shattered something inside him. It was as if he'd awakened to every sin, ever misdeed, every evil, hateful, cruel and sadistic act he had ever committed.

Psychologists would say he is a product of his upbringing, and because he was raised in an abusive home it was inevitable that he would be an abuser himself. The world would say he can't help the way he is—that because of lack of proper counseling and help, he can't be blamed for his acts. They would allow him to skate through life, taking no responsibility for his actions because it is not his fault that he turned out the way he has. None of it is his fault.

But he knows the truth. *He* made the choice to abuse, to defile, to permanently alter lives. There is no escaping that.

Only now, when his body is broken and his health is failing, does he truly understand.

Those acts are costing him dearly.

Forty-two

The months have quickly passed and Christmas is fast approaching. I am especially excited because we will be having a guest; Jessica is coming to spend the holidays with us.

I thoroughly enjoy decorating the house with Adagio. I've been feeling a little under the weather, but I still manage to get out and get the Christmas shopping done and do some of the baking. When I wake up too sick to get out of bed one morning, Adagio is worried. I just smile and assure him I'm fine. I am actually better than fine because I already have an idea of why I'm sick. In fact, I purchased a pregnancy test yesterday.

Leaning against the vanity, I stare at the positive result through misty eyes, knowing Adagio will be overjoyed. Opening the bathroom door, I find him sitting on the edge of the bed, waiting patiently and I smile through the nausea. "Merry Christmas, my love, we are going to have a baby."

His smile is wide as he draws me to him, holding me close. "This is wonderful!"

"I think so too. I've wanted this so much."

"So have I." He caresses my cheek. "I love you."

"I love you, too." Another wave of nausea rolls through me and I move to the bed, needing to lie down again.

Pulling the covers over me, Adagio says, "Just rest for a while. Can I get you anything?"

"Maybe a croissant and some juice, if you don't mind."

"All right, and don't worry about Ingo. I will take care of him."

"Thank you, Adagio."

"You are welcome, *amore*." He bends to kiss me before leaving to get my breakfast.

Adagio

After taking the croissant and juice up to Cisely, Adagio heats a bottle of the breast milk Cisely had stored in the freezer to feed Ingo. Pouring some rice cereal in a bowl, he mixes in some of the milk and a little applesauce, then puts a clean bib on the squirming little boy and gets him settled in his chair. As Adagio feeds their son, now six months old, he can't stop smiling. The thought of becoming a father for the second time brings him a happiness that cannot be put into words. Only this time is different. Though he loves little Ingo with all his heart, this baby will be a product of the love he and Cisely share, and he can't ask for a more wonderful gift for Christmas.

Having been an only child himself, Adagio remembers how lonely he sometimes felt growing up, and he'd always held to the dream of one day marrying and having a large family of his own. Gazing into the face of the precious little boy God has already sent to bless his life, he believes he is off to a good start.

When Ingo has had his fill, Adagio wipes the cereal from his cherubic face and cleans up the breakfast dishes before going to check on Cisely.

When the two loves of my life enter the room, I smile, releasing a sigh of contentment. Feeling a little better having eaten something, I am able to sit up now without feeling too bad. Adagio places Ingo on the bed and sits next to me, reaching for my hand.

"How are you?"

"I'm better." For days I suspected I might be pregnant, but I dared not hope because I wanted it so badly. And though I know it is going to be a challenge taking care of two children so close together, I am ready for it. I love little Ingo more than I can say, and having Adagio's child will only add to my happiness because it will be a part of him.

"I think I'm okay enough to take a shower and get some things done this morning."

"Are you sure? I can take care of things for you."

"I'm sure," I say, leaning forward to kiss him. "I've done this before, remember?"

"I remember," he says, touching my face. "But I am here and willing to do anything I can to make things easier for you."

267

"I know." I urge him closer. "And I love you for always thinking of me, but I can't stay in bed all day. I have to get going."

"All right, but if you need me, I'll be here."

I kiss him again. "Are you really okay with this?"

"I am, Cisely," he answers, brushing his lips against my temple. "You have given me a wonderful gift."

Forty-three

I spend the final days before Christmas baking and preparing for the big day. I am always ill in the mornings for a short while, but I'm usually better after eating something. By evening I am exhausted and fall asleep as soon as my head hits the pillow. Still, for me it's a happy exhaustion.

On the day before Christmas Eve, I wrap Adagio's gifts while he is at the airport picking up Jessica. The underlying morning sickness I experience most of the time keeps me from going for drives longer than fifteen or twenty minutes at a time. Otherwise, I would have gone with him. I miss Jessica immensely and can't wait to see her.

When they finally arrive, Jessica and I tearfully hug each other. How I have missed that motherly smile and those twinkling blue eyes! I can't believe we are together again.

Jessica cuddles Ingo a bit, marveling at how much he has grown. I know she has missed him and I feel bad about that. At times, I can't help wishing we lived a little closer to one another. Still, I wouldn't trade my home in Italy for anything.

After giving Jessica a tour of the house, I show her to her room. She tells me how much she loves our home, and she says it's wonderful that Adagio only has to go to the other side of the house to work. While she unpacks, I fill her in on what has been going on in our lives, and when I tell her about the baby, she is ecstatic. We relax on a cushioned bench by the window.

"I'm glad to see you so happy, Cisely. It's as if you two have always been together."

"Sometimes it feels that way. I guess we've both gone through so much emotionally, and now we are growing together." I pause, a familiar sense of wonder entering me. "You know, I can't explain it, but it just feels so right being with Adagio. In the beginning when I first discovered my feelings for him, I wasn't so sure. I wasn't sure of much of anything. I really was afraid of growing to love him more than Ingo, like I would be betraying him. I'm sure Adagio felt the same. But now . . ." Intense emotion surges through me. "That man is everything to me. He's a part of my very soul. I know I will always love Ingo because of what we shared. He taught me how to see the good in myself. I had never known such love and I will always treasure the time we had together. But . . ."

"But," Jessica presses, squeezing my hand gently.

"What Adagio and I have . . . the love, the passion . . . there are no words. Whenever I look into his eyes . . . Jessica, I see forever. I see myself being with him for eternity. I can't imagine *not* being with him. I am tempted to feel guilty at times for feeling this way, but I don't. I can't."

She smiles, brushing a tear away. "I think you and Adagio were growing together long before you discovered you loved each other. You shared a special bond having lost the dearest person in your lives. Your courtship with him was different from yours and Ingo's, just as the growth you two experienced both emotionally and romantically was not the same."

I brush a tear away. "It really was different," I agree. "My courtship with Ingo was a whirlwind, filled with magic and excitement. I had never known love before he came into my life. He made me so happy, and nothing will ever diminish or minimize what we shared."

"I know how deeply you loved each other. I could see it each time you two were together. And had he lived, I'm sure your love would be even greater now. He lived a good life, but he's gone. And now you are experiencing a different kind of love."

"Yes," I say, marveling at how much Jessica understands. "It is a love that was completely unexpected. And now . . . with Adagio . . . every time he looks at me, I can feel how much he loves me. Just a touch from him warms my entire being. I can't even be in the same room with him without being close to him, without touching him in some way or having him touch me. His love is overpowering, and sometimes emotion fills me so much, it overwhelms me to the point of tears. It's a desperate kind of love that consumes me." I sigh, wiping my eyes. "How can I feel like this so soon? How can I feel this way at all?"

Jessica smiles. "Because it was meant to be. Don't question it, and don't feel guilty. Just accept it and be grateful."

Nodding, I smile. She always knows just what to say. "Thank you, Jessica, for once again being a mother at a time when I truly need one."

She hugs me. "Thank you, my dear, for giving me the joy of being your mother. I couldn't love you more if you were truly my own flesh and blood." Drawing back, she wipes her face again. "Now we had better stop all this crying or Adagio is going to wonder what he has gotten himself into by getting the two of us together again."

"You're probably right."

Forty-four

On Christmas Eve, Anna stops by with her arms full of gifts for our family. I introduce her to Jessica and Jessica is immediately taken with her. Sometimes I wonder if Jessica has ever met a person she didn't like. We visit for a few minutes, then Anna leaves to get back to her own family celebration.

In the evening, we gather in the family room and sing Christmas carols, and Adagio reads the Nativity story from the Bible.

As I listen to him, I can't help remembering the previous Christmas we spent together, except it was Ingo who read the story of Christ's birth. We had been so happy to have Adagio with us. He hadn't been able to bear the thought of spending another Christmas alone and we didn't want him to. I had even talked with Adagio that night about getting together the following year for Christmas.

As Adagio's soothing voice brings me back to the present, I find it both poignant and fitting that we are indeed sharing this

Christmas together, only not as just friends, but husband and wife.

Coming to the end of the nativity story, he smiles lovingly, pulling me close, and I can tell he is remembering as well. We both loved Ingo. I loved him as a spouse and Adagio, as a brother, and now we share a love for each other that grows with each day that passes. The time of feeling guilt and uncertainty has passed. Our life is as it should be.

After having some eggnog and Christmas treats, Adagio pulls several large boxes from the storage room down the hall. They are filled with wrapped presents. While I get Ingo ready, Adagio tells Jessica what we planned and she is excited to participate in this opportunity. After loading the boxes into the back of the large van used by his employees to pick up produce for the restaurant, we leave.

Ten minutes later, we arrive at an old Catholic Church just outside of Treviso. I knock and the large door is immediately opened.

"Merry Christmas, Signor Giovanni!"

"Well, Merry Christmas to you, Mrs. St. John!"

"We're sorry to be so late," Adagio says, carrying the first of the boxes in and quickly going back for another one.

"Oh, you are just fine." He holds the door open for us and we enter the large, beautiful old building. This particular church is no longer used for worship, but instead houses families in transition, offering them help until they are able to get back on their feet. Looking around, my mind wanders back to the day Adagio and I met Signor Giovanni. We were shopping at one of the markets a couple of weeks ago when we met two older women picking up supplies. They were both weighed down with bags and we offered to help them carry the groceries back to their vehicle. The women graciously accepted.

On the way to their car, the women told us about the non-profit organization they volunteered for and the families they were trying to help. We listened with sadness as they told us about these families and how hard things were for them financially, and my heart ached for them. The parents had no money to buy Christmas for their children because there were so many other things they needed more.

I told Adagio I wanted to help them and he felt the same. We have been abundantly blessed and couldn't think of a better way to use our abundance than helping others. We followed the women back to the old church where we were introduced to Signor Giovanni. He and his wife, Theresa were grateful for our willingness to help.

"Are all the families here?" I ask.

"Yes, they are. My wife is reading them a Christmas story in the great hall downstairs."

While Adagio grabs the last box from the van, I introduce Signor Giovanni to Jessica. Thankfully he can speak a little English and Jessica is able to converse with him. However, I know the language well enough and continue to speak to him in Italian.

When Adagio returns, we follow Signor Giovanni down to see the families, meeting all the parents and their children. A few of the children are withdrawn, but most are friendly and eager to get to know us. I place Ingo on the floor and the children immediately begin playing with him. Jessica and I visit with the group of parents while Adagio brings in the gifts.

"Look what the St. Johns brought for you, children!" Signor Giovanni says excitedly.

Each child's eyes brighten as Adagio helps Signor Giovanni and the other women give out the gifts. I made sure to mark each gift ahead of time with their names, so the right gifts would go to the right children. After everything is handed out, we stand with the parents and watch the children open the packages, their happiness evident with each gift they unwrap.

Signor Giovanni gives us a teary smile. "I can't tell you how much this means to us. We had so little money to help out this year and the donations have been few. Having you come into our lives has been a miracle." He grips Adagio's hand. "Thank you both from the bottom of my heart." Each of the parents tearfully express their gratitude as well.

"There is no need to thank us," Adagio says. "This is what we are here for. This life is all about helping others." He pulls an envelope from his pocket. "We hope this will help to get things that are needed."

"Thank you so much." He hugs us both.

"Adagio is right," I say. "Helping each other really is what this life is all about."

We say goodbye to the families and wish them all a Merry Christmas. I blink away tears as each child hugs us. Signor Giovanni thanks us again, sending us off with a basket of fruit and some of Theresa's homemade *biscotti*.

Except for an occasional sniffle, the ride home is mostly quiet as we each contemplate the wonder of the evening.

Jessica tells us that she can't remember having a more special or meaningful Christmas, and she will remember this one forever. She is grateful to have been able to be a part of such a special opportunity.

Adagio takes my hand and smiles. We have both experienced something truly amazing and neither of us can ever remember feeling so at peace. I am blessed to even be in the position to help others this way. I definitely remember what it is like to have to go without, and I'm grateful for the opportunity to give back.

Before we go to bed, Adagio and I discuss how the service has affected us and decide this will be a tradition in our family from now on.

The feelings from the night before linger in our hearts and Christmas morning is filled with joy as presents are exchanged and opened. We all laugh as Ingo goes after the wrapping paper each time a gift is opened. He isn't old enough to crawl yet, but he can roll and scoot to get where he wants to go. Grabbing the camera, Adagio takes lots of pictures, promising to send Jessica copies.

We enjoy a wonderful Christmas dinner and stay up until late talking about the special time we shared last night.

Jessica tells us how grateful she is to have been able to spend Christmas with us and we feel the same. Adagio promises her we will try to return to the states for a visit before I am too far along to travel.

Before going to bed I receive a phone call from Gloria and Patrick. They are traveling to Verona, Milan, and Rome for an after-Christmas vacation and want to come by and see us on the way. We eagerly say yes and anticipate their visit. Though it is late, I knock on Jessica's bedroom door to tell her the news and she is ecstatic!

Gloria and Patrick arrive the following day and it is a tearful reunion. I hadn't realized how much I missed them until now. They cuddle little Ingo and marvel over how much he looks like their son while catching up with Jessica, and we open the gifts they brought for us.

Gloria said the twins and their wives gave them some wonderful news before they left. Both couples are expecting. My heart is full of happiness for them and we offer our sincere congratulations. I am sure this news had been a priceless gift for them because they have waited so long for more grandchildren.

They spend the night and head out the following morning, expressing their gratitude and happiness for the opportunity to visit us and see Ingo. We embrace them both, assuring them they are always welcome.

When we finally have to say goodbye to Jessica, she and I are in tears. I will miss her so much, and I wish she could stay longer, but she needs to get back to the boutique. Adagio again tells her we will try to come back and visit.

I give her a final hug and a kiss before Adagio takes her to the airport. I wave goodbye until the car is out of sight, and look forward to the day we will see each other again.

Forty-five

I am now well past the days of morning sickness. At seven months along I feel huge, but Adagio continually tells me there is no one more beautiful, and his longing and desire for me never wavers. Our nights are full of passion, and every day our love for each other deepens.

Adagio

Adagio gazes across the room at Cisely as she rocks Ingo and softly sings to him. A little over ten months old, Ingo is starting to walk and venture through the house. They'd quickly had to install extra safety gates to keep him out of trouble. Their son's antics never cease to make them smile. As he continues to watch her, he is more content than he has ever been. At times like this, he sometimes ponders his life before Cisely.

Adagio will always miss Ingo, and he never feels guilty whenever he thinks of Cisely once being his friend's wife. He will forever treasure the memories of the time he shared with them when Ingo was alive. But as he gazes at Cisely now, his love for her again overwhelms him to tears. She means everything to him, *is* everything to him. She is the very air he breathes and he loves her more than his own life.

He sometimes wonders how this can be, especially knowing she had been the love of his best friend's life. And what if something happened to her and death separated them? Or if death took them both? Would she meet Ingo again on the other side and choose to be with him again? Would Adagio be able to cope with losing her to Ingo after loving her so desperately and completely?

He has no answers, and he doesn't want to think about it right now because it is physically painful and too unsettling. He only knows she truly and completely owns his heart.

When Cisely looks over at Adagio and smiles, he again glimpses forever in her eyes and it startles him. The feelings that just a look from her stirs inside him . . . it just amazes him.

"*Ti amo*, Cisely," he says, smiling at her.

"I love you, too," I say back, blissfully happy with my life. Everything is so good with us that I sometimes have to push away nagging fears that things won't always be this way. Sure, our life isn't perfect and I know we will still have trials, and I pray that I can handle them when they come. But I only have to look into Adagio's eyes and I know that as long as he is by my side, I can face anything.

The ringing of the phone breaks into the quiet stillness of the house. Adagio answers it and I continue to rock Ingo.

"It is for you," he says, sounding surprised. He brings me the phone. "It is your cousin, Velma."

I am surprised as well. I hand Ingo to him and he leans down to kiss me before taking him outside to play, giving me some privacy.

I have not talked to Velma in a long time. The last time was about a month after Ingo died to let her know what happened. Velma had been so sorry to hear the news. She said she really liked Ingo and thought he was a great guy. During that same call, Velma told me she had gotten a job as a nanny and would be moving to Florida. I was so happy for her. We've been keeping in touch with one another through letters. When I wrote Velma about Adagio and told her of our plans to be married, she was happy for us and very supportive.

Right now, she is still in Florida. This is the first time she has called since moving and I pray she is doing well and everything is okay.

"Velma, how are you?"

"I'm fine. It's so good to talk to you."

"It's good to talk to you too." I can already tell something is wrong just by the tone of her voice, and I'm amazed that I have grown to know her so well. "How is the nanny job going? Is everything okay?"

"Everything is fine. I'm doing great and keeping busy. Of course, with looking after three kids under six, there is never a time when I'm *not* busy." I smile, understanding. She pauses. "I received some news from home, Cisely, and I have something very important to tell you. It's actually a message I'm supposed to give you."

"A message . . . from whom?" I ask her, my curiosity piqued.

"It's . . . from your father, Cisely."

I feel as if the wind has been knocked out of me. I am suddenly ill and bile rises in my throat, but I swallow hard against it. As my mind reels, the same question repeatedly races through my thoughts.

"What message could he possibly have to give me?"

Velma is quiet for a few seconds and I can sense her wishing she didn't have to be the one to do this.

"He is in a hospice, Cisely. He is dying of AIDS . . . and he wants to see you."

You've got to be kidding! How could he even request such a thing? I can't believe it. My father mentally tortured and sexually abused me for half my childhood, causing so much emotional pain, I hadn't thought I would ever heal. What right does he have to request this or anything else from me? *How dare he do this to me now!*

"Cisely, are you okay?"

I shudder. Velma still doesn't know the full extent of my childhood with my father and I have never desired to tell her. "I don't know," I answer honestly. "And I don't think I can grant him that request."

Velma sighs. "Cisely, I don't know everything about your life with your father. I do know he hurt your mother, and I can understand that you might still have ill feelings toward him. Even still, Cisely, he is your father and he is dying. I mean, as much as I dislike being around my mother and am glad to be away from

284

her, I can't help but care about what happens to her. I can't hold her mistakes against her the way she has held mine against me."

I want to scream, *"You have absolutely no idea what my father did to me! You have no clue of what kind of man he really is!"* Instead I calmly say, "I'll think about it."

"Okay. If you do decide to go, he is in the hospice center over off Montford Avenue."

"Okay," I say, wanting to be done with the conversation. "Thank you, Velma," I mumble sincerely. I know she is only trying to help and I really can't be upset at her. *I guess she's a better person than I am right now.*

Sighing, I sit with my head in my hands long after the call ends, the dull ache in my temples growing as painful memories I've long since tried to bury return to the surface. In my heart, I have tried to forgive my father. I've tried so hard to let the past go, but the pain and anger that have resurfaced at the mere thought of his request brings a heaviness to my heart that I have not felt in a long time.

Oh, God, I voice silently as warm tears slip through my fingers. *Why now? Why is this happening now after all this time? I've been so happy. Why must I deal with this now?*

J. Adams

Forty-six

Adagio

Adagio enters the family room, having left Ingo in the nursery.

"What is it, *amore*," he asks, kneeling down, pulling her to him. She presses her face to his shoulder and cries, prompting his own eyes to burn as he holds her shaking body close. Lifting her in his arms, he carries her over to the sofa. Sitting with her cradled on his lap, he continues to hold her in silence until she is able to stop crying enough to speak. He wipes her tears. "Please, baby, tell me what is wrong."

Cisely finally looks at him. "You know, before I received that phone call, I was thinking about how good my life is now, and I thought that as long as I have you, I would be able to face any trial that came, but . . . I don't know if I can face this one." Her voice breaks.

"What trial?" he asks, trying to keep his voice calm, fearing something terrible has happened.

"My . . . my father wants to see me."

Adagio's brow creases, anger immediately rising inside him until she continues. "He is in a hospice back home. He had AIDS and I guess he won't be around much longer."

Holding her close, Adagio tries to understand what she must be feeling. Her father had hurt and defiled her, causing scars that would always be there. Her nightmares, though infrequent now, bear witness of those scars.

Like so many times before, Adagio's mind drifts back to the conversation he had with Ingo when Ingo shared Cisely's painful past with him. He couldn't understand how a parent could do something so sick. He remembers the sorrow he he'd felt as Ingo told him what Cisely had gone through, and how angry he himself had been on her behalf.

"What should I do, Adagio?" she asks, breaking the silence. "I don't know what to do."

Pressing a kiss to her brow, he tightens his embrace. He can share what he thinks, but in the end, it will be her choice. It will be painful, but he has no doubt she will make the right one. It's hard for him to think about her even being in the same room with the man, but he knows it's wrong to hold on to such feelings. "What does your heart tell you?" he asks softly.

Cisely brushes fresh tears away only to have them replaced by more. "I don't know because my heart hurts too much right now to listen to it."

"I'm so sorry for all the pain he has caused you, *amore*," he whispers against her brow. "But maybe he wants to make peace with you before he dies."

She pulls back abruptly. "Am I supposed to forget about everything just like that?" Her voice is emotional and unsteady.

"Am I supposed to grant him his dying wish so he can go in peace while I'm left holding the pain?"

Adagio takes her hand, pressing a kiss to the back of it. "I love you more than anything, Cisely, more than life itself. And one of the reasons I love you, the most important reason, is because you have so much love in you. You are the most giving and caring person I know. Yes, you have pain in your heart, but there is no hatred." Placing a hand on her cheek, he looks into her eyes. "An unforgiving heart is a heart full of hate and that is not you, *amore*. Sometimes I have been so angry, I've found myself wanting to hunt the man down and beat him senseless because of what he put you through, but as much as I want to hate him and any other person that does such terrible things, I can't because that is not the way we should be. And if your father wants your forgiveness, do you not think you owe him that opportunity? Does not everyone in this world deserve the chance to be forgiven for the hurts they inflict on others when they truly seek forgiveness?"

I press my face against Adagio's neck as the tears begin anew. I know he is right, but my heart hurts so much, I don't know how to handle it. In the past I would have handled the pain by numbing myself with drinking and drugs. But I can't do that now. I have come too far to go back down that road, and I would rather die than give in to such weaknesses.

"You need to heal, baby," he whispers against my ear. "Maybe this is the way to do that."

Broken in spirit, I continue to cry as Adagio stands, cradling me in his arms. Carrying me upstairs, he gently places me on the bed. Covering me with a light quilt, he sits on the edge of the bed and kisses me tenderly.

"You rest. This is a very hard thing you are facing. I wish I could make it all go away somehow and take away the pain, but I can't."

"I know," I whisper hoarsely. I can see how much my hurting is affecting him, and I hate putting him through this.

"I will take care of Ingo. Just try and rest." He presses another soft kiss to my lips and leaves.

Adagio

After closing the door, Adagio checks on Ingo. Finding him content in his playpen, he heads to the den, and with tears filling his eyes, he kneels to pray. He knows if he can do nothing else to help his wife with the trial she is facing, praying for her is the one thing he can do.

Forty-seven

I awaken the next morning with a heavy heart, wishing I could shake the pain, but not knowing how. I had spent a good while on my knees last night, praying and begging for God's comfort, but nothing has changed. There is no hate for my father present, none at all, and I truly want to forgive him. I just don't know if I have the strength to speak the words to him, or even face him.

I pray throughout the day for peace, but by evening, my heart is still heavy, the burden too great to bear.

Staring out our bedroom window at the River Sile in the distance, I try to draw upon the comfort that usually comes with the view, but it eludes me. After another moment, I finally lie down and try to rest, then I sit up on the side of the bed, deciding that trying to sleep is futile. Closing my eyes, I attempt to clear my mind. But images of my father beating my mother by day then standing over my own bed by night flash before me and my eyes open abruptly, releasing the hot tears trapped behind them. I struggle to push the images away and replace them with good ones, but they continue to intrude and will not leave me. By now the agony inside me is so intense, I immediately slip to my knees beside the bed, desperation filling my whole being. I feel like I will die from the pain.

Remaining on my knees, I cry softly, not caring about the ache in my back from the extra weight I carry. Nothing matters except ridding myself of these feelings.

After a while, I drift to sleep.

I am again sitting in the grassy countryside, staring out at a small lake in the distance. The little boy from the dream I'd had previously is beside me. We don't speak, we simply sit quietly, enjoying the serene view before us. Glancing at his profile, I take in his familiar features. A gentle breeze tousles his black wavy hair and his olive skin shimmers in the sun. He is a beautiful boy and I find myself longing to see his eyes.

He must sense my thoughts, because in the next moment he turns, fastening his emerald gaze on mine. Then he speaks.

"Forgive him, Mama."

I wake up with a gasp.

"Our son!" I whisper. The boy I had just dreamed of for the second time is our son. Mine and Adagio's. My mind reels in amazement.

And he urged me to forgive my father.

With this thought, a feeling of peace slowly enters me, and with this peace comes the start of true healing. I am again overcome with emotion, but it is sweet and soothing instead of painful.

I know what I have to do now. It will be hard, but there is no other choice.

Adagio

When Adagio enters the room, Cisely is still on her knees. "Are you all right, *amore?*" he asks, kneeling down beside her.

She wipes her face and smiles. "I am now."

He presses a hand against her cheek, wiping another tear away with his thumb. "I can tell," he says, marveling at the peace radiating from her. Offering up a silent prayer of gratitude, he helps her to her feet and holds her close, kissing her cheek. "Does this mean I need to make plane reservations?"

"I think it does. And since we are going back to the States, do you think we could spend a couple of days in Utah with Jessica?"

"I think we can arrange that."

Her expression sobers. "I'm so sorry about yesterday."

"It is all right, angel," he soothes. "You had a right to be upset. Anyone in your position would have been."

"But I'm not upset anymore."

"I know."

She buries her fingers in his hair. "I love you," she says breathlessly.

He smiles, allowing her silky voice to flow through him. "I love you." Pressing her as close as possible, he kisses her, reveling in the way her body melts against his. Tightening his embrace, he continues to feast upon her warm mouth, wishing he could somehow make up for all the hurt and pain she suffered in the past. Though there will still be trials, for now, he only wants her to know love—his love.

"Where is Ingo?" she whispers as his mouth sensuously explores her face and neck.

"Sleeping," he murmurs.

"Good."

Drawing back slightly, he smiles, releasing her just long enough to turn on the baby monitor and close the door.

Forty-eight

Asheville, North Carolina

After grabbing our luggage and picking up the rental car, we check into our hotel. By the time we are settled, it is late, so we decide to wait until morning to go and see my father.

As I close my eyes and try to sleep, my thoughts travel across the states to little Ingo. I hope he is doing okay without us. Jessica is taking care of him to make things easier, and under the circumstances, we felt it was best to leave him in her care. I don't know how this visit with my father will affect me, and not having to worry about exposing our son to my emotional state makes me feel a little better.

I continue to stare up into the darkness, not able to turn my mind off. I am both nervous and afraid to see my father. Yes, I have done the right thing by coming, but I am still scared and can't seem to calm down enough to sleep.

"Adagio," I whisper.

"Hmmm?" he answers sleepily.

295

"I'm sorry to wake you, but could you do something for me?"

"Anything, *amore.*" He awakens fully.

"Would you tell me again that I've made the right decision in coming back?"

He turns on the lamp and rubs his eyes, then props himself up on his elbow. "You have made the right decision. And I admire your bravery."

"But if it hadn't been for our son appearing to me in that dream, I don't know if I would be able to do it."

Pressing a hand to my face, he looks at me intently. "I think God knew that, which is why he gave you such an amazing experience. I am still awed by it, and that our son appeared to you twice . . . it just blows me away every time I think about it."

"Me, too," I say as I think back on sharing the experience with Adagio a couple of days ago. His reaction had been the same as mine.

"But even if you had not had that experience, deep down you have always had the courage to do what is right. You would have found that courage."

"How can you have so much faith in me?" I ask softly.

Drawing me close, his lips rummage my brow. "Because I know you, Cisely. Better than I have ever known anyone. No one has a kinder heart or more beautiful soul."

I smile. "I can think of one person. I'm fortunate enough to be married to him."

His mouth travels to my jaw. "You have made me a better man," he whispers as his kiss moves to my neck. "You are the part of me that was missing for so many years." He draws back slightly, looking into my eyes. "I am so glad you are mine."

"And I'm glad you are mine. You will never be without me," I whisper, burying my fingers in his hair and meeting his mouth with mine.

The heat building between us is now a steady burn and we quickly lose ourselves in one another. I am unaware of anything except his kiss and his touch. Whenever he makes love to me, the rest of the world ceases to exist.

"Thank you," I say after a long while.

He turns out the light. "You are welcome."

Secure in his arms, I rest my head against his chest. After a while, the familiar rhythm of his heartbeat against my ear slowly lulls me to sleep.

The next morning, I pace the floor nervously, trying to calm down. After last night, I thought I would be fine, but this morning the feelings are fresh. Except for glimpsing him in the distance the day of my mother's funeral, I haven't seen my father in almost twelve years, which has always suited me fine, but now the thought of being in the same room with him again has my stomach tied up in knots, even though I know I've made the right decision in coming.

Adagio
Adagio can understand his wife's feelings. Not many women would choose to see their abuser again, much less forgive

him for the hurt he caused. *But then again,* he muses, *not many women are like my Cisely.*

When Cisely finally stops pacing, Adagio approaches her from behind, wrapping his arms around her. She leans back against him wearily.

"Everything will be all right, *cara,*" he whispers against her ear.

"I know. As long as you're there with me, I know it will be okay." She turns in his arms, and he kisses her. "Thank you," she murmurs.

He smiles, pressing his forehead to hers. "You're welcome."

Forty-nine

Could you please tell us which room Mr. Alton Matthews is in?" Adagio asks the receptionist at the information desk. I wait nervously while she looks up the room number.

"He's in 236. Just take the elevator to the second floor and turn left."

"Thank you."

Adagio's hand is firm around mine as we step into the elevator. I can tell he is a little nervous as well, not for himself, but for me, and I feel the connection between us. I sense him trying to send me his strength.

Breathe. Just breathe, I tell myself over and over. Adagio also whispers words of comfort. When we reach my father's room, I am literally sick inside. I turn to my husband.

"I don't know if I can face him!" I whisper in desperation.

"Yes, you can," he soothes. "I will be right here with you." He presses a hand to my cheek. "You are much stronger than you think you are, *amore.*"

299

No, I'm not! I nod, taking a deep breath. I have to go in; there is no other choice. Putting my hand on the knob, I hesitate.

"Would you hold me for a moment?"

"You don't even have to ask." As his warm arms come around me, I cling to him, comforted by his tightening embrace.

Closing my eyes, I try to draw from him as much strength as I can. I finally move back a little and he presses a kiss to my brow.

"I'm ready," I finally whisper.

Taking another deep breath, I open the door, gripping Adagio's hand as we slowly approach the still form on the bed. Except for the blip of the monitor and our soft footsteps, the room is silent.

My father is hooked up to an IV and an oxygen mask covers his nose and mouth. He doesn't even look like the same man. This small, frail, thin man looks nothing like the large one that used to tower over and terrorize me and my mother. His cheeks are now sunken and hollow, his dark skin gray and pasty looking. I can't believe this man who was once so strong and healthy is now lying in a hospital bed totally helpless.

He can't hurt me anymore. He will never be able to hurt me or anyone else ever again.

As I stand looking down at him, something tugs at my heart. I can't explain how or even pinpoint the exact moment, but I truly feel sorry for him.

And there it is.

I have forgiven him. Almost instantly, I no longer see the monster that stole my childhood. Instead, I see a man who had somehow gotten lost along his way through life. While I will probably never truly know whether he has changed, it isn't my place to judge, only to forgive.

As if he senses my presence, my father opens his eyes. He turns his head slightly and looks at me, and then he smiles. I saw my father smile many times when I was younger, and most of the time I thought it an evil smile. But there is nothing familiar about the one he wears now. It looks like a smile of contentment, and love.

He continues to stare, maybe waiting for me to speak, but I don't know what to say. What can I say? I can't pretend the past never happened, and I will not pretend I am overjoyed to see him either. I am trying to think of something to say when he moves a frail hand to his face and weakly slides the mask to the side. His breathing grows more labored as his mouth begins to move. I move to the head of the bed and strain to hear, but his voice is barely above a whisper. I bend forward until my ear is positioned above his mouth, and this time I understand when he speaks again.

"Forgive me, please," he whispers feebly.

Moving back a little, I look into his eyes, grasping the depth and importance of this moment. Never in my wildest imaginings could I have fathomed this would happen.

"I do forgive you," I finally say.

He looks at me for a moment and another slow smile spreads across his face. He turns his head, looking toward the ceiling and a tear rolls back into his gray hair. Looking at me once more, his eyes seem to say thank you. Then he closes them and does not open them again. He sucks in a slow rattling breath and exhales once . . . twice. Then he goes still.

And that's the end of that story, I muse sadly, staring down at him a moment longer. The man who had been the source of a great deal of my pain has now made me the source of his peace. "Goodbye," I whisper before moving into Adagio's waiting arms.

The tears I shed now are not really for my father, but are the result of the peace in my heart. I have finally let go of the fear and anger and have truly learned to forgive.

"Are you all right?" Adagio asks, wiping my tears.

"Yes," I answer with a smile. "I am finally okay."

Fifty

Adagio

Adagio lay in bed next to Cisely, contentedly watching her nurse their son. Adagio Philip St. John II was born in the middle of July weighing in at eight pounds, ten ounces, and once again they thought there wasn't a more beautiful baby in the world. They decided to call him Philip to avoid confusion when he is older. At three months old, his dark hair and emerald eyes are just like his father's.

Philip finally finishes, having fallen asleep while nursing. Cisely burps him and takes him to the nursery. When she returns, Adagio is sitting up looking at a framed photograph of their family.

Adagio can't believe how much his life has changed in the past two years. He is the husband of an amazing, beautiful woman and the father of two adorable children. Life is wonderful, and he can't ask for anything more.

Slipping under the covers, I rest my head against Adagio's chest. He circles his arm around me and I smile, marveling at how blessed I am. I've dreamed of many things in my life, but I never dreamed I could be so happy and blessed with so much love in my heart. The peace I now carry inside is indescribable. At times like this, I think my heart will burst with the overwhelming joy I feel.

As if he is reading my mind, Adagio replaces the picture on the bedside table and lifts my chin, looking into my eyes. "There are no words to describe how happy I am." He caresses my cheek. "I love you so much."

"I love you too. Sometimes those three words aren't good enough to describe what I feel for you, but they are all we have."

Pressing a hand to my face, he caresses my lips with his thumb. "I know." His continues to reverently gaze at me another moment before lowering his head and kissing me passionately. As his mouth sensuously plies mine, heat fills my insides. Through this kiss, he expresses to me everything he feels. There truly are no words to describe our love.

Clinging to him, I again feel forever in his arms. And for the moment, there is nothing but bliss.

Asheville, North Carolina

Brooding like the angry storm clouds darkening the evening sky, Gladys sits on the back-porch steps of her home holding a cigarette in one hand and a can of beer in the other. She is alone now, her daughter abandoning her over a year ago, leaving her to take care of herself.

Gladys is angry.

And it is all Cisely's fault.

If Cisely hadn't come back to Asheville, pretending to be Miss High and Mighty, Gladys would be sitting pretty. Somehow, she would have gotten the insurance money from Geneva's death, and Velma wouldn't have developed a backbone and left to chase after the "white man's" life.

Yes, this is all Cisely's doing.

And one day she will pay.

Gladys will make her pay if it is the last thing she does.

We are told that trials help to make us stronger, that we have to go through pain to really savor the experience of joy. I have known this for a long time, but I also know something else. The strength that comes from those trials is actually faith refined; the joy that comes after the pain, celestial favor.
Cisely St. John's journal

Fifty-one

Five years later.

Carrying a small tray of homemade *biscotti* out to the veranda, I place it on the table next to the pitcher of raspberry lemonade. After making sure there are enough napkins and glasses, I sit in one of the padded iron chairs, and with deep contentment, watch Adagio play with Ingo and Phillip. It is a beautiful day. The sun is out and there isn't a cloud in the sky. Thankfully it's not as hot as it has been the past couple of days. Of course, being raised in a similar climate, I had adapted to Treviso the moment I moved here.

I laugh at Adagio feigning weakness as Ingo and Phillip wrestle him to the ground and climb on top of his back laughing. Turning over, he growls loudly and tickles the two little terrors. The children squirm away from his reach, then dive back in and repeat the process. I am amazed at the amount of energy they possess, and I can't believe how fast they are growing.

Adagio surrenders, pleading for a timeout. When it is obvious the boys are not going to give in to his pleas, he tries a different tactic, which always works.

"Hey, let's go and see what Mama brought out for us, okay?"

"Okay," they say, hopping up and running to the veranda.

Adagio

Adagio heaves a deep sigh of relief mixed with joyful contentment as he watches them take off up the hill. He enjoys the time he is able to spend playing with his boys and is grateful for a job that allows him this time.

Standing and stretching for a moment, he looks down and smacks the grass from his clothes. There are stains on the knees of his jeans, but he doesn't mind. It seems these afternoon wrestling matches with the boys always warrant a change of clothes, but it's worth it. He leans his head over and brushes the grass from his hair as well.

When he looks up again, he sees Cisely coming down from the veranda heading out to him. Even after six years of marriage, the sight or mere thought of her never ceases to make his heart skip a beat. He continues to gaze at her as she comes closer, the sun setting off the highlights in her dark auburn hair and adding a shimmer to her brown skin. Her every move is graceful, and just being in her presence is intoxicating. He would be thirty-nine in a few months, almost ten years older than Cisely, but he finds his age easy to ignore because she makes him feel so young, and he is thankful every day to be blessed with her as his wife.

Watching Adagio as he watches me causes my heart to flutter. He will always be the most handsome man in the world to me, and I frequently admire how lean and muscular he still is, thanks in part to chasing our sons around. Well, that and good genes. His gaze warms me as I approach him. When he looks at me that way, the rest of the world just falls away. I wonder sometimes if the effect will ever fade. But I only have to look into his eyes and I know it never will.

"It looks like they wore you out," I say, plucking the grass from his tousled hair.

He grins, pulling me into his arms. "You heard my surrender, huh?"

"I did. For a moment there, I thought I was going to have to come and rescue you."

"I was almost ready to call you." He presses me closer, whispering seductively in my ear, "You know, you could have joined us and it would've been even more fun."

"Maybe later," I growl softly and he laughs.

Arm in arm we walk back up to the veranda to be with the boys. By the time we get there, half the tray of *biscotti* is already gone.

"I see you got a head start on us," Adagio says, smiling at the two, their cheeks full.

"But they're so good," Ingo says before biting into another one.

"Well, thank you," I say, pleased they turned out so well.

I sit down and Phillip automatically moves to my lap. "Are you going to eat one, Mama?" he asks, holding a chocolate covered cookie out to me.

"Now when have you ever known me to turn down chocolate, little man?"

"Never, Mama," he says, grinning.

"That's right, and I never will." I take it from him. "Thank you."

Adagio smiles at me as we watch his namesake watching me eat the offered cookie. Both boys look like little chipmunks with their cheeks stuffed and we can't help chuckling.

"Well, I guess that's it," I say as Ingo and Phillip polish off the last of the *biscotti*. "If you two keep this up, you are going to look like cookies with legs." I pinch their cheeks, provoking a laugh from both.

"I have to agree with them, *amore*. These are very good. I could not have made them better."

"Thank you, my love. I've had a good teacher."

Adagio winks and kisses my hand. "Why don't we help Mama take everything in," he says to the boys.

Ingo immediately takes the empty tray into the house and Phillip collects the used napkins. I smile at their promptness. We have been doing our best to raise them to be obedient and I am grateful they are so helpful to me. I hope they will always be that way. Like all kids, they have their moments and give us fits, but I wouldn't trade motherhood for anything in the world. I want to be the best mother I can be, and I never want our children to doubt my love for them or feel neglected in any way. I saw and experienced enough neglect in my own childhood to ever let them suffer those feelings. I try to enjoy every moment with them, and I look forward to having more children one day.

After taking everything to the kitchen, the boys head to their rooms to play for a while and Adagio goes to checks on things at the restaurant. Since everyone is occupied with other things, I decide to use the time and go through some of the clothes Ingo and Phillip have outgrown and take them down to Signor Giovanni to give to children in need. By the time I am done, I have filled two boxes with both clothes and shoes. I can't believe how fast they are growing, especially Phillip. Even after keeping a few clothes handed down from Ingo, it seems we have to purchase new shoes and pants for Phillip often.

Pondering this for a moment, I again feel a deep sense of gratitude that we are able to afford to get the things we need for our family. I often think about growing up poor and what it was like to have to go without. I never want that for our children. I want them to have all I never had and more, without spoiling them, of course.

Having taped the boxes shut, I take them downstairs to put them in the back seat of my car. Adagio returns just as I am taking the first one out.

"Let me get that for you, *amore*," he says, taking the box from me.

"Thanks. I wasn't going to take them to the church until later, but I just wanted to get them loaded ahead of time." I smile. "You know me."

"Yes, I know you. You are the most organized person I know."

"Oh, I don't know about that, but I do like to get things done."

"Well, thank you for always being one step ahead of me."

"Anytime." He snorts and kisses me. I am about to follow him out with the second box when the phone rings.

"You go ahead and get it," he says, "and I will come back for that one."

"Thank you." I put the box down and head back into the foyer to answer the phone.

Fifty-two

Ciao, Cisely. It's Velma."

"Ciao!" I am both surprised and delighted to hear from my cousin. "How are you?"

"I'm doing great!"

Picking up on the excitement in her voice, I'm instantly curious. "You sound like you're doing better than great. What's happening?"

"Well, that's the reason I called. I could let you try and guess, but I'm too excited for that."

"I can definitely tell. So, what's up?"

"I'm getting married!"

"Really? I can't believe it! Congratulations, Velma! I'm so happy for you."

"Thanks. I'm so excited I can't sit still. I feel like I'm about to jump out of my skin."

"I can hear it in your voice. He must be a great guy."

"Oh, he's the best."

"Well, tell me about him."

Velma sighs softly. "His name is Ted Wright and girl, he is definitely Mr. Right."

Shaking my head, I chuckle at the pun.

"I met him during my nanny job in Florida. We were having lunch in the same restaurant and were sitting across from each other. After five minutes of staring and smiling at one another, he came over, introduced himself and asked me to join him. He was there on vacation for a couple of weeks. We had a great time and went out a few times after that. Then he went back to New York. I liked him a lot, and I never expected to see him again, but I've thought about him over the years. Then three months ago I ran into him at a motivational seminar downtown. Can you believe it? He was visiting a friend here and suddenly there we were, face to face."

"It looks like you two were destined to be together. I'm so happy for you."

"Oh, Cisely, I can't wait for you and Adagio to meet him. I know you'll love him."

"I'm sure we will, but of course, not as much as you do."

Velma laughs. "Nobody will love him as much as I do. But I guess you feel that way about your husband, too."

I sigh dreamily. "Every second of the day and every day of forever."

"That definitely sounds like celestial love to me. Oh, by the way, I have two questions for you."

"Ask away."

"I would love it if you and Adagio could come to the wedding. And if you can, I was wondering if you would be my maid of honor."

"I'm honored that you asked me. We would be delighted to come and I would absolutely love to be your maid of honor."

"Thank you so much, Cisely. You're the only person I wanted to ask. You have been such an example to me. I appreciate all the support you've given me through the years."

Her sentiments make me a little teary. I treasure the good relationship I have with my cousin. "You're an amazing person, Velma, and I'm grateful for your support as well. Thank you for inviting us and for always thinking of me."

"You're welcome. Now we come to question number two."

"Okay, shoot."

"Well . . . I know it's a lot to ask, but . . . would you perform at my reception? It would mean so much to me if you would."

"I would love to," I answer, flattered that she asked.

"Thank you!" Now I know it will be a wonderful reception. You are definitely the most talented person I know."

"Oh, I doubt that, but thank you for the compliment anyway."

"I'm just speaking the truth. The wedding will be three weeks from tomorrow. Will that be enough time for you to prepare and get arrangements made?"

"That should be plenty. We all have valid passports and the boys' tutor isn't scheduled to come for another couple of months, so there shouldn't be a problem."

"Thank you so much for doing this for me, Cisely."

"You're welcome. I'm just so excited for you."

"Me too. Are you sure all of this will be okay with Adagio?"

"I know it will. And he will be just as happy for you as I am. There's no way we would miss this." I smile as Adagio's arms encircle me.

"Happy about what, *amore?*" he whispers against my ear.

"It's Velma. She's getting married."

"Congratulations, Velma!" he says.

She laughs. "Tell him I said thanks."

"I will. We'll call you back as soon as we get the arrangements made."

"I look forward to hearing from you. And Cisely?"

"Mmm hmm?"

"You're the best."

"The feeling's mutual. *Ciao.*"

Hanging up, I turn in Adagio's embrace. "I can't believe she is really getting married," I say, slowly caressing his arms, feeling the contour of solid muscle through his shirt.

"I think it is wonderful she has found someone. She is a special lady. I think she has some of your strength."

"Sometimes I don't feel very strong, but I try." I touch his face. "The wedding is three weeks from tomorrow. She invited us and asked me to be her maid of honor."

"That's great. You mean more to her than you know. It is good that you two have each other."

I nod, pondering the truthfulness of his words. Thinking back on the next to nonexistent relationship we had when we were younger, I never could have guessed she and I would be so close now. "She means a lot to me too and I feel pretty honored. She also asked me to perform the music at the reception."

Adagio's smile widens. "Even better. You know how much I love hearing you sing."

"I know. And I love singing for you."

When he draws me even closer, I press my face in the hollow of his neck, breathing in his cologne. The masculine scent is intoxicating and always fills my senses with nothing but him. Of course, just being with him has the same effect.

"We should be able to get everything arranged in time, shouldn't we?"

"If I start right now."

He tightens his embrace; I never tire of being in his arms. "Well, maybe you'd better get going." Drawing back a little, I give him a coy smile. "I'll save your place."

He presses a light kiss to my lips. "You promise?"

Drawing his head down, I whisper, "I promise."

J. Adams

Fifty-three

After dinner is done and everything is put away, I make myself comfortable on the veranda and gaze out across the land. This is my favorite place to sit and ponder things. There is a slight breeze in the air. It carries the scent of the rose bushes I planted a few years ago that are now in bloom. How well I remember undertaking the project. It was the first time in my life I'd ever planted anything, and the feeling of satisfaction I felt after accomplishing the task was priceless.

When the roses finally began to bloom that year, I would awaken twice a week to find a single red rose in a small vase sitting on my bedside table. Adagio told me he wanted me to thoroughly enjoy the fruits of my labors. When the weather changed that year and the roses were no longer blooming, Adagio made a trip to the flower shop once a week, bought two roses and placed them in a vase by the bed every Monday. And every year since then, he has continued this ritual. His love never ceases to amaze me.

Gazing down at the roses, I again ponder my life and how far I have come. If someone had told me ten years ago that I would one day be living in Italy and married to a painfully-handsome Italian man, I would have considered that person out of his or her mind. Then I probably would have offered the person a drink to help them regain their sanity, because that was how I always handled things back then; a drink and an occasional drug to go with it could cure anything. Thinking about that part of my life always makes me shudder. Back then, I never could have fathomed living such a life now.

Sighing deeply, I gaze out at the water-colored sky, grateful for these times of reflection. I need to remember where I once was and how far I have come, and even though the past had been painful, I will never let myself forget. I can't, because every trial I overcame served to bring me here, sharing my life with a man I love more than life–a man I can't imagine not being with, one that I could *never* be without.

I turn and smile as the object of my thoughts comes through the doors.

Adagio leans down to kiss me. Grabbing a chair, he pulls it close to mine and takes my hand.

"You know, I think Italy has the most beautiful sunsets in the world," I tell him. "I know I haven't been all over the world, but I still think so anyway."

"I think you are probably right. However, any sunset I get to look at with you is beautiful."

I smile, squeezing his hand. "Thank you, my love. You know, you should be a poet. You always say just the right things. I could see you doing greeting cards."

"Sure," he says with a chuckle. "Whatever you say, *amore*. If I say the right things, it is only because you bring out the romantic in me. Besides, my words of love are reserved for you and you alone."

"I wouldn't want it any other way."

Adagio

Adagio gently pulls Cisely from her chair onto his lap. Holding her close, he closes his eyes, resting his forehead against her chin. He never tires of being near her, never tires of touching her. He sometimes feels like he was born for the specific purpose of loving her, the feelings are so strong. Breathing deeply, he inhales the soft scent of her perfume.

There are no words to describe Adagio's feelings for his wife. She has become a part of him, a part of his very soul—so much so that whenever he is away from her for one thing or another, he literally feels like he is missing a part of himself.

Adagio's thoughts shift to Ingo. He still misses his friend, even after all this time. He will always miss him. But would he change anything if it was in his power to go back?

No, he wouldn't.

Not if it meant he wouldn't have Cisely.

Adagio knows he shouldn't, but sometimes he wonders if the love he and Cisely feel for one another ever pales in comparison to what she and Ingo shared. He briefly wonders who she loves more. If Ingo were still alive . . .

He quickly steers his mind away from the 'what if' thoughts. None of it matters. Cisely is his wife now. She's *his*.

Cisely's silky voice draws him from his thoughts. "I'm really looking forward to the wedding."

"I am as well. Velma deserves to be happy."

"She is definitely reaping the blessings. I've never heard her sound so alive. I could hear in her voice how much she loves him."

"Well, he must be a great guy. I look forward to meeting him."

"Me, too." She places her hand on his cheek, letting her fingers travel over the soft stubble covering his jaw. "If he is even half as wonderful and amazing as you are, she's got it made."

"Now who should be writing greeting cards?"

"I was just returning the earlier compliment."

"Thank you, *amore*."

"You're welcome. And speaking of cards, we should go shopping this week for one, and wedding gifts."

"We can go any time you want."

"Maybe I'll even pick up a couple of new outfits for the trip. Would you mind?"

"You don't even need to ask. Buy anything you want. Do you need a dress for the reception too?"

"No, she's having them made."

"Well, I hope she doesn't have them made too pretty," he says with a sigh.

"Why do you say that?"

Smiling slyly, he answers, "Because we would not want you to outshine the bride. Then again, it really doesn't matter what you wear, because you won't be able to help it."

She grins, kissing him. "You really are amazing, you know that?"

"So are you, angel."

They sit for a few moments longer, watching the sun slowly sink into the horizon and Adagio ponders his earlier comment. Holding his wife in his arms, the sunset truly is more beautiful because he is watching it with her. Her presence always enhances his enjoyment of even the simplest things.

Fifty-four

Adagio

Adagio and Cisely spend some time with Ingo and Phillip before getting them ready for bed. After stories are read and they are settled for the night, Adagio heads over to the restaurant for a few moments to speak with the manager on duty about their upcoming trip. His staff is very capable of handling things without him and he usually never worries about anything when he and Cisely need to leave.

As Adagio sits behind the desk in his office, he can't help speculating a little about their upcoming trip back to the states. He had taken the family to North Carolina for a vacation a couple of years ago and they visited with Velma while they were there. During the weeks of preparation for that trip, he'd kept the hope that maybe Cisely's family's hearts had softened and he would finally get to know them, but his hope had been futile, just as hers had been. He couldn't believe how they shunned her, despite her efforts to reach out to them. It angered him to see her hurt, and watching her strive to make peace with her family had been very painful. Not only had they refused to speak with her, they wouldn't even acknowledge her presence. He just couldn't understand how a family could be so cruel and heartless.

Remembering the sadness that filled Cisely's countenance when she could make no progress with them causes his heart to ache for her all over again. Adagio has always thought it a little sad that he doesn't have family living himself, but having family members who don't even want to associate with you is much worse. He hated to see his wife in pain, and though she put on a brave front while they were there and did her best to hide it, she couldn't hide it from him and it broke his heart.

Maybe things will be different this time, he hopes silently. *Miracles do still happen.*

Thinking about Cisely produces in him a sudden strong need to be with her. He quickly finishes up and heads back.

I am sitting at the piano playing a soft ballad when Adagio returns. He takes a seat next to me on the bench and watches my hands as I play. After finishing the tune, I ask, "Did you get things taken care of?"

"I did. And I am sure everything will be fine. I think they are used to our little trips by now."

"I'll have to find something else unique to bring back for those guys."

Adagio chuckles. "You mean, more unique than those cans of potted possum you brought them the last time we went."

I snort. "They were pretty surprised, weren't they?"

"Surprised is an understatement. The reactions varied from Sam's words of 'Hmmm, interesting,' to Alonzo's 'Awesome!'"

"I know. I'll definitely have to think of something good to top that."

"I am sure you will come up with something." He presses his hand to my face, brushing my hair back, exposing my neck to his soft caress. "So, did I ever tell you how beautiful you are?"

I smile shyly because he asks me this frequently, and it never fails to remind me of how lucky I am to have him. "Yes, but if you want to tell me again, it's okay."

He leans closer, softly brushing his lips against mine. "*Sei bella*, baby. *Ti amo*."

"I love you too."

Drawing me closer, our mouths merge as we drink in the flavor of one another, our instant passion and longing for each other growing steadily. After a few minutes of drowning in his heated kisses, I finally move back a little and read the burning desire that is almost always present in his emerald eyes. He lifts me in his arms and I continue to kiss him as we make our way up the stairs to our bedroom. As soon as the door is closed, we let passion have its way.

Afterward, I lay with my head against Adagio's chest, looking into his eyes. For me, the intimacy we share is always indescribable, the emotional intensity never fading.

He caresses my face softly and smiles. "I told you on our wedding day I would never tire of making love to you. I still feel that way."

I touch his lips, sighing dreamily. "So do I." Looking at him quietly for a few moments, I marvel at the emotions churning inside me. Even after all this time, they still feel new.

Everything inside me desperately wishes I could tell him how completely I love him, how the strength of it burns within me, but I again come to the conclusion that there are no words to describe my feelings; no words are good enough. I continue to stare into his eyes.

He returns my gaze in silent adoration, and the complete love in his eyes brings tears to my own. It is almost more than I can take.

"Promise me we will always have this. Promise me that no matter what we go through in this life, we will always have these times, these moments, and they won't ever fade." I touch my fingers to his lips. "Promise me."

Adagio silently stares into my eyes for another moment, then presses his mouth to mine and kisses me with so much passion, I melt in his arms. I cling to him, infused with a rush of silent desperation I can't begin to define. When he parts his lips from mine, the same emotion is there in his misty eyes.

"I promise, Cisely," he finally says, resting his forehead against mine. "We will always have this. With everything in me, I promise."

Fifty-five

Asheville, North Carolina

Looking across the reception hall, I watch Velma and her new husband shaking hands and hugging their guests. The two absolutely glow as they accept heartfelt congratulations from friends and loved ones. Since neither Velma nor Ted have parents present, they decide to forgo a formal receiving line and just mingle and greet everyone, and the place is full of well-wishers. The hall is decorated in ivory and peach colored hues, from the floral arrangements adorning each table in the hall, to the beautiful four-tiered wedding cake. Everything is lovely and romantic.

It had been a glorious morning for the newlyweds. Their wedding ceremony in the gardens behind the reception hall was wonderful, and Velma and Ted make an attractive couple. Velma is breathtaking in her silky white gown. Her shoulder-length, black hair is styled in deep waves. Her facial features are similar to mine, as well as her figure, but she is three inches shorter than my height of five-feet-ten. Her skin tone is a shade darker, but it is still easy to tell we are cousins. Ted is equally attractive, though his complexion is closer to mine. He is tall and lean with short, neatly-trimmed hair, and his big brown eyes sparkle every time he gazes at Velma.

We have enjoyed the time we've been able to spend getting to know Ted during the last couple of days. And even if I hadn't already known where he was from, I could have guessed he was a New Yorker the first time he spoke because his upstate accent was so prominent. We learned that Ted is also the only member of his family to ever move away from New York. His parents and his sister were saddened by his decision to settle in North Carolina, but they still supported him, and they fell in love with Velma the moment they met her. Ted's parents couldn't come for the wedding because his mother recently had heart surgery and is not well enough to travel. His sister is a nurse and needed to be there for their mother. Under the circumstances, I am even more grateful that we can be here to support the happy couple.

Once the reception is underway, I seat myself at the grand piano on the stage in front of the reception hall, and the members of the band I have practiced with for the last few days move to their instruments. I was thrilled when Velma told me she had asked a few of her talented friends to play backup for me. I've never had an opportunity to sing with any accompaniment other than the piano, and I was very pleased with the way the rehearsals had gone.

Adagio

Cisely and the band begin playing a medley of love songs. She is lost in the music, her silky voice resonating through the hall, and it is obvious to Adagio that everyone is touched by how beautifully she sings. Pretty soon, the floor is filled with couples dancing to the soft ballads. He smiles as he watches her. Glancing to his left, he grins as a few young men cease talking, their attention fixed on Cisely, and he is again thankful to be her husband. Turning heads is something she definitely does often, yet she never seems to be aware of how she affects other men, only how she affects him.

Feeling a tug on his hand, he looks down into a cherubic face with laughing brown eyes and rosy cheeks, and he smiles.

"Will you dance with me?"

"I would love to dance with you."

Adagio makes his way to the front with his eleven-year-old partner who is wearing an infatuated grin as she looks up at him. Smiling slyly at Cisely, he winks. He watches her smile widen and wonders if she will be able to get through the song without laughing. When she does finally finish up the set, she informs the guests that she is taking a break, which brings some disappointed sighs, but she promises to continue in a few minutes. Approaching him, she slips her arms around his waist.

"It looks like you sure made a little lady's day," I say, smiling at him. "Stepping out on me, huh?"

Adagio pulls me close. "Are you jealous?" he whispers close to my ear.

"Maybe."

"Well, when she asked me with that adorable little smile of hers, I couldn't say no."

"I suppose not. But I could hear her sighing above the music. She was like putty in your hands."

"I can assure you that I only have eyes for you, *amore*. Besides, she is not my type."

"Oh really?" I continue toying with him. "What, Mr. St. John, exactly is your type?"

He tightens his embrace. "I am holding my type right now."

"Good answer," I say and he chuckles softly.

Velma and Ted had hired a young man in their church to play music in between sets. The next song he chooses is Motown. As the familiar Gladys Knight tune fills the reception hall, Adagio's eyes meet mine and we smile, our expressions melancholy. It is the song we danced to years ago at my wedding reception when I married Ingo. Memories of that day rush back to us both. It was the first dance I had ever shared with Adagio, and the fact that I had just married his best friend makes this moment even more sentimental.

"Come, *amore*," he says, leading me out on the dance floor. Grinning, I eagerly follow.

Adagio and I share a great love for dancing. We go dancing quite a bit, and sometimes we even dance at home with the boys. Ingo has learned a lot of good moves from watching us, and though Phillip's rhythm still needs a little work, it never stops him from joining in the fun with his own special talent of bouncing around.

After the song ends and before I begin another set, we go to check on the boys in another room down the hall and find them both very content, coloring with several other children attending the reception with their parents. A couple of the young women from Velma's church volunteered to keep an eye on everyone.

"How are you doing?" I ask, kneeling down between Phillip and Ingo.

"Fine, Mama," Ingo answers. He holds his drawing up and Adagio and I tell him how beautiful it is. Caressing his hair, I watch him as he continues to color, his concentration deep.

"Look at my picture, Mama," Phillip says, holding his drawing up for me to see. "I drew a dinosaur."

"That is a wonderful picture, honey," I say, ruffling his wavy hair. He grins and kisses my cheek, then his father's.

"Can I hang it in my room when we go back home?"

"Sure, you can," Adagio answers. "As a matter of fact, why don't you both save your pictures and we can frame them when we get back to Italy."

"Okay, Papa," the boys respond together.

We stay with the boys for a few more minutes before heading back to the reception hall. We take our time, walking slowly, enjoying being close to one another. Before entering the hall, Adagio pulls me aside, holding me a moment.

"I don't think I am ready to share you again just yet." He smiles. "You know, we could . . . What is that American phrase? Oh, yes. We could blow this joint and take a drive through the country or something."

I laugh. "Feeling a little lonely, are we?"

"More than a little." He brushes my hair back and kisses my ear.

"A drive does sound pretty nice. Tell you what. You hold on to that thought and I promise you, after this last set of songs, I'm all yours."

"All right," he whines. "I guess I will just have to wait."

I laugh, but I can hear the longing in his voice through the teasing. He kisses me before reluctantly releasing my hand. I smile and head back up front.

Adagio

As Cisely returns to the piano, Adagio takes in all the anxious faces in the crowd. He is so proud of his wife for continuing to cultivate her talents by sharing them with others. She has even begun teaching Ingo and Phillip to play. Ingo doesn't show much interest, but Phillip is a natural, almost a prodigy. Adagio figures he must have gotten the musical gene from Cisely, because he definitely enjoys singing and playing with her. He'd found it interesting that while Ingo had inherited her musical rhythm, Phillip had inherited her musical ear.

Cisely starts the next set of songs with one that had become hers and Adagio's personal love song. Her eyes shining, she begins singing Minnie Riperton's emotional ballad, *Loving You*. As her silky voice caresses the lyrics, Adagio closes his eyes, letting his mind drift back to years ago when she first sang the song to him for his birthday. He remembers the tears he had swallowed back because it stirred his emotions for her so, and he could feel how deeply she loved him as she sang.

Even now, emotion churns inside him as he listens to the words. Smiling, he lets his thoughts drift to memories of last night and the special evening he and Cisely had together.

Last night

The daughter of one of Velma's friends offered to watch the children at the hotel and give Adagio and Cisely a chance to go out for a while. They gratefully took her up on her offer. They went to dinner, then took a drive through the city. Adagio loved again exploring the place of his wife's birth. Cisely pointed out more places of interest and they revisited some of the places she used to spend a lot of time.

One of those places was the botanical gardens at the university. Since the weather was warm and comfortable, they decided to stop there and take an evening stroll. They kept an arm around each other as they walked through the winding paths, admiring the beautiful flowers and landscaping. Cisely told him the place brought back a lot of memories for her. She had spent a great deal of time there contemplating her life and where it was headed.

"I used to come here a lot to think because it was so peaceful."

"What kinds of things did you think about?"

She sighed, her eyes becoming distant. "Just about the different ways my life had changed. Before giving up the party life, I never really felt worthy of much of anything because of how I was living. Nor did I ever think about the future. Nothing in my life seemed to be important, except surviving and finding my next drink or fix. I didn't have any aspirations at all, and you never would have found me in a place like this. Even after I changed, I still didn't feel that my life was worth much because of all the mistakes I'd made. I was pretty lost. All I could see in my future was loneliness." She paused in her thoughts, her eyes holding a subtle sadness at the memory. "I discovered this place one day when I was taking the bus to see a friend and immediately asked the driver to stop. It was as if . . . it was calling to me. I came to love coming here after that because I almost felt like God lived here, and it made me want to be here, to feel Him near. Back then, I never felt as close to Him as I did when I came here." She chuckled. "Sounds kind of silly, huh?"

"It doesn't sound silly at all. I am sure He really was here for you, and He probably kept pulling you here. You needed this place and the peace that you felt here. There are times we all need such places."

They continued to walk in comfortable silence. After a few moments he turned to find Cisely gazing at him intently. "What are you thinking about, amore?*"*

She smiled. "Oh, I was just remembering our wedding day and how happy I was to finally be your wife."

He also smiled, remembering the joy he felt when they were married. Stopping on a small wooden bridge, he drew her into his arms. "I needed you in my life so much. I was tired of being alone, of never having anyone to come home to or share my days and nights with." He sighed, looking into her eyes. "I can honestly say the day we married was the happiest day of my life, because it changed my life forever."

Her eyes grew misty. "For me, too. You were, and still are, everything I could ever want."

"And having you makes me the most blessed man in the world. I can't imagine not being with you." Touching his lips to hers, he kissed her slowly.

She finally drew back and looked into his eyes, a slow grin spreading across her face. "Tell me again when you first knew you loved me."

He leaned back against the railing, pulling her firmly against him, smiling as he thought about the moment that he lost his heart to her. "Well, it was something that happened slowly, but the moment I truly realized I loved you was the day I came in from the kitchen to let you know lunch was ready. You were standing in front of the living room window deep in thought. I remember quietly gazing at your profile, unable to move. You looked so beautiful just standing there." He paused, softly caressing her lips. "I remember my heart pounding so hard that it was hard to breathe. Then you turned and looked at me and smiled, and that was it. You claimed me, heart and soul."

Cisely pressed her face against his neck and sighed, and Adagio sensed the warm memories washing over her as she remembered that moment.

"You know," she said, "the look in your eyes at that moment nearly took my breath away."

Smiling, he tightened his embrace. "You took my breath away by looking at me as well." When she drew back slightly and met his steady gaze intently, he grinned and said with warmth, "Yes, just like that."

"I'm glad I still have the same effect."

"And you always will, bella. *Now," he said, kissing her brow, "tell me again when you first realized you loved me."*

"Okay," she drawled. "I guess it is only fair." She laughed at his boyish grin. "Well, my love for you grew over time, too, but the moment I truly knew I loved you was the morning of the day you came over and proposed. I was standing in front of the window again looking out at the city, and I started thinking about you. Only instead of fighting it, I gave in to it. I had only been lost in my thoughts of you for a few minutes when I suddenly remembered the very moment you stood in the doorway of the living room the week before staring at me. I remembered the look in your eyes and how it made me feel."

She caressed his face. "The memory of the way you looked at me affected me so much, it intensified the feelings I already had for you, and I knew I was fighting a losing battle. I saw the longing in your eyes. I knew the feeling because I felt the same that day and every moment after that. That's when I knew I truly loved you, and my heart was no longer my own."

Adagio closed his eyes and pressed his forehead against hers a moment before tightening his embrace and kissing her passionately. At that moment nothing else in the world existed. Just her. He finally drew back and looked into her eyes, relishing the feel of her warm breath on his face. His entire being was full of longing for her. "Devo amarlo," he whispered. He pressed his mouth lightly to hers and again whispered the words in a raspy voice.

"I need you, too," she whispered back. She kissed him once more and without another word, took his hand and led him back to the car.

When they got back to the hotel, the children were already in bed. They thanked the sitter and Adagio paid her. After she left, he went to the bedroom and found the room lit only by the moonlight shining through the opened curtains. Cisely smiled at him through the darkness. "I thought since we don't have any candles, this will have to do."

"It is perfect." He undressed and carried her to the bed, and they made love as the rays of the moon filled the room and surrounded them.

Adagio's thoughts return to the present and he again gazes at his wife, longing to hold her in his arms.

As I sing the final chorus, I meet Adagio's emotional gaze. Through this song, I express my love for him to everyone present. When I am finished, I receive a standing ovation from the guests. Brushing a tear away, I smile lovingly at Adagio and he smiles back, blowing me a kiss.

Our love is truly a thing to behold.

Fifty-six

Gladys watches Cisely through the cracked door, her cold heart seething with anger and bitterness. The niece she hates with never-ending passion had become a thorn in her side long ago, and that hate has burned hotter with the passage of time.

In Gladys' eyes, Cisely completely ruined her life and took her meal ticket by convincing Velma to move away, as if Velma didn't have a mind of her own and couldn't think for herself. Since her daughter left, there has been no one left for Gladys to rule over or take advantage of, and this makes her angry.

So now anything and everything that goes wrong in her life is Cisely's fault. It is Cisely's fault that Gladys doesn't have enough money to fuel her nicotine and alcohol addiction. It is Cisely's fault that Velma is no longer living under Gladys' roof, supporting her and jumping at her every beck and call. And it is Cisely's fault that Gladys had not been able to see her daughter get married. Velma had chosen not to invite her mother, but in Gladys' mind, it is still Cisely's fault.

339

J. Adams

Gladys continues to watch her niece, jealous of her looks, her talent, and the life she now has. She had managed to avoid seeing her niece during her previous visit to Asheville. Before that, she had heard about Cisely's first husband dying. Even then, Gladys didn't have one sympathetic thought for her niece. Why should she? After all, Cisely is trash, and Ingo was white. It just wasn't right for them to be together. Then Velma told her about Cisely remarrying and living happily in Italy.

Looking around the large hall, she immediately spots Adagio, recognizing him from the picture Velma had shown her of him and Cisely with their two children. Gladys has never been into men who are not of her race, but she cannot deny that Adagio is handsome. Ingo had been handsome as well, but to Gladys, Adagio is even more so. For a white man, he is walking perfection. This fuels her hatred for her niece even more. She looks back at Cisely and once again begins to seethe.

Look at that tramp! She doesn't deserve to be happy. She doesn't deserve any of it, the little skank! Gladys glances over at Velma and Ted. *I should be in there with them. After all, I am still her mother, whether she likes it or not. She just didn't want me around her snobby friends.*

Blood boiling, Gladys closes her eyes for a moment, then opens them, fixing her stare on Cisely once more, a subtle smile curving her discolored lips.

You won't get away with this, Miss Better Than the Rest of the World. You're gonna to pay for everything you've done to me. And you're gonna to pay dearly.

I finish up with a few more songs, again receiving a standing ovation. Through the years, I have grown to enjoy performing for others, and I am happy to have been able to do this for Velma. People often tell me I should pursue a professional singing career, but I've never given it a thought. I am completely content with my career of being Adagio's wife and a mother to our children. I want nothing more than that.

After taking a final bow, I stop and talk with a few guests, thanking them sincerely for their compliments and praise of my performance. It means a lot that they enjoyed the music. Walking over to the DJ, I request a song, hoping that he has it in his music collection, and he does. I turn, scanning the hall for my husband, wanting to share a slow dance with him. Adagio's eyes meet mine through the crowd and he moves toward me, his gaze producing instant butterflies in my stomach. I again marvel that he never ceases to affect me that way.

"Have I told you how incredible you are?" He repeats one of his usual questions, pulling me close, pressing his lips against my ear.

I close my eyes and smile, relishing the feel of being in his arms again. "Yes, but I am no more incredible than you are."

"Okay, then have I told you how much I love you?"

"Yes, you have, but you can always tell me again."

He moves back a little and stares into my eyes, gifting me with one of his heart-stopping smiles. "I love you, Cisely, more than anything in this world."

"I love you too," I sigh, resting my head against his shoulder.

Adagio

Holding her close, Adagio lets the words of Nat King Cole's *Unforgettable* flow through his mind and heart.

The song has become one of his favorites, because it describes exactly, how much he loves his wife. She truly is unforgettable in every way and he is moved by everything about her, and that will never change.

After we dance for another couple of minutes, Velma and Ted approach us and we hug them both.

"Thank you, Cisely, for making our reception so special," Velma says.

"Well, thank you for asking me to do this. It was a lot of fun and I really enjoyed it."

Adagio shakes Ted's hand. "We were honored to be invited. It was a beautiful ceremony and we wish you both all the happiness in the world."

"Thank you. We're glad you could come. It wouldn't have been the same without you." Ted smiles at Velma. "I guess we should get going if we want to make our flight." Ted's friend owns a private plane and offered it and the services of his pilot as a wedding present. They are going to the Bahamas for their honeymoon.

Velma hugs me once more. "I have always prayed for the kind of love you and Adagio have." She gazes at her new husband. "And now I have it."

Adagio wraps his arms around me, his smiling eyes meeting mine. "We are very blessed," he says softly.

"I'll call you when we get back," Velma tells me as they turn to go.

"I'll look forward to your call." I give her hand a final squeeze. I am truly going to miss her when we return to Italy.

After the newlyweds make their final rounds and say goodbye to everyone, Adagio and I follow them out to their car, which is now covered with shaving cream and ribbons. We wave goodbye as they drive off, laughing when Ted gives a loud whoop out the window as he pulls out of the parking lot.

Leaning back against Adagio, I gaze down the road until their car is no longer in sight. Reaching up, I press her hand to his face. "This was so great. Thank you for bringing me and for being so good to me."

"I will always be good to you, *amore*," he says, kissing my cheek. "There is no way I would have let you miss your cousin's wedding. In a way, I feel like she is my cousin as well."

"I think she feels the same," I say, grateful that Velma and Adagio get along so well, and pleased that Velma was also born with the desire to love people for who they are. Skin color and ethnic background have never been an issue. This fact about Velma had surprised me at first, especially considering the racial views Gladys holds near and dear to her heart. However, it seems Velma had been determined she would never share her mother's views, on that subject or anything else. Her strength makes me love her even more.

Adagio tightens his embrace a little and I sigh deeply, relishing the closeness we share. Smiling, I ponder Velma and Ted's wedding ceremony. As the two spoke their vows, I had again been overwhelmed by the memory of our own wedding and the pledge Adagio and I made to love and cherish one another always. But when they had repeated the words "Till death do us part," I briefly experienced the familiar pain that always comes whenever I think of being separated from Adagio. It's not that I ever dwell on that thought, but most of the time, I can barely remember what my life was like before him; my love for Adagio is so intense and deep, it is sometimes hard to remember that I did love before. I loved before, and I lost that love. If I were to ever lose Adagio, I honestly do not think I could survive. I could not go on.

It frightens me sometimes, this powerful love that consumes my heart. And whenever my thoughts betray me and remind me that nothing in life is ever certain, including having a long life with him, it hurts so much, I feel physical pain.

Adagio

When the silence between them stretches a little too long, Adagio senses there is something was wrong. Turning Cisely to face him, he knows her thoughts the moment he looks into her eyes. He has seen that look before. She is afraid of losing him. He knows this because he has experienced the same feelings about her, and each time the thoughts intrude, he pushes them away because he cannot bear to dwell on them even for a moment.

Adagio sees the subtle pain in Cisely's eyes, even though she tries to hide it and it literally tears at his heart, but he understands exactly how she feels. He remains quiet for a moment, contemplating what he can say to her, needing to comfort her as much as himself. Closing his eyes, he rests his forehead against hers, needing her warmth. Drawing back slightly, he presses a hand against her cheek and smiles, his emotion-filled gaze capturing hers.

"We will never lose each other, baby." He caresses her face gently. "We will have a long and happy life together, and we will be together even after that. I know we will."

Cisely nods, smiling at the conviction she hears in his voice "I believe you."

They stand for a while longer in silence. "Are you going to be all right?" he finally asks.

"I'll be fine. As long as I have you, I will always be all right."

He kisses her, feeling her smile against his mouth. "You will always have me," he whispers, deepening the kiss, wanting more than anything to take her back to the hotel and lose himself in her arms.

"I guess we should go and get the boys," Cisely says with a longing sigh.

"I suppose," he agrees with a smile, taking her hand. "I only hope the young ladies watching all those hyper little people have not gone crazy."

She laughs. "I know what you mean."

Fifty-seven

We find Ingo sitting with some of the children who are still waiting for their parents. They are at a small round table putting together some puzzles.

"It is time to go," Adagio says, kneeling down. He takes a moment to watch how quickly Ingo is able to fit the pieces together.

"Did you two have a good time?" I ask, caressing his hair.

"We had lots of fun, Mama, and lots of good food, too."

I laugh. If there is one thing our kids have an absolute appreciation for, it's food. Standing, I look around the room. "Where's Phillip?"

"I don't know," Ingo answers looking around as well.

"Excuse me." I approach one of the girls in charge of watching the children. "Where is Phillip?"

She looks surprised by my question. "We thought he was with you."

"What do you mean you thought he was with us?" Adagio asks, standing and moving next to me.

"Well, a woman came and took him. She said you asked her to bring him to you. She told us she was your wife's aunt, and she said it was okay."

My blood instantly chills. Adagio reaches for my hand. "What woman? What did she look like?" I fight to keep my voice calm and the feeling of desperation in check.

The girl looks at us nervously. "She was a large black lady. She said she was Velma's mother."

The violent pounding of my heart increases. "No! God, please no," I whisper frantically. "Please no!"

I turn to Adagio just as the color drains from his face. He bolts through the door and I trail close behind him. We race through the halls, frantically calling Phillip's name, shoving doors open throughout the building. Running back into the main hall we find employees putting chairs and tables away. The reverend is also still here.

Adagio's voice is shaky. "Has anyone seen our youngest son, Phillip? The girls said a woman took him claiming to be bringing him to us, but we never saw her."

The women in the room gasp. One of them nervously approaches us. "I saw a heavy-set woman leaving a good while ago and it looked like she had a child, but . . . I didn't stop to question it." She places her hand over her mouth. "I'm so sorry."

The room slowly begins to spin before my eyes. "No, not my baby," I whisper as my legs give out and everything goes dark.

Adagio

Adagio catches her before she hits the floor.

"Cisely!" he cries as tears fill his eyes. He lifts her in his arms, cradling her against him, his insides tearing in two. "Someone, call the police! Please, hurry!"

I come to before the police arrive. They immediately begin questioning the girls, as well as a few of the employees that are still here. Two other sets of officers begin a search of the building and surrounding areas. One of the officers, a female, takes Ingo into another room and tries to keep him occupied while her partner, Officer Ed Payne, gets as much information as he can.

Adagio holds me and we both shed sorrowful tears as the young girls tell the officer what they know. By now they are also crying. After getting what he can from them, he lets the girls and everyone else leave. The reverend stays, just in case he is needed for anything.

Officer Payne turns to us. "Mrs. St. John, I need all the information you can give me about your aunt."

I try to calm myself enough to speak, but my emotions are so unstable, I don't know if I can. Adagio keeps his arms around me, lending me his strength. I finally pull myself together enough to tell Officer Payne about Gladys and how much my aunt dislikes me. Only I can't for the life of me understand why she would do something so awful.

By the time I have finished sharing my history with Gladys, he has come to some conclusions of his own.

"I think this is most likely some sort of revenge on her part. I really don't think she will hurt your son, but I feel the longer she is out there, the harder it will be to find her and get him back."

While Ed calls and has an all-points bulletin put out on Gladys, as well as a car sent to her address, I press my face against Adagio's shoulder and silently utter the same prayer over and over again–that we will get Phillip back safely and quickly. The thought of my aunt being cruel to my baby boy brings a pain so great, I can't bear it. Never would I have imagined anything like this happening to us. In the past, we have seen kidnapping stories on the news and in the papers, and it always broke our hearts to think of what the families were going through. But it has always been one of those things that happened to *other* families. Well, now *we* are one of those *other* families. I continue to plead with God for Phillip's return.

Adagio holds me tightly, whispering prayers of his own. He gives Ed a wallet-size photo of Phillip as he'd requested to have posted everywhere. Then we wait in silence as the minutes slowly tick by.

About thirty minutes later, Ed is called over his radio and told that Gladys hasn't been seen at or near her home in the past two hours, which leads him to believe she has most likely left town. He tells the officers to continue patrolling the area. Then he looks at us sadly.

"Mr. and Mrs. St. John, we are going to do everything we can to get your son back. Why don't you go on back to your hotel and we will keep you posted and call you the minute we hear or discover anything."

I turn to Adagio as tears again fill my eyes. "I don't want to leave here. What if she brings him back?" I know it isn't rational thinking, but I can't think rationally. "We have to stay here."

Officer Ed Payne is saddened by the anguish on Cisely's face and his heart is quickly filled with compassion. Having three children of his own, he doesn't know how he and his wife would handle it if one of their children was abducted, and he can only imagine what they must be going through. He kneels in front of Cisely and speaks softly.

"Mrs. St. John, I know this is hard, but I promise you, we will do everything we can to find your son. I really don't think there is a chance of Ms. Baker coming back here." He looks up at Adagio. "Take your family back to the hotel. We will call as soon as we find out anything."

Adagio nods wearily. "Come on, baby," he whispers. "Let's get Ingo."

I continue to cling to him in desperation as we walk down the hall to get our son, tears blinding my vision. I try to dry them before going into the room, but it is a futile attempt.

The drive back to the hotel is filled with anguished silence. I feel as if I have fallen into a deep dark hole with no way to come back out. I close my eyes as hot tears again spill onto my cheeks, still unable to believe one of my worst fears has actually happened. We have constantly prayed for the safety of our children. Now one of my babies has been snatched away from me and the pain is too much to bear.

Adagio

Adagio's heart is in turmoil. He wishes he could turn back time and change what happened. How he wishes he had gone back to check on the children again, but he knows such thoughts are useless. He doesn't know how to handle the pain, and he continues to fill his mind with prayer.

Once we are back in our suite, we sit on the sofa, placing Ingo between us, and with a prayer in our hearts, explain to him what happened.

"Will Phillip be back?" Ingo asks, tears filling his eyes.

"Yes, he will," Adagio assures him. "We need to pray that the police find him and bring him home soon."

"I want Phillip," he cries, his bottom lip trembling. I hold him close and caress his hair, unable to speak. My eyes meet Adagio's sorrowful gaze and I know he understands.

"Phillip with be back with us really soon. I promise you. Maybe even by tomorrow."

When he says the last, I glare at him as my thoughts and emotions prompt a sudden irrationality I cannot explain. I want our son back more than anything, but how can he promise something he doesn't know for sure will happen? I know I should also try to think positive, but my emotions are not letting me. There is no telling how far Gladys is by now.

I read the hurt in Adagio's expression and a wave of guilt sweeps through me. This is not his fault and I should not have reacted that way. His eyes plead with me to understand that he needs to give Ingo as much hope as he can. He wants to give me hope as well.

We comfort Ingo a little longer before finally putting him to bed. When we enter our room, Adagio suggests we have a prayer of our own. I ask him to offer it because I don't think I can. For the first time in a long time, my faith is wavering and I don't know how to stop it. My heart is so full of fear and anger, I honestly do not think any words I utter at the moment would get very far.

Holding hands, we kneel by the bed. Fresh tears roll down my cheeks as Adagio pours his heart out to God, praying for our son to be found safe and well. When he finally utters an Amen, I sit on the floor and sob. Moving next to me, Adagio takes me in his arms and cries with me.

Adagio

Adagio feels completely helpless. Their son could be anywhere. He wishes he could do something—anything instead of just waiting for a phone call.

"I am here, baby," he croons softly, his voice breaking with emotion. "I'm here. Everything will be all right."

When Cisely's sobs quiet and he manages to get his own emotions under control, he stands and gently lifts her, holding her against his chest for a moment before placing her on the bed and taking off her shoes. She turns to her side and continues to cry silently. They have the strength nor the desire to undress. He takes an extra blanket from the closet and spreads it across her. Turning off the light, he lay with his arm draped over her and his face pressed into her hair. All he can do is listen to her painful whimpers and be there for her.

Neither of them will find sleep tonight.

Fifty-eight

Adagio

The next morning, Officer Payne stops by Adagio and Cisely's hotel room to show them a copy of the flier being posted everywhere in several states with Phillip's picture on it.

Adagio watches his wife's eyes tear up as she gazes at their son's photograph. It is hard for him to believe the photo they had taken only two months ago is now on a missing child poster. Her tears fall onto the paper as she reads the information printed below Phillip's picture. Saying nothing, she hands it to him and leaves the room.

Ed shakes his head sadly and says he wishes there was something else he could do. He tells Adagio that he had questioned Cisely's uncle and his wife and they seemed pretty shocked to hear about what Gladys had done. And after questioning them further, he knew they had no knowledge of where she was.

"So, what do we do now," Adagio asks wearily.

"Aside from posting these and doing another search of Asheville and surrounding areas, we wait," Ed answers with a tired sigh. "At this point, it's about all we can do. She's bound to make a move sooner or later, and when she does, we'll get her." He pauses. "There have been many missing child cases here in Asheville, but this is the first one I have personally been involved in investigating. We'll do all we can."

"We appreciate your efforts. We are willing to do whatever it takes to help get our son back."

"I know. I'll keep you updated."

Adagio

A little before noon, Adagio calls their friend, Sam. His head chef is emotional as Adagio tells him about Phillip. Sam and the rest of the staff at the restaurant love Adagio and Cisely's children, and Sam is almost like an uncle to the two little boys.

"Would you like me to come there?" Sam asks, taking Adagio by surprise. "I know Angelo and Tony will cover my shifts for me, and the new guy, Dominic, is even doing well enough that he can take a couple of extra shifts."

"You would really come here?" Adagio didn't think Sam would ever leave Italy, not even for a vacation. He had never even ventured out of the Veneto region.

"You need support right now and I want to be there for you and Cisely. I wouldn't be able to stay long, but I know a week would not be a problem. I think any longer than that and your kitchen will fall apart."

Adagio smiles, wiping at the tears that come. "It would mean a lot to me if you would come."

"I will get the arrangements made and be there as soon as I can."

"*Grazie*, Sam." He appreciates the sacrifice his friend is making more than he can say.

After Adagio ends the call, he goes back in to Cisely and sits on the edge of the bed. Her back is turned to him, but her breathing is deep and he is grateful she has finally drifted off. She had not slept last night, and he hadn't either. Leaning over her, he presses a kiss to her forehead, then stands and walks to the door, turning for a moment to gaze at her slender form once more. He has been doing his best to comfort her, but for the first time in their marriage, his presence seems to make no difference to her and nothing he says seems to help. He is beside himself as to what to do. She continues to slip further into despair and it is becoming harder to hold himself together.

Cisely has been in bed the entire day. She seems to have no strength to even function and Adagio has never seen her so distanced from the world. He decides to keep his distance for a while and give her some space, but by evening he is so worried about her, he doesn't know what to do. He had prayed throughout the day for a way to help her and is again on his knees when the answer finally comes to him.

Taking Cisely's address book from her purse, he quickly looks up Jessica's phone number. If ever there was a time Cisely needed Jessica, it is now. He slips into the other room and dials her number, becoming a little emotional when he hears her voice.

Fifty-nine

"*Ciao*, Jessica."

"Adagio, my boy! What a wonderful surprise! How are you? And how is Cisely?"

"She is . . .we are . . ." Adagio cannot continue as his emotions quickly cave in again.

"Adagio! Adagio, what is it? What has happened?"

He hates that he can't keep himself from falling apart. He should be stronger than this, but he has no strength left. When he is finally able to pull himself together, he tells Jessica where they are and about Phillip's kidnapping, and then waits quietly as Jessica cries. He knows how much she loves their children, as if they were her own grandchildren, and the thought of Phillip being out there somewhere with someone as evil as Gladys hurts her terribly.

"How is Cisely?" she asks, the emotion in her voice under control.

He sighs, wiping at the fresh stream of tears. "She is not good, Jessica. I try to comfort her, but she is in so much pain, she won't let me near her. I don't know what to do. Ingo is also having a hard time. I don't know how we will make it through this."

"You will make it. It will be hard, but I promise you will. I will try and get a flight out tomorrow. I want to be there to help in any way I can."

Adagio heaves a grateful sigh. "Thank you, Jessica. I think Cisely really needs you right now. One of our good friends is coming as well, but it still will not be the same for her as having you come."

"Tell Cisely I love her and everything will be all right."

"I will. I know having you here will mean a lot to her."

After talking for a few more moments, Adagio hangs up, grateful for the inspiration to call Jessica. He hopes her being there will make a difference. He only wishes he didn't feel so helpless. All he can do for his son is pray, and all he can do for his wife is be there for her.

Adagio sits with Ingo for a while, watching him color in the new coloring books he'd bought for him earlier. He had also purchased an assortment of toys and puzzles, trying to find things to keep their son busy and his mind occupied. Ingo has said very little since Phillip's disappearance and Adagio is worried about him as well.

Wishing he had something to occupy his own thoughts, Adagio leans back on the sofa and rubs his tired eyes as a different sadness fills him. His heart is heavy, his soul wearied, and it is taking all his strength to keep from breaking down again. He is handling his emotions as best he can. He thinks about

Jessica coming to stay with them and her willingness to be there for Cisely, and he is again grateful.

Even still, he wishes with all his heart he could be the one to comfort Cisely. He is her husband and it is his place. And right now, he desperately needs comfort from her.

Sixty

One month later

Staring through the large bedroom window, I absently finger the silky green drapes. Until Phillip is found, we will not leave the country or even the state. After a few days of looking for a place to live, we rented a lovely and spacious condo in Biltmore Forest. I find it ironic that I am now temporarily living in an area I spent so much time dreaming about when I was younger. Under different circumstances I would thoroughly enjoy my surroundings, but I am no longer able to find much joy in anything.

Even after a month, the police still have not come up with any leads and are no closer to finding Phillip. I continue to go through the motions of thinking positively, but my faith is so shaken, I feel utterly lost and nothing can comfort me. Various people we met at the wedding occasionally stop by and offer their support, bringing food and kind words. I appreciate their efforts, but no amount of comfort can soothe my aching heart.

Adagio

Adagio manages to get through the days, but it is hard. He continually prays his son is okay and will return soon, but he also prays for his wife to return to him as well. She has been so distant and he misses her more than he can say. He misses the closeness they had always shared. He misses holding her, being loved by her. This whole ordeal is beyond painful and he needs her love and strength to help him through this, and he desperately wants to comfort her.

Jessica's presence has helped to make things better for Ingo, but sadly, it has done little to comfort Cisely. Still, Adagio can tell she is grateful Jessica is there, and so is he. He is also grateful for the week Sam was there. He had needed good friends more than he realized, and he appreciated Sam's love and support.

Adagio does his best to fill the void that both Phillip's absence and Cisely's distance leave in him by keeping busy with little projects around the house, as well as trying to do what he can to help locate their son. Whenever he is engaged in the latter, Cisely eagerly does what she can to help him. Those are the only times they seem to be able to connect. But he needs more than that.

Staring deeper into the woods, my thoughts travel to the next room where I left Adagio sitting alone earlier. He had tried to carry on another one-sided conversation, just as he has over the last few weeks. I can't seem to find anything to say these days. I am like a book that has had the pages ripped out, a blank slate.

What's worse is I clearly see the pain I am causing my husband every time I look into his sad eyes, but I don't know how to stop it. I can't handle my own pain enough to comfort him. I try to pray for strength to be of some comfort, but how can I help him when I cannot even help myself?

I turn slightly as Adagio enters our bedroom and closes the door. I meet his eyes briefly before returning my gaze to the window, though I really look at nothing in particular. Our bedroom window faces the back of the condo, which is totally wooded. The only view is a forest full of trees, with the exception of a squirrel or two on the window ledge every now and then. I even spotted a deer once. Under different circumstances I might go exploring in the beautiful woods. At another time I would find the prospect romantic. But I will not allow my heart to soften enough to delve into such simplicities. I can't. I tense slightly as Adagio moves beside me.

"Velma and Ted took Ingo to the mall. Jessica went with them."

"That was nice of them," I say, grateful for all they do to help.

When Velma and Ted came back from their honeymoon and were told what happened, Velma couldn't stop crying. She could not believe her mother could do something so cruel. She knew Gladys hated me and blamed me for all the things that went wrong in her life. She even knew her mother blamed me because she moved out and found happiness, but like me, she could never have imagined Gladys was far gone enough to kidnap our child as a way to exact revenge.

Velma immediately began to blame herself, despite Adagio and I doing our best to assure her none of it was her fault. She could not have known how deeply her mother's hatred was embedded, and even if she had, there was still no way Velma could stop Gladys from doing whatever she wanted. And what she wanted was to punish me. Sadly, I know Gladys better than Velma, despite the miserable years she lived under her mother's rule. Velma and Ted come over every other day and always try to help in any way they can.

My Uncle Pete and his wife, Dona, have also started coming by a couple of times a week. They feel terrible about everything, including the way they treated me in the past. They offered no excuses, they simply asked me to forgive them. Though I had forgiven them in my heart a long time ago, I am thankful for the chance to tell them. And despite the sadness that fills me, I'm grateful for the opportunity to get to know them better.

"I guess I should go and prepare something for lunch," I finally say, breaking the silence. "Ingo will probably be hungry when he gets back."

Adagio reaches for my hand to stop me. "Lunch can wait, *amore*. I really think we need to talk." His voice is soft and full of longing.

"About what?" I ask, trying to hold on to the distance that feels so safe.

"About us. About our son."

I lower my eyes. "Our son is gone. There's nothing to talk about." When I try to pull my hand away, he holds it firmly. I manage to keep my voice calm, but a familiar turmoil fills my heart. "What do you want from me?"

Adagio

Adagio struggles to bite back an angry retort and control the emotional anger now hovering close to the surface. Lifting Cisely's chin with his free hand, he forces her to look into his eyes. He can clearly see the emotional struggle in hers, but he needs to say this.

"I miss you, Cisely. I desperately miss my wife. And right now, I feel more alone than I have ever felt in my life. I hate this feeling and I don't want to do this alone anymore. I can't." He waits for her to say something. When she doesn't, his frustration works its way to the surface. "Say something! Say anything!" His voice softens as his gentle fingers move to her cheek, caressing it softly. "Tell me you miss me too."

Freeing my hand from his, I turn my face away as tears flood my eyes and spill down my cheeks. "I'm sorry, but . . . I don't have anything to give you right now." I know I am not being fair to him, but I can't seem to break through the wall I have built around myself.

He releases a sorrowful sigh, tears filling his eyes. Wiping them before they can fall, he slowly moves to the door. When he turns back, my eyes meet those of a broken man—and I know it is my fault.

"Cisely, you have so much to give, but you will not give it, and you won't let me get close enough to comfort you in any way. I have tried, but I cannot force you to accept my comfort, and I can't force you to give it. I shouldn't even have to. And I am not talking about a physical need, but an emotional one." When I say nothing, he again sighs sadly.

"Cisely, I know your heart is aching, and I know the pain is unbearable thinking about our son and what he must be going through. I know this because I go through exactly the same emotions every minute of every day. I cannot heal your heart and I can't take the pain away. All I can do is be your husband and love you. But you have to let me. You have to let me into your heart."

He wipes his eyes once more. "I need you, Cisely, more than I have ever needed anything in my life, and I know you need me, too. Handling this alone is killing me, but I haven't had a choice. When you can finally see that you need my comfort as much as I need yours, let me know . . . and I will be here."

I press my face in my hands, unable to say anything, and unable face him right now. When I finally hear the door open and then close, I look up. Adagio has left, leaving me to tearfully ponder his words.

Adagio

Velma and Ted drop Jessica and Ingo off just as Adagio comes through the front door. He thanks them before they leave, appreciating every effort they make to help. He smiles as Jessica walks up.

"Did you have a good time?" Adagio asks, squatting down to hug Ingo.

"Yes, Papa," his son answers, holding out his new action figures for Adagio to see.

"Wow! Those are pretty cool!"

"I got this, too," he says. Opening his bag, he pulls out a gray teddy bear in a little white and black tuxedo. "I got this for Mama. Maybe it will cheer her up and help her feel better."

Adagio gives him a teary smile. "I think Mama will love it. You should go in and give it to her."

"Okay," he says, his innocent smile shining some light into his father's heart.

Jessica squeezes Ingo's shoulder. "Why don't you go on in and show her your treasures. I will be in in a few minutes, okay?

"Okay."

Jessica closes the door after him, then motions for Adagio to sit with her in one of the cushioned chairs on the porch. "How are you?" she asks, squeezing his hand gently.

He releases a weary sigh. "I don't know, Jessica. I have not felt so alone since before we were married." He pauses, rubbing his eyes. "I am so tired, and I am trying with everything in me to have faith that we will get Phillip back, but . . ."

"But?" Jessica presses.

"It would be so much easier to deal with this if I didn't feel like I have lost my wife, too." He releases a frustrated breath, tugging a hand back through his hair. "She is so far away from me, Jessica, and I don't know how to bring her back. I know she is in pain, but I am, too. I miss her so much. We should be helping each other through this, but I can't even get near her. Each time I try she just pulls away."

Jessica sits quietly for a moment, waiting for inspiration, which quickly comes. "I would like to share some thoughts with you if that's okay."

"Of course," Adagio says, willing to listen to any insight she can give. He is desperate for something that will help because he is at a complete loss.

"I remember the day I introduced Cisely to Ingo like it was yesterday. The two were instantly taken with each other. And when they finally married, I didn't think there was a happier couple in the world. I could see how much they loved each other every time I looked at them."

Adagio is surprised at the direction of the conversation. He smiles, remembering the time he spent with Cisely and Ingo. "I could see it as well."

"You were a constant support to Cisely after Ingo died. I used to marvel at the way you were always able to get through to her and comfort her when no one else could. She grew to depend on you for your strength. You brought joy back into her life, and you helped her to realize she would make it and everything would be okay. After a while I could see how inevitable it was that you two would fall in love."

Adagio smiles as the memories come rushing back. "I tried to fight my love for her, but I couldn't. I was fighting a losing battle the moment the feelings began to grow."

"I know. And she fought hers as well. When you two finally married, I was so happy for you both. I knew you were supposed to be together."

"We did too," Adagio says, again remembering the joy he felt on their wedding day to know that Cisely was finally his. "I had fallen so desperately in love. I felt guilty because of Ingo, but I could not help my feelings. When I finally accepted that it was okay to love her, she became everything to me. All I could think about was making her mine. I wanted that more than anything, and when we were finally married, her happiness became all that mattered."

"And she felt the same. You became her whole world." She pauses, staring out across the tree-lined street. "Do you remember the first Christmas I spent with your family in Italy?"

"I will never forget it. It was very special because it was the start of our tradition of taking Christmas to families in need."

"It was wonderful and one I will always treasure. But I also remember something else." She squeezes his hand. "I remember observing you and Cisely and how happy you both were. Every time we were in the same room, I could feel the love between you two radiating all over. I could feel it throughout your home, like a warm blanket on a cold winter day. I had never witnessed that emotion as strongly as I did when I was around you two. Cisely and I talked quite a bit while I was there, but one thing she said always sticks out in my mind, and that thing is the most important thing I can tell you now."

She looks at him intently. "Adagio, she told me that though she loved Ingo with all her heart when they were together and would always treasure the time that she had with him, there were no words for what she felt for you. She told me each and every time she looked into your eyes . . . she saw forever, and she couldn't imagine being without you. Don't you see, Adagio? Even then her love for you had already grown deeper than her love for Ingo."

Adagio remains quiet, letting the words sink into his heart. He knows the emotions intimately and they match the intensity he feels whenever he looks at his wife. That Cisely's feelings for him were just as strong at that time in their marriage leaves him in awe. Neither of them had spoken of this to each other then, but they felt it.

Jessica smiles and leaves him with one final thought. "Adagio, Cisely loves you and that will never change. Just be there for her and love her. If you do, I know with all my heart she will come back to you. You own her heart, just as she owns yours. You two were destined for each other. I'm as sure of that as I am about anything. You have years invested in your love for each other—years of growing together, and years of being a strength to one another. Hold on to that."

Adagio nods and lets the truthfulness of her words echo in his mind and settle in his heart. "Thank you, Jessica," he says, finding it hard to speak."

"You're welcome."

After a few moments, he stands and pulls his car keys from his pocket. Helping Jessica up, he kisses her cheek. "I am going out for a while and will be back later." Before opening the car door, he adds, "Tell Cisely I love her more than anything."

Sixty-one

Adagio

Adagio takes a drive up the Blue Ridge Parkway, hoping to clear his head and gain some clarity. As he cruises up the scenic byway, he is even more amazed at the beauty of North Carolina. The leaves have changed to their various colors of red, yellow, and orange, and the air is rich with the feeling of fall. He spots a view area off the side of the road and quickly pulls over. Getting out, he leans against the car and gazes down into the vast tree-covered valley, feeling as if he is viewing a depth-filled painting.

This is amazing! He wishes he could share this view with his family, especially Cisely. How he misses the special times they shared!

Closing his eyes, Adagio lets his thoughts drift back to last year when he and Cisely took a two-week-long trip to Rome and Tuscany. Sam and his wife took care of Ingo and Phillip at their own home, so it was just the two of them.

They spent their days sightseeing and shopping. They had picnics out in the countryside and took walks through the vineyards of Florence Hills and Chianti, and along the shores of Camaiore. They dined at elegant restaurants, saw plays and went for romantic moonlit walks through the city. Even though Adagio had taken Cisely to some parts of these regions before, exploring them with her again so fully was like seeing them for the first time. From the coliseum of Rome to the museums to Vatican City, to the sculpture of Michelangelo's David and the Uffizi Gallery in Florence, everything excited her and it was like he was seeing it all anew through her eyes.

Blinking away rising tears, he remembers how they stayed up all night their last night in Rome, making love and talking endlessly. There was nothing and no one for them to think about except each other, and they treasured each and every second. He marveled at how good their marriage was. It can be that way again. Of this, he is certain.

He stands for a few minutes longer, lost in the memories. At the moment they are all he has.

Getting back into the car, he drives off with a prayer in his heart that they will find Phillip so their family will be whole again.

I cling to the bear Ingo gave me as tears stream down my face. I love my little boy so much, and I feel awful for not being there for him more through this whole ordeal, but I don't know how to rid my heart of these terrible feelings. Fear and despair have become my constant companions and they consume my entire being to the point that I can't think of anything other than my own grief. And every time I think about what I am putting

Adagio through, my heart aches even more. He is my husband and needs me. Why can't I give him the comfort he needs? Why can't I let him comfort me? I desperately want to, and I crave the closeness we have always shared.

I can't even remember the last time I showed him affection. He told me he needs me, but I have only felt my own pain. My oldest son needs his mother. I manage to see to his physical needs, yet I remain emotionally detached. Ingo's brother is missing and he needs my comfort and my assurance that everything will be okay. Why can't I give it to him? Over and over I have reminded myself it is not the trial that is important but what I do with it. And what have I done? I let it completely consume me.

Weeping, my soul cries out, desperately yearning to be freed from the cage around it and my heart. Trembling, I fall to my knees by the side of the bed. Never have I felt so lost. Closing my eyes, I slowly begin to pray. I am so sorry for the way I have been and for not being there for my family. I plead for the strength to endure this trial. I plead for comfort.

Over and over I plead, determined to stay on my knees for as long as it takes. I need to feel whole again, not only for myself, but for my family as well. And they need me to be whole. Especially Adagio.

"Your husband needs you, Cisely. He loves you more than you know."

Sucking in a breath, I gasp. The voice comes from nowhere. It is faint, but it is as familiar as my own. I have not heard it in years, but I could never forget the sound of it.

It is Ingo's voice.

With this discovery, my tears are renewed tenfold, because I know that not only is God listening, but the love Adagio and I share truly is the forever kind.

Sixty-two

Pressing her forehead against the cool windowpane, Jessica closes her eyes as her thoughts linger on Cisely.

She loves Cisely so much and hates to see her hurting this way. But she can only imagine what she is going through. Jessica has never had children of her own and she loves Ingo and Phillip as only a grandmother can. It hurts to think of Phillip being out in the world somewhere, kept from his family and suffering who knows what. But her feelings are those of a grandmother. Cisely had given birth to him and is connected to him in a way no one else could ever be.

Jessica smiles as memories of Cisely and Adagio's two-month long visit to Utah two years ago comes to mind. At the time, Phillip and Ingo were three and four. She remembers how amazed she was at how well Cisely and Adagio were able to keep up with the rambunctious little boys. She was exhausted just watching them as they played together. Jessica ponders the happiness that radiated from Cisely every time she gazed at

Adagio and their children. She was living the life she was born to live.

Two years ago.

Jessica went out to the back yard that evening after clearing away the last of the picnic dinner they all shared and found Adagio and Cisely dancing barefoot in the grass to a soft ballad playing on the portable stereo. As she quietly watched the two gazing into each other's eyes, she concluded there was enough love between them to cover the globe and light up the world.

A few weeks later on Halloween, Adagio crept up behind Cisely dressed in a Gorilla suit. Cisely jumped across the room and screamed so loud, Jessica thought she would have a heart attack. The boys laughed as their father chased their mother around the kitchen. Cisely giggled when he finally cornered her and began tickling her. Then when he pulled the mask off and pick her up and kissed her, the children clapped. Cisely whispered something in his ear and he grinned widely before kissing her again and putting her down. He flashed Jessica a wicked grin before putting the mask back on and she immediately took off running with Ingo and Phillip right behind her. She could hear Adagio growling as he chased her through the house.

Jessica wipes her eyes, smiling at the memory. *What a marvelous time we had!*

She turns from the living room window as Cisely emerges from the hallway. Though her eyes are red and swollen, Jessica immediately notices the peace shining through them. Cisely smiles and Jessica gives her a teary smile in return. She holds her hands out and Cisely takes them.

"You're okay, aren't you?" Jessica asks me.

"I am." I squeeze her hands. "And I know now that everything will be all right."

She releases a soft sob as she embraces me and tells me she's grateful to have me back. "I'm so glad you're all right."

Drawing back, I look into her loving face. "Thank you, Jessica, for all you have done for me. Thank you for being here, for loving me so much, and for again being my mother when I've needed one, even though I couldn't see that."

"I wouldn't want to be anywhere else, my dear." She presses a gentle hand to my cheek. "You and your family mean more to me than you could ever know."

I hug her again and draw back, concern creasing my brow. "Did Adagio say where he was going or when he would be back?"

"He didn't say either. I'm sorry, dear." She pauses a moment. "But he did say to tell you he loves you more than anything."

I smile sadly as a tangible ache fills me. "Oh, Jessica, I have been so awful to him and he has been trying so hard. He's been hurting just as much as I have, probably more because of me, but I couldn't see past my own grief." My voice breaks along with my heart. "He has needed me and I haven't been there for him. For the first time in our marriage, I have not been there for him." Hanging my head, I let the tears fall. "I feel so ashamed. How could I do that to him?"

Jessica wipes my tears. "He loves you more than life, Cisely, and he knows how hard this has been for you. He also knows you love him."

Walking over to the window, I look down the tree-clad street as my insides churn with regret. "I have to make it up to him," I say, turning to Jessica. "I need to set things right between us."

She smiles. "You two need an evening alone to reconnect and I've got just the solution."

"Really?"

"Yes. Velma and Ted offered to take Ingo for the night and give you and Adagio a little break. They invited me to come along. I was going to mention it to you earlier, but I didn't know how you would feel."

"I think that would be perfect!"

"Good. I'll call Velma and let her know. She and Ted were pretty excited about the idea. I think they are looking forward to having children of their own. They certainly do enjoy spoiling your son."

"They will make great parents."

"I think they will too." Jessica looks at her watch. "Well, I'll go and call them now." She smiles, squeezing my hand. "I'm so happy you are all right."

"So am I, Jessica. So am I."

Sixty-three

Dublin, Georgia

Gladys sits in an over-sized leather chair smoking a cigarette, her free hand cradling a tall can of beer. Closing her glazed eyes, she smiles contentedly, thinking about Cisely and what she must be feeling now. Gladys imagines the grief she is probably experiencing and relishes the thought. Picturing her niece crying and falling apart makes her smile take on an even more demented appearance. Gladys wants her niece to experience pain, and she is sure Cisely is doing just that. She intends to make her suffer for as long as possible.

She releases a low, throaty chuckle, completely pleased with herself. Turning her beer up and downing the last swallow, she sneers, realizing the can is now empty. If there is one thing Gladys cannot stand, it is an empty beer can or liquor bottle.

"Sadie," she calls to the kitchen. "Bring me another beer."

A minute later, a young brown-skinned woman of nineteen enters the living room, which is only lit by the television, and hands her another can. Gladys looks up at the thin woman and takes the beer, not offering a thank you. "Has the boy eaten anything?"

"Not today. I'm taking something to him now. He's stubborn sometimes and refuses to eat, but by night time, he's usually so hungry he gives in."

"Well, it don't matter none to me. It saves me money."

You mean it saves me money, Sadie voices silently. *You've never paid a dime for anything.* She looks at Gladys, her disgust for the woman evident, though Gladys doesn't seem to notice. She wouldn't have cared anyway. The only person Gladys is ever interested in pleasing or even cares about, is Gladys.

Heading to the kitchen to dish up a plate of spaghetti for the boy, Sadie silently wonders how she ever let herself get into this situation.

Sadie is the product of infidelity on her father's part, a man who happened to be Gladys' now deceased husband. For months, he cheated on Gladys with Sadie's mother, never bothering to tell her he was married. A little over eight years ago, he was killed one day while robbing a liquor store. Sadie and her mother attended his funeral when Gladys discovered the truth. Sadie wondered if Gladys ever told anyone. Probably not. She figured Gladys was most likely saving the information to use at another time. And she was right.

Sadie's mother died of cancer a year ago, and the insurance money that was left after paying for the funeral was enough to pay off the house and other bills. She works four days a week at the local grocery store as a checker and has been able to take care of herself pretty well. She is wise with her money and has never needed to depend on anyone. Her mother taught her to manage her finances well.

Sadie does not go out much, which means she doesn't have much of a social life. There is no one special in her personal life, and truthfully, she doesn't know if there will ever be. She is basically alone in the world and has resigned herself to the fact that she may always be.

When Gladys landed on her doorstep a month ago with the little boy in tow, she thought it was only going to be temporary. Gladys told Sadie the boy's name was Michael and he was her daughter's child by one of her ex-boyfriends. She said her daughter did not want to be a mother, especially to a half-white child and she ran off, leaving Gladys to care for him. Gladys also told Sadie she came to her because she had lost everything and had nowhere to go.

Now, as Sadie has observed how little she seems to care for the child, she isn't so sure Gladys is being truthful. There is something far beyond resentment in the woman's face every time his name is spoken. Sadie had tried talking to the boy several times when Gladys was passed out, but he would not speak. In all the time he's been there, he has never uttered a word, but she can see the fear and sadness in his beautiful green eyes and it tears at her heart. Gladys told Sadie he is mentally slow and the only time he talks is when he is pretending to be someone else, but some part of Sadie does not believe it. There has to be more to it.

Sadie puts the food on a tray and takes it in to the little boy. He is lying on the bed curled up on his side as usual, but he sits up when she enters. She sets the tray on a small table, and once again he moves to the chair, picks up the fork and eats ravenously. She smiles sadly as she watches him. Sitting in the chair next to him, she softly caresses his dark hair, all the while wishing she could somehow get him to talk to her. There just has to be more to his life than this.

Sixty-four

Lighting the last of the candles placed around our bedroom, I survey the small table set for two and decide everything is perfect. I want the evening to be as wonderful as I can make it for Adagio. I hate the way things are between us, and sadly, I know it is my fault. I never meant to hurt him and my heart is full of regret. I wish so much that I could take back all the pain I have caused him. I have a lot to make up for and I hope he can forgive me for not being there for him and Ingo when they really needed me. But all of that will change. I will never neglect them again.

Walking over to the mirror once more, I check my reflection. Smoothing my hands down the silky, ivory chemise, I try to calm the butterflies in my stomach. Not since the day I realized that I was in love Adagio have I felt so nervous. Or so afraid.

Adagio

Adagio is surprised to walk into the condo and find no one home. The last thing he needs right now is to be alone, though in a sense, he has been alone for a while now. He feels terrible about leaving Cisely the way he did earlier. Never in all the years of their marriage had he ever left without saying goodbye or telling her where he was going. And because of this, he had been anxious to get back home to her, if only to be in the same room with her. He knows she is still in pain, but he needs to be near her. He wants her to know he will always be there, and he hopes she will soon open her heart to him again. The distance between them is painful, but he will wait. He will wait forever.

He is about to call Cisely's cell when his ears tune in to soft music coming from their bedroom. This is something he has not heard in a long time. Walking down the hall, Adagio stops at their door, hesitating for a moment, not knowing what to expect. Then his heart begins to race in a way it has not been allowed to in a long while. Slowly, he opens the door. The dim room is lit by several candles. His gaze is immediately drawn to Cisely's silhouette standing in front of the window and his heart threatens to leap from his chest. She is also wearing a gown he hasn't seen in a while.

Oh, angel! he breathes silently. As he slowly approaches, he notices her forehead is pressed against the window, her eyes closed. She looks so beautiful standing there. He loves her so much, and watching her, his longing increases with an intensity that makes his breath catch. Moving close behind her, he presses his face into her hair, wrapping his arms around her waist.

As Adagio's arms close around me, heat rushes through my entire body. Releasing a breathy sigh, I lean back against him as a long-suppressed longing fills my entire being.

"Cisely," he whispers against my ear. His voice is raspy, emotion-filled and painfully seductive. "Baby, I love you."

I close my eyes as the warmth of his breath and the softness of his lips against my cheek intoxicate my senses. Turning in his arms, the longing in his gaze makes me want to weep. Wrapping my arms around his neck, I gently pull his head down, brushing my lips softly against his. Tears roll down my face as he kisses me. The sensation is like a heavy rain after a long drought. I bury my fingers in his hair, relishing the burning desire I have denied myself for so long.

As his mouth sears a path from my ear to my neck, every part of me is on fire. Being in his arms is so perfect, I don't know how I could have been without their warmth for as long as I had.

I undress him as our urgency increases. Pressing me tightly against him, his mouth continues to devour mine and an uncontrollable frenzy of emotion overtakes us both. The tears that spill onto my cheeks mingle with his as passion consumes us. And in his arms, I am finally home.

Adagio

Adagio lay wrapped in Cisely's arms with his head against her shoulder, and quietly contemplates the long absent contentment, relishing the closeness they now share. Their intimate union has completely rejuvenated him, and though he knows the trials are far from over, he can make it through them now, as long as they face them together. With each gentle caress of her hand against his face, Adagio marvels anew at the oneness that is again present.

"*Ti amo*, Adagio," Cisely says.

He smiles. "And I love you, so much." He stares into her eyes, watching them quickly tear up. "What is it?" he asks, raising up a little.

"I'm so sorry for not being there for you and Ingo. I'm sorry about everything."

He presses his hand against her cheek. "It is all right, *vita mia*. I understand."

"I wish I did," she says with a sigh. "No matter how hard I tried, I couldn't seem to stop myself from shutting everything down inside."

Adagio nods, understanding how she felt. Though he has tried to think positive and not let things get him down, it is still very hard. "I am sure self-preservation of the heart is still deeply ingrained in you. And it will probably always be because of all you have been through in your life. I really do understand." He smiles. "But you are okay now."

"Yes," she says, smiling serenely. "Now I am." She pauses. "I need to tell you something, my love."

"All right." They both sit up and lean back against the pillows. Taking her hand between his, he looks into her eyes, grateful for the peace he sees there.

"Each day that passed with no word or leads about Phillip pushed me further into despair. The pain became so bad, the only way I could handle it was to completely shut down." She squeezes his hand. "I needed you so much, but I didn't know how to tear down the walls. I wanted you near, but I couldn't let you close. This morning after you left, I spent a long time on my knees, begging God to help me."

Adagio wipes her tears with his fingers. It feels so good to have her sharing her feelings with him.

"You may not believe this, but I heard Ingo's voice telling me you needed me."

"Really?" he says, surprised and grateful at the same time. Given her past visions, he really could believe it.

Cisely nods. "It calmed me and I finally realized that I have never been alone, even though I have tried to face this alone."

Adagio smiles, tears filling his eyes. "I know each day Phillip is away from us will still bring pain, but we will find him, *amore*. I know we will."

"I know too," she says with a small sob. "I do."

Adagio pulls her close and they lay quietly for a while, holding one another, each giving the other the comfort that has been needed for so long. He silently vows to never let anything come between them again. She is too important to him, and he loves her too much to allow anything to push them apart.

"Are you hungry?" she finally asks, breaking the silence.

"I think I have worked up an appetite," he says, smiling slyly and she grins at him.

Slipping from under the covers, she walks into the bathroom and grabs their robes from behind the door. And as usual, Adagio can't help letting his gaze roam over her. She has always stayed so trim and keeps herself in shape, and motherhood has only enhanced her perfect figure.

Cisely hands Adagio one of the robes. "Just make yourself comfortable at the table and I'll be right back."

He restarts the disc in the player and waits for her. She returns a couple of minutes later with a large tray of take-out cartons.

"Mmmm, Chinese," he says as he helps her put the food on the table. "I love Chinese."

"I know," she says, smiling lovingly. She'd ordered the food earlier and had it delivered while she was preparing for the evening.

"Thank you." He takes her hand and kisses it. Then deciding it isn't enough, he leans over and captures her mouth with his. "Thank you," he again whispers.

"You're welcome."

As we eat, we spend the time reconnecting, each of us sharing the fears that have plagued us, as well as the peace we now feel. We know everything will be fine and somehow Phillip will be brought back to us. We treasure this time of talking everything out and giving support and comfort.

I marvel at how wonderful it feels to share my feelings with my husband instead of keeping everything bottled up inside. Why have I waited so long? Why had I let my fear get the better of me and needlessly wasted so much time?

There is nothing I can do about what is past, but this will never happen again. I won't let it.

Pretty soon we both have our fill of the food. Adagio follows me to the kitchen and helps me put the leftovers away. Then we get back into bed and talk more.

Adagio

Remembering his stop earlier, Adagio reaches over his side of the bed and pulls a small velvet box from his jean pocket.

"I have something for you, *amore*." He hands Cisely the box. "I know we celebrated our anniversary a couple of months ago, but I wanted to get this for you."

"You didn't have to do that," she says, her eyes moist. "I've missed out on so many things with you, but you never stopped thinking about me. I'm so sorry for what I put you through. I was so unfair to you and you didn't give up on me."

"Don't be sorry. I am just happy to have you back. And I could never give up on you. You are a part of me, Cisely." He wipes her tears and looks at the box. "When I saw this in the store window earlier, I just wanted you to have it."

She smiles. "I promise I will make everything up to you."

"You already have. Being with you like this has given me more joy than I can possibly express. Just being able to touch you again and express my love for you is enough."

She leans over and kisses him before opening the box. Her vision blurs as she gazes at the beautiful diamond eternity band. Looking into her husband's eyes, she understands why he bought it and what he is saying by giving it to her. She fully absorbs the ring's meaning and all that it symbolizes.

Adagio takes it from the box and slips it on her finger with her wedding rings.

"It's very beautiful," she whispers.

He smiles. "You and I are forever, angel. *Sei l'amore della mia vita.* You are the love of my life."

She nods, touching her fingers to his lips. "*Ti amo con tutto il cuore.* I love you with all my heart. Thank you for being so good to me."

"Always." He pulls her close and passionately captures her mouth with his again, reigniting the fiery need between them that can only be assuaged by their mutual love.

In the quiet darkness, I lay nestled in Adagio's arms, mentally tallying the blessings that have come from this trial. Before this, I never had extended family I could be close to besides Velma. Now, I am developing a relationship with my uncle and aunt, and I'm getting to know them better than I ever have. I consider that a miracle in itself, and I continue to keep a prayer in her heart for a second miracle.

That miracle will be manifested the moment we find our son.

Sixty-five

By November, the weather turns cold and I find myself having to readjust to the frigid winter of North Carolina after being spoiled for years by the mildness of Italy. I miss our home in Treviso, and I long for our family to be whole again soon so we can go back. But I also accept that for now, this is home.

Thanksgiving is in a couple of weeks, but it is hard to get in the spirit of the holidays. We recognize all we have and are grateful, but without Phillip with us, the holidays just cannot be the same and the sadness lingers.

Occasionally I look through the dresser drawers at Phillip's things, overwhelmed by his absence. Sometimes I stare at his photo and hug his clothes to me, trying to find comfort, desperately wanting to hold him in my arms. I long to feel his small arms around my neck and ache to have him give me one of his affectionate kisses that always brightens my day. Adagio sits with me during these times and we talk about our son and some of the things he does to make us laugh or smile. Though the ache is always there, having each other to lean on helps us cope with Phillip's absence.

With practice, I have become very good at being cheerful around Ingo. We have even managed to get him excited about the upcoming holiday, which helps to lift our own spirits a little more. Though it is an American holiday, I have always insisted that we celebrate Thanksgiving, and everyone in our family enjoys it. The boys always look forward to me making lots of treats, some of them American and some Italian. And except for Phillip's absence, this year will be no different. After all, we still have much to be grateful for.

On the Monday before Thanksgiving, Adagio and I take the whole family out to dinner. Velma and Ted dine with us, as well as my uncle and aunt. We all meet at the restaurant and enjoy a wonderful evening together. I am experiencing a little fatigue, but it doesn't keep me from enjoying myself. I love listening to Pete's stories about his childhood with my mother and the things they did together. He carries a photograph of the two of them as teenagers in his wallet.

Adagio and Jessica examined the photo and comment on how much I favor my mother. Since I have never seen a picture of my mother when she was younger until tonight, I am also surprised at the resemblance.

"She was very pretty," I say, handing the photo back to Pete.

"She was a looker in her younger days," Pete agrees, rubbing his bearded chin. "Even the years of drinking didn't diminish her looks like with most alcoholics."

I silently agree. Most of the alcoholics I've seen look worn and much older than they are. But Geneva Matthews never looked a day over thirty.

"Yeah, she was definitely beautiful," Pete says, looking at the photo once more before returning it to his wallet.

"Like mother, like daughter," Adagio whispers, smiling lovingly at me. I smile back, squeezing his hand. I turn my attention back to Pete as he tells us more about his and Geneva's experiences growing up. Though he doesn't go into much detail because of Ingo being present, he says it was hard growing up with two alcoholic parents. Their childhood was difficult, but they handled things as best they could.

I can definitely relate and understand. I knew alcoholism was the reason my grandparents died so young, and it saddens me that the pattern continued through my own mother, as well as Velma's. But I am also grateful Velma and I have broken the pattern. We chose a better path. And I hope every day for the strength to stay on that path.

Somehow the conversation steers clear of Gladys and her name is never mentioned, which is fine with everyone. The last thing we want is to add more gloom to the sadness already present. It has truly turned out to be a great evening, one that I will always treasure.

Sixty-six

This morning, I awaken experiencing more nausea than I have ever felt in my life. I have only been sitting up for a moment before I run to the bathroom and lose everything that I ate last night.

Adagio appears at my side, rubbing my back. "Are you all right, baby?" he asks, concern etched into his handsome features.

"I think so." A sense of melancholy fills me, despite how sick I feel. "But I think I need to lie back down." I rinse and splash cold water on my face before heading back into the bedroom.

When I am settled in bed again, Adagio slips under the covers and cradles me in his arms. Resting my head against his chest as he holds me close, so many thoughts flow through my mind. I am pretty sure I'm pregnant and the thought brings great comfort to me, especially now when I need it most. Though it does puzzle me a bit that I am feeling sick so soon. In the past, I was usually further along than I or the midwife suspected, but this time I know I can't be because of the month we hadn't made love–unless it happened before Phillip's kidnapping. Some women are pregnant for months before showing the usual signs. Maybe it has happened to me this time.

Looking up at him, I ask, "Would you mind getting me a piece of toast and maybe a small glass of juice?"

"Not at all, *cara*" Adagio sits up and pulls on a pair of sweat pants, then he stops. He turns and looks at me, his eyes full of wonder. "Cisely?" When I smile, he knows there is no need to finish the question. Instead he asks, "Would you like me to make a trip to the store, too?"

"I think that's a good idea."

He leans over to kiss me. "*Ti adoro.*"

"And I adore you."

He grins and I chuckle. Dressing quickly, he brings me the toast and juice. Then making sure I have everything that I need, he grabs the car keys and leaves.

Twenty minutes later, we both laugh and cry as we examine the positive test result. Adagio hugs me tightly and happiness fills a part the empty space in my heart.

Dublin, Georgia

Sadie enters the house and finds Gladys passed out in the chair as usual. She never bothers to enter quietly because Gladys usually sleeps so hard, no amount of noise ever wakes her up. Sadie stands for a moment looking at the grossly-overweight woman and her contempt grows.

She is tired of this whole situation and wants her home back. She is fed up with having to pick up after this woman, and tired of spending her entire shift every day worrying about the little boy in the back room. Each time she leaves the house, Sadie prays he will be all right until she gets back. Gladys is supposed to be his grandmother, but she acts like he does not even exist most of the time. And Sadie wonders what kind of mother would just dump her child off on someone and leave, if that is what really happened.

Taking her purse and coat to her room, Sadie hurries to check on Michael. Thoughts of him had consumed her throughout the day and she could not get home fast enough, needing to make sure he was okay. She muses over how motherly she has become. How had she become so attached to this child? He has never spoken, yet she can feel his sadness. She can see it in his eyes, and she would give anything to see him smile, just once.

When Sadie reaches the bedroom, she cracks the door open slightly and freezes, unable believe what she is seeing. The sight she beholds is as much of a shock as a surprise, and it immediately brings tears to her eyes.

This sweet boy is on his knees with his head bowed, praying softly. It is the first time she has heard him speak. His voice is so soft, so innocent and pure. Sadie covers her mouth with her hand, trying to muffle a sob. She knows absolutely nothing about this child, yet he has ingrained himself in her heart even more with this innocent act.

When she sniffles softly, the boy looks up and jumps to his feet. He crawls back on the bed, backing into the corner.

"It's okay, Michael." she says, hating that she'd frightened him. The last thing she wants to do is scare him into silence again. "It's all right. I'm not going to hurt you. I would never hurt you."

She slowly moves toward him and kneels by the side of the bed. "I want to be your friend."

Phillip hedges himself in the corner, still too afraid to believe her. The only thing that has helped him to cope this long is praying. He remembers his mother telling him anytime he is scared or sad, he can talk to God and he would never be alone. The sound of her silky voice as she said this fills his heart every day and has helped him get through the lonely days and nights he's lived through. He would give anything to be in his mother's arms again.

Saddened beyond words by the fear in his eyes, Sadie brightens and smiles at him, hoping she can somehow gain his trust. "Are you hungry, Michael?"

Phillip looks at her for a moment, trying to decide if he can really trust her. Sadie has always been nice to him and seems like she cares. She isn't at all like Gladys. Every time Gladys even looks at him, he wants to cry, he is so afraid of her.

Sadie continues to look at him, her eyes pleading. "Wouldn't you like something special for dinner today? I can make anything you like, and if I don't have it, I'll go and buy it." When he continues to silently stare at her, she sighs and moves to get up, but what she hears next stops her.

"My name is not Michael."

Her emotions are mixed, but she isn't too surprised by this. She has felt that something was not right for a while now. She speaks to him again, except softer this time. Gladys usually sleeps pretty hard, but she doesn't want to take any chances.

"Would you tell me your real name?"

"Phillip. Phillip St. John."

Sadie is again surprised by the sound of his sweet voice, and his accent is beautiful. She decides to get all the information she can from him while she has the chance. Hopefully, Gladys will not wake up any time soon. She lowers her voice to just above a whisper.

"Phillip is a very nice name. I like it."

Phillip considers her words for a moment and decides that maybe he can trust her a little. "My name is the same as my papa."

"Really? I'll bet your papa is nice, huh?"

"He's the best papa in the world," Phillip says, slowly coming out of the corner and his shell.

Sadie thanks the heavens for the information she had gotten from him. "What about your mama? I'll bet she's nice too.

When Phillip hesitates, Sadie wonders about his mother until he says, "My mama is the best mama ever. And she is the prettiest too."

She smiles. It is obvious the little boy loves his parents and they probably love him just as much. She looks at Phillip, really looks at him, and decides he can't possibly be Gladys' grandson. "I'll bet you miss your mama and papa, don't you?"

Phillip's eyes tear up and he nods. "I want to go home."

She covers his small hand with hers. "Where is your home?"

"In Italy."

"Italy?" She briefly wonders if he is indeed making up a story until he speaks again.

"I went to a wedding with Mama and Papa in North Carolina. Mama sang there."

"Really?" she says, growing more intrigued with each thing he reveals. "I'll bet she has a beautiful voice."

Phillip again nods as tears trail down his cheeks. "I want to go home."

"I know," she soothes. "How did you come to be with Gladys?"

"She took me. My brother was there too, but she just took me."

Sadie's heart breaks at his words. For some reason Gladys ripped this little boy from his parents. She wonders how the woman could do something so cruel. *How could she do this to his parents?* Pondering the anguish that they must be going through, her heart aches even more. *Those poor people. What they must be going through. I can't even imagine.* Looking at Phillip, she knows she has to do something. Somehow, she has to get him back to his family.

"Listen, Phillip. I'm going to get you out of here. I've got to get some help somehow."

His eyes light up. "I get to see my mama and papa again?"

"Yes," Sadie whispers, smiling. "I promise you that you will be with them again. Maybe even by Thanksgiving. It's the day after tomorrow. Would you like that?"

"Yes!" Phillip whispers excitedly, his eyes sparkling.

Sadie pauses for a moment to think. She must think of a way to get him out of the house. She could leave now and go to the police, but Gladys will be awake soon and would wonder where she was, and she doesn't want to give her any cause for suspicion. Of course, she did promise Phillip anything he wanted to eat, even if it means going out to buy it. She could go to the police then, but she hates the thought of leaving Phillip alone with Gladys again.

Glancing back at the door, she listens a moment for Gladys, then leans closer to Phillip and whispers, "I'm going to go to the store. While I'm gone, I will try and get help. You just stay quiet like normal and I will be back as soon as I can. Okay?"

Phillip nods quickly. "Please hurry," he whispers. His eyes are drawn toward the door and fear instantly seizes him.

Sadie's heart pounds violently as she slowly turns, her eyes meeting the face that frightened the boy into silence. Taking on a calm facade, her mind quickly works up a story. She hopes it will sound convincing enough.

"What are you doing in here, girl?" Gladys growls, her glassy eyes suspicious.

Sadie's smile is tense. "I was just asking Michael what he would like for dinner tonight. I was going to go out and buy him something special."

Gladys moves her hateful eyes to Phillip. "What did he say?"

Sadie clears her throat. "He said he wanted pizza."

"What else did he tell you," Gladys asks, moving closer, staring at her through hardened eyes.

Sadie rears back a little to avoid the stench of alcohol permeating around the woman. "He didn't say anything else, just pizza. He never says anything, and frankly I was surprised he even answered me." She manages to keep her voice calm.

Gladys stares at Sadie a moment longer. Her head is still fuzzy, but she doesn't believe her, and she isn't willing to take any chances, just in case Phillip told her anything. "That boy don't need no pizza tonight. Just fix him something else." She isn't about to let Sadie out of the house now that Phillip has spoken. Until now, she'd never worried much because he had been too afraid to talk, but she will have to be more careful now.

Sadie remains expressionless, but her stomach is in knots. Her plan for the moment is blown. She turns to Phillip. "I guess you will just have to deal with hot dogs again tonight, kid." She keeps her voice monotone, but a casual wink, unseen by Gladys conveys to Phillip she had meant what she said to him. She will find a way to get him back to his family.

Sixty-seven

Sitting at the kitchen table with a steaming cup of hot chocolate, I make a list of things I need to buy for our Thanksgiving meal. I will probably be sick in the morning, but I am determined to get all the cooking done. Thankfully, I have a whole day to prepare, and I have Adagio and Jessica here to help, which will make things easier.

Last week I invited Velma and Ted, as well as Pete and Dona to spend the holidays with us, but they all have plans. Velma and Ted are heading out tomorrow morning to spend Thanksgiving with his family in New York. Pete and Dona are driving up to Virginia to spend the holidays with their son. I am a little sad they will all be gone because I have grown so used to having them around now, but I do understand that they have their own lives.

Checking my list over, I add a few more things like crackers, croissants, and more juice, because I will definitely need them for a while. Smiling, I press a hand over my flat stomach.

We had hoped for more children, and this pregnancy has come right when I need something to help lift my spirits. When we told Jessica the news earlier in the day, she was so happy for us, she cried. I am so grateful to have her here, and once Phillip is found and we return to Italy, I will miss her more than I can say. I will have to talk with Adagio about taking another trip to Salt Lake City next year.

Stirring my chocolate, I take a sip, savoring its sweet warmth while my thoughts again turn to our missing son. I pray he is somewhere warm and getting enough to eat, and I hope he remembers what I taught him about praying when he is afraid or sad.

Closing my eyes tightly, I try unsuccessfully to fight the tears that come as I picture Phillip on his knees offering up humble prayers to heaven.

He is all right. He will be back with us soon.

I remind myself to remain positive and have faith. Willing away the sadness, I dry my eyes and shift my thoughts elsewhere. I am startled by the sound of the doorbell. A moment later Adagio sticks his head in the kitchen.

"*Amore*, someone is here to see you. She said she was a guest at the wedding, but I do not recall seeing her there."

I am instantly curious. "All right, I'll be right there." I fold the list and put it in my pocket before going to the living room. The young woman is sitting on the sofa. I don't recognize her from the wedding, either. Of course, there *were* a lot of guests.

"Hello."

The woman stands. "Hello. "I'm Janet Cook." She extends her hand and I shake it firmly. "I'm an old acquaintance of Velma's and I wasn't at the reception long, so I didn't have a chance to meet you."

"Well, I'm glad I have the pleasure of meeting you now."

"I'm happy to meet you, too. I hope I'm not keeping you from anything, but I just felt the need to see you."

"No, I'm not busy at all." I gesture to the sofa. "Please, have a seat."

"Thank you."

"Well, thank you for coming to visit. I'm always happy to meet new people. What brings you by?"

"Well . . . I uh . . . I just wanted to tell you how sorry I was to hear about your little boy."

"Thank you." I am moved by this woman's compassion for someone she has never met until today. The support we've received from new friends and neighbors means a great deal, and we will never be able to repay their kindness. I notice Janet wringing her hands nervously.

"Do you have children?"

Tears fill her eyes. "I had a little girl. I lost her about four years ago. She was only three."

"Oh, I'm so sorry." I lean forward and squeeze her hand gently, my heart going out to her. "Do you mind if I ask what happened?"

"Not at all. That is why I felt such a strong need to meet you. You see, my ex-husband was a very hard man. He was abusive, not physically, but verbally and emotionally. When I finally divorced him after three years of dealing with his abuse, he swore he would get even with me." She chuckles bitterly. "Well, he got even with me all right. He took Kelly from me. He took her from a friend's home one day while I was at work. The police were never able to find him. They think he left the country."

I wipe at the tears that come nonstop before moving to the sofa and hugging her. We know nothing about each other, yet we share a common bond. That her story is so much like mine is uncanny. I move back, looking into the woman's eyes. "I'm so sorry."

"Thank you. It's a little easier now, not much but a little. I still pray every day that he is taking care of her and keeping her safe. In my heart I feel she is okay, but it's still hard knowing she is out there in the world somewhere and I might not ever see her again." She squeezes my hand. "I hope things turn out different for you. I hope you get your son back."

"We pray for that every day as well. And I hope you will get to see your daughter again."

Janet nods, her voice catching in her throat. "I want that more than anything."

I smile sadly, aching for her. I have just finished drying my face when Adagio walks in.

"Is everything okay?"

"Everything is fine." I motion for him to join us. He sits next to me and I tell him about Janet's missing daughter. Compassion immediately fill his eyes, and he expresses his sympathy to Janet.

We talk with her for a while longer and a friendship quickly forms between us. Her visit helps me to remember I really am not the only mother in the world suffering the pain of having a child taken from her. I am grateful she came, and grateful for the opportunity to get to know her.

"Do you have plans for the holidays?" I ask.

"Actually, I do. My sister has invited me to spend Thanksgiving with her family in Nashville."

"That's good. But if something should happen and your plans fall through, you're definitely welcome here."

"Thank you," Janet says with a smile.

Before she leaves, I hug her and thank her again for coming to see me. She promises to keep in touch.

Moving to the window, I watch her drive away, again grateful to have made a friend.

"She is a great lady," Adagio says, moving behind me, wrapping his arms around my waist.

"She is." I sigh, leaning my head back against his shoulder. "But she has no one to lean on." Reaching back, I press a hand to his face. "Thank you for being a steady rock, for loving me through it all and not giving up on me."

My eyes slip shut as his lips rummage my ear, the sensation sending instant heat through me. I release a breathy sigh as his mouth languorously explores the side of my neck, searing a burning path to my temple. Oh, what he does to me!

"That will never change, *cuorcino mia*," he finally whispers against my ear, producing a warm shiver. Turning me in his arms, he lightly presses his mouth to mine, whispering again, "That will never change."

J. Adams

Sixty-eight

Dublin, Georgia

Sadie turns over in the darkness and looks at the clock. It is just past midnight. Getting up, she quietly dresses in the jeans and tunic sweater she had placed on the chair earlier. With thoughts of what she'd planned running through her head earlier, she had known she wouldn't be able to sleep, but she had dressed for bed anyway. The last thing she had wanted to do was give Gladys any cause for suspicion.

Sadie had felt Gladys watching her throughout the evening, and remembering the hateful way the woman looked at her before she went to bed makes her shudder. She shakes her head, still not able to believe she is having to plan an escape from her own home.

She quickly puts on some socks and a pair of running shoes, and locates her purse and jacket. Opening her dresser drawer, she takes a large wad of cash from under the folded clothes and stuffs it into the front pocket of her jeans. Taking a deep breath, she turns off the bedroom light and quickly moves down the hall to Phillip's room.

Sadie quietly opens the door and whispers Phillip's name. After shaking him gently, he sits up and rubs the sleep from his eyes, trying to adjust them in the darkness.

"Come on, honey. I'm going to get you out of here." He had slept in his clothes and he slips on his shoes. She unfolds a small blanket and wraps it around him, wishing she had a coat that would fit him. She places her hand against his cheek. "Everything is going to be okay. But we have to be really quiet, all right?"

Phillip nods and grips her hand, anticipating being with his parents again. Thoughts of seeing them and his brother had made it hard for him to fall asleep.

"Are you ready?" she whispers and Phillip nods, holding tightly to her hand. Sadie turns toward the door, and they begin quietly making her way down the hallway when something hard crashes against her head. The last thing she hears is Phillip's scream before losing consciousness.

I silently lay in bed next to Adagio and gaze out the window at the moonlit forest. I don't know why I have awakened, and the harder I try to go back to sleep, the more sleep eludes me. Not wanting to wake him, I quietly slip out of bed and head to the kitchen, deciding a cup of chamomile tea might help. I do not normally have a problem sleeping when I am pregnant, but staying awake is usually a challenge.

Taking my tea to the living room, I stretch out on the sofa and try to relax. Sipping my tea, I mentally go over all the things

I need to do to prepare for Thanksgiving. I am glad for all the work because it keeps me busy and my mind occupied. It would be so easy to dwell on the fact that our son will not be sharing the holiday with us, but I can't allow myself to do that. I want to make the day as special as I can for my family, and I need to be emotionally intact to do that.

I run a hand back through my shoulder-length hair, still trying to get used to the new length. I got it cut last week after years of wearing it down my back. The stylist I went to did a good job and I am pleased with my new look. I still wear it straight, but the layered ends are slightly turned under, softly framing my face. I also have wispy bangs, which give me a youthful appearance. Smiling, I remember the look on Adagio's face when I came home. He told me over and over how beautiful I looked and couldn't stop staring. Of course, he always thinks I am beautiful. I just felt like I needed a change. And being pregnant, it will grow out again soon.

Rubbing my tired eyes, I look around the spacious living room, sighing as I take it in. It truly is a beautiful condo and I am grateful to finally be emotionally whole enough to appreciate its beauty. I remember how often I rode the bus through this neighborhood when I was younger, gazing at the elegant homes. I recall passing these very condos, trying to imagine what the interior of one was like, and I ponder the irony.

I could never have guessed I would again be living in the town I grew up in. It had not been a part of my plans. But things don't always go quite the way you plan. I am forever discovering this fact the hard way, but I also know this life is a learning process, and I am okay with that.

I am just finishing my tea when Adagio appears in the doorway. He doesn't sleep well when I am not beside him and I am the same. He pushes a hand back through his disheveled hair. "Can you not sleep, *amore?*"

"I'm having a hard time relaxing. Can you believe it? Me, pregnant and not able to sleep?"

Joining me on the sofa, he begins to gently massage my shoulders. "Things are different with this pregnancy. You are going through so much right now. We all are." He sighs wearily. "And things are not the same without Phillip. How can they be?"

I close my eyes against the burning tears, but they escape anyway. "I miss him so much." Pressing a hand against my mouth, I sob.

Adagio turns me and pulls me against his chest as his own tears come. "I miss him too, baby" he says pressing his lips into my hair. "I miss him so much it hurts. But I know everything will be all right."

Drawing back a little, I look into his eyes. "Me too. But thank you for reminding me and for being strong enough for the both of us."

"I draw a lot of my strength from you these days." He kisses my brow.

Smiling, I rest my head against his chest, basking in the love we share. I finally close my eyes and try to clear my mind, focusing only on positive things. I can't dwell on the negative and still keep my sanity.

When Cisely's breathing deepens and she is asleep, Adagio tilts her head back slightly and gazes down at her face. Pulling her closer, he presses his lips to her brow, breathing in the scent of her hair. How he loves this woman! She is in his every thought, his every dream, and he needs her like he needs air to breathe. He can't even sleep unless she is within his reach. Her presence fills him, and he can barely remember what his life was like without her.

"I love you, baby," he whispers against her brow. "*Il mia bella angelo.*" His lips linger on her forehead a moment longer before he stands, lifting her in his arms.

She awakens and smiles sleepily as he carries her, wrapping her arms around his neck. "You're so good to me," she says softly.

He kisses her lips and gently places her on the bed. "And I always will be."

Sixty-nine

Dublin, Georgia

Sadie presses her hand to the back of her throbbing head, the pain growing worse with each movement. Though she had never been hit by a truck, she can't imagine it feeling any worse. Pushing herself up enough to reach the light switch, she leans against the wall to keep from falling. Tears seep from her closed eyes as she thinks about Phillip and the danger that he is in.

It's all my fault. How could I have been so careless?

Holding the back of her head, she staggers to the bathroom and turns on the light, not surprised to find blood on her hand when she pulls it away from her head. *If she did this to me, there's no telling what she will do to Phillip.* She moans as pain shoots through her whole head. *I have to get help.*

Sadie presses a towel to the wound and winces. She picks up the phone on the table near the bathroom door to call the police, but the line is dead.

I should have known.

Pulling on the cord, she finds that it has been cut, certain the other two probably are as well. Staggering back down the hallway, she picks up her purse, futilely searching for her car keys, then moves as quickly as she can to the front window only to discover her car is no longer there.

It figures.

Sadie lives so far away from town, she will have to walk two miles to get to the nearest bus stop, and there are no buses running this time of night. She realizes the remote location of her home is probably one of the reasons Gladys chose to stay there. Feeling her pocket, she sighs with relief, grateful Gladys hadn't thought to search them. She still has the cash she had stuffed in them earlier.

With a great deal of effort, Sadie pulls on a heavier coat and some gloves. The walk will be hard, but she has no choice. She needs to get to the police and tell them about Phillip. And she is determined to make it to the station.

Even if it kills her.

Sadie collapses onto the bus stop bench. She is in so much pain, she wonders if she will make it into town. Leaning forward, she holds her head in her hands, trying to catch her breath and find some relief. Closing her eyes, she begins to cry, unable to believe her life has come to this. For over two months now, she had most likely been harboring a fugitive. She had housed an evil woman who kidnapped a child and caused misery to a family.

Slowly lifting her head, Sadie takes a deep breath. She is miserable but continues to fight thoughts of her own discomfort. She has to, because there is a little boy out there somewhere who needs her to fight for him. She is the only one who can.

Biting back the pain, she focuses on the Christmas advertisements posted on the acrylic shelter around the bench. She had never taken the bus, because she'd always had reliable transportation, and even if she did not, the prospect of a two-mile walk to the bus stop every day was not very appealing. Each time she passed this stop on her way to and from work, she glimpsed advertisements for one thing or another, and she wondered how many people in her neck of the woods ever ventured to any of the expensive stores advertised there. She doubted many could afford it. She definitely couldn't.

Turning and letting her eyes scan the various posters, her heart literally stops for a second, her eyes growing large as Phillip's face stares back at her from a missing child poster next to a photo of Gladys. Her voice catches as she reads the information under the pictures.

Adagio Phillip St. John II
Age: 5
Race: Biracial – Black/Italian descent
Height: 3 feet
Hair: brownish-black
Eyes: green
Last seen with: Gladys Baker
Age: 57
Race: Black
Hair: Black
Eyes: Brown

Call if you have any information
Reward offered.

Closing her eyes, Sadie lifts her face heavenward as hot tears spill down her cheeks, her hands forming fists. "How could I have been so stupid? Because of my stupidity, Phillip has been kept from his family, and now they might not ever see him again." Her voice breaks. "God, please help me. Help me to help Phillip."

She presses her face into her hands and cries helplessly, feeling alone and hopeless. She will never be able to live with herself if anything happens to Phillip, so she continues to plead to the heavens for help. She needs to make it to the station, but she is in so much pain, she can hardly move.

Taking a deep breath, she makes an effort to get up when a car approaches and stops.

"Are you all right, honey?" a woman calls through the window.

Sadie wipes her face. "I need to get to the police station."

The woman's brows draw together in concern. "Well, come on and I'll take you."

"Thank you," Sadie says with a grateful sob. As she stands and moves toward the car, her knees buckle and she falls. The woman jumps out and helps her to walk around to the passenger's side.

"I think maybe I should take you to the hospital instead," she says, seeing fresh blood roll down the back of Sadie's neck. "I work in housekeeping there and I'm on my way in now."

"No, please," Sadie says as she practically drops into the seat. "I need to get to the police. I have information about a kidnapping."

"Good heavens!" The woman closes the door. As she pulls out onto the road, she introduces herself. "My name is Helen Grant."

"Sadie Roberts." Sadie continues to hold her head. The pain is excruciating and she is just barely hanging on to consciousness. "I'm grateful for your help, Helen. It was a miracle you came when you did. You were an answer to my prayers."

Helen gives a small smile. "I'm happy I can be an answer to someone's prayers. I've certainly had plenty of mine answered lately."

When they finally arrive at the station, Helen walks around and opens the door for Sadie, helping her to stand. Sadie leans against her and they walk into the building. The officer at the front desk looks up just as Sadie's legs give out and she goes down, almost taking Helen with her.

"What happened?" he asks, rushing to them.

"I was driving by and saw her sitting at the bus stop. She told me she was trying to make it here, but she was in so much pain, she had to stop."

The officer gently lifts her head and examines the bloody mass on the back. "Someone got her pretty good."

Sadie loses consciousness and the officer calls for an ambulance. While they wait, he questions Helen and she tells him all she knows. When the ambulance finally arrives and leaves to take Sadie to the emergency room, Helen follows, hoping she will be okay.

J. Adams

Seventy

Adagio

As morning light spills into the room, Adagio lay watching Cisely sleep. He wishes he could see her dreams and longs to be a part of them. How he loves just looking at her! He gently brushes her hair back, unable to resist touching her, and he marvels that she never ceases to take his breath away, even when sleeping peacefully. Despite all they are going through, their love for each other is continually growing, and her happiness is everything to him.

Adagio is so proud of Cisely for her strength and awed by her determination to continue their family Thanksgiving tradition, even though Phillip is not with them. There is still a great deal of pain every time he thinks of his little boy, and his hope for Phillip's return never ceases. But his faith is strong and he knows in his heart their son is all right.

As Cisely slowly awakens, Adagio continues to caress her face, as if she were a priceless treasure. Opening her eyes, she smiles, the deep love in her eyes evident.

"Good morning, my love."

"Good morning," he says with a smile. "How are you feeling?"

"About the same."

"I will go and get a croissant and some juice for you, okay?" He sits up, pushing back the blanket.

She nods. "Thank you."

"You are welcome."

"Adagio?" she says, reaching for his hand as he stands. He sits on the edge of the bed. "I love you. Thank you for loving me so much."

Leaning over, he presses a gentle hand to her face. "You don't need to thank me. You are very easy to love. I can't imagine not loving you or having you in my life."

"I can't imagine not loving you either." She stares into his eyes and he reads a multitude of emotions in them. "It seems like we have always been together, like I have always been yours."

"You were meant to be mine," he says, his voice gentle, yet his gaze is intent. "And you will always be mine." Pressing his lips to hers, he kisses her possessively. *You will always be mine.* The statement embeds itself deeper into his soul as her mouth continues to soften under his.

I melt under the power his kiss holds. I really am his. I completely belong to him. Everything about his love is perfection.

"I will go get that juice and croissant for you," he whispers against my lips. He draws back a little, meeting my misty eyes with his own tear-filled gaze. *"Ti amo con tutta me stessa/tutto me stesso."* He kisses me again and heads to the kitchen.

Sliding over to his side of the bed, I contemplate his words. Pressing my face to his pillow, I breathe in his scent. This powerful passion I harbor for him completely fills me, and he holds my heart in the palm of his hand. He is everything to me, a literal part of my soul.

I smile, thinking of the new life growing inside me that is another product of our love. Brushing a tear away, my thoughts linger on Phillip and how happy he will be to know he is going to be a big brother. Pressing a hand to my chest, I sob softly as sadness again overwhelms me. I miss my little boy immensely and it isn't getting any easier.

Adagio returns with a tray for me. Setting it down beside the bed, he gets back under the covers, immediately pulling me into his arms.

"I'm sorry," I tell him. "I didn't mean for this to happen this morning."

"Shhh," he soothes, pressing a kiss to my brow. "It is all right. Anytime you need to cry, it is okay." His voice cracks. "And I will be right here."

As if his permission is all I need, I bury my face against his chest and cry without restraint. Adagio can do nothing but hold me and cry with me.

J. Adams

Seventy-one

Sadie slowly awakens as early morning light seeps through the blinds of the hospital room. The pain she had felt previously is gone, replaced by a lightheartedness she had never experienced. Lifting a hand to her head, she finds it securely wrapped in bandages. She tries to remember what happened last night, but her mind is still fuzzy and her brain cannot seem to function. The one thing that does stand out in her mind is Phillip is in danger. She has to help him.

She pushes the call button attached to her bed. After a moment, the doctor enters her room, and she finds herself doing a double take, taken off guard by his attractiveness. Taking in his expression, she wonders if she only imagines the look of relief in his eyes.

Blue eyes, she muses. *Eyes as blue as the sea. Whoa! Where did that come from? Oh, yeah, my head is still fuzzy.*

"Good morning, Miss Roberts," he says softly. "I'm Dr. Grant. I can't tell you how glad I am to see you awake. I know you probably don't remember much and I will try and fill you in. But first, how are you feeling?"

"My head is kind of fuzzy, but it doesn't hurt anymore."

"That's good. It means the pain medication we gave you is still working. As soon as it wears off and you start to feel pain, don't hesitate to ask for more." His eyes grow more serious. "That was a nasty gash you received and you got a slight concussion along with it." He places a gentle hand on her arm. "Would you like to tell me how it happened?"

Sadie's arm tingles under his hand and she forces herself to keep from reacting. "Yes, I'll tell you, but I need to speak with the police too. I have some important information for them."

"I thought you might. There has been an officer waiting out in the hall for a while now to speak with you. I said I would let him know the moment you awakened. I'll go and get him now if that is all right."

When Sadie nods, he leaves, returning seconds later with the officer. Sadie vaguely remembers him from last night.

Dr. Grant sits on a stool next to the bed. He isn't sure if he should stay or not, but he doesn't want to leave Sadie just yet. A deeper part of him needs to know who would do such a thing to her.

"Miss Roberts, last night you came to the station because you had some information about a kidnapping. I would like to take your statement now."

Taking a deep breath, Sadie tells the officer about Gladys kidnapping Phillip and bringing him to her house, pretending he was her grandson. She tells him about her history with Gladys, explaining that even though she did not like the woman, she had no reason at first to doubt her story. Then she observed the hateful way Gladys treated the boy. Sadie tells the officer that until yesterday, Phillip had not spoken, so she didn't know he had been kidnapped. Then she saw the missing child poster at the bus stop. She repeats to him what Phillip told her about Gladys taking him from the wedding reception of a relative in North Carolina.

She wipes her eyes. "Gladys came in and caught me talking to him and became suspicious. That was when I made up my mind to get him out of there. She watched me for the rest of the evening. When I tried to get him out of the house in the middle of the night, she hit me from behind. The next thing I knew, I was waking up on my hallway floor. And now . . . now she's taken Phillip to who knows where . . . and it's all my fault."

Dr. Grant places a box of tissue on the bed. Seeing the guilt and grief etched into Sadie's face, he wishes he could say something to help. He places his hand over hers and squeezes.

Sadie looks into the doctor's eyes, her own conveying how much she appreciates him being there. She doesn't know this man, and she is sure this is not a part of his job description, yet for the first time in a long time she doesn't feel alone.

The officer tells Sadie she is not responsible for any of this and it is good that she came forward as soon as she'd made the discovery, but his words do nothing to ease her conscience. She should have known Gladys wasn't telling the truth. She should have done something sooner. The guilt is tearing her up inside.

When the officer leaves to call the information in, Sadie heaves a sigh of relief, holding to the hope that they will find Phillip before it is too late.

Seventy-two

Charleston, South Carolina

With one hand gripping the back of Phillip's shirt, Gladys knocks on the door of the secluded old trailer, musing that it pays to have friends in low places. Looking around the area, she has to admit, this place is even lower than her own. The rusty old trailer is out in the middle of nowhere surrounded by trees. There are junked cars and trucks everywhere and the road leading to the place is unpaved.

Yeah, no one will look for me here, she muses with a smile.

When there is no answer, she bangs on the door again.

"I'm coming!" yells a gruff voice. "Hold your horses!"

A minute later the door opens. Phillip looks up at the big, rough looking man and cringes.

"Well, if it ain't Glad Gladys. What are you doing in this neck of the woods?"

"I just thought I'd come and hang out with my old drinking buddy for a while." She eyes the tall Indian and smiles. "How you been, Tom?"

"As well as can be expected. Ya'll come on in, then."

"Go on in there, boy," Gladys says, shoving Phillip through the door.

"So, what you been up to?" Tom asks, fixing his eyes on Phillip as she shoves him into an old chair in the corner of the cluttered room.

"Not a whole lot. My daughter dumped her boy off on me and I've been trying to take care of him. But it's hard when money is low."

"Yeah, tell me about it. My ex tried to leave the two young'uns with me, but I wouldn't stand for it." He eyes Phillip again. "That's a good-looking boy, but I know his daddy ain't black, is he?"

"No, he ain't."

"You want something to eat, boy?" Tom asks him.

Phillip nods slowly. Normally he wouldn't have answered, but since he hasn't eaten anything since dinner yesterday, he is hungry.

"Well, I got a can of peaches and some bread. Come on in the kitchen." Phillip timidly follows Tom.

While Tom is getting the food for Phillip, Gladys starts looking through his cabinets for something stronger than water to drink.

"I got a bottle stashed in the bottom cabinet over there." He points to a greasy door in the corner.

"Ah, jackpot!" she says as she pulls the almost full fifth of vodka from the cabinet. She takes a dirty glass off the table and fills it, then quickly takes a swallow, grimacing as the burning liquid rolls down her throat.

"I'm guessing you needed that."

"You guessed right," she says, smiling before taking another swallow.

"Well, pour me a glass." He takes another dirty glass from the table and hands it to her. She fills it half way and holds it out to him. Tom takes a large swallow and sets the glass down. "So, how long you plan on staying?"

"Just for a few days. I'll keep out of your way and the boy won't be a problem. I'll make sure of it." She shoots Phillip a hateful look.

Phillip fights the sudden burning in his eyes, determined to not cry. It makes Gladys angrier when he does, and that's the last thing he wants.

"He don't look like he'll be too much of a problem."

Gladys looks over at his now empty bowl. "That boy would eat me out of house and home if I let him. That's why I ain't got any money left now."

"I hear what you're saying. Young'uns take every dime, that's for sure." He turns to Phillip. "Hey, boy, go on back in the bedroom and turn on the television while me and your grandma talk."

Phillip does as he is told. Secretly, he is eager to watch television. He hadn't been allowed to at Sadie's. Gladys hadn't allowed him to do anything, except sit quietly in the bedroom all day. And he'd read the picture books Sadie bought for him so many times, he had the pages memorized.

He turns on the television and sits in a wooden chair in the corner, but instead of watching the cartoons on the screen, his thoughts travel to Sadie. Tears fill his eyes as he recalls her lying on the hallway floor. Never during this whole ordeal had he been as frightened as he was at that moment. Gladys has always been hateful to him, but to know she actually hurt Sadie completely terrifies him. He feels like it is his fault. Sadie was only trying to help him, but she ended up getting hurt instead. He quickly wipes at the tears.

"Please let her be okay, God," he whispers. "Please let Sadie be okay."

Seventy-three

Sadie lay awake staring up at the ceiling, futilely wiping at the endless stream of tears. She has been praying unceasingly that the police will be able to track down her car and catch Gladys, and her heart is aching for Phillip. She will never forgive herself if anything happens to him. Truthfully, she doesn't know if she can forgive herself now for letting things get this far. She had always considered herself a somewhat intelligent person, but not anymore. At the moment she feels as far from smart as a person could be.

Dr. Grant enters the room, wanting, more than needing to check on Sadie. There are nurses in his charge that can do it, but when he is not busy with another patient, he wants to be with her. There is no way he can explain how she had touched his heart the moment she was put in his care. In the five years he has been a doctor, nothing like this had ever happened to him. It is as if her spirit had spoken to his.

435

Earlier, he talked with his mother about what he was feeling, and she said she understood. She had also felt an unexplainable closeness to Sadie when she picked her up at the bus stop last night. Helen told him she had a special feeling about Sadie. She had no idea her son's life would be affected by the young woman as well.

When Peter sees the tears rolling back into Sadie's hair, he again places his hand over hers. "How are you doing?" His voice is soft.

Her pain-filled eyes meet his. "How could I have been so stupid?"

The young doctor rolls a stool over by the bed and sits down. "Sadie, you are not now, nor were you ever, stupid. You thought you were helping someone. You didn't know."

"Oh, I helped her all right. I helped her to keep a little boy from his family." She looks into his eyes. "Oh, Dr. Grant, what am I going to do?"

He smiles. "Well, the first thing I want you to do is stop calling me Dr. Grant. My name is Peter."

Sadie wipes her eyes and looks into his, her own laced with subtle humor. "Is that allowed?" she asks almost mischievously.

"For you, it is."

She gives him a slow smile that melts his heart. He squeezes her hand. She returns the gesture, her smile fading slightly.

"The second thing I want you to do is try and relax. You did everything you could and no one blames you for anything. In fact, the police think what you did was very brave. I know I do."

She sighs as fresh tears come. "I don't feel very brave. Right now, I am more afraid than I have ever been in my life."

436

She tries not to cry, but it is no use. "I pray that they find him soon," she says as she turns to her side and lets the tears come. "I just don't know what I'll do if anything happens to him."

Peter wants so much to take her in his arms and hold her and offer comfort, but he can't. She is his patient and such actions are not permitted. Instead, he presses his free hand against her cheek, caressing it softly. Even this action is crossing the line, but at the moment he doesn't care. "Everything will be okay," he says softly.

Sadie covers his hand with hers, pressing it against her face, trying to draw strength from him. "I hope you're right."

Seventy-four

Adagio

Cisely and Jessica's hands are covered in pastry dough when the phone rings.

"I'll get it," Adagio says, wiping his wet hands on his apron. "Hello."

"Yes, Mr. St. John, this is Officer Ed Payne. I have some news about your son."

Adagio reaches for a chair, suddenly feeling a little weak. Cisely has just finished washing her hands and is about to put a new batch of rolls in the oven when she sees Adagio's face go pale. "What is it?" she asks moving to his side.

He takes her hand. "It's about Phillip."

She sucks in a breath and moves a chair next to his. He puts an arm around her, holding her close. Jessica quickly retrieves the other cordless phone from the living room and hands it to Cisely, then stands with her hands clasp together tightly, waiting to hear about Phillip.

"Go on, officer," Adagio says.

"It looks like Ms. Baker has been holed up in Dublin, Georgia with Phillip. She turned up on this young woman's doorstep and told her Phillip was her grandson, only his name was Michael. Then she fed the woman some sob story about losing everything and having nowhere else to go. The woman believed her and took her in. Her house is a good distance from town and I'm guessing that's why Gladys picked her in the first place."

Adagio closes his eyes as tears fall down his face, and he tightens his arm around Cisely. Their son is alive. They have waited so long to hear those words, to know for sure.

When Cisely is finally able to get hold of her emotions she asks, "Is Phillip all right?"

"Well, truthfully right now we don't know."

"What do you mean, you do not know?" Adagio says, his heart dropping a little. "Does Gladys still have him?"

"Yes, she does, but they are no longer in Dublin. It appears that Miss Roberts, the woman Gladys was staying with, was finally able to get Phillip to talk last night after two months of silence and managed to get him to open up about who he really is and what happened to him. Gladys walked in on them and immediately became suspicious. Last night, Miss Roberts tried to get Phillip out of the house. She was about to take him to the police when Gladys attacked her from behind and knocked her unconscious."

"Good heavens," Cisely says, her voice full of compassion for the woman. "Is she all right?"

"She's in the hospital. She has a concussion and a fair amount of stitches, but she will be fine. She was pretty brave, though. Because Gladys took her car, Miss Roberts had no

440

choice but to try and walk to town. She had barely made it two miles when someone saw her sitting at a bus stop. She couldn't have made it any farther with the shape she was in. She asked the woman to bring her in to the police station and collapsed right after walking in."

Adagio sighs. While he feels terrible about what Sadie had gone through, he is grateful for what she tried to do. "So, now what?" he asks the officer.

"We are keeping a lookout for Miss Roberts' car, and we've begun a search of Dublin and surrounding areas. We're doing everything we can to find your son. We will keep you posted and notify you the minute we find out anything else."

"Officer, is there any way we can contact Miss Roberts?" Cisely asks. "I would like to tell her how much we appreciate her efforts to help Phillip."

"I think that would be a good thing. She is worried sick over him. She's feeling pretty down right now and believes this is all her fault."

"Nothing could be further from the truth," Adagio says.

"I agree, and I'm sure hearing it from you two will make all the difference in the world right now." He gives Cisely Sadie's full name and the hospital and room number she can be reached at. Before hanging up, he again assures them the department will do everything they can to track Gladys down and get Phillip back to them.

Adagio continues to hold Cisely as he fills Jessica in on what happened. Jessica sheds tears of her own, for both Phillip and Sadie. A little while later when their emotions are under control, Adagio and Cisely sit with Ingo, and without going into too much detail, tell him about Phillip. He cries a little, but they do what they can to assure him everything will be okay.

Cisely tells Adagio she feels a need to talk with Sadie. Adagio agrees and sits with her as she dials Sadie's hospital room number. He gets on the other extension.

Seventy-five

The ringing of the phone startles Sadie. She hesitantly picks it up, wondering who would know she is there.

Maybe it's a wrong number.

"Hello."

"Hello, is this Sadie Roberts?"

"Yes," she answers, taken off guard by the silky voice on the other end.

I somehow manage to steady the emotion in my voice. Adagio squeezes my hand in support. "My name is Cisely St. John. I'm Phillip's mother."

When I am answered with silence, I know Sadie is probably struggling with her emotions just as much. "My husband is here as well. We just wanted to tell you how much we appreciate what you tried to do for our son, and how grateful we are that you were there for him." When I am unable to speak anymore. Adagio holds me close and takes over.

"Our children mean the world to us, and we have been in constant agony over Phillip. We are truly grateful you were there to watch out for him."

"I didn't do too good a job. Gladys managed to get away with him anyway. I should have known she was lying about everything."

"Oh, Sadie," I say softly, "how could you have known? Gladys is my aunt and I know her well. She can make anybody believe anything to get her way. She's evil and vindictive and you did what you could. You are not responsible for any of this. It's not your fault. I know in my heart Phillip is okay and will be found soon. I know it as surely as I know God used you to look out for him."

Sadie begins to cry. We listen quietly, shedding more tears of our own. When she is finally quiet, I ask, "Would you tell us about Phillip?"

"I would be happy to." For the next half hour Sadie answers our questions, then she tells us how Phillip had been, starting with the day Gladys brought him to her house.

I cry silently as I listen to Sadie describing how Gladys treated Phillip. And when she tells us about finding Phillip on his knees the previous day praying, Adagio has to move the phone away from his ear as emotion overtakes him. He had been there the day I talked to the children about praying when they were afraid. As he cries silently, I hold and comfort him while continuing to listen to Sadie. After a few minutes, he is able to pull himself together.

When Sadie has told us everything she can, I begin asking her questions about herself and her life. She tells us about her

444

mother dying of cancer and her father being shot years ago while robbing a liquor store.

Sadie is about to say more but stops as sudden realization dawns on her.

"I can't believe it," she says softly.

"You can't believe what?" Cisely asks.

"You said that Gladys is your aunt?"

"Yes, I did, though we've never been even remotely close. Her hatred of me is the reason she took Phillip in the first place. She wanted to get back at me for reasons that don't make sense to anyone but her. She wanted to hurt me in the worse way, and she did. Why do you ask?"

"Well, you're not going to believe this. I'm having a hard time believing it myself." Sadie laughs, then figures she had better explain.

"I'm sorry, but this is pretty amazing. You see, Gladys' husband had an affair a little over nineteen years ago."

"I'm not surprised," Cisely said. "But how do you know?"

Sadie smiles sadly. "I know because it was with my mother. I'm the product of that affair."

When I look at Adagio, I'm not surprised to see him wearing one of his, '*God moves in mysterious ways*' smiles. "Well, I guess that means we are cousins in a way." My mind is reeling.

"And that means I was looking out for a member of my family and didn't know it." There is fresh emotion in Sadie's voice.

After a moment of contemplative silence between us, a whole new conversation begins. We talk about our family ties, each of us asking the other questions. I tell her about her half-sister, Velma, and Sadie eagerly looks forward to meeting her.

Though there is a ten-year difference between us, it seems Sadie and I have a great deal in common, and I want to meet her more than I can say.

Adagio breaks in. "Ladies, excuse me for interrupting, but I was just wondering how long Sadie had to stay in the hospital."

"My doctor said I could be released in the morning."

He smiles at me and I grin in return, knowing exactly what he is thinking and loving him for it. "Sadie, I think my husband just had another of his many genius moments." He makes a face and I laugh.

"Sadie," he continues, "I know you are recuperating, but how would you feel about coming and spending Thanksgiving with us?" I squeeze his hand, grateful that he'd thought of it.

"I . . . I don't know what to say. To actually have family to spend the holidays with would be a dream come true for me. And being with you would also help me feel closer to Phillip somehow. I would love to spend Thanksgiving with you. But I don't know if I can get arrangements made in time."

"Just let us worry about that," Adagio says. "We will take care of everything. And we will call you back as soon as everything is arranged."

"I can't believe how kind you are being to me." Sadie's voice cracks. "Thank you."

I wipe a tear away. "There's no need to thank us. You are family and we are excited to have you come."

"I'm excited, too."

After talking a few more minutes, I ask Sadie if there is anything else that we can do for her. She tells us no and thanks us again for inviting her to come up.

After hanging up, Adagio quickly makes the arrangements while I fill Jessica in on everything. I count Sadie as another blessing that has come to us through this trial.

J. Adams

Seventy-six

Charleston, South Carolina

Tom watches Gladys as she downs the last of the vodka, amazed that one woman can put away so much liquor. Then again, that is how she earned the nickname 'Glad Gladys.' She can down a fifth of booze within minutes, and if there is more to be had, the grin never leaves her face.

He disappears for a moment and returns from the back room with another bottle, and just like clockwork, the woman's face breaks into a wide grin.

"You're right on the ball, Tom," she says, immediately opening the bottle.

"I aim to please." He reaches across the table and pulls an old flannel shirt from the back of one of the chairs. "I gotta go help a man across the way fix a wire fence, so you're on your own for a little while." He looks at her and grins. "I gotta earn a little money to keep us swimming in drink."

Gladys raises her glass. "I'll drink to that." Then they both laugh.

Tom heads back to the bedroom to get his coat, casually glancing back at Gladys. Her eyes are closed, but her hand is still cradling the glass.

That's a good sign.

Entering the bedroom, he turns the volume on the television up slightly. Then he quickly squats down in front of Phillip, catching the little boy off guard. He keeps his voice low as he speaks.

"I want you to listen to me. Now I know you ain't got no reason to trust me, but you have to do exactly as I say. I'm going out the front door in just a minute. You see that door right there?" he asks him, pointing to the side door in the hall.

Phillip nods, warily.

"I'm gonna leave it open a little. While I'm going out the front, I want you to slip out that door. My truck is parked out back. Run to it, understand me?"

Phillip only hesitates a moment before nodding. Tom has been nice to him so far, despite his rough appearance, and Phillip sees no reason not to trust him, especially if it means getting away from Gladys.

Tom grabs his coat and motions for Phillip to do exactly as he'd told him. He walks into the hallway and opens the side door slightly before heading to the front door.

"I'll be back in a couple of hours," he calls to Gladys. "I guess I don't have to tell you to make yourself at home."

Gladys smiles, raising the glass to her discolored lips. "That's already been done."

That's what I'm counting on. He glances at Phillip as the boy quietly slips out the side door unnoticed. Tom casually opens the front door and leaves. When he reaches his truck, Phillip is already there, hiding on the outside of the driver's side. Tom opens the door.

"Get in," he whispers, "and stay down until I tell you it's safe."

Phillip immediately obeys. And it isn't until they have pulled onto the paved road and he is able to sit up on the seat that he asks, "Where are we going?"

Tom glances over at him and gives him a half smile, ruffling his hair. "We're gonna get you home."

Heaving a contented sigh, Sadie mentally goes over her conversation with Cisely and Adagio. Her mind is still reeling over the fact that she and Cisely are related. Even though it is not a total blood relation, they are still family, and Phillip is her cousin. This only intensifies her love for the little boy. Her thoughts go to him again and she continues to pray for his safety. It is about all she can do.

Peter enters and Sadie smiles, her heart lightening even more. When he approaches and again takes her hand in his, she ponders the emotions stirring inside her.

How can this be happening to me?

This is something she thought only happened in movies, and she briefly wonders if it could be a Florence Nightingale effect, or in this case, a 'Peter Nightingale' effect. How can she actually be falling for her doctor? If she didn't know any better, she would swear this is a sign that she needs to get out more. But then, what is Peter's excuse? She is sure he sees female patients every day, yet for some reason he seems to connect with her. The thought makes her feel warm inside. She continues to smile, remembering his earlier visit.

When Peter had come back earlier in the afternoon to visit Sadie, he told her more about himself and his life, and now it is as if she has known him for years instead of just a day. She had been relieved beyond words that he wasn't attached to anyone. Peter told her he is thirty-three years old and has been a doctor for five years. After his father died, Peter convinced his mother to move in with him so she wouldn't be alone. His parents had worked hard to help put him through medical school and he will always be grateful to them for their sacrifices. He has two sisters. One is an attorney, the other a model, and it isn't hard for Sadie to imagine the good looks running in the family. She can't help staring at him every time he is near.

His straight blond hair is neatly cut and his chiseled face is adorably-handsome. And every time his blue eyes looked into hers, she has to fight to calm her racing heart.

"Are you okay?" Peter asks.

Sadie pulls her thoughts back to the present. Smiling again, she squeezes his hand. "I'm actually doing okay now."

Peter notices a sparkle in her brown eyes that was not there before, and he silently hopes he has something to do with it. He marvels at the raw emotion she brings out in him. Smiling inwardly, he remembers their conversation earlier and the warmth that grew in his heart as they got to know each other more. He had learned more about her in that small amount of time than he has about most of the friends he's known for years.

Sadie told him about her life, her dreams and the aspirations she once had of being a youth counselor. But with everything that has happened in her life recently, she now thinks she is the last person that should be counseling teens. Peter assured her nothing is further from the truth. He can see her doing great things with her life.

When Sadie continues to smile, Peter asks, "Did something happen?"

"Yes, actually. Something truly amazing." Sadie tells him all about the phone call from Cisely and Adagio. When she is done, he shakes his head in wonder.

"That really is amazing! To think something so tragic could produce such wonderful blessings."

"I know. I would never have imagined such a thing. And that they actually want me to spend Thanksgiving with them just leaves me in awe."

"I'm very happy for you, Sadie. You deserve all the happiness in the world."

Noticing the subtle sadness in Peter's eyes, Sadie lifts her hand to his face. "Peter, what is it?"

Peter closes his eyes at the gentle touch of her hand. Placing his hand over hers, he holds it against his face. This too, is inappropriate, but his heart is already too far across that line to care anymore. "Please tell me I can still see you when you come back."

Sadie is touched by the emotion in his eyes. "I would like that very much." *More than you know.*

He sighs, relieved. He continues to stare into her eyes, his yearning to kiss her growing steadily with each passing second. He caresses her smooth skin, brushing back the short hair peeking from under the bandage on the sides of her head. He remembers how her hair looked before the bandages. Sadie's hair is styled in a chic layered cut that flips at the ends, and it is easy to see she is a woman who cares about her appearance. Peter longs for the day that he can run his fingers through the soft tresses.

A knock at the door startles them both. Peter reluctantly moves away from Sadie, the disappointment in her eyes matching his. They both turn as Helen enters the room and heave sighs of relief.

"Hi, Sadie. I just came by to make sure my son was minding his manners."

"Actually, Mom, I wasn't." He takes Sadie's hand again.

"I suspected as much." She smiles at Sadie. "But I must admit, in this instance it's okay. To me, anyway."

"It's okay with me, too," Sadie says, gazing at Peter.

"So, I hear you're getting out of this place tomorrow."

"This is true."

"Do you have any plans for Thanksgiving?"

"As a matter of fact, I do. I was invited to spend Thanksgiving in North Carolina." Sadie then repeats what she told Peter, amazement filling her voice all over again.

"Well, that's definitely one of the most incredible stories I've ever heard."

"It truly is. I'm looking forward to getting to know Cisely and Adagio, and my half-sister."

"I'm really happy for you," Helen says. "I had hoped to invite you to spend Thanksgiving with us, but spending it with family is more important, especially in this instance."

"I would have liked that," Sadie says, meeting Peter's gaze. She is excited for the opportunity to get to know her family, but she is also a little saddened that she will not be able to see Peter for a few days, and she again wonders how this all happened and what she has done to be so lucky.

Peter's eyes convey his feelings to her as well. He doesn't want to be away from her either. But his gaze also tells her there will be plenty of opportunities to come for them to see each other. He squeezes her hand.

"Well, my other patients are probably wondering where I am. I guess I had better go and make my rounds. That's what I get paid for."

Helen grins. "I'm glad you haven't forgotten that, son. And I guess I had better go and make sure things are getting done in housekeeping."

Sadie smiles at mother and son. "Thank you again, Helen, for picking me up last night. Thank you for everything."

"You're very welcome. And thank you for giving my son a reason to smile."

Sadie's gaze returns to Peter as he raises her hand to his lips, kissing it softly. "The feeling is definitely mutual."

Seventy-seven

Charleston, South Carolina

Gladys fights to keep her droopy eyes open as she sloppily pours another glass of liquor. The clear liquid splashes over the sides, leaving a puddle around the bottom of the glass. Not wanting to waste a drop, she presses her mouth to the table and slurps up the excess.

She had successfully found another place to hide, and for the moment she is content. The booze that comes with the place makes it even more appealing.

As usual, Gladys' thoughts turn to Cisely. She is not finished making her niece pay, and the longer she is able to keep Phillip away, the longer Cisely will suffer. However, it is becoming harder to keep Phillip because of lack of money, and Gladys now despises the boy even more because of it. Having had to leave so quickly, she had been unable to get the few pairs of clothing and underthings she'd conned Sadie into purchasing for him.

Smiling, Gladys hazily remembers how she had told Sadie her daughter dumped Phillip on her with no extra clothing. She recounts with pleasure how bad Sadie felt and how she had immediately gone out and bought him a few things. Gladys despises her dead husband's illegitimate child almost as much as she does Cisely, and she was glad to hit her last night. Sadie was just another person to use and abuse. Gladys thought the con game would go on forever since Phillip had never spoken to make Sadie believe anything other than what she'd been told.

But it hadn't. And this angers her.

Phillip *had* started speaking. Now everything has changed.

"Hey, boy!" Gladys yells, her speech slurred. "Get in here!" She intends to punish him for what he put her through. She had never hit him before, but that is about to change. He will pay just as Cisely is paying now, only his pain is about to get physical.

When Phillip doesn't appear, she yells again. "Boy, you better get your behind in here!" After a moment, she hefts her large body up and staggers to the back of the trailer. Looking around the cluttered room, she curses loudly.

Now I know why Tom was so generous with his liquor.

Swearing again, she futilely tries to clear her head enough to think. Wobbling back down the hall, she struggles to put on her coat, then slowly moves to the front door. Staggering down the rickety stairs, she grabs the railing, somehow managing to keep herself from falling. Just as she makes it to the car, three police cars appear in a cloud of dust and surround her. Gladys squints her eyes against the sunlight as two of the officers get out and slowly approach, their hands on their weapons.

"I guess this is it, then," she says as one officer handcuffs her while the other reads her rights. "Could one of you boys go in and get my bottle for me?" she asks with a grin.

The officer shakes his head at her lack of remorse. "I'm afraid not. By the look and smell of you, I'd say you've had too much of the bottle already."

Gladys laughs. "I can never have too much. Besides, you boys look like you could use a good drink."

"Let's go, Ms. Baker."

She is so intoxicated, it takes both the officer and his partner to get her situated in the car, and they have to hold their breath while doing it. The other officers shake their heads as Gladys leans back in the seat and immediately passes out.

J. Adams

Seventy-eight

"Happy Thanksgiving, *amore*." Adagio places the breakfast tray over my lap.

"Thank you, my love."

"You're welcome."

I smile at my husband, grateful for his thoughtfulness. It seems the morning sickness is twice as bad with this pregnancy and I am having to force down more than just a croissant and juice to feel well enough to get up. I am also becoming even more exhausted during the day than normal. Adagio is always there, taking extra care of me, making sure I have everything I need. I cannot ask for a more loving or attentive husband.

I take a sip of the juice and touch his face. "Thank you for loving me so much, and for taking such good care of me."

He smiles tenderly. "I was born to love you, Cisely," he says with strength.

"There you go again, being a poet."

"You always bring it out in me."

461

"And you make me so happy."

"The feeling is mutual, angel."

He kisses my brow and leaves me to eat while he gets breakfast ready for Ingo.

Eating as much as I can, I am finally able to get up and shower. After getting dressed, I head to the kitchen to get started on dinner preparations. Adagio and Jessica are a big help and it isn't long before we have everything done.

"What time should we leave to pick up Sadie?" I ask, practically dropping into a chair from exhaustion. I can't believe how low my energy level is this morning.

Adagio looks at me, his brow furrowing. "Jessica and I will leave in a few minutes. However, you, my love, will stay here and rest. We will take Ingo with us."

I want to argue that I am fine to go, but I have to admit I'm not. "I guess I really could use a short nap," I say, getting back up. "But promise me you will wake me as soon as you get back."

"I promise, *amore*." Adagio scoops me up and carries me to the bedroom, placing me gently on the bed. As he leans over me, I hold his face in my hands.

"I love you, Adagio."

"And I love you." He kisses me tenderly. "I will be back soon."

I smile, then turn to my side, immediately falling asleep.

Seventy-nine

Sadie checks her reflection in the compact mirror as the plane slows on the runway. Peter had agreed to her request and removed the bandage around her head that morning with strict instructions not to let her head get wet. With a little work, she was able to maneuver the hair on the back of her head since it is slightly longer than the sides, and covered her stitches somewhat. She is grateful for a capable hairdresser who always keeps her short and trendy style looking just right.

Filled with nervous excitement, Sadie exits the plane, then enters the terminal and heads to the baggage claim area. She lets her eyes quickly scan the crowd when she sees an attractive man holding a sign with her name printed in large letters. With him is an older woman and a little boy. She approaches them.

"I'm Sadie."

Adagio smiles, taking her hand. "I am Adagio St. John, and it is truly an honor to meet you and have you as our guest for the holidays."

463

Sadie smiles tearfully. Looking at Adagio is like seeing Phillip in the future, the little boy looks so much like his father. "Truthfully, I'm the one who is honored, and it is a pleasure to meet you."

"My wife is sorry she could not come. She is pregnant and has been sick, but she is waiting at home and looking forward to seeing you."

"I am looking forward to meeting her as well."

After Adagio introduces Sadie to Jessica and Ingo, they retrieve Sadie's luggage and are soon on their way.

When they reach home, Jessica and Ingo visit with Sadie while Adagio puts her suitcase in the den. They will be using it as a second guest room since the small sofa folds out into a bed. He heads to their bedroom to awaken Cisely.

"*Amore,*" Adagio whispers, pressing a kiss to the back of my hand. "Sadie is here."

Smiling sleepily, I sit up. "Thank you, my love. Just give me a minute and I'll be right out."

"Are you feeling a little better?" he asks as I head to the bathroom. "Can I get you anything?"

"No, I think I'm okay."

When I come back out, Adagio is still waiting for me, his eyes expressing a mixture of love and worry. "Is something wrong?" I ask.

He smiles, pressing a hand to my cheek. "I am just a little worried about you. I really think we need to get a checkup scheduled."

I silently agree. Normally I would already have one scheduled back home in Italy. I am very fond of my midwife in Venice and we have become good friends through the years. I dread having to find one in Asheville because it makes our situation somehow seem a little more permanent, but I do know how important it is to get a healthy start for myself and the baby.

"I suppose I have been putting it off," I admit.

"I know, baby," he says softly.

"But I'll start calling around in the morning and get an appointment scheduled, all right?"

"Okay." He kisses me. "I just want to make sure you are all right." His eyes hold mine and I see the love reflected in them. "I couldn't bear it if anything ever happened to you."

Wrapping my arms around his waist, I pull him closer. "Everything will be all right. I promise I'll take care of myself, and I will find a midwife right away. Okay?"

"All right." He rests his forehead against mine a moment. "Well, are you ready?"

"Yes. Let's go and meet my cousin."

J. Adams

Eighty

"It's so good to finally meet you!" Cisely says, hugging Sadie. "You and Velma look a lot alike, and you're just as beautiful."

Sadie accepts her warm embrace, then draws back, taking in her features. Cisely is without a doubt the most beautiful woman she has ever seen, and her kindness again leaves Sadie in awe. "Thank you. It's good to finally meet you, too." Emotion rises in her voice. "I can't tell you how happy it makes me to have family to spend the holidays with."

Cisely hugs her again. "We're very glad you're here. And we're so glad you were there for Phillip." She swallows against rising emotion, squeezing Sadie's hand. "You are more of a blessing than you could possibly know."

"Thank you," Sadie says softly, not trusting herself to speak anymore.

The family spends a little time getting to know each other more. Sadie loves hearing about Cisely and Adagio's life in Italy, and after Jessica shares the history of her relationship with Cisely, she is even more amazed. She can't believe they now consider her a part of their family. It is a dream come true. The only thing that will make her happiness complete is for Phillip to be found and brought back to his family.

To our family, Sadie affirms.

After visiting for a while, Cisely, Adagio and Jessica head to the dining room and set the table for dinner while Sadie keeps Ingo company. She cannot get over how warm and accepting they are to her, and the love she'd instantly felt for them is growing with each passing minute. Her offer to help in the kitchen is flatly refused and Cisely insists that she rest since she is still recuperating from the terrible ordeal with Gladys.

When the table is set and the food is placed out, Sadie and Ingo join us in the dining room and we all take our places around the table. I smile at Adagio and he takes my hand.

As Adagio blesses the food, he gives thanks for the blessings we have received through this long ordeal, including having my family in our lives. His voice cracks with emotion as he prays for Phillip's well-being and expresses the hope that he will be found. He asks God to help our son know how much we love him, and he also gives thanks for the new baby that will soon join our family and prays all will be well.

Ending the blessing, Adagio looks up to find us all drying our eyes. He leans over and kisses my cheek.

"I love you, angel," he whispers.

"I love you, too."

Dishes of food are passed around the table while Adagio carves the turkey. I pour lemonade for Ingo and help him fill his plate, kissing his brow. Though I miss Phillip terribly, I am grateful for this beautiful little boy, and I do my best to show him how much he is loved.

As Sadie watches the scene before her, she can't help thinking of a Thanksgiving painting she'd seen hanging in an art store earlier in the year. It was a picture of a family sitting around a large table just as they are. The father stood at the head of the table carving a turkey and smiling lovingly, just as Adagio is doing. Every time she saw the picture, she thought of it as an elusive dream. She didn't think anyone really lived a life like that. She did not believe there was really such a thing as a happy family. How wrong she had been. Because she is sitting with such a family. And despite all they have gone through and are still going through, their very countenances express a peace she had never seen, and being here with them brings her that same peace. She had never felt anything like it.

Jessica watches Sadie and smiles, almost reading her thoughts. She knows the look on the young woman's face well, because it is the same look Cisely wore when she came to stay at her home in Utah. Jessica places her hand on Sadie's arm. "We're so glad you're here."

Sadie smiles back. "Thank you. So am I."

The meal is relaxing and conversation flows freely. Gazing around the table, I smile, trying to hide the sadness that comes when I think of Phillip's absence, but I am grateful for every person present.

Thinking back on how I closed my heart to my husband and everyone around me, I am still a little saddened to think of all the time I spent buried in my own grief instead of sharing my feelings with Adagio and offering him comfort. But he is a patient man and I am grateful. There is no way I could have continued to make it through all this without Adagio's love and comfort.

The object of my thoughts takes my hand in his. He can see the subtle sadness behind my smile and I know he understands. We are sharing the holidays with family, the people we love, but our family is not complete, not without Phillip. Only when he is finally with us will we be whole again. Adagio continues to gaze at me, sending me silent words of comfort.

And I do feel comforted. I am always amazed at how connected he is to my feelings, and I consciously will the sadness from my eyes, wanting to convey to him that I am okay.

The ringing of the doorbell surprises us all.

"I will get it, *amore.*"

"All right." I wonder who could be stopping by on Thanksgiving Day. In Italy, we are usually prepared for unexpected company during the holidays, and people occasionally stop by. But this is unexpected.

Eighty-one

Adagio

When Adagio reaches the door, he opens it and freezes. From somewhere deep inside, a sob erupts as he drops to his knees and pulls Phillip into his arms. Phillip wraps his arms around his father's neck and cries.

"Oh, thank you, God!" Adagio cries, lifting him. "Thank you!" He looks at Officer Payne, who also has tears trailing down his face and grips his hand firmly. Finally finding his voice, he says, "Please, come in."

Ed follows Adagio in and closes the door. Phillip's arms are still tightly wrapped around his father's neck and Adagio relishes the feel of them. "We have missed you so much," he says, looking into his son's eyes.

"I missed you, too, Papa. And I missed Mama." Phillip hears the familiar beloved voices coming from the dining room. "Where's Mama, Papa? I want Mama."

"I will take you to Mama now. She will be so happy to see you. We've both missed you so much."

"I love you, Papa."

"I love you, too, son." Adagio kisses Phillip's cheek as tears streak his own face. "I love you so much."

Adagio silently holds Phillip in his arms as he stands in the doorway of the dining room, watching Cisely wipe Ingo's face. Her back turned to them. When the room suddenly goes quiet, she looks up.

"Phillip!" Ingo cries.

I quickly turn and gasp, my vision blurring at the sight of my little boy. "My baby!" My voice is barely a whisper. "My baby!" My knees weakening, I reach for a chair and quickly sit down.

Adagio puts Phillip down and he runs to me, crushing himself against me. As soon as he wraps his small arms around my neck, I wrap him in mine and cry without restraint. Adagio kneels beside me, enfolding us both in his arms. Ingo runs to us and Adagio pulls him into the circle, holding us all. I can hear Jessica and Sadie crying and Ed sniffling.

Phillip finally draws back and smiles, placing his hands on my face in the way that is so endearing to me. "I remembered to pray, Mama, and God was listening, just like you said."

I repeatedly caress his face and hair. "I'm so proud of you. You're such a good boy, so brave, and we've missed you so much." I can't say anymore, overcome by a fresh bout of tears.

"I missed you, Phillip," Ingo said, his face wet with tears.

Phillip moves from my embrace long enough to hug Ingo. "I missed you, too." Then he returns to my lap and Adagio softly caresses his back.

Jessica moves to my side and kneels. "I'm so glad to see you, Phillip," she says, smiling through the tears.

Phillip reaches over and hugs her. Then he glances over my shoulder. "Sadie!" he cries, jumping down from my lap, running to her.

Sadie drops to her knees and scoops him up in her arms. "I worried about you so much," she says with a sob. "I'm so glad you're okay."

"I'm glad you're okay, too. It scared me when she hurt you." His lips tremble.

"I know," she soothes. "I know. But I am fine, and now you're back with your mama and papa. Everything is going to be okay."

Phillip nods, hugging her again and immediately returns to me. I hold him close, silently sending up prayers of gratitude.

When all emotions are under control, Ed finally gives us the details of Phillip's whereabouts and how they came to find him. He tells us Gladys took Phillip to Charleston, South Carolina to the home of one of her old friends. Little did Gladys know that the friend knew about the kidnapping from the newspapers. He'd also seen posters of Phillip and recognized him the moment he saw him. He said if there was one thing he couldn't stand it was the thought of a child being taken from their family and being abused. He kept Gladys ignorant of his knowledge long enough to sneak Phillip out and get him to the police. They immediately went out and captured Gladys, which wasn't too hard because she was so intoxicated when they found her, she wouldn't have made it very far.

Phillip is still clinging to me as Ed concludes the details. There are no words to describe how grateful we are that it is all over and Phillip is home and safe. We thank Officer Payne profusely for all he has done and ask him to convey our gratitude to the police department.

Phillip sits between Adagio and me as we finish our meal. Watching the ravenous way that he eats moves us both to tears. It breaks my heart to think of him going hungry. After he has finished, he takes a bath, smiling as he exits the bathroom wearing his own familiar clothes.

We gather around the table again and have dessert. At one point I notice Phillip looking from me to Adagio with quiet thoughtfulness. Then his expression changes to one I can't discern.

"What is it, honey?" I ask, caressing his hair.

He tearfully looks up at me. "Will she come back to get me again?"

My eyes meet Adagio's and his sad expression mirrors my own. We mourn the innocence our son has lost. Before this happened, he'd been so carefree and full of life. I hope he will one day be that way again.

"No, baby," I finally answer. "Gladys will never take you from us again. She is in a place where she can never hurt anyone else."

Adagio presses a hand to Phillip's cheek. "We promise you son, that we will always keep you safe."

We know it will take time for Phillip to adjust, but he is back with us now, and I can think of no greater blessing to have received this day.

J. Adams

Eighty-two

After the boys are in bed asleep, we stand in the doorway of their room and gaze at our youngest son. We are grateful beyond words to have him back and I am constantly sending up prayers of thanks for his return. I also thank God for helping us endure this whole ordeal. Never again will I hear of another child being kidnapped without feeling a deep sorrow for that child and his family.

Striving to be strong has taken more out of me than I realized. As I continue to watch Phillip sleep, a strong wave of emotion comes over me. I turn to Adagio as tears splash down my cheeks.

"It's all right, *amore*," he whispers, taking my shaking shoulders in his hands.

I manage to hold everything inside just long enough to make it to our bedroom. Then the flood of emotional grief that has filled me for so long comes forth. Adagio pulls me into his arms, sinking to the floor with me as I weep.

"Everything is all right," he whispers against my ear. "It's okay."

Adagio

Adagio understands her tears and knows her feelings well because his are the same. They are grateful the ordeal is over, and they can now get on with their lives. But the pain will take time to fade. He is sure this time of letting go of their emotions is a good start. Leaning back against the bed, he cradles Cisely against his chest until her sob subside.

"I'm sorry," she finally says, her raspy, silky voice softly filling the silence. "Must be hormones."

Adagio presses a kiss to her brow. "Then what is my excuse? I am not pregnant and I don't get PMS often."

She chuckles and takes in his soaked shirt. "It seems like I'm always wetting your shirts these days."

"And like I told you years ago when Ingo died, I have many and you can cry on them all. I just want to be here for you."

"And you always have been. You helped me through one of the hardest times of my life."

"Even then, there was no other place I wanted to be than with you."

"I don't know what I would have done without you."

Smiling, he presses his forehead to hers. "You would never have had the chance to find out." He looks into her eyes. "I was supposed to be there for you, Cisely."

"I know," she says, touching his face. "Through all these years you have never let me down." She brushes a hand back through his hair.

"And I never will."

Snuggling closer, she buries her face in the curve of his neck, sighing deeply. "How can I be so happy and still feel so much pain? How can I feel so much love and gratitude and still have this ache?"

"I don't know, *amore*. I also wonder about those things because I feel the same."

After a few moments of silent contemplation, Cisely says, "I guess we just have to believe that the joy we feel now will slowly replace the rest of the hurt because it is stronger than the pain. I know we will never forget the pain, nor would I want to because it has been spiritually refining. And that refinement will continue to add to the joy, making it that much greater later on. A little while ago I couldn't see that. But I do now."

"And because of your strength, I now see that too." Tears fill his eyes. "I'm so grateful for you."

"And I'm grateful for you." She touches her fingers to his lips before pulling his head down.

As Adagio becomes lost in her kiss, he feels his life can be no more perfect. His family is whole again, and the woman he loves with all his heart and soul again has his child growing inside her. Soon they will go back home to Italy, and he promises himself that he will always treasure each and every second of his life with his family, because that is how often the blessings come, each and every second.

J. Adams

Eighty-three

Treviso, Italy

Holding hands, Adagio and I gaze at one another as Sadie and Peter repeat their vows and are pronounced husband and wife. I have always considered the veranda the most romantic spot at our home, and it is the perfect place for my cousin's intimate ceremony.

Before we moved back to Italy, Sadie and I kept in touch with each other through phone calls every few days. Sadie told me about Peter Grant and their growing feelings for each other. Before long the two fell in love and became engaged. We invited them over for dinner, and as soon as we met Peter, we could tell he was a great guy. It was easy to see how much the two loved each other.

Velma was overjoyed to get to know her sister. Pete and Dona were also happy to meet the niece they never knew existed, and they welcome her to the family.

The day before we were to move, Sadie called me with some exciting news that would bring me even more joy. Peter had received a phone call from an old colleague whose wife was from Venice. They moved back to Venice last year to be near her family and he opened a medical practice a few miles outside of the city. He offered Peter a partnership, and after pondering long and hard about it, Peter and Sadie felt he should accept the offer. Peter's mother, Helen, would be moving with them as well. She and Sadie had become very close.

Sadie and I were ecstatic about the move, and Adagio and Peter were equally happy because they knew how close we had become. I insisted that they have the wedding at our home and the couple happily accepted. Peter told us about the home that came with the practice. They would only live thirty minutes away from us. And the thought of actually having family close brought me a joy I could not describe.

Velma was a little saddened to see Sadie move so far away after just developing a relationship with her, but she and Ted promised to visit, which meant we would get to see them again. Adagio surprised them with tickets to come to the wedding.

Adagio kisses my hand just as Sadie and Peter share their first kiss as husband and wife. The love radiating from them is so tangible you can feel it, and we know the feeling well. Finding the person who makes you whole is everything.

Adagio

Cisely turns to Adagio and smiles, and he can see a peaceful glow radiating about her. She is so beautiful and he never tires of looking at her. Almost seven months along now in her pregnancy, she can't get around as well as she could with the other pregnancies because she is larger than usual. This is due to the fact that she is carrying twins.

They could not believe it when her midwife told them. Cisely told Adagio that when she was younger, her father mentioned there were several sets of twins in his family, but she'd never had reason to think about it and had actually forgotten. Adagio never imagined they could be so blessed. It is a dream come true.

J. Adams

Eighty-four

After the festivities are over and everyone has gone, we relax on the veranda.

"It was a wonderful wedding," I say as Adagio takes my hand.

"It was. I can tell they will be very happy together."

"I can too. And it's truly amazing how many miracles we've been able to see this past while."

He smiles. "And to think, some people say miracles don't happen anymore."

"Well, if those people were to spend a little time with our family, they would know different." I ponder a moment on all the wondrous things we've witnessed. Meeting Adagio's quiet gaze, he presses a kiss to my hand.

"I have always believed in miracles," he says. "I have seen too many to doubt them. And now I am married to one of those miracles." He leans over and kisses me, caressing my face softly. As he draws back, I take in his handsome face and flawless masculine features, still convinced that I'm married to the most beautiful and amazing man in the world, and I am the most blessed woman.

I yawn as the day's festivities catch up with me. Adagio stands, holding a hand out to me. "Come, *amore*. Let's get you to bed."

"You always take such good care of me."

"And I always will."

When I get up, he lifts me, cradling me against his chest. "You know, sometimes I think I'm married to Mr. Universe. I feel like I weigh a ton and you lift me without a grunt. You sure you're not hiding a body building title somewhere?"

He chuckles. "Hardly, angel. I just never pass up an opportunity to sweep you off your feet."

"You definitely do that," I agree as he carries me inside and up to our room. He places me on the bed, then he kneels and we pray.

"I will get the children settled for the night." He leaves to take care of the boys.

After changing into a gown, I slip beneath the covers and flip through a magazine, waiting for Adagio to return.

"You are supposed to be sleeping, *cara*," he says, entering the room. He begins to undress. "You need your rest."

"I know. But I wanted to talk to you about something."

"All right." He slides under the covers next to me and props his pillows up. "Now, tell me what is on your mind."

"Well, Phillip came to me a few days ago and asked me a question. His exact words were, "Are you and Papa still mad at Gladys?""

"Really?" Adagio says, surprised. "What did you tell him?"

"I told him no. I said that despite what she did, we had to forgive her. And do you know what he said?"

"No, *amore.*" He touches my face. "Tell me."

"He said he was glad we weren't upset with her anymore because . . . because there is still good in her, and she only acted the way she did because . . . she had *forgotten* how to be good."

Adagio rubs his eyes. "I cannot believe it," he says, reverently.

"Don't you see, love. To have him come through such a terrible ordeal feeling this way—to have a child that loves so unconditionally is more than I could have ever hoped for. And just think of the strength he will bring to our family and his own when he's older. What a legacy of love we will have!"

"And to think that strength started with you and your willingness to forgive your father. Despite all the hurt and pain that you endured, you forgave and never looked back." He smiles. "You will always be my inspiration." Lying down, he pulls me into his arms.

"I love you Adagio," I breathe, raising my lips to his.

"I love you, too, angel," he whispers against my mouth. "And thank you for sharing that with me," he adds before deepening the kiss.

"You're welcome." Resting my head against his chest, I snuggle against him and quickly drift off to the feel of his gentle fingers in my hair and his lips against my brow.

J. Adams

Eighty-five

Sitting on the veranda, Adagio and I cuddle our two-month-old babies and enjoy the beautiful sunset, while Ingo and Phillip play happily in the distance.

Phillip is doing well and thriving again. There will still be hidden emotional scars for a while, but he is young and will have a lot of time to heal. Thank goodness for Ingo. He has always been close to his little brother, but the kidnapping ordeal seems to have increased that closeness tenfold. And though they are almost the same height now, Ingo is ever-protective of Phillip and never lets him out of his sight whenever we are on family outings, determined to never lose him again.

I gaze down into the cherubic face of our little girl. After a month of strict bed rest, Isabelle and her brother, Ian, were born healthy and strong with no problems during labor or delivery. In fact, the midwife was amazed at how smoothly everything went, especially having been on bed rest. She said I must have an angel watching over me. I said there were probably many.

Adagio

As Adagio gazes down into little Ian's face, he marvels at the blessing of having these two new precious additions to their family. Life could not be better. Turning his gaze to Cisely, she smiles as if she'd read his thoughts.

"My heart is so full," she says, looking into his eyes. "I didn't think life could be any better, but it does get better with each passing day."

"It takes a valiant heart and a strong spirit to see the good in life after all you have gone through in yours, and you possess both, *amore*."

"If I am strong, it is because I have you as my husband. A lot of my strength comes from you." She reaches for his hand. "You raise me up, Adagio. Every time I feel like I'm falling, you're always there to catch me. Whenever my heart is heavy, you know, and somehow you always seem to lighten it."

"You are all those things for me as well." He leans in, touching his lips to hers.

As I melt under my husband's kiss, I relish the warmth of love that surrounds us, and the wealth of heavenly favor radiating like a Venetian sunset.

I know I am young, but I do know what true love is. My knowledge doesn't come from any experience of my own, but it is the result of the lessons ingrained in my twelve-year-old heart from watching my parents. Their love is real; it is what heaven is made of. I'm grateful that my father has set the example for me to follow.

Phillip St. John's journal

Eighty-six

Salt Lake City
Six years later.

With my husband's arm around me, I kneel on the cool grass and place a large bouquet of red and white carnations next to the tall granite headstone. The morning sky had been cloudy, the weather dreary, but now the sun's rays are bursting forth and the day is starting to warm. Adagio gives my arm a comforting squeeze as I reverently brush my hand across Jessica's name. It has been four years since she passed away, but kneeling in front of her grave now, it feels like it was only yesterday.

I had been devastated when I received the call from a mutual friend and was told that Jessica had a stroke. Adagio immediately made arrangements and our family flew back to be with her. Sadly, our time together was short. Jessica died a week later and I was crushed.

Jessica's family flew in from Australia and helped me with the funeral. I had kept in touch with them through the years and was glad to see them. Since Jessica had informed her family years ago of the contents of her will, everything was settled. Still, nothing could, or will ever compensate for her loss.

We decided to sell Jessica's clothing boutique. Since our home is in Italy, it would have been too hard to try and keep it. Wendy Wang, a friend I'd made while working at the boutique, bought the shop. I was happy with the way things turned out, and I could not think of a better person to buy the business. Wendy worked for Jessica for years and loved her very much. I knew the shop would be in good hands.

In the week that followed, we boxed up most of Jessica's personal belongings and sent them to her family. I kept some things that were very sentimental to me. I also kept the house because I could not bear parting with it. There were so many wonderful memories for me there, I couldn't possibly sell it. And now I am glad I didn't. Every time we come back to the beautiful old home, I feel closer to Jessica, and the memories we shared in the home always warm my heart.

Wiping my tears, I sigh as my thoughts return to the present. "Oh, how I miss you, Jessica! I love you so much. You brought more joy to my life than you could ever know." I smile. "Then again, you probably do know."

Adagio

When Adagio stands, he helps Cisely up and she moves into his arms. Holding her close, he blinks back tears of his own. He still misses Jessica too, and often reflects on all he'd learned from her. He will always love her and be grateful for her mothering ways.

Pressing a gentle hand to Cisely's face, he brushes back a wisp of her auburn hair, continually in awe of her beauty. She is thirty-six now and has not changed at all. Her brown skin is still satiny smooth, and there isn't a line on her face. "Are you all right?" he asks softly.

She looks into his loving eyes and smiles. "I'm fine."

Keeping his arm around her, they walk back to the car. As he opens the door for her, Cisely turns and gazes across the cemetery once more at Jessica's grave.

I love you, Mama. Drying my tears, I get in the car, keeping my gaze on the grave until Adagio is in.

He squeezes my hand. "I love you, *vita mia,*" he says before starting the car.

"And I love you." We lean in, our lips meeting. Drawing back, I press a hand against his face, marveling at how blessed I am. Approaching his forty-sixth birthday, Adagio doesn't look a day over thirty-five, even with the graying at his temples, and I am still convinced there isn't a more handsome man in the world. I smile, brushing my hand back over his wavy hair. He wears it longer now and there isn't a trace of thinning anywhere. I love pressing my hands into its softness.

"Thank you for coming with me today. You're always so good to me."

"That will never change, *amore.*"

When we arrive back at the house, Ian and Isabel come running out to the garage. The two six-year-olds usually stick together like glue and are as close as any twins can be. Both have inherited Adagio's dark, wavy hair, but their honey-colored eyes definitely come from me. Isabelle looks like me while Ian's features are a mixture of Adagio's and mine. We frequently study all our children and tell each other we do good work.

"Hurry, Mama!" Isabelle says, taking my hand. "We have to get ready for Aunt Wendy's party!"

Adagio laughs as Ian echoes his sister's sentiments. He squats down and ruffles his hair. "The party is still two hours away. You don't want to be there before everyone else, do you?"

"We don't mind," Isabelle says, her voice a younger version of mine. "If we get there early, we can eat as much of the good food as we want before everyone else does."

I look at Adagio and we laugh. "So, that's what the game plan is, huh?" The two nod, huge grins spreading across their faces, which makes me laugh even more. "You two are pretty clever."

"I would have to agree with you," Adagio says. "Tell you what. Why don't we go into the house and have a snack and maybe you will be all right until the party, okay?"

"Okay," they both agree, running back into the house.

I shake my head. "Where do they learn these things?"

"I am guessing it was inherited from their brothers, especially Phillip."

"You're probably right," I agree, remembering how excited Phillip was about food at parties when he was their age, and he still is. "Then I guess I will have to accept part of the blame. I've always had a love affair with food. Especially anything you cooked."

"So," he says, drawing me close, "that's why you married me, huh?"

"Well, you have to admit, you do make the best creme brulee in the world."

He grins. "Well, my mother did tell me the best way to a woman's heart is feeding her dessert."

I chuckle and kiss him. "Well, remind me to thank your mother when we see her in the next life."

"I will, *amore.*" I look forward to introducing you to her someday."

"Do you think she will like me?"

He brushes my hair back. "She will love you." Kissing my brow, he holds me close a moment longer before we head into the house.

When we enter the kitchen, Ian and Isabelle are sitting at the table, waiting anxiously for me to heat up some of the leftover pizza from last night.

"*Grazie, Mama,*" they say as I hand them a slice.

"You're welcome."

"Where are your brothers?" Adagio asks, taking a bite of the pizza.

"Ingo is next door playing with Scott, and Phillip is in his room reading."

"I should have known," he says, smiling.

Phillip is the avid reader in our family, and he is rarely found without a book in his hand. Given the choice of hanging out with friends or reading, Phillip chooses the latter most of the time, preferring to stay close to us. For a while we wondered if he was still a little traumatized from the kidnapping ordeal, but it soon became clear that this is just Phillip's personality, and we don't mind at all.

Phillip and I share a special closeness and I love having him around more, but I try not to shelter him too much, and I do what I can to encourage his independence. Our children are growing fast and will be gone one day. All we can do is try to prepare them for the world they will go out into.

Once the children are finished, I put a slice of pizza on a plate and take it up to Phillip. Knocking softly, I stick my head in the room. Phillip looks up and flashes one of his heart melting smiles that is so much like his father's.

"I brought you some pizza."

"*Grazie*, Mama," he says, closing the book. He puts it on the table and takes the plate from me.

I pull the chair from the desk and sit down facing him. "How are you, honey?" I ask, squeezing his knee.

"I'm okay." He takes a bite of the pizza and smiles. "I'm excited about Wendy's party."

"You and everyone else. She's the only person I know who would turn her own birthday party into a going away party for her friends."

"She really is a neat lady." He pauses. "Her daughter doesn't seem too friendly, though."

"I think she's probably going through a tough time right now. I'm sure her parent's divorce was pretty hard on her."

Phillip is thoughtful for a moment, which leads me to believe the conversation is about to turn serious. I know his look of contemplation well. It is one of the many things he inherited from his father.

"Mama, how could Paul leave Wendy for someone else? I mean, why would he do that?"

Despite preparing myself, I am caught off guard by his question. He has a way of doing that. I have often pondered Wendy's situation over the past couple of years and the marital problems she confided in me about, and Adagio and I have always kept Wendy and Paul in our thoughts. When we brought the kids back to visit a year ago and Wendy told us her husband left her for someone else, I was extremely sad on her behalf. I couldn't believe their marriage was over just like that. Paul had immediately filed for a divorce and it was finalized a few months before we arrived this time.

Since then, Wendy and I have spent a lot of time talking. Wendy confided in me about her concern for her daughter. Mali has gone through some changes since the divorce. She is sullen and withdrawn, refusing to talk much with anyone, except for a few rough kids she hangs out with. Wendy is afraid her daughter is heading down the wrong path, and she doesn't know what to do. I am also afraid for her. Mali is a beautiful girl and could do a lot with her life if she will just follow her mother's advice and guidance. But right now, that seems to be the last thing she wants to do.

"Why would he leave her, Mama?" Phillip asks again, drawing my thoughts back to the present.

"I don't know, honey. It's hard for me to understand too. But since I'm not in his shoes or Wendy's, I couldn't even guess. I do know though, that infidelity is wrong, no matter what the problems are in a marriage."

Phillip is quiet for a moment, letting my comment settle. After another moment he asks, "Do you think they still love each other?"

I sigh. I have never known a twelve-year-old so sensitive to matters of the heart. "I don't know about Paul, but from what I know of Wendy's feelings, I think she still loves him. But, honey, sometimes love isn't enough to keep two people together. It should be if it's truly unconditional love, but a lot of times it isn't. And only God knows what is in our hearts. Am I making any sense?"

"I think so." He again silently ponders my words. "Mama, you and Papa love each other unconditionally. I can tell."

I smile, placing my hand over his. "Yes, I would say our love is definitely that. There is nothing we wouldn't do for each other, and nothing could ever come between us." I blink away moisture rising in my eyes. "There isn't another man on this earth like your father, Phillip. He has supported me and been there for me through some of the hardest times of my life. And I have tried to do the same for him." I smile. "He treats me like a queen."

Phillip holds his mother's hand, his expression thoughtful. Having grown up witnessing the love between his parents, he has always watched the way his father treats his mother. To him this is the way it is supposed to be, and he truly does believe nothing will ever come between them. Determination fills his eyes. "I will be like Papa when I grow up. I will love my wife unconditionally and treat her like a queen, too."

500

Smiling tearfully, Cisely presses a hand to his face. "I know you will."

Phillip kisses his mother's cheek, then hugs her. "I love you, Mama."

She returns his embrace with fervor. "I love you, too."

J. Adams

Eighty-seven

Sitting with my hand in Adagio's, I absently finger his wedding band as we watch the guest slowly file through the side gate onto Wendy's large patio. Each family presents the hostess with a birthday gift. She accepts them graciously and places them on a table by the patio door. But through Wendy's smile, I can see the emotional strain hidden behind her beautiful Asian features.

Most of Wendy's friends consider her a strong woman, but at the moment, I am privy what she is feeling, and it is not strength. Only forty years old, she is convinced her life is basically over. As I watch her, I ponder what I know about her life.

Raised in the United States by parents who moved here from Japan when she was just an infant, Wendy had always thought her life a good one. After attending college for two years and receiving a bachelor's degree in fashion and interior design, she moved to Salt Lake City and went to work for Jessica.

When Wendy met Paul, the connection was instant. Having moved from Japan to Salt Lake himself, Wendy thought their meeting each other was destiny. The day they married had been the happiest of her life. She thought they would be together forever.

Sadly, she had been wrong. In an instant, her dreams were gone, and in that same instant, her daughter's world had been shattered. Now Wendy feels her daughter slipping further away from her and she doesn't know what to do about it.

Once she has greeted all the guests, Wendy excuses herself and heads to the kitchen. Deciding that this is the perfect opportunity to talk to her, I squeeze Adagio's hand.

"I'm going to go and see if Wendy needs any help, all right?"

"Sure, *amore*. I think I will go check on the kids as well."

I find Wendy pouring more chips into a bowl. "What can I do to help?"

"Absolutely nothing. This party is for your family, too, remember?"

"I know and you are the sweetest person in the world for doing this, but if the birthday girl has to work during her own party, so can I."

Wendy feigns annoyance. "I should have stipulated that you had to sit and enjoy this party to be able to attend."

"And let you have all the fun of having your hands moisturized in potato chip grease alone? Never."

She snorts, then laughs. "Oh, all right. My little helper seems to have disappeared, anyway."

"How is Mali today?"

"About the same." Wendy washes her hands and leans against the counter and sighs, pushing a hand back through her short ebony hair. "I don't know what to do anymore, Cisely. She is becoming more withdrawn by the day. And what makes it even worse is Paul occasionally makes plans to pick her up and spend time with her, then he doesn't show up. She doesn't believe him anymore, and she doesn't trust him. Truthfully, I can't blame her."

"What does she say when you try to talk with her about her feelings?"

"That's just it. She won't talk to me. She won't say anything. If she would, maybe we could get somewhere. The one thing I do get from her when her father's name is mentioned is anger. It's like she hates him now. Sometimes I feel like she hates me too."

"I'm so sorry," I say, putting an arm around her shoulders. "I wish I could help in some way." I can't begin to imagine what she is going through.

"Thanks. I guess just having you here to listen to me is enough." Closing her eyes, she heaves a frustrated sigh. "I love my daughter, but I almost feel like I need a break from her. Does that make me a terrible mother?"

"No, Wendy. It makes you a normal one. We all need time for ourselves sometimes, and I think you are especially deserving of it, considering what you are facing." I squeeze her shoulder, wishing I could do or say something to help.

While Wendy fills a pitcher with water, I ponder her predicament. There just has to be something I can do. But what? A moment later, inspiration comes.

"I have an idea. It's something I would need to talk over with Adagio, but if you're willing, I really don't think it would be a problem, and I would actually quite enjoy it."

"Okay, you've got me totally curious. Out with it."

"Well, how would you feel about letting Mali come to Italy for a month? It would give you a break and also get her away from the crowd she hangs around. Plus, Mali would definitely have some neat experiences for the rest of the summer and hopefully come back changed for the better."

Wendy swallows hard, her eyes growing misty.

"So, what do you think?"

"I think you are the most wonderful and giving friend I've ever had. If it's okay with Adagio, I think Mali spending a month in Italy is a wonderful idea. She needs to be away from here for a while."

"Well, hopefully she will agree to it."

"She'd be crazy to pass up a chance to go somewhere so exciting. If she doesn't agree to go, then I will."

I chuckle. "Well, no matter how this works out, you're welcome anytime."

Wendy hugs me and wipes her eyes. "Thank you so much. You will never know how much your friendship means to me."

"Your friendship is very important to me too. I want to do anything I can to help. And speaking of helping, that's exactly what I came in here for."

She smiles. "Okay, if you really have to do something, let's get these chips and platters of hot wings out there. The rest can wait."

Once we have the food on the table, I head back to the kitchen to see if there is anything else that I can do. I contemplate looking for Adagio to tell him my idea but decide to wait until later. It will be wonderful to have Mali stay with us, and I have no doubt he will agree.

Adagio

Adagio locates Ian and Isabelle. They are in the family room playing a video game with a few other children. Satisfied that they are doing okay, he goes in search of Ingo and Phillip. He finds Phillip sitting on the front porch with Mali while Ingo plays basketball in the driveway with two other boys his age. After talking with Maria and Phillip for a moment, Adagio heads back into the house. Then he stops. Unable to help it, he stands just inside the screen door and listens to Phillip's conversation with Mali. Normally he would never do such a thing, but it is the conversation that stops him.

"I hate my dad. He doesn't love me or even care, so why should I care about him?"

"I'm sure your father does care," Phillip says, his voice compassionate. "And you can't possibly believe their breakup had anything to do with you."

Mali's eyes are filled with doubt and her heart is closed to any other option. In her mind it *is* all her fault. She is sure her actions caused her father to leave. And now her mother is alone. Mali will never be able to forgive herself for that. She remains quiet for some time, then looks at Phillip intently.

"You are lucky to have parents that love each other so much."

Phillip is thoughtful before speaking again.

"Mali, I really do think that your dad cares . . ." When Mali opens her mouth to interrupt, he puts a hand up to stop her. "But, if he doesn't, then it is his loss. Your mom still loves you and she's still here for you. That's all that matters." Pausing again, he meets her intent stare. "Trust me, it really will be okay." He looks down at his hands a moment before lifting his eyes to hers again. "God also knows what you are going through, and He will never leave you alone, either. Believe me, I know."

As Mali looks into Phillip's eyes, she sees the truth of his words reflected there and wonders what had happened in his life to give him so much faith. "I believe you."

Phillip places his hand over hers, the boyish grin that is so much like his father's lighting his face. "Okay, that's enough serious talk for now. It is time to go and chow down on some serious food."

Mali smiles and nods and Phillip stands, helping her to her feet.

Adagio quickly and quietly moves from the door before they enter, thinking he had never felt more pride in his son than he does at this moment.

Adagio enters the kitchen just as I am breaking up another bag of ice.

"Let me do that for you, *amore*."

"Thank you," I huff, handing him the bag. "It's all yours. This is the third bag and my hands are freezing."

Moving close to me, he says in a low, seductive voice, "I could warm them for you if you'd like." He presses several warm kisses to the back of my neck, producing goosebumps over my entire body.

"Later," I breathe.

"I'll hold you to that," he says with a smile that instantly thaws my frozen hands.

I sigh, taking another bottle of pop from the fridge. "So, did you find the children?"

"Yes, and they are all behaving themselves." He empties the ice into a large pitcher on the counter, then leans back against the counter, folding his arms. "I just witnessed something amazing. Well, I did not actually see it, but I heard it."

"Oh? What was it?" I turn and give him my full attention.

"Well, Phillip and Mali were sitting on the front porch visiting."

"Really?"

"Really. Mali was expressing her feelings about her father. She is very angry with him. And apparently, she blames herself for his absence. She thinks it's her fault that Paul left."

"Oh, that poor girl! Why would she think such a thing?"

"I don't know, *amore*. But I could hear the anger and hurt in her voice. Phillip did his best to comfort her. I was very proud of him. He reminded her that not only does her mother love her, but God loves her as well."

I'm surprised. "Really? Our Phillip?"

"Our Phillip," he says, smiling.

"Do you think it made a difference?"

"I think it did. It definitely did to me. Our son will be a great man one day."

I smile. "He's always been very perceptive to the feelings of others. He takes after you in that and many other ways. He is going to make someone a wonderful husband one day. After all, he is learning from the best."

Adagio grins, kissing my cheek. "Thank you, *cara.*"

"You're welcome."

"What else can I help you with?"

I scan the kitchen counters. "All that's left to take out are the two trays of vegetables."

"I think I can handle those." Adagio heaves an arrogant sigh, flexing his muscles a little.

I chuckle. "I'm sure you can, but let me know if you need help. I wouldn't want you to hurt yourself."

Feigning indignation, he reaches for the larger platter and walks by me, pretending to trip and lose his grip, making my heart jump. He laughs and I swat at him with a dish towel as he heads out the door. I shake my head and laugh. How I love that man!

Later in the evening, I finish the last of the packing. I am actually able to fit all the extra things we are taking back home into our suitcase. It seems no matter where we go, we always manage to take back twice as much stuff as we bring with us. I suppose it always helps to pack light in the first place.

Having that taken care of, I slowly wander through the large house, taking in every detail, letting the memories wash over me. Looking back to the day I received Jessica's initial invitation to visit, I could never have guessed how coming to stay with her would change the course of my life. Thinking on all that has happened since, I can hardly take it in at times.

Sitting on a wooden bench in the hallway, my mind drifts back as it has so many times before, to the dream I had before coming to Utah the first time. I am still amazed at how similar the things that Adagio's mother told him were to the things spoken by our son in my dream. Just as I was told that I would face times of sorrow before receiving blessings beyond measure, Adagio had been told literally the same thing pertaining to his own life by his mother. Looking back over the years, I can see that those things have come to pass several times over. Even still, the trials have been few, and the joys definitely outweigh the sorrows. I would not trade any of the experiences I've had because they each had a part in shaping my life.

My eyes move to a framed picture of Adagio and me. It sits on a small table by the bench. We'd had it taken when we came back for a visit last year. There is also a copy of it in Italy in our bedroom. I lightly run my fingers across the glass, my gaze fixed on my husband's face. I can't help smiling as ponder all we have gone through together and how our marriage came to be. Our love is as constant as the day is long, and I know it will always be, because the love we share is a rare one. It is a gift. Of this, I am certain.

Leaning back, I close my eyes and let my thoughts once again drift back to the morning after our wedding.

I stood looking through the balcony door of our suite, wrapped in a long, thick bathrobe. I was still reeling over the fact that I was Adagio's wife, and the happiness enfolding me was indescribable. As I gazed out at the large buildings scattered all over downtown, I was freshly amazed at the course my life had taken. It was almost as if I had lived multiple lives. The life I lived before coming to Salt Lake had in part consisted of terrible choices, which brought both pain and misery. The life I'd lived since moving there had been full of joy, then grief unlike anything I had ever experienced.

Then Adagio claimed my heart and now a new life had begun. Though I was moving away, I would always love this city, and I am sure Adagio probably loved it just as much. It would forever be a special place for us because it was here that we had both lost someone we loved very much. I lost a husband, he lost a best friend and brother, and subsequently we found an even greater love in each other.

Turning my head to the side, my eyes slipped shut as Adagio pressed a warm kiss to my ear and softly said, "I feel like a new man with you, amore. You have totally changed my life." He sighed, tightening his embrace a little. "Being with you like this feels like home, like this is where I was always meant to be."

Turning in his arms, I looked into his eyes, pressing a hand to his face. "I feel the same." I was thoughtful for a moment. "You know, the first time you held me in your arms and kissed me, it was as if everything made sense, like the pieces of my life suddenly fit. It was an amazing feeling."

Pressing his lips lightly to mine, he whispered, "Our love is amazing. And our life together will be as well." He released a breathy sigh before fully claiming my mouth with his.

As my thoughts return to the present, I am again grateful for my life. I have the love of a good man, and I have my children. I cannot ask for anything more. And I know that no matter what trials come in the future, we will continue to make it through them. We will face them and survive. Of this also, I have no doubt.

"What are you doing, *amore?*" Adagio's loving voice breaks through my pondering.

I look up and smile. He is standing before me barefoot with his hands in his pockets. I silently let my gaze roam over him a moment, admiring the way the jeans and t-shirt fit his lean, muscular form. Other than the graying at his temples and the length of his hair, he has not changed.

"Just remembering," I finally answer.

Sitting next to me on the bench, he draws me into his arms. I hold one of his strong hands in mine and relax against his solid chest. His lips graze my brow. "Good memories I hope."

"Very good memories. This house and city are filled with them."

"It is always nice to come back."

"It is," I agree. Closing my eyes, I snuggle deeper in his embrace. "But it will be good to get back home."

He sighs, resting his head against mine. "I miss home as well."

"Well, everything is packed, except for what we will need in the morning."

"I am guessing the suitcases are probably bursting at the seams."

"Just about. But at least I didn't have to sit on them this time. That's progress, isn't it?"

"That *is* progress," he agrees with a tired chuckle. "I think I will turn in now. Are you coming?"

"I'll be there in a moment, okay?"

"Okay." He kisses me, then stands and stretches.

As I watch him walked away, I am again full of gratitude for his love. We share the same life force and are connected in a way that can never be explained. And I don't know where I would be without him.

Adagio

Standing in front of the open bedroom window, Adagio stares up at the stars in the night sky and waits for Cisely. As always, he has enjoyed their time in Utah, but he really is looking forward to returning home. He reflects on their decision to have Mali come and stay with them for a month and feels sure they made the right choice.

He hates to admit it, but deep down, a part of him is angry at Paul for what he has put his family through. Adagio and Paul have never been as close as Cisely and Wendy are, but they had been friends. Adagio always enjoyed the times he and Cisely spent with Wendy and Paul in the past, and he had felt he knew Paul pretty well. Now, as he contemplates their friendship, he realizes he did not know the man nearly as well as he'd thought. He will never be able to understand how Paul could leave his family. How could he give up a wonderful life with the people who loved him so easily? Nothing is worth that, not even another pretty face, no matter how bad things are at home. True, Adagio has never walked in anyone's shoes but his own, and he was never present in Wendy's home to know what went on in their daily lives, but he does know this: no one, and absolutely nothing will tear his family apart. He won't let it. Cisely and their children are his life. And his wife, the woman who holds his very soul in the palm of her hand, is worth everything.

"*Siete gioia della mia anima, amore.* You are my soul's joy," he whispers into the breeze softly blowing through the window. "My soul's delight."

"And you are mine," Cisely whispers behind him. Adagio slowly turns and she smiles at him, and he is completely warmed by the love in her eyes. "*Ti amo*," she whispers, opening her arms. "*Ti amo*," he breathes, moving into her embrace.

J. Adams

Eighty-eight

Treviso, Italy

"Do you two have everything you need?" I ask, straightening the back of Phillip's collar.

Phillip checks his backpack once more. "I've got the water, sandwiches, and cookies."

"And I have the cups, napkins, and apples," Mali says, closing her bag.

"Then I guess we're ready." Phillip puts his arms through the straps of his backpack.

Following them to the door, I smile and wave as the two leave for their outing. It seems a picnic in the park every few days has become Phillip and Mali's favorite past-time.

Mali has been in Italy for two weeks now and I can already see marked changes in her. She is thriving in her new surroundings, and being away from the crowd she hung around at home has made a definite difference. The young girl's countenance has softened, making her even lovelier. And the smile that now graces her face after being unhappy for so long warms my heart.

I call Wendy regularly to keep her updated on her daughter. The few times Wendy has talked to Mali, she could tell how much her daughter has changed just by listening to her voice. I know Wendy misses Mali, but having her in Italy with our family has been worth the heartache. Mali needed this change. She needed to be away from the problems she'd had to face daily. And she needed to think about something else besides her father.

We hope that Mali being here will somehow help her shed the unnecessary guilt she has carried around since the divorce. She has never said anything, but I can sense her feelings of guilt, I just have no idea why. As I watch her blossoming more and more each day, I hope the young girl will continue on the path of healing. Having faced my own set of trials growing up, I understand how traumatizing life can be for a twelve-year-old, especially one dealing with an unstable home life.

"Where are you, *cuoricino?*" Adagio approaches me from behind and wraps his arms around my waist.

"I was just thinking about Mali. I was also thinking of how blessed our children are to have both their parents. There are so many kids out in the world facing the same trial Mali is."

"It is a sad situation. She seems to be doing a little better now."

"She is," I agree. "I'm so glad she came here. I think it has helped her more than she realizes." Reaching back, I press a hand to his face. "I want our children to always feel secure, to know that regardless of what happens in our lives, nothing will ever tear our family apart." Closing my eyes, I soak in his closeness. "They need to know that."

"They will," he says with a husky sigh, pressing a kiss to my ear. He tightens his embrace gently. "I promise you, angel, they will." He holds me for another moment before drawing back and taking my hand. "Come with me."

"All right." I let him lead me upstairs.

Adagio

When they enter their bedroom, Adagio leads Cisely across the room to face the large, gold-framed family photo hanging over the fireplace in the sitting area. He moves behind her, wrapping his arms around her waist. Pressing his cheek against hers, he says, "Each and every time I look at this picture, I am freshly reminded of my goal, and that goal is forever, *amore.*" He points to the picture. "This is everything to me, Cisely. Everything. Nothing with ever stand between me and my family. Nothing but death will ever separate us, and I hope that will not be until we are old and gray. And even then, I hope the separation will not be very long. I mean, I know realistically, I will probably go before you, being almost ten years older, but the separation would still be hard. It is hard to even think about." He presses his face into her hair, inhaling deeply the floral fragrance of her shampoo. "I need to be with you too much."

Closing my eyes, I absorb my husband's words, my heart taking hold of the promise in them. "I think God knows we wouldn't be able to stand being apart. He knows I would be lost without you."

"And I would be lost without you as well." Tightening his embrace, he presses his lips to my ear and whispers, "You are mine forever, baby. It is what I want more than anything. It always has been and that will never change."

Turning in his arms, I echo his sentiments. He kisses me then, and all other thoughts are abandoned as I am swept away in the security of his arms and the safety of his love.

Phillip and Mali sit underneath an iron gazebo in the park, eating their lunch, watching people come and go. The sky is a brilliant blue and the warm weather is the perfect temperature. A slight breeze fans their faces, rustling the leaves on the trees. They could not have picked a more wonderful day for a picnic.

"I can't believe I've been here for two weeks already," Mali says, brushing her hair back from her face.

"Neither can I. Time is passing pretty quickly." Phillip pauses, smiling. "You are having a good time, aren't you?"

She smiles back. "Oh, yeah. I can't remember ever having so much fun. And I really love visiting Venice and going on the gondola rides."

"So do I."

"I think by the time I go back home I will know lots of Italian."

"I bet you will, too," Phillip agrees, not wanting to think about her going home just yet.

In the two weeks Mali has been in Italy, she and Phillip have grown very close. They share a love for both reading and food, as well as music and dancing. Mali occasionally spends time with the rest of Phillip's siblings and they have become good friends, but she and Phillip share a special bond, a connection that is unexplainable.

Every now and then, Phillip can sense when Mali's thoughts are on her father, and at those times the sadness inevitably returns. He is perceptive to her feelings and within minutes, he usually has her smiling again and thinking about happier things. Mali told Phillip she has never had a friend like him before. And until Mali, Phillip never had anyone he could truly call a friend besides his brothers, his sister, and his parents. For this reason, he hates the thought of her leaving. He will miss her more than he can say.

When the two finish their lunch, they take a walk through the park. After a few minutes, they stop, pull some bread from Phillip's backpack, and feed the pigeons. This is another one of their favorite things to do.

"So, are you excited about going back to school?" Phillip asks, breaking another slice of bread into small pieces.

"Not really."

When Mali says nothing more, he asks, "Why? Do you not like school?"

"I like it okay, I guess. But I would love to have tutors at home like you guys."

"I'll admit I love it too. It is the only thing we have ever known. But what about your teachers?" The sudden darkening of her eyes catches him off guard. "What is it?" he asks, touching her arm.

"Nothing." She shakes her head slightly. "I will have new teachers this year, so everything should be fine."

"What was wrong with the ones last year?"

"Nothing," she says, dropping her eyes to the grass.

Deciding not to press the issue, he changes the subject. "Mama and Papa have decided to throw a barbecue for you this weekend." He smiles when a wide grin lights her face.

"Really?"

"Really."

"Your mom and dad are so cool!"

"They are. I'm pretty lucky." As Mali's head lowers, Phillip lifts her chin with his finger, adding, "So are you. You have a great mom."

"I know. And I feel really bad about the way I treated her before."

"I think she knew you were having a hard time."

"I know. But I still should have been nicer."

Phillip squeezes her hand trying to offer what comfort he can. "You can tell her that when you get home. And tell her you love her. Since you can't change the past, all you can do is start now."

"You're right." She smiles, giving his hand a squeeze. To Mali, Phillip seems so much older than twelve. Sometimes he is like an adult trapped in a young boy's body. And he always has a way of making her feel important, like she really matters. "I will apologize to Mom the next time I talk to her," she finally says.

After spending another few minutes at the park, they pack up and head home, taking their time, keeping lively conversation going. Talking with Phillip is Mali's favorite thing to do. When they are together, everything seems better.

They are about to enter the house when Adagio opens the door and smiles. "Another fun afternoon, I take it," he says as Mali laughs at something Phillip just said.

"It was awesome," Phillip answers. He tells Mali he will see her later and follows Adagio to help him with a project.

Mali heads to the kitchen to wash the empty containers their lunch had been packed in.

"Well, hello there," Cisely says, standing at the stove, stirring the sauce she is preparing for dinner."

"Hi, Aunt Cisely. Thanks again for fixing lunch for us."

"You're very welcome." Covering the pan, Cisely walks over to the sink and puts an arm around Mali's shoulders. "Are you still enjoying yourself?"

"Definitely. I told Phillip I can't remember ever having so much fun. This is the best summer I've ever had."

"Good. We'll have to have you back next year, if you would like to come."

"I would," Mali says eagerly. "It would be great!"

"I think so, too. I'll talk to your mom about it in a couple of months. Maybe we could even get her to come next time."

"I hope so. I think Mom would really like it here." Her expression is suddenly sad.

"What is it?" Cisely asks, squeezing her shoulder.

Mali turns away as guilt over her father leaving fills her heart. It resurfaces whenever she thinks of her mother being home alone. She wishes she could make things the way they once were, that she could take back the things that were said between herself and her father. If she had only kept her mouth shut, her parents would still be together. But there is really nothing she can do now to change any of it.

"Mali," Cisely presses. "Are you okay?"

"I'm fine," she answers, forcing a smile. "Do you think we could go shopping tomorrow? I would like to find something special for Mom."

"I think we could manage that. I never turn down an opportunity to go shopping."

"Neither does my mom," Mali says with a smile that isn't forced.

"We'll make it a girl's day and have lunch out. How does that sound?"

"It sounds like a lot of fun."

"All right. Why don't you go and make a list of some things she might like and I'll let Adagio know our plans."

"Okay." She takes a few steps, then turns back and hugs Cisely. "Thank you, Aunt Cisely."

Smiling, Cisely returns her embrace. "You're welcome."

Mali grins and heads to her room.

Indulging in our evening ritual, Adagio and I sit on the veranda and watch the sunset while I share my plans for tomorrow with him.

"It sounds like you ladies are going to have a good time."

"I hope so. Mali really needs this. I think she's been pretty happy here, but I can still tell when the memories get her down.

I hope she can soon heal enough to deal with her parent's divorce and move on."

"She will, *amore*. She is still young and it will take time, but I think eventually she will be fine."

I smile, squeezing his hand. "I love you."

Adagio gently pulls me from my chair onto his lap. "I love you, too. I love that you care so much about everyone."

I press a hand to his face, caressing his lips. "You always give me more credit than I deserve." Touching my lips to his, I kiss him slowly, relishing the feel of his arms around me. Each kiss we share conveys a thousand words and feelings. Our spirits literally merge in every aspect of our life, and it always amazes us both how well we seem to know each other's thoughts, and how deeply we are connected. That emotional connection grows stronger with each bit of time that passes.

Adagio draws back slowly, looking into my eyes. "I think we are due for some time alone." He gently runs his fingers down through my long ponytail. "How would you feel about getting away for a few days after Mali leaves?"

"It sounds wonderful," I agree. I treasure the time we are able to spend alone together. "As a matter of fact, I had been thinking about how much fun it would be to go back to Tuscany. Could we go there for a few days?"

"We can go anywhere you want. I will make the arrangements tomorrow."

"And I'll ask Anna if the kids can stay with her family. I know Sadie and Peter would be happy to keep them, but I'm afraid it would be too much for her, being so far along in her pregnancy."

"I think you are right. Besides, they probably have their hands full already with little Joshua, even if they won't admit it."

"He really is a ball of energy," I say, thinking of Sadie and Peter's two-year-old son and the miracle he is.

After being married for three years and being unable to conceive, Sadie had begun to give up hope of ever having a baby. When she did finally become pregnant, she and Peter were ecstatic. And now their new little one is due in a couple of months.

When little Joshua was born, Peter's mother Helen was there to help. Sadly, during Sadie's third month of pregnancy with the baby she now carries, Helen passed away after a year-long battle with breast cancer. Peter and Sadie still miss her and occasionally still struggle with her loss, but they are getting better.

I often visit Sadie and do what I can to help when Peter is working. When he is not working, he is always by his wife's side. Since Peter is also Sadie's physician, she is getting the best care possible. As far as Sadie is concerned, there isn't a better doctor than her husband.

"I think I'll give her a call and see how she's doing," I finally say, drawn from my thoughts by Adagio.

"Mmm hmmm," he murmurs, as his mouth thoroughly explores my neck. Sighing, my eyes slowly close as warmth spreads through me. I press my hands into his hair as his kisses sear a burning path up my cheek and his lips finally capture mine. We are lost in one another for some time before he finally draws back slightly and his raspy voice whispers, "You can call her later, *amore*."

I draw him back to me, my desire matching his. "What about the children?"

"They are playing video games. They will never miss us."
He smiles against my mouth, then stands, taking my hand in his
and I follow.

The whole house is asleep, but I am awake. For some
strange reason I can't seem to fall asleep, and the harder I try, the
more anxious I feel. I quietly get out of bed, put on my robe, and
go downstairs.

Entering the kitchen, I walk over to the sink and flip on
the under-cupboard light. I take a small glass from the cabinet to
get a drink of water. Taking a few swallows, I set the glass in the
sink, pausing a moment to straighten a framed floral print
hanging on the wall above the sink. I stand motionless for
another moment, trying to figure out why I am so restless. There
aren't any pressing issues or problems filling my thoughts, and
for the moment, my mind is basically stress and worry-free.
Normally if I can't sleep, these are some of the reasons, but not
tonight.

I move to the patio door and stare out into the night.
Sighing, I walk out onto the patio and down the steps. Standing
on the cool grass, I lift my eyes to the clear sky and gaze at the
stars, marveling at their brightness and beauty. I am continually
amazed by God's handiwork and the many undisputed evidences
of His existence.

Keeping my face raised toward the heavens, I close my
eyes and relish the soft breeze gently lifting my hair. Taking in
the sensation, I imagine Adagio's gentle hands caressing my hair
because it feels so similar. Even in nature I am connected to him.

He is the very air I breathe, the lifeforce that keeps me going. Wrapping my arms around my middle, I try to calm the sudden rush of emotion entering me as thoughts of my husband fill my mind. All at once, various memories of our life together slowly consume my every sense. Warm tears fill my eyes and roll down my face as I relive treasured moments, and I am again awed by the life I have been given.

Staring up at the moon, memories the drive Adagio and I took last week through the Dolomite Mountains fill my mind. We stopped in a few of the small country villages to shop, then had a picnic in a secluded area. We spent those peaceful moments eating calzone and cheesecake, and talking about our children. The rest were spent in each other's arms. Oh, how I love being in his arms!

Brushing the tears away, I wonder where this strong bout of emotion is coming from, and why it is hitting me at this time of night. Lightly pressing a hand over my heart, another feeling hits me, almost as if I am experiencing some sort of premonition. *There is another storm coming*, my mind whispers. The thought is not as disturbing as it has been before. We have been through many trials and have always handled them together. The feeling does however, bring about a sudden need to be with my husband. Closing my eyes once more, I breathe the night air in deeply.

As I turn to go back into the house, the patio door opens and Adagio walks out.

Adagio
When Adagio had awakened and found Cisely gone, he'd immediately gone in search of her. Now, as he watches her

standing barefoot in the grass, the silky white gown billowing around her slender form, her auburn hair shimmering in the moonlight, it is as if he has stumbled across an angel. He opens his mouth to ask her if she is all right, but the look in her eyes stops him.

Standing on the lawn gazing at my husband, I find I can't move. I watch him as he silently walks down the steps, my heart beating faster with each step he takes, and I am quickly filled with an intense longing for him, one that is so strong, I can hardly breathe.

Adagio

By the time Adagio reaches Cisely, his heart is pounding as well. Something is happening. He does not know what, but looking into her eyes, he feels it. Maybe that is why he had awakened. They are so in tune with one another, he can almost feel what she is feeling. And what he is experiencing now is something beyond description. Reaching out, he brushes a tear from her cheek and takes her trembling shoulders in his hands.

"*Amore*," he breathes.

With that one softly-spoken word, she is in his arms. They fuse together, almost as if their souls are merging. Their kisses are frenzied and desperate, each touch of his mouth to hers stoking the fiery passion that is raging to consuming proportions.

He marvels anew at the taste of her kiss, her softness and warmth. He finally draws back and again wipes the tears from her face.

Cisely stares into his tear-filled eyes. "I love you so much," she whispers emotionally.

"I love you," he breathes, lifting her in his arms.

Wrapping her arms around his neck, she clings to him. Feeling the desperation of her embrace and warmed by the burning desire in her eyes, he kisses her again and carries her back into the house.

Eighty-nine

I thoroughly enjoy my outing with Mali and quickly dub the young woman a shopping queen. We spend the bulk of our time in my favorite department store. I have always thought of it as Italy's version of *Macy's* because a lot of the name brand merchandise is discounted. After helping Mali find something for her mother, I buy Mali a new outfit and treat myself to one as well. I also purchase a few shirts for Adagio and some gifts for the rest of the children.

We have lunch at a pizzeria in downtown Treviso. The beautiful bustling area is one of my favorite places to eat during the warmer seasons.

I listen as Mali chatters on excitedly about when she will wear her new clothes. As I take in the innocence of her simple musings, my thoughts drift back to when I was twelve. For me, there were no such conversations. There were no worries over wardrobe or fashion. No sleepover parties or innocent talks about boys or secret crushes. No hair styling sessions with friends on the weekends or passing notes back and forth in class. No such innocence existed for me at that age. I never really had the chance to be a child. I was forced to grow up fast, too fast.

Even still, looking at the beautiful young woman before me now, I feel fortunate to be her friend, and blessed to be a part of her life, to bask in her innocence.

"Excuse me?" I say as a deep male voice breaks into my thoughts.

"I was just wondering if you ladies would care for anything else."

"No, thank you. I think that will be all."

The young waiter smiles, his eyes roaming over my face. "In that case, I will be right back with your check."

"Thank you very much."

After hovering for another few seconds, he finally pulls his eyes from me and leaves.

Mali watches the waiter glance back again at Cisely.

"I've really enjoyed today," Cisely says.

"Me, too."

"Shopping is definitely one of my favorite things."

Mali is about to respond when the waiter returns. She silently watches him give Cisely the check, his smiling eyes once again drinking her in. Though she cannot completely understand what he is saying, she does understand his actions. He continues to turn on the charm as Cisely takes money from her purse and pays him.

"Thank you. It has been a pleasure serving you."

"Well, thank you. We enjoyed our meal very much."

The young waiter moves back as Cisely stands, his dark eyes raking over her body. He adds in impressive English, "I hope I can serve you ladies again."

I bet you do, Mali thinks.

I am puzzled by Mali's expression as we walk to the car. "Are you okay?" I ask, touching her shoulder.

"I'm fine," she says, lowering her eyes.

"Are you sure?"

Reaching the car, Mali finally looks at me. "Doesn't it bother you to have other guys looking at you like that?"

Where did that come from? "No, Mali. It doesn't bother me because I usually ignore it. The only looks that matter to me are the ones my husband gives me."

"I'll bet if Uncle Adagio had been with us, that guy wouldn't have been looking at you like that."

"Sometimes it happens even when Adagio is with me," I say, confused by Mali's reaction. "He just smiles when it does."

"Why?" Mali asks. I hear frustration in her voice. "Why doesn't he say something to the guys when they do that?"

I take her hand, keeping my voice gentle yet firm. "Mali, people have the right to look at others if they want. It's normal and it happens every day. Every now and again I do notice when men look at me, like today, even when Adagio is with me. But Adagio knows he owns my heart. He's the only man that matters to me."

When Mali's expression doesn't change, I decide I will definitely have to talk with her about these feelings later. She is holding something in, something very painful. I change the subject for now. "Would you like to go anywhere else? We can stop at a few more shops if you'd like, maybe have some *gelato*."

Mali shakes her head. "Can we just go back home now?"

"If that's what you want," I answer. "We will have to do this again before you go home. We can make another day of it."

"Okay." Her voice is devoid of enthusiasm.

The drive home is silent. When we enter the house, Mali absently thanks me for taking her, then takes her bags up to her room, leaving me staring after her pondering what happened. I wish I understood.

Taking another moment to contemplate the afternoon, I seek out the children and give them the gifts I bought for them. Phillip tells me their father is at the restaurant and will be back in a few minutes, so I take the rest of the things up to our room and wait for him. I place everything on the bed, pausing to touch the silk shirts I purchased for Adagio. I am sure they will look good on him. Of course, to me, *everything* looks good on him.

Walking over to the large window, I stare out over the land as thoughts of Mali fill my mind.

It is obvious the waiter's attention to me had truly bothered Mali. I only wish I knew what is going on inside the young girl's heart. If I could only figure out a way to reach her.

Maybe she will talk to Phillip . . . Probably not.

Mali and Phillip are close, but even as close as they are, there are still things she isn't likely to share even with him. Phillip and I have shared many conversations about Mali. I have tried to offer him advice and insight, but I am sometimes at as much of a lost as he is. What I do know for sure is somehow Mali will be a part of our future, a very important part. I feel it deep in my heart.

I turn and smile as Adagio enters the room.

"How was your day out with Mali?" he asks, pulling me close.

"It was great. We had a fun time together."

"What is bothering you, *amore*?"

How does he do that? I sigh, shaking my head. "How do you do that?"

"Do what?"

"How do you always know when something is bothering me?"

He smiles, touching my chin. "Because I know you."

"Phillip is taking after you, you know."

"Is that a good thing?"

"Most definitely."

Taking my hand, he guides me over to the sofa. "So, tell me what is wrong."

"I'm just worried about Mali."

"Why? I thought she was doing okay."

"I thought she was, too, but after today I'm not so sure."

"What happened?"

"Well, it's not so much what happened, but how she reacted. We were having lunch and everything seemed to be fine. The young waiter started paying a little too much attention to me."

Adagio grins slowly. "There is nothing unusual about that, angel. It happens every time we are out together. It can't be helped."

I smile, grateful that he thinks I'm beautiful. "Today is one day I wish it could have been helped."

"Why? What happened?"

"Well, I ignored it as usual, but the waiter's attention upset Mali a great deal. I noticed the way she watched him, but I didn't really think anything of it. She commented about it when we reached the car. I told her it didn't matter to me what other men thought and you were the only man that mattered. After that, she seemed to close up. I know these feelings are somehow connected to her parent's breakup."

"I am sure you are right. Did she say anything else after that?"

"No. She was quiet the rest of the way home. When we got here, she went straight to her room." I sigh, tucking a lock of hair behind my ear. "I just wish I could get her to open up to me. I think it would help if she did."

He presses a hand to my cheek. "You will, baby. I know you will find a way somehow."

I rest my head against his shoulder and caress his face. "You have more faith in me than I deserve, my love."

"Only because I know you so well. You can do anything you set your mind to." When I look up, he smiles, kissing the corner of my mouth. "You definitely have me wrapped around your finger."

"As you have me wrapped around yours," I whisper, raising my lips to his.

Adagio

As Adagio loses himself in her kiss, immersed in the softness of her warm mouth under his, he finds it easy to push away memories of the unsettling feeling he had experienced earlier this morning as he watched her drive away with Mali. It had scared him, affecting him so deeply, he literally had to stop himself from shaking. It is a feeling he will never forget and he hopes he will never experience again.

Ninety

Once dinner is ready, I go upstairs to get Mali. She had not come down from her room since we returned from shopping. I had been concerned, but I thought it best to leave her alone for a while. Now I am not so sure it was the right thing to do.

I knock on Mali's door. When there is no answer, I open it slightly and stick my head in. My eyes are immediately drawn to the corner where Mali sits in a chair with her arms wrapped around her knees, crying. Looking up, she quickly dries her face and my heart aches for her all over again. Slowly approaching, I kneel next to her.

"What's wrong?" I ask, squeezing her hand.

"Nothing," she answers with a small sob.

I try again. "Mali, honey, please tell me what's wrong. You can talk to me." I try not to sound as desperate as I feel.

Mali opens her mouth to speak, but a sob escapes, preventing her from talking.

Grabbing a chair from the desk, I sit next to her and put my arms around her, trying to offer what comfort I can. Mali clings to me and continues to cry. When she finally calms down a little, I lift her chin and dry her tears. "Tell me what's making you so sad, Mali."

She raises her eyes to mine and I see the fear in them. I can feel it. She is afraid to share whatever it is that she has carried inside for so long. But I know she needs to tell someone, and I send up a silent prayer that she will trust me enough to open up.

Taking a deep breath, Mali closes her eyes and says, "It was my fault that my dad left my mom. It was all my fault."

I open my mouth to disagree but stop myself. Instead, I remain quiet, praying that I can say the right thing. I try to keep my voice gentle. "How was it your fault, Mali?"

Mali wipes at her face again and takes another deep breath, her eyes taking on a faraway look.

"Last year I had this teacher—Miss Sims was her name. She was young and beautiful. She had blue eyes and blond hair, and her skin was always perfectly tanned. All the boys in school would stare at her when she walked through the halls, and the boys in her classes could barely get any work done because they were too busy looking at her. I thought she was pretty nice. She always tried to make sure I understood everything and sometimes even spent extra time with me during the class period, giving me help when I needed it. I thought she was the perfect teacher." Her expression hardens. "How stupid I was!"

"Why do you say that?"

"Because . . . because there was a reason that she was being so nice to me." Her hands form fists. "I was so stupid, Aunt Cisely! Everybody knew it but me! People hinted around but never said anything. Everybody knew!"

"Knew what?" I press, doing my best to keep my voice calm.

Mali drops her eyes, hesitating to answer, but there is no disguising the smoldering anger she has been suppressing since arriving in Italy.

"Knew what?" I ask again.

"That my father had been cheating on my mother with Miss Sims!"

What? I am stunned. Paul had been unfaithful to his wife with his daughter's school teacher? Wendy never mentioned the other woman was her daughter's teacher, nor did she say how she found out. I try to keep unkind thoughts from my mind, but it is hard. How could he hurt his family that way? I remind myself of what I told Phillip during our first conversation. I was never involved in their day to day life, and I have no right to judge. But that knowledge still does not stop me from being angry on Mali's behalf.

Keeping my voice soft, I ask, "How did you find out about it?"

When her eyes meet mine, they express a mixture of emotions, and I can't discern any of them. Then to my surprise, she snorts.

"Oh, it was pretty easy. One day I went back to the school to see Miss Sims because I knew she worked late sometimes. Imagine my surprise to walk into the room and find her half dressed in a lip-lock with my dad."

I gasp, covering my mouth. I can't even imagine the shock and hurt Mali must have felt at that moment.

"They both turned and looked at me," Mali continues as if in a daze. "They didn't say anything. They just stood there for a moment, looking at me, wearing shocked expressions. Then they straightened their clothes and my dad whispered a few words to her before taking my arm and guiding me out to his car."

By now, I am in tears. I want to comfort Mali, but I hesitate, wanting her to get everything out. We are so close to the heart of her problem and I cannot let her stop now. Holding her close, I caress her hair, giving her a moment with her thoughts. I can't even begin to comprehend the storm raging in the heart of this beautiful lost soul.

Releasing her, I press a hand to her tear-streaked face. "Mali, what did your father say to you?"

She sniffs, wiping her face. "He asked me not to tell Mom."

"He what?" I am incredulous! Completely incredulous! I cannot believe he would put his own child in such a position.

"He said he still cared for Mom, but he was in love with Miss Sims. He said as long as Mom didn't know, he would stay, but as soon as she found out, it would be over between him and Mom."

I fight to keep my voice calm and my anger in check. *How could he be so selfish? The little jerk! How could he do that to his own child?* "What did you do, Mali?"

"At first, nothing. But then . . ."

"Then what?" I press gently. I sense that we are so close to the source of the problem.

She looks at me, tears again welling in her eyes. "I got more and more upset as the days passed . . . and I needed to tell someone, so I told a friend. I told her not to tell anyone else, but she told her mother. And somehow it got back to Mom. Mom had no idea that . . . it all started with me. But Dad knew. I should never have been so stupid." She squeezes her eyes shut as fresh tears trail down her cheeks. "It was all my fault."

I hold her hands firmly. "Mali, it wasn't your fault. Your father made the choice to be unfaithful to your mother. And it was wrong of him to ask you to hold something like that inside."

"No!" she shouts, ripping her hands from mine. "I shouldn't have said anything! Because I did, my dad left her! Now she's all alone and it's my fault!"

I growl inwardly. *That weaselly little scumbag!* "Mali, that's exactly what your father wants you to think. He doesn't want to accept the blame or the consequences for his actions."

She shakes her head and stands, wringing her hands in her hair. "It's my fault! It's all my fault!"

"No, Mali," I say again, my heart breaking for her. As I reach out for her, she pulls away, running from the room.

"Mali, wait!" I cry, running after her.

Adagio

Adagio blesses the food so the children can start eating. He wonders how Cisely's conversation with Mali is going and is pretty sure that is why they have not come down yet. He hopes she is successful in getting Mali to open up. If anyone can get through to the young girl, she can. He smiles. *My Cisely can do anything.*

Looking back over his life, Adagio wonders what he'd done to be worthy of having Cisely as his wife. There are no words to describe the happiness she has brought to him. Through the years, they have faced trials, both separately, and then together, and they have made it through them, becoming stronger with each one. He can handle anything life throws at him as long as Cisely is by his side.

Adagio is startled by the sound of Cisely's frantic voice calling Mali's name, and he jumps up just as the girl runs past the entrance of the dining room. Cisely passes a few seconds behind her.

"Cisely!" he calls, rushing to the door. He turns to the children. "Ingo, watch your brothers and sister," he says before going after her. Phillip jumps up from the table.

"I'm coming with you, Papa!" he says, following his father out the door.

"No, Phillip!" Adagio says, panic seizing his insides. "I need you to stay here." He squeezes his son's shoulder firmly. "Everything will be all right."

The rain is coming down in sheets. I continue to run, trying to catch up with Mali. The large drops beat down hard, making it difficult to see, but somehow, I am still able to make out her green blouse in the distance.

"Mali!" I continued to yell, "please wait!" I don't know how much longer I can keep up this pace. "Mali, please stop!"

Mali is in agony as guilt continues to eat away at her heart. Somehow, she had felt that running would help her escape the pain, but it only follows her, and there is nothing she can do to stop it. She tries repeatedly to drown out Cisely's pleas, but the growing fatigue in Cisely's voice finally gets to her. Forcing herself to slow down, she crosses the street a short distance and stops. As weariness takes over, she sinks to the ground and sobs as the cool rain mingles with her tears.

I sigh with relief as Mali sits on the ground in the distance. I am tired, but now that she has stopped, I am able slow my step. As I get closer and can hear her rain-muffled wails, my heart aches anew for her and I again quicken my pace. Thinking of nothing except making it to the trembling form in the rain, I continue running down the small embankment, then across the street.

Mali presses her face in her hands, her shoulders trembling. Then she hears Adagio's voice screaming Cisely's name, followed by the sound of screeching tires, and her head jerks up. A single-syllabled scream tears from her throat.

"Nooo!"

Adagio

Adagio continues to run after Cisely. When she finally slows, he is able to gain a little ground. Through the rain, he spots

Mali sitting on the ground with her head in her hands and his heart goes out to her. He does not know what was said between them, but he figures Cisely must have gotten to the heart of Mali's problems. Just thinking of it fuels a rush of anger at Paul for deserting his family. If he hadn't left, Cisely would not be running after Mali in the rain. She would be home, safe and dry and having dinner with him and the children. Adagio knows he isn't thinking rationally. But right now, he is afraid—more afraid than he has ever been in his life.

He notices Cisely picking up her pace again to get to Mali and his heart threatens to pound through his chest. Cisely steps from the curb, and when she does, his whole world turns upside down and crashes upon him. He watches in slow motion as a car speeds up the road, opening up a river of rain in its path, and hears himself scream her name as the vehicle slams into her.

"No! No! No!" he cries over and over, running to her, half sliding down the embankment. As he reaches her still form, the rain stops. Sinking to the pavement, he leans over her, and what starts as a cry comes out as a hoarse sob instead. "Cisely! Oh, Cisely!"

Cisely slowly opens her eyes, struggling to focus. Looking down at her through grief-stricken eyes, he watches a tear fall from the corner of her eye back into her hair. Her mouth begins to move.

"Don't try to talk, angel," he says as she struggles to say something. "Just hold on." Her eyes slip shut and he panics. "Cisely!"

The shaky driver is standing outside his car, calling an ambulance.

Adagio looks up at him, barely able to see through the tears. "Please tell them to hurry!"

Mali slowly approaches them, her expression a mixture of horror and shock. When she reaches Cisely's still form, she can no longer move. She tries to speak, but no words come. Tears fall down her cheeks as she watches Adagio lean over and press his face to Cisely's, whispering the same thing over and over.

Adagio

"Please don't leave me, Cisely," he cries softly. "Please don't leave me. I can't lose you. I just can't." He squeezes his eyes shut. "Oh, God, please do not take her from me." He fights the desperate urge to move her. He wants so much to hold her, but he is afraid of making her injuries worse. Raising up a little, he stares at her bruised face, his mind willing her eyes to open as tears splash down his face onto hers. "Please do not leave me. Oh, God, please don't take her from me."

He sucks in a breath as Cisely struggles to open her eyes, and he gently places his hands on both sides of her face. "Stay with me, baby. Stay with me." Her lips begin to move and he again tells her not to try to talk, but she is insistent. Leaning down, he turns his head, positioning his ear above her lips.

"I will never leave you, . . . my . . . love," she whispers before slipping into unconsciousness.

A soft sob escapes his throat, and he continually fights the desperate longing to pull her battered body into his arms. Every part of him wants to die, his fear of losing her is so unbearable.

Hearing soft sobs, he turns to Mali, suddenly remembering she is there. Taking in her grief-stricken face, he pulls her down to him.

Mali buries her face in his wet shirt, crying bitterly. "I'm sorry, Uncle Adagio. This is all my fault. I'm so sorry."

Moving back a little, he presses a hand to her face. "Listen to me, Mali. This was not your fault. Please believe me, it was no one's fault." As Paul's face enters his mind, he swallows against the renewed anger burning his insides. Closing his eyes tightly, he tries to rid himself of these feelings, knowing there is no good in them. Holding Mali close again, he gazes tearfully over her shoulder at his wife's face, willing the paramedics to come soon. Then he remembers the children.

"Mali, I need you to go back to the house and tell Phillip to call Anna. Will you do that for me?"

Mali nods. She wipes her eyes and stands. He reaches for her hand once more. "It is not your fault. You must believe that."

Nodding solemnly, she looks down at Cisely once more. "I'm so sorry," she whispers again before starting back to the house.

Adagio again leans over his wife and places a gentle hand on her face. "Oh, God," he pleads, "please help them to get here soon." He wipes his face. "I cannot live without her, God. I can't."

Ninety-one

Adagio

Siting in a chair by the hospital bed, Adagio watches the first rays of morning sun seep into the room. The soft light casts an illuminating glow on Cisely's face. He had been in the same position all through the night. He hadn't slept at all, having spent the entire night gazing at his wife's face and holding her hand. Even with her bruised, swollen cheek, he has still never seen a more beautiful face. And after talking with Peter earlier and hearing the extent of her injuries, it is a miracle she is still alive.

Rubbing his tired eyes, he squeezes them shut as he mentally goes over the prognosis he'd been given.

Cisely has two cracked ribs, a broken leg, a broken wrist, and a severe concussion. Peter told him that because she has not regained consciousness, it is very possible for her to slip into a coma. He also said there is a chance she may never wake up. This thought brings him unbearable pain.

Moving closer to the head of the bed, he rests his head next to hers as his tears wet the pillow. "I love you so much, baby," he says softly. "Please come back to me. I need you more than you could ever know, more than words could ever express. I could not bear it if I lost you. You are my whole life, and if I lost you, I would die, too. I know I would."

He presses a hand to her face, caressing it softly. "I need you to come back to me, *amore*. Our children need you. They need their mother. I need my wife. I need the love you give to me, the joy you bring to my life every day."

As he tenderly traces the outline of her lips with his finger, then softly touches the bandaged spot on her temple, his thoughts travel to two nights ago when they stood together on the back lawn. He remembers the passion that had burned between them. It was unlike anything he had ever experienced. Intimacy between them has always been amazing, but that night it had been something else entirely. Holding her, touching her, kissing her was . . . it was as if they became one person. Her heartbeat became his, their emotions moving through each other. English abandoning him, his thoughts had all been in Italian, his whispered words against her skin producing shivers as she burned beneath his touch. It was a beautiful and terrible need that had stolen all breath from them both. And as he held her warm body in his arms afterward, he had drifted to sleep with tears clogging his throat, wishing they could stay wrapped up in one another forever, never leaving the haven of love encircling them.

Drawing his thoughts forward, he ponders the feeling he had experienced earlier yesterday. Was God trying to prepare him to lose her? He prays this was not the case because he would be lost without her.

"We still have so many years left, angel," he continues. "So many years to live and love on this earth. We need to grow old together, to watch each other's hair turn white and watch our children raise their children." He sobs softly. "I can't do any of those things without you. I have to have you here with me. I know you will always be mine even in death, but . . . I need you here with me now." Sighing, he swallows hard. "You are my everything, *vita mia*." Raising up, he presses a gentle kiss to her lips, grateful they are still warm.

A short while later, Peter comes in to check Cisely for any changes. After examining her, he suggests that Adagio go home and get some rest. Adagio shakes his head, refusing to leave his wife. He wants to make sure he is there when she awakens, and he cannot possibly sleep in their bed without her there beside him.

After some major coaxing, Peter convinces him to at least go home and change and get something to eat. He promises Adagio that he will stay with Cisely until he gets back, and he will call him if there is any change at all.

Sitting on the veranda steps, Mali rests her head against Phillip's shoulder. Neither of them had gotten much sleep and were up with the sunrise.

Mali is sick with regret. She feels responsible for the accident and had spent half the night futilely wishing she could turn back time and change what happened, as well as her part in it. She wishes she had not run away. If she had stayed calm, Cisely would be home and safe. Each time she looks into Phillip's grief-stricken eyes, her guilt is magnified. His mother should be home preparing breakfast, greeting everyone with her beautiful smile.

Phillip squeezes Mali's hand, sensing her thoughts. Blinking against threatening tears, his own thoughts travel to the hospital where his mother lay. He loves her so much, and the thought of possibly losing her is more than he can take. His thinks of his father and what he must be going through. Phillip has never seen two people more in love than his parents, and he knows this is tearing his father up inside. He had cried and prayed through the night for them both, futilely wishing the accident had never happened.

Still, even wading through the sadness and worry, he does not hold Mali at fault. He'd spent the entire night trying to convince her she is not to blame. Sometimes things just happen. And witnessing her suffering breaks his heart. He cares for her more than he can say, and he wishes he could help her somehow. All he can do is be there for her and let her know he cares.

Adagio

As Adagio walks through the veranda doors, Phillip jumps up and runs into his open arms. Pulling back, he anxiously looks at him. "How is Mama?"

Cupping his son's cheek, Adagio swallows hard. "She has not awakened yet." His voice is strained, but he draws forth a smile. "But I think she will soon."

"Do you really think so, Papa?"

"That is what I keep praying for." He caresses Phillip's hair. "We have to have faith that she will be well." He says this for himself as much as his son. He must force himself to think positively, otherwise, he will go out of his mind. Watching Cisely sleep through the night had taken a toll on him, but his prayers for her have never ceased because he can't bear the thought of losing her.

"Uncle Adagio," Mali says, slowly approaching him, "I'm so sorry."

Smiling sadly, Adagio pulls her close, embracing them both. "There is nothing to be sorry about, Mali. You are not responsible. It just happened."

"That's what Phillip keeps saying," she confesses, wiping her face. "But I can't believe that."

"You should listen to Phillip. He is the smart one in the family." Giving his son a slow smile, Adagio's eyes mist over. "He takes after his mother."

"I love you, Papa," Phillip says tearfully.

"I love you, too, son. I love you as well," Adagio says, returning his gaze to Mali.

Mali buries her face in his shirt and cries.

Keeping his arms around them, Adagio draws as much comfort as he gives. "Are you two going to be all right?"

"Yes, Papa," Phillip answers, drawing strength from his father.

"I need to go check on Ingo, Ian and Isabelle. Then I am going to shower and get back to your mother." He kisses Mali's forehead and places a firm hand on his son's shoulder. "Anna is going to stay and take care of things, and Sadie will be by later. I need you to take care of Mali, all right?"

"Yes, Papa."

Phillip's father takes his face in his hands and kisses his cheek before turning to go back into the house. Watching his retreating form, Phillip knows there is not a better or braver man in the world.

And I will be like him.

Ninety-two

Slowly awakening, I struggle to adjust my eyes to the dimly lit surroundings, but the throbbing pain accompanying the attempt makes it difficult to focus. The pain that reenters my body is a stark contrast to the sweet peace I'd felt only moments ago, but the memory of the experience fills my heart with warmth. Turning my head slightly, my eyes meet Adagio's sleeping form leaning against the bed. He looks so exhausted and I cannot begin to imagine what he has been through.

Oh, amore. Tears blur my vision as I gaze at his handsome face, and I want so badly to hold him. Ignoring the pain, I lift my uninjured hand and softly caress his hair, unable to resist touching him.

Adagio

Feeling a gentle touch, Adagio awakens. When he raises his head and finds Cisely staring at him, tears immediately fill his eyes and spill down his cheeks, and emotion wells in his throat, rendering him unable to speak. Even if he could, there are no words—no way to describe what he feels looking into her beautiful eyes—eyes he had not known if he would gaze into again in this life.

Cisely wipes his tears, caressing his face. "I told you I would never leave you." Her voice is slightly hoarse.

Moving to the head of the bed, he presses his face into the pillow next to hers, unable to suppress the sobs that come. "Oh, angel, I thought I was going to lose you." He rests his cheek against hers, relishing her warmth. "Thank you, God," he whispers. He finally draws back and kisses her hand. "How are you feeling, *amore?*"

Cisely weakly pulls his hand, bringing him closer. "My head hurts and I'm achy, but I'm so happy to see you, none of that matters."

"Oh, Cisely," he says, kissing her hand again. "I was so afraid. I don't know what I would do if I lost you."

Loosening a finger, I catch one of his tears. "Never, my love." I close my eyes against the pain, knowing I need to request something for it, but right now I need him more. "*Baciami. . . .* please."

Smiling through a steady stream of tears, Adagio softly touches his lips to mine. I long to be closer, and I sense him fighting the urge to hold me. His warm breath against my skin only makes my yearning increase. An emotional moan escapes me as his mouth molds to mine. His kiss is powerful and leaves me completely breathless. After a long moment, his lips move to my cheek.

"*Ti amo*," he whispers against my skin.

"And I love you."

He draws back slightly and we silently gaze at one another. I take in every feature of his face—his handsome brow, his tousled hair, his full lips, and his beautiful, emotion-filled emerald eyes. I just *need* to look at him, to be lost in his beauty, his perfect masculinity.

Closing my eyes, I groan softly, losing the fight against the increasing pain. "Adagio, could you go and ask someone to bring me something for the pain?"

"I will go right away." Adagio is only gone a moment and the nurse arrives right after he returns. She injects the pain medicine into my IV and within minutes, I begin to feel relief. I thank her before she leaves and she tells us the doctor is on his way. Adagio again takes my hand, moving as close to me as possible.

"How is Mali?" I ask softly.

His smiling eyes are tinged with sadness. "She will be all right," he assures me. "Don't worry. Just concentrate on getting well."

I squeeze his hand. "Adagio, please tell me."

He heaves a resigned sigh. "She is not good, I am afraid. She blames herself for the accident."

"She needs to understand it wasn't her fault."

"I know, *amore*. I tried to assure her of that, but she has grown used to being hard on herself. I don't understand it."

"I know, but I do," I say with a yawn. "I need to tell you about the conversation we had. Mali blames herself for things she has no control over." Yawning again, I gaze at him sleepily as the medication kicks in. "I also need to tell you something else. Some . . ." I pause, fighting the drowsiness.

"Don't try to tell me now, baby. It can wait." He caresses my face. "You need your rest. After all, we still have a trip to Tuscany to plan."

I smile sleepily. "Don't worry. I'll be back up and ready in no . . . time."

"I know, angel," he says, kissing my brow.

"Are the children okay?"

"They are fine. Anna is with them. Don't worry."

"Okay."

Adagio

When Cisely's breathing deepens, Adagio assumes she has fallen asleep, but he is surprised when she opens her eyes slightly and squeezes his hand.

"Stay with me, my love."

Lifting her hand to his face, he kisses her palm, holding it against his mouth. "I will stay with you forever, baby," he whispers. "I am not going anywhere."

Ninety-three

Phillip lay on his back with his hands clasped behind his head, making a futile attempt to fall asleep. For hours, his mind has been completely focused on the room down the hall. Thoughts of Mali consume him and he cannot stop worrying about her.

Unable to stay there any longer, he finally gets up. Pushing a hand back through his hair, he quietly makes his way down to the kitchen for a glass of milk, surprised to see the kitchen light on. He is even more surprised to find Mali sitting at the table with a glass of water. There is a distant look in her eyes as she stares at a painting on the wall.

"How are you?" he asks, sitting beside her, placing his hand over hers.

"Okay, I guess," she answers, looking down at their hands.

Phillip lifts her chin with his finger, looking into her eyes. He knows she is *not* okay, but he doesn't know what to say to help. Her sadness affects him in ways he can't begin to explain and his heart aches for her. He has never felt so much pain for another person before.

As he continues to stare into her eyes, deep emotion fills him. Words that have hovered in the back of his young mind fight their way to the surface, bringing with them feelings so pure, yet so intense, his heart threatens to thump through his chest.

By the way Mali is staring back at him, he senses that she feels the change. He hears her take a deep breath and watches her press a hand to her chest. Swallowing hard, he tightens his fingers around hers. "Mali . . . I need to tell you something, something important."

When she says nothing, he takes a deep breath, exhaling slowly. His voice is soft. "I love you, Mali. I love you very much." He watches her eyes widen and plunges ahead. "You are more special than you could ever know. And one day . . . when I am older, I will come for you, Mali, and make you my wife."

Tears of disbelief blur Mali's vision. Never would she have dreamed of him saying these things to her. She is young, but she cannot deny the feelings his words stir in her heart. She has guy friends at home and in school, but she has never felt as close to anyone as she does to Phillip. He treats her special. He makes her believe she matters. And he seems so much older than his years. She continues to stare at him through glistening eyes.

Phillip glances down at Mali's hands in his for a moment before lifting his eyes to hers again. Not knowing what else to say, he swallows hard, then slowly leans forward and brushes his lips lightly over the corner of her mouth. The kiss is brief, yet it is as soft and gentle as the flutter of a butterfly's wing. He moves back, staring into her eyes intently. "I promise, I will come and find you. Please tell me you believe me."

Lifting a hand to her lips, Mali slowly smiles as a tear trails down her face. Though his lips had only touched part of hers for a second, it is the first time she has ever experienced something so amazing. And no matter how many summers she spends with him after this, this is the one she will remember forever. She squeezes his hand. "I believe you, Phillip."

Ninety-four

Adagio

Cisely begins to heal, her progress slow but steady. Adagio hardly ever leaves her side, seeing to her every need. And each morning when he awakens and gazes at her sleeping form lying next to him, he gives thanks to God for sparing her life and allowing him more time with her on the earth. He wants to grow old with her and prays that they will have many more years together in this life—many years to laugh and love.

Ian and Isabelle often draw pictures and make cards to cheer their mother up. Ingo helps out by keeping an eye on his brother and sister and sharing in the housework. Phillip spends most of his time sitting with his mother when his father has to take care of other things. Adagio is proud and grateful for all their children and every effort they make to help. He could not have made it through this ordeal without them. God had truly blessed him.

Cisely and the rest of the family keep in touch with Mali through letters, cards and emails, wanting her to know she is loved and missed. And despite all that had happened, Mali is doing better. She always responds to their letters, telling them how much they all mean to her as well. She keeps them informed on what is going on in her life. Her letters to Phillip are usually longer, because there's always so much more to say between them.

Six months after the accident, other than having a slight limp, which I am told will most likely be permanent, I have completely healed, and Adagio and I are finally able to go on a two week long trip back to Rome and Tuscany.

Though I love taking in the wondrous ancient structures of Rome, I had forgotten just how much I've missed the beautiful Tuscan region. I have always considered Italy a laidback country, but life in Tuscany's rolling hills and countryside moves at an even slower pace, which is what I need right now. Still, both are equally beautiful and we savor every moment together.

Having finished dinner, we relax out on the bedroom terrace of the secluded villa we have rented for the week. The elegant old country home is surrounded by acres of trees and is bordered by a small stream. The villa is set high on a hill overlooking numerous vineyards, orchards, and olive groves. It is larger than we need, but we enjoy the privacy of having the place all to ourselves, especially during times like tonight.

Watching the stars slowly appear in the darkening sky, we talk about the past two weeks. When night has completely fallen, I light several candles and placed them on the table. Then, sitting next to Adagio on the bench, I take his hand in mine, running my thumb over his knuckles. His emerald gaze is illuminated by the flickering flames.

"Adagio, there is something I need to share with you. It is something I have wanted to tell you since the moment I awakened in the hospital, but for some reason the time just never felt right, until now."

"What is it?" he asks, looking into my eyes. I say nothing for a moment, so he remains quiet, studying my face.

"I had an amazing experience while I was unconscious. It was brief, but it will stay with me forever. At first, I thought maybe it was a dream, but I know without a doubt it was real." I give him a slow smile. "I saw your mother, Adagio."

His grip on my hand tightens. "You saw my mother?" His voice is thick with emotion.

"I did," I say, touching his face. "I knew her before she even told me who she was because you look so much like her."

Emotion fills his eyes. "Tell me, *amore*, how did she look?"

"She looked beautiful," I answer, remembering the lovely petite woman with laughing emerald eyes, deep dimples, and a long, dark, thick wavy mane. Dressed in spotless white, Marcella St. John looked like I supposed an angel would look.

Adagio closes his eyes. "Your description is perfect. I always thought my mother was beautiful. And since you have never seen a picture, I have no doubt you saw her."

"My time with her was brief," I continue, "but I remember everything she said to me. I remember the warmth I felt from her. She never touched me, but just being near her was indescribable."

"What did she say?"

"She said she loved me, and you . . . and that our marriage was meant to be. She told me the love we share is the purest kind, and that the Lord brought us together for a reason. She said that out of our posterity will come some of God's choicest spirits, and that we would be blessed, that many on the other side are praying for us. She also told me that I may not fully understand this now, but one day, I will, that we both will." Pausing, I wipe the tears from his cheeks. "She said nothing more, but she stayed with me until I awakened."

Adagio

Silently absorbing all Cisely had shared with him, Adagio says with reverence, "I am glad you were able to meet her and still be here to share this experience with me. My mother is an amazing woman." He presses his hand to her face. "And so are you." Staring into her eyes, he caresses her cheek and moves closer, gently taking her face between his hands.

"It is a beautiful agony, this powerful hold you have on my heart. To love you so much that everything in me aches to be where you are. I have often wondered why sometimes I cannot tell where I end and you begin, how I can feel so connected to you that my every sense is consumed with you. There have been times when my need for you has been so strong, I literally could not think, function or even breathe unless I had you in my arms."

He traces a caressing finger over her lips. "And when I thought I was going to lose you I knew I would die. I could not have survived. I have asked myself over and over how I can be so integrated with you, how you can be such a part of me that I can't even exist without you." Releasing a shaky breath, he touches his lips to hers, then draws back slightly. "Now I know why. You really are supposed to be mine, *amore*," he whispers breathlessly against her lips. "*Siete stati promessi me.* You were promised to me," he continues to whisper against her mouth. "That is why you are such a part of me. So much so that I can literally feel you moving inside my soul. I know now that my heart has always belonged to you, and it always will, just as God intended. And apart from God, everything I am is yours, Cisely."

There are no more words as their kiss becomes moist and heated.

I shiver as a heady warmth rushes over me, through me, a product of the passionate words spoken. A small sob escapes me as his mouth devours mine with a kiss that is demanding, possessive, and infinitely filling at the same time. Deep within, my heart burns as his soulful words wash over me, my entire being suddenly crying out for him, and the strength with which these emotions come is almost frightening. How can this man love me so much? How can I love him beyond all reason?

I relish the feel of his gentle hands on my face and in my hair. And as he pulls me firmly against him, the love and longing that surges through me makes me weak with a great and terrible yearning that is beyond words.

Adagio

Adagio is drowning in delirium as Cisely's softness and warmth consume his every sense. He cannot hold her close enough, cannot kiss her enough. Each kiss, and each moment in her arms only fuels his burning need for her. It is as if he will die if he waits any longer to make love to her.

Drawing back, he stands, lifting her in his arms. Their gazes are locked as he carries her into the house, their eyes conveying to one another that no more words are needed.

When we finally arrive home, we are showered with hugs, and we in turn shower our children with gifts. Phillip, in particular, has missed us greatly. From the day I was released from the hospital, he had stayed close to me, and it had been hard for him to see us leave.

Adagio and I are grateful for the time we had away, but we are happy to be back with our family. And though we know there will be many more vacations alone in the future, this particular one will always be especially treasured.

Mali returns the next summer for two months and we are thrilled to have her back. Emotionally, she is still healing but doing much better, and I watch the bond between her and Phillip grow even stronger. Wendy joins her daughter for the last two weeks and we have a marvelous time.

Once again, Phillip is sad to see Mali go, but there will be another summer, and the promise he made to Mali last year will stay in his heart, never letting him forget her part in his life, or his goal to have her share his future.

I have held the hope in my heart for some time that Phillip would follow in my footsteps. All of our children are striving to live good lives, and they make me proud. But watching Phillip is truly like viewing my younger self, only he has grown into a better man than me. I cannot ask for more than that.

Adagio St. John's journal

Ninety-five

Ten years later

After checking off everything he needs, Phillip places his neatly-folded clothes in the large suitcase, adding the toiletry bag last. Having finished, he looks over his list once more and smiles, musing over how much he has taken after his mother. She makes lists for everything and he had adopted the habit as well because he hates forgetting anything. When he is sure he has everything he needs, he sits on the edge of the bed and stares out his window down into the front courtyard, pondering with irony what he is about to do.

Phillip was sixteen the last time he saw Mali, and seventeen when he received her last letter. That was the year he was told by her mother that she left home and ran off with a guy she knew in school who had graduated that year. Wendy, being left with no choice, had given her consent for Mali to marry.

With that news came a sorrow that crushed Phillip's world.

Thanks to a lot of inspired wisdom from countless conversations with his parents, Phillip was able to bury the pain and get past the heartache, but deep down, it never completely went away. Mali's choice to marry someone else caused him a pain unlike anything he had ever experienced, but he could not let her go. He was still young, but he could not get her out of his heart.

Then, two years ago, his mother received a call from Wendy. She told Cisely that Mali had been in a car accident the week before. Mali's husband had been driving while intoxicated and crashed into a large tree. Neither of them suffered any major injuries, but a piece of glass from the shattered windshield had sliced into Mali's face, leaving a large scar going down the side of her cheek. Because her face was scarred and she was no longer perfect to her husband, he quickly decided he did not love her anymore and soon left her for someone else. Mali then moved back in with her mother. A month later, Wendy called Cisely and told her Mali's divorce was final.

Closing his eyes, Phillip ponders what Mali had gone through, unable to imagine her pain. He had wanted so much to go to her when he first learned of the accident but decided that letters would be better, especially when her emotions were still so raw. If he had gone to her, he would not have been able to leave. He knew he wouldn't. Instead of helping, he might have just made things worse. Besides, he got the impression that she didn't want to see him.

Phillip started writing Mali weekly and was discouraged when there was no response. Nevertheless, he continued to write. Every day for a year, he searched his mail, hoping for a letter from her, but there never was. Yet his letters were never returned. He also emailed her twice a week, but she never answered. He wished he could shut his feelings off. He had tried to give up the dream he'd kept locked inside since childhood, but his heart could not give her up.

Even now with everything that had happened, he knows with every fiber of his being he and Mali are meant to be together. Every desire in his heart is centered on her, and he feels driven to make this trip. Just as his mother owns his father's heart, Mali owns his. She claimed it when they were twelve, and he has never desired to have it back.

Sighing, he zips the suitcase shut. He does not know what the outcome of this trip will be, he just knows he must go to her. Everything else is in God's hands. He is moving the suitcase next to his bedroom door when his mother enters.

"Do you have everything?"

"I think so. No, correction, I know so," he says, holding up his list for her to see. He chuckles at her soft noise of approval.

Watching his mother scan his bedroom, he can guess her thoughts. There is a great deal of his personality in the room. Two walls are lined with floor-to-ceiling bookshelves. On the other two hang framed photos of his family. A cushioned bench sits beneath the large window and a thick, beige down comforter covers the bed. His desk is topped with a stack of books. The ambiance is very cozy.

"I'm sure the house will probably need a bit of dusting when you get there."

"Probably," he agrees with a smile. "But don't worry, Mama, I will take care of it."

"Are you sure you want to stay in that big place alone? You could probably stay in a cozy room somewhere."

"I don't mind being there alone. I love the memories we made there, before Jessica died and after. Besides, I'll feel closer to you and Papa."

She touches his face. "I know it's only for a month, but I will still miss you."

He smiles, embracing her. "I will miss you too. But I will be back before you know it, and hopefully not alone."

Drawing back, I look into his eyes, meeting the emerald gaze that is so like his father's. To me, looking at him truly is like looking at a slightly tanned, younger version of Adagio. "Are you sure a month will be long enough?" I ask him.

"All I can do is hope." He pauses, and I know he is remembering his conversation with Wendy last week. He had shared details of the call with me.

Wendy told him how withdrawn and self-conscious Mali had become. She spends her days working in the stockroom at the boutique, hiding her face from customers. Wendy also told him Mali said she doesn't want to see him, despite the energy her mother exerted trying to talk her into it. Phillip spent close to an hour talking with Wendy about Mali and his feelings for her. Wendy is sure Mali still has feelings for him as well, but her daughter has become too afraid to trust anymore. Of course, neither of them can blame her since her father had also abandoned them for someone else years ago. Phillip let Wendy know he is coming and asked her not to tell Mali. She was only too happy to keep his secret, hoping he will be able to get through to her daughter.

"I have to believe," he finally says.

"Your father and I will keep you both in our thoughts and prayers. We really feel that she is meant to be a part of our family."

Phillip squeezes my hand. "Sometimes I think I could live on your faith and be fine, because it is so strong."

I chuckle softly. "Oh, I have my moments, believe me. Sometimes I think I would be a lost cause if it wasn't for your father. He keeps me steady."

As Phillip quietly looks at me for a moment, his face bears a mixture of emotions I can't discern. He squeezes my hand, saying with emotion and strength, "I want what you and Papa have."

"You already have it," I say, pressing a hand over his heart. "Right here. You always have. Like your father, you have perfect love." I pause a moment, allowing my gaze to roam over his handsome features. "I remember a conversation you and I had when we came back home after the ordeal with my aunt. I was sitting out on the veranda one day thinking about what we had gone through, and you came out and sat next to me. You placed your hand on my stomach and quietly sat, enjoying the feel of Ian and Isabelle moving around. After a few moments, you asked me something. Do you remember what it was?"

Phillip smiles somewhat sadly. "Yes, I do. I asked you if you and Papa were still mad at Gladys. You told me you weren't."

I nod. "We really weren't, because we had to forgive her and let it go. It was hard, but we had no choice." I squeeze his hand. "Do you remember what you said to me?"

"Kind of, but I'm sure you remember exactly what I said, don't you? You never forget anything, especially anything pertaining to the family."

"I do remember," I say softly. "You said you were glad we were not still angry with her because there was still good in her, and she only acted that way because she had forgotten how to be good." I touch his face. "In that moment I knew the kind of man you would be. At almost six years old, you retaught me what I already knew but still struggled with from time to time. I never struggled with it again after that." Sighing, I place my hand over his heart again. "So, you see, you already have everything you need right here, just like your father. I think you were both born with the ability to love unconditionally."

Phillip looks down, swallowing hard. "You give me more credit than I deserve, Mama. I mean, I still have my moments."

"Oh, I know you do," I agree with a chuckle. "Honey, look at me." I touch is chin and he raises his eyes to mine. "I know you're not perfect and I'm not trying to put you on a pedestal. I'm just telling you what I've observed. Throughout your life, you have been able to get along with everyone, and you have handled every situation you've been faced with well. Your brothers and sister are like that, too, but you have always been especially strong."

"I try," he says humbly.

"I know, and I can't ask for more than that. I know that characteristic about you will never change. That is why I know Mali will finally see into this heart she unknowingly claimed years ago. When she does, she will know what real love is."

Phillip embraces me, pressing a kiss into my hair. "I long for that as well." He draws back, touching my face. "Thank you, Mama, for everything."

"Thank you for making me so proud."

"I second that," Adagio says, standing in the doorway, surprising us both.

Phillip smiles as his father joins them, putting an arm around his shoulders. He watches his mother gaze at his father before reaching out and softly brushing her hand back through the graying waves. His father smiles, taking her hand, pressing a kiss to her palm.

Witnessing these displays of affection between them each day makes Phillip marvel and know of a surety that real love never fades but continues to grow stronger with each passing day. He supposes that is why he has never been able to get over Mali. He continues to watch his parents. *With one look, their eyes convey a thousand words.*

"I only have one request for you, son," Adagio says, turning to him with feigned sternness.

"And just what would that request be?" Phillip asks with equally feigned seriousness.

His father grins boyishly. "Don't come back here without her."

"You can count on it."

"I'm glad you will be spending some time with Ingo and his family," his mother says with a sigh.

"I am too. It's been a long time." He reflects on his brother's decision to leave Italy.

Ingo met his spouse while attending Arizona State University and they decided to make their home in Phoenix. Ingo and his wife, Erika, have a one-year-old baby girl. The whole family went to see them a few weeks after she was born. Ingo had grinned proudly when everyone declared Beth looked exactly like him. He and his family came back to Italy for Christmas last year and try to visit whenever they can, but his parents still miss them. School and work take up a lot of Ingo's time, so he is unable to come back home as often as he would like.

"Well, hopefully there will be a wedding sometime in the near future and we can get them back here for that," Adagio says.

"Amen to that," Cisely agrees, putting her arm around her husband's waist and they laugh.

"Well, I promise you both I will do my best," Phillip assures them.

Adding a sprig of parsley and a lemon wedge to the two seafood platters he'd just prepared, Phillip places them in the steel pickup window under the heating lamps. He taps the bell, feeling a familiar sense of satisfaction that comes whenever he masters another of his father's popular dishes.

Phillip's love for cooking developed at an early age and has grown steadily through the years. He spent countless hours learning everything he could from his father. By the time he was sixteen, his culinary skills were exceptional. Then two years later, Adagio made him a chef in the restaurant. His father frequently tells him how proud he is, and Phillip cherishes every opportunity he gets to work side by side with him. In Phillip's opinion, he has learned from and is working with the best.

Ian and Isabelle's playful bantering draws him from his thoughts. His seventeen-year-old siblings help out in the restaurant for a few hours three days a week, and they both work longer shifts on Saturdays. Ian buses tables and Isabelle hostesses. Phillip smiles at the two as they wave, thinking how valuable their family's work ethic is. His parents have always taught them to work for what they want and not expect anything to be handed to them. He will always be grateful for that lesson. It makes him want to work hard for everything he desires in life.

Including a life with the woman I love.

By the end of the evening after the restaurant is closed and the kitchen is in perfect order, Phillip sits at one of the tables in the silent dining area. Pulling off his chef's hat, he rakes his fingers back through his hair and heaves a tired sigh as his mind drifts to tomorrow and what it will bring. This is the first time in his life he has ever lived for that word.

Tomorrow. The beginning of my future.

Salt Lake City, Utah

As the sun begins to set and the hot day starts to cool, Mali shifts in the cushioned chair on their covered patio, making herself more comfortable. Combing her fingers back through her shoulder-length, layered black hair, she closes her eyes and ponders the direction her life has taken.

Once upon a time, she had great hopes for her future, but due to a series of turns, some of which occurred because of poor choices, she is convinced her life is basically washed up. At twenty-three, her life is a mess and her future will be as well. She will never understand how she could have been so naive when it came to men. But then again, if the guy whose name she took had been a real man, she would not be in this situation.

But why should things be any different for me? After all, Dad did leave Mom for what he considered a more perfect version of a soul mate. And I am my mother's daughter. What comes around goes around.

Mali brushes a tear away as she thinks of Jake. From the beginning, he had said and done all the right things, and she had been convinced that marrying him was right. In fact, she had been so convinced that he loved her, she had given him that most precious part of her before marriage–that part of her that had not yet been hers to give. What a fool she had been. Jake's promise to love her forever was cut short the moment the broken windshield cut into her face.

So much for promises. They are nothing more than words to her now.

Closing her eyes against the stinging tears, memories of another promise comes to mind–a promise spoken by a perfect boy and received by a not-good-enough girl. A promise entered into by two young people who had been innocent enough to believe in fairy tales, yet too naive to realize that fairy tales are like elusive dreams. No matter how much you believe in them, no matter how much you want them to come true, they simply will never be.

Mali is smart enough now to know this.

And no one will ever make me believe otherwise.

Adagio

Adagio lay awake, staring up at the faint moonlight shining on the ceiling over their bed, his thoughts traveling to their son. He is sure Phillip had probably experienced nervous anticipation throughout the day thinking about his trip tomorrow . . . well, he glances at the clock, *today*, and he understands. Wanting so badly for this to work out for Phillip, he can definitely imagine what he is feeling. Adagio knows what it is like to be consumed with love so strong for someone, your heart is literally driven to make the person who claimed it yours. He knows the feeling well.

He smiles as he thinks back to the day that he realized he was in love with Cisely. The emotions that surged through him that day had been intensely deep. She was all he could think about. Even as he had wrestled with his feelings, he'd known they were meant to be together, and the thought of actually making her his had been exciting and frightening. He had needed her in his life so much, yet the thought of her rejecting him was more than he could bear. In the end he had simply hoped for the best. And his prayers were answered with the gift of her love.

Yes, Adagio understands what his son is going through, and he hopes all will be well for him and Mali. She is meant to be his daughter-in-law. He only hopes she will recognize and accept Phillip's love, and open her heart to him in return.

Tightening his arms around his sleeping wife, Adagio presses his lips into her hair. Closing his eyes, he soaks in her warmth. He and Cisely have been blessed with a lot of years together, and he has treasured every moment through both good and bad times. He realizes he is not getting any younger and the years are beginning to pass quickly. Focusing on the woman in his arms, his heart is again full of gratitude. She is his, his heart, his soul, and the love of his life. And she will always be.

Still, sometimes he is tempted to mentally will time to slow down. It is hard to think about being separated at the end of their mortal lives for a single day or a single minute, because even that would be too long. He is healthy, yes, but he is so much older than Cisely. Even if they live until they are old and gray, it will be her that is left alone, and even that thought hurts. He just has a problem with separation, period. And if his son is as much like him as he seems, his love for Mali will surely grow to run as deep.

"What are you thinking about, my love?" Cisely's silky voice is soft and soothing in the silence.

"I did not mean to wake you, baby," he whispers, kissing her brow.

She snuggles closer. "Maybe I sensed you needed me."

Sighing, he smiles in the darkness, marveling at how intimately and emotionally connected they are to one another. He presses his forehead to hers. "I always need you, *amore*."

Her hand moves to his face. "And I will always be here. Now, what were you thinking about?"

"I was thinking about our son and his quest to win his true love. I hope he is successful in getting her to open up and accept his love."

She caresses his hair, "Well, he takes so much after you, I have no doubt he will succeed. He loves her too much to give up. He will fight for her."

"I am sure you are right."

"Now," she says, raising up and leaning on one elbow, resting her head against her hand, "what else were you thinking about?"

"How do you know I was thinking about something else?" he asks, pressing a hand to her face.

"Because I know you well enough to know that your thoughts usually consist of multiple things." She smiles. "So, spill it?"

He chuckles. "Boy, you can get pretty feisty at one o'clock in the morning, can't you?" When she snorts, he laughs.

"It comes with age, *caro*. By the time I'm seventy, I'll be fearsome."

"Thank you for the warning. I will make sure and be on my guard."

"Noted. But you're avoiding the question."

He sobers. "I know." He sighs. "Truthfully, I was also thinking about getting older. Time is passing so quickly, and sometimes I wish it would slow down a bit." He pauses, not wanting to say more, but he is sure she understands his heart. "I just think about that sometimes."

I *do* understand, more than he realizes because I have these moments as well. Willing the thoughts away, I lean down, kissing his lips lightly. "You know what I think? I think you think too much."

"You are probably right," he agrees, pulling me closer. "I don't want to think anymore." His voice is thick with emotion. "And I don't ever want to be away from you."

Moving my face closer to his, I whisper, "You won't. I'm right here." I place my hand over his heart. "And when we are not together, I am here."

Returning the gesture, he pushes the hair back from my face, brushes his lips over mine and whispers huskily, "Let us not think anymore, *amore*, not talk anymore." Then he takes me fully in his arms.

I immediately melt against him as the heat of his kiss and the touch of his hands light a fire inside me, a fire that is only kindled when passion roams free.

Ninety-six

Salt Lake City, Utah

Phillip is surprisingly calm as he enters the boutique. Standing just inside the door a moment, he lets his eyes scan the female faces until he finds one that he recognizes. And just as he spots her, Wendy's wide-eyed smile meets his. She runs to him, embracing him tightly.

"It's so good to see you!"

"It's good to see you too," he says.

Wendy pulls back, taking him in from head to toe, causing him to blush. "You look great. As handsome as ever."

He grins shyly. "Thanks. I only hope your daughter feels the same."

Wendy squeezes his hand, pulling him aside. "I really believe that deep down, those feelings are still there, though she adamantly denies it." Pausing, she cautiously looks around a moment. "She's afraid, Phillip. Not only has she lost her trust in others, she doesn't trust herself or her feelings, either." Her brow furrows slightly as she releases a small frustrated sigh. "Jake the jerk, as I fondly call him, really did a number on her, and she is still beating herself up over the choices she made. But I know you can help her see how amazing she is. I just know it."

"I pray you're right. All I can do is try." He takes a deep breath. "Where is she?"

Wendy points to the door her daughter imprisons herself behind daily, her expression growing sad. "She never comes out until we close. I usually take lunch in to her, otherwise she wouldn't eat." She pushes a hand back through her hair, swallowing in frustration. "She would rather go hungry than face anyone. And I just don't know how to help her."

Shaking his head, Phillip looks at his watch, a slow smile spreading across his face.

"Why don't you let me take care of lunch today?"

Wendy grins, admiring his quick thinking. "I think that's a wonderful idea."

"Let's just hope she doesn't throw it back in my face," he says, only half serious.

"Well, if she does, then I guess she will go hungry, won't she?"

He laughs. "I guess so."

Mali slowly runs the steamer down the silk skirt a final time before placing it on the rack with the other finished garments. Brushing her hair back from her face, she takes a deep breath, momentarily gazing off into space. Her mother will be in with her lunch at any moment. She is tempted to feel guilty for keeping herself secluded this way, and she knows she should be braver and get out more. She cannot expect her mother to do this forever.

Mali needs to reclaim her life. But how can she face anyone so disfigured? How can anyone ever look past the scar that has taken away any chance of her having a normal life? Even as her mind reasons that it is wrong to feel this way, she pushes the thought aside, telling herself to accept her fate. She is not being shallow, just internally stating a fact.

Putting her mind back on her work, Mali takes another blouse from the rack and hangs it on the hook. She is just beginning to steam the wrinkles from it when she hears the door open. "Thanks, Mom," she calls, her back facing the door. When there is not the usual response of "You're welcome," she glances back and freezes.

"*Ciao*, Mali." Phillip's voice is calm.

Completely speechless, she turns off the steamer, her heart racing wildly. In an effort to overcome her shock, she lowers her eyes and turns away from him. "Hello," she finally responds, her voice unsteady.

Phillip walks over and places the Subway bag and tray of drinks on the table. When Mali tries to turn away again, he gently catches her arm.

With a sigh of defeat, she faces him fully. Bravely lifting her chin, there is a hint of quiet defiance filling her eyes. She has never felt more vulnerable in her life, but she refuses to let him see it. And having him standing before her now, looking so painfully handsome that it hurts her heart doesn't help matters.

Remaining silent, Phillip lifts his hand to her face, pausing when she tenses slightly. His fingers gently move over her skin, his thumb caressing the three-inch scar lining her cheek. "I've missed you, Mali." His voice cracks a little.

Mali closes her eyes against stinging tears, soaking in his gentle touch. She marvels at the emotion that just a single touch from him produces.

"Oh, Mali," he says with quiet reverence, "you're so beautiful, even more so than I remembered."

At his heartfelt statement, Mali abruptly moves away from him. "Don't patronize me," she returns vehemently.

Phillip keeps his voice soft. "You should know me well enough to know I don't say things unless I mean them."

Her eyes are angry. "I thought I did, but maybe some things have changed."

Struggling to keep his rising anger in check, he swallows hard. "So, are you calling me a liar now?"

She winces, then sighs, taking a deep breath. "I'm sorry, Phillip. You didn't deserve that. But you don't know what I've had to deal with." She tugs a hand back through her hair. "I'm not the same person anymore. We aren't the same two kids."

At the risk of her pulling away, he reaches for her hand. When she doesn't, he plunges ahead. "First, I know things are not the same. We've led totally different lives. But I am a man now and you are a woman—a woman I have loved since we were children. For me, the only thing that has changed is that my love for you has only grown stronger." He touches her face. "And I know that this," he says, tracing her scar, "will never change who you are inside unless you allow it to." He pauses. "Second, I can't begin to understand what you have gone through. But I want to." His eyes delve into hers. "Please, Mali. I've come so far to be with you. Don't push me away. Just open up a little and let me into your life."

Mali looks away as tears fill her eyes, her defenses crumbling. "Oh, Phillip," she whispers. "I'm so sorry for hurting you."

"Hey," he says softly, drawing her into his arms. "It's all right. You did what you thought was best. It's over now."

A combination of desperation, loneliness and confusion causes Mali to cling to him. Burying her face in his shirt, she cries, drawing comfort from his muscular arms and soothing warmth. It had been so long since she had just been held, so long since she had felt such comfort. After a few moments, she draws back. Phillip wipes the tears from her cheeks with his fingers and she cannot help being touched by the gesture. As she looks into his eyes, all of the feelings she'd buried long ago come rushing back. There is still confusion, but the feelings are there.

Phillip gazes into Mali's eyes, clearly reading the emotions there, and feels a renewing of the connection they once shared. He senses her fear and his heart goes out to her. Earning her trust is going to take some time, but he will be patient and wait for her. He has already been waiting for half his life.

Moving back, he takes her hands. "Why don't we have some lunch and you can tell me all about what's been going on in your life. I want to know everything."

Mali gives him a faint smile. "I was going to say I will tell you only if you tell me about yours, but I already know everything from your letters." She hesitates. "I'm sorry about not writing you back. I guess . . . I was a little afraid. I didn't want to know how much I hurt you."

Looking down at their joined hands, he pushes away the painful memories of Mali marrying someone else. He had never mentioned in his letters how her decisions had practically gutted him—he had said nothing. It had taken a while, but he had finally begun to heal. He refuses to let those wounds be reopened. "It helps to know you read my letters. I didn't know at the time if you ever did."

She smiles. "I devoured every one you wrote. Jake was . . . he was gone a lot. Reading your letters help me to not feel so alone."

He squeezes her hand, saddened to think of her being alone with only his letters for company. "I'm glad they were of some comfort."

"Thank you for writing me." She is about to say more, but the sudden rumbling of her stomach causes them both to laugh.

"I think that was an official announcement that it is lunch time," Phillip says. He hands her a sandwich from the bag, and for the next hour, listens as Mali shares the details of her painful marriage.

How Mali longs go back and change things. Sometimes it seems her whole life had been full of regrets. One mistake had led to another, and now her days are empty, with only misery and grief for company. And every time she glimpses her reflection in the mirror, she is reminded of the consequences allotted to her because of the choice she made to get into the car with her intoxicated husband.

During the first year of Mali and Jake's marriage, Jake was wonderful to her and she was happy. But as time passed, he changed. He started drinking heavily and stayed away from home more, preferring the company of his friends over Mali.

Even now, Mali often asks herself why she didn't leave him when the drinking began to get out of hand. Truthfully, she knows why. She had been determined to make their marriage work so she would not wind up feeling like a failure. She had hoped he would change. But her hope had been in vain. Even after the accident, Jake made no attempt to change. And since Mali was no longer the perfect-looking adornment for his arm when he felt inclined to spend time with her, he decided he could do better. A three-inch scar had sealed her fate.

"Hey," Phillip says, startling her. "Where were you?"

Mali shrugs absently. "Nowhere."

They finish their lunch in silence.

"Thank you for lunch," she finally says. "I need to get back to work." She stands, turning away from him.

"Okay," he says, taken off guard by her sudden mood change. He can literally feel her closing herself off to him again, and he wonders what triggered it. Still, he is not about to let that happen. He can't.

"Mali," he says softly, taking her hand. "I would like to take you out to dinner this evening. Will you go with me?"

She turns her face away, discreetly touching the scar. "I uh . . . I can't. I'm sorry."

"All right," he says, a little disappointed, but unwilling to give up. "Well, can I come by and see you later?"

"I don't know. I . . ."

"I will not let you shut me out, Mali. I am going to be here for a while." He touches her face, staring into her eyes intently. "And I'm not going back to Italy without you."

Mali is rendered speechless, not only by the statement but the intensity of his gaze as well.

Could he really care for me that much? She continues to look into his eyes, doing her best to ignore the fluttering of her heart. "I won't make you any promises, Phillip. Too much has changed."

"I know." He caresses her cheek. "And I don't expect any promises. But I will make one to you." He draws her into his arms, whispering against her ear, "I will never hurt you, Mali. Never. And if it takes me forever to prove that to you, then so be it. Because that is how much time I am willing to wait for you. *Forever.*"

Ninety-seven

Over the weeks, Mali and Phillip spend a great deal of time together and Mali slowly emerges from her shell, occasionally covering her scar enough with makeup to brave going out in public with him. She had finally decided that it was time to reclaim her life, and she could not do that hiding in the shadows. She also understands now that if she and Phillip are going to have any chance at all, she has to make an effort and at least meet him half way.

The two spend time taking long walks in the city and drives through the canyon. They share picnics in the park and go to a few movies. Phillip even gets her to go dancing, which is a major step for her. Other times, they relax in the family room at his place and simply talk. She knows that to Phillip, anything they do is fine. He just loves being with her. She treasures that knowledge.

Phillip senses Mali's confidence growing daily, little by little, and each moment he is with her only deepens his love. He knows this is all taking her far beyond her comfort zone, but it will be well worth it in the end, so he will continue to exercise patience.

He takes things slow, never pushing his affections on her, leaving her each night with only a hug or a kiss on the cheek. Though everything inside him aches to take her in his arms and kiss her in a way that would surely betray the passion and longing he feels for her, he keeps himself in check. They have become so close again and have come so far, the last thing he wants to do is scare her away.

They spend a few days in Arizona with Ingo and his family and have a great time.

One day while Mali is out shopping with Ingo's wife, Erika, Phillip and Ingo enjoy some bonding time, and Phillip gives his brother more details about Mali's previous trials.

"What a total jerk," Ingo says about Mali's ex. "After watching her mom being treated so badly and abandoned like that, I can't even imagine how devastating it must have been for Mali to go through the same thing."

"I know," Phillip agrees.

"But at the same time . . ."

"What?" Phillip prompts when Ingo hesitates, guessing what he is about to say. He knows his brother well.

"If she had waited for you . . ." Ingo doesn't finish.

"Trust me, that is a direction I have to fight constantly to keep my thoughts from traveling. I cannot ever go there."

Ingo looks at Phillip for a long moment, maybe searching for a sign of the pain that he had witnessed in his brother during those tender years when emotions were so raw. When he smiles and nods, Phillip knows he understands.

"So, how was it for you and Erika?" Phillip asks. "When you fell in love?"

Ingo pushes a hand back through his blond waves. "I've found that falling in love is a fickle thing, bro. It happens so many different ways. For me, I guess it was like Mama said my biological father told her it was for him. I mean, I was leaving the school library and Erika was walking in. She looked at me and smiled and boom! Man, I was a goner. That smile got me. My heart was gone then and there."

Phillip chuckles, imagining the moment. His brother was always a sucker for a pretty smile, and Erika has a beautiful one, but he knows there had to be a lot more to her to have captured Ingo. Many had tried and failed. Erika had definitely been *the one.*

"Now, as for you and Mali, it was more like Mama and Papa, a friendship that merged into a bond far deeper than either of you ever expected, and from there grew into a love you *never* expected."

"I think you just described it more perfectly than I ever could."

"Just trying to keep up with you. You're the one who usually has a way with words."

Phillip snorts. "No, that would be Papa."

"True," Ingo agrees with a chuckle. "At least, according to Mama. In any case, I'm happy for you, bro." He squeezes Phillip's shoulder. "We love Mali, and we hope she will soon be a part of the family."

"So, do I, brother. So do I."

Mali finds herself dreaming of a future with Phillip. With each day that passes, her feelings for him grow until she can no longer deny her heart what it wants—what it needs. She loves him, deeply. For the first time in her life, she truly knows what it feels like to be in love.

When Mali married Jake, she did not really love him. She cared for him and her feelings grew during their marriage. Had things been different, she might have fallen in love with him, which is what she had hoped for from the beginning, but it was not to be. And deep down, what she had felt for Phillip when she was younger had never truly gone away. She is grateful now that it hadn't.

Looking back now, she understands and readily admits to herself that her only reason for marrying Jake was because of her own feelings of unworthiness at that time. She had settled for Jake because she felt so unworthy of Phillip, because of the pain she had caused him and him and his family. She was never able to forget her part in Cisely's accident that summer.

Now she knows that she has to let go of everything in the past if she is to ever have a future with Phillip.

Phillip also begins to sense Mali's growing feelings for him. He can see it every time her eyes met his. He just isn't sure when to begin taking things further. Afraid of moving too fast, he keeps himself in check, waiting for a sign from her.

Then, out of the blue, it happens.

He and Mali are sitting together on the patio steps one evening watching the sunset. Both are silent, each lost in their own thoughts. Phillip is scheduled to return to Italy in less than a week and he still does not know where things stand with Mali. He loves her so much, and he cannot allow himself to think of leaving without her, or at least without knowing for sure she is his. Every moment he has to refrain from expressing his feelings for her is agony. Still, he waits.

Mali studies Phillip's profile as a light breeze blows through his dark, tousled waves. She takes in his every feature— his strong handsome brow, his olive skin, his deep dimples and full lips, and his chiseled build. He is walking perfection, and owning the affections of such an amazing man is unbelievable at times.

She ponders the love in his eyes whenever he looks at her. She knows he is doing his best to be patient and she is grateful to him for allowing her some time. It had been exactly what she'd needed. Still, with all his patience, she senses his underlying passion, and the desire that burns in his eyes when he gazes into hers almost undoes her at times. Never in her life has she ever felt so loved or wanted.

Sitting with him now, her feelings are so strong, she can't hold them back any longer. He needs to know how she feels, and she needs to tell him.

Sensing Mali's gaze, Phillip's eyes meet hers, his heartbeat quickening as she takes his hand. Timidly, she presses her other hand against his cheek, letting her thumb slowly caress his lips. He closes his eyes, releasing a shaky breath, and marvels at the sensation of her touch.

"I love you, Phillip."

One lone tear rolls down his face. He has waited so long to hear these words from her. Taking her hand from his face, he presses a lingering kiss in her palm.

"I love you, too," he breathes. "So much that my heart can't hold it all. I cannot remember a time when I didn't love you."

Mali smiles. "I've never been able to completely get over you, you know. I tried, but I couldn't." She pauses, looking into his eyes. "Maybe it was because I wasn't supposed to."

Phillip smiles back, marveling that she really does love him. Unable to wait any longer, he gently takes her face between his hands and presses his lips to hers. The second her mouth softens under his, he is lost. Trying to keep his passion in check is futile. Moving his hands from her face, he slides them down her arms and caresses her silky skin before pulling her firmly against him, his arms enfolding her as the kiss becomes heated.

As Phillip's mouth devours hers, Mali is sure she's never experienced anything so intensely right. She feels herself weakening as he continues to weave a kiss unlike any she has ever received. With this one thoroughly overpowering kiss, he has claimed her. She is all his, and he is hers.

Drawing back slightly, Phillip rests his forehead against hers, trying to slow his breathing and his racing heart. No words can describe what he feels being with her this way. He tightens his arms around her, loving the way her body molds so perfectly to his. Moving his lips to her ear, he whispers, "Marry me, Mali. Be mine forever."

Mali smiles through the tears. "I would be honored to be your wife, Phillip."

Smiling widely, Phillip kisses her again, his whole being brimming with joy. After another moment, he laughs.

"What is it?" Mali asks with a chuckle.

"I'm just so happy."

"I'm happy, too," she says, laughing. "I feel so blessed."

"So do I." He heaves a contented sigh, tightening his embrace and presses his face into her hair. "Mama and Papa will be thrilled. They have wanted this for us more than you know."

Mali snuggles closer. "Your parents are so amazing. I'm looking forward to being a part of your family."

"I am as well, which means we need to be married as soon as possible."

She smiles up at him. "I agree. How's tomorrow?" she asks with a chuckle.

Phillip grins. "If I knew my mother wouldn't have my head, I would. Even tomorrow isn't soon enough." He trails a finger down her cheek. "But I guess we should at least give our parents the benefit of a wedding."

"I suppose you're right," she says, feigning disappointment.

Smiling, he softly brushes his mouth against hers. Mali wraps her arms around his neck, pulling him closer, savoring the sweetness of his kiss. She could kiss him forever. She sighs, thinking that since they are getting married, she really will be able to kiss him forever. And other than finally giving herself to him fully, she cannot think of anything more wonderful.

The next morning, Phillip and Mali share their news with Wendy and she is ecstatic. She cries and hugs them both, grateful for their happiness. She had always felt they were meant to be together, and she is glad her daughter finally realizes it as well.

Phillip calls his parents and tells them he and Mali are engaged. Adagio and Cisely are overjoyed for their son, and they look forward to him bringing their future daughter-in-law home.

"I am very proud of you, son," Adagio says

"Thanks, Papa. I can't tell you both how happy I am."

"You don't have to. We can hear it in your voice."

"I knew deep down she really loved you," Cisely adds on the other extension. "How could she not? You are your father's son, and you are as completely irresistible as he is."

Even though Phillip can't see it, he can still picture the wide grin that is surely gracing his father's face at the moment. "Well," he says playfully, "I don't know about Papa, but I am pretty irresistible, aren't I?"

"Whatever you say, Mr. Irresistible," his father says.

Phillip chuckles. "I want to thank you both for having so much faith in me, and for helping me through this. I couldn't have done it without you. I love you both."

Leaning my head against Adagio's shoulder, I wipe my eyes. "We love you too, honey. Very much."

"And we can't wait to see you," Adagio adds before our call ends. Hanging up the phone, he pulls me close. "Well, it looks like we have another wedding to look forward to."

"I can't wait."

"So, I guess the men will have find things to keep ourselves busy and out of the way while you women go into a wedding planning frenzy."

"Oh, no you don't. You're not getting out of it that easy."

Growling under his breath, he presses his face against my neck. "That's what I was afraid of."

I chuckle. "Oh, you know you love looking at color swatches and picking out flowers. Admit it."

"All right. If you're going to make me." Before I can reply, he kisses me, immediately silencing my words, and I eagerly return his affections. Drawing back slightly, he breathes, "Okay, you don't have to make me."

"I know," I say triumphantly, claiming his kiss once more.

Phillip takes Mali out to dinner and presents her with the beautiful engagement ring his father had helped him pick out before he left home. When she leans over and kisses him, he forgets for a moment that there is anyone else in the restaurant. After dinner they go dancing.

Before he takes her home, they stop by an all-night diner and share a piece of cheesecake, basking in their love for each other and talking of the future. He leaves her at her door with a kiss that neither of them wanted to end. And as Mali waves goodbye to him through the living room window, Phillip sighs contentedly, unable to remember ever being so happy.

Ninety-eight

Excited about going to Italy with Phillip, for the first time in a *long* time, Mali allows herself to daydream of the future. Sitting in front of her dresser brushing through her hair, she lets her thoughts flow freely, imagining her life with Phillip, picturing their children, seeing herself growing old with him. She smiles at her reflection, trying to see what Phillip sees when he looks at her.

"You're beautiful, Mali." Phillip tells her this every day, and slowly, his words—no, his love—has started to penetrate, healing that broken part of her. However, she knows she will still have her moments of insecurity; she also knows that Phillip will never let them stay.

She is smoothing a little more foundation over the scar when the doorbell rings. Thinking Phillip has arrived early, she rushes down to answer the door, a wide smile lighting her lovely face. However, upon opening the door, the smile completely disappears.

"Hello, baby." Jake grins at her shocked expression. "Surprised to see me?" He enters uninvited.

"I wouldn't exactly say that," Mali says, annoyed by his usual brashness. Her ex-husband is the last person she wants to see and yet here he is, standing in her home. And nothing about him has changed. He is still as full of himself as ever. "What are you doing here, Jake? No, correction, what do you want?"

He chuckles. "Do I need a reason to come by?"

Mali takes a deep breath, tempering her anger. "I haven't seen you since I left the courthouse after our divorce was final. Of course, you have a reason. You have an ulterior motive for everything you do. So, spill it." His sly smile unnerves her even more. Why she married him, she will never know. Even his beach-boy good looks have no effect on her the way they once did. Everything about him is repulsive.

"Well, I did hear about your new boyfriend. I came by to congratulate you on actually nabbing someone. Is there anything wrong with that?"

She snorts. He is so predictable it's laughable. "Well, thank you for your heartfelt good wishes. They mean about as much to me as you do."

Shaking his head, he again chuckles softly. "Ah, Mali, baby, that's what I miss about you. You always gave it to me straight." His demeanor sobers. "I really have missed you."

Yeah, I'll bet you have. "What do you want?" she asks, all patience gone.

He shoves his hands deep into his pockets, finally coming to the point. "I want us to get back together."

What?! "You have got to be kidding me. What, are you bored with your latest conquest already?"

He looks away. "We decided it wasn't there for us anymore. Besides," he says, reaching out and touching her hair, "I realize now how wrong I was to let you go."

Mali recoils from his touch. "I get it," she says acidly. "You're bored with your new toy and now you want your old one back since someone else is interested in it." She shakes her head. "You are pathetic, you know that? Even if I weren't involved with someone else, there's no way I would ever take you back. It wouldn't be worth the heartache."

His eyes move to the scar on her face and he smiles. "No, you are the one who is pathetic. And as far as heartache goes, I'm sure you will have your fair share soon enough. When the poor sap you've managed to get your hooks into finally stops feeling sorry for you and really takes a good look at you, you will wish you had taken my offer."

"Like you are so great! At least I know he loves me, imperfections and all."

"Yeah, you keep telling yourself that and you might actually convince yourself. But you'll learn soon enough, and by then it will be too late. And my offer will be void."

Squeezing her eyes shut, she clenches her hands, her knuckles turning white. "Get out of my house," she said with quiet vehemence.

Jake's smile is triumphant. "Don't worry, baby. I'm going. But you just remember what I told you. One day you'll regret not giving us another chance." And with that, he turns and leaves.

Mali slams the door and leans against it, fighting to calm her nerves. Swallowing against the nausea rolling through her, she heads back up to her room.

Picking up the brush, she starts to run it through her hair again, then stops. Taking in her reflection, she squeezes her eyes shut against the tears.

It's not true! None of it is true! She mentally chants this over and over again. But as she touches her fingers to the raised line of skin on her cheek, doubt again enters her heart.

Is Phillip's love spurred by pity? She suddenly wonders how she can be sure he really loves her. Will he one day get tired of her and leave in search of someone else? Someone prettier? Someone perfect? Logically, she knows Phillip deserves her trust. He has given her no reason to doubt his love, yet distrust has become such a part of her, she wonders if she will ever be rid of it. She wants a normal life with a family of her own and a man who truly loves her. She had hoped that man was Phillip, but confusion now clouds her thoughts, replacing the hope with doubt.

Oh, why did he have to show up today? Why couldn't he have stayed under the rock he'd slithered beneath when they divorced, or better yet, disappeared from off the face of the earth?

Walking over to the window, Mali watches the storm clouds slowly darken the sky. Closing her eyes, she presses her forehead against the cool glass. She hates the rain. Her hatred of rain began years ago. Each and every time the storm clouds occur, she is reminded of the day Phillip almost lost his mother.

And it had been because of her.

She had caused him so much pain back then, and through the years her choices had hurt him even more, yet he continues to profess his love for her. How can he love her after all she has put him through?

My life is such a mess. I'm a mess!

A burst of anger fills her, and before she knows it, she is running down the stairs out into the rain. Standing in the middle of the backyard she raises her face heavenward crying, "Why is this happening? I know my life is a mess, but don't I deserve a little happiness?"

Lowering her head, she softly cries, her shoulders shaking as the cool rain mingles with her tears.

She feels so lost.

Phillip taps his hands against the steering wheel, waiting impatiently for the light to turn green. He is not supposed to be at Mali's for another hour and had been heading to the store when the sudden feeling that she needed him made him do a U-turn and head toward her house. He doesn't know what has happened, but he does know she needs him.

When he reaches Mali's house, he knocks hard on the door, his clothes drenched from the short run.

"Mali," he calls and knocks again. Still there is no answer. Leaning over the side of the porch, he peers through the window, raking a hand through his dripping hair, combing it back from his face.

Where is she?

Thinking that he should try the back door, he walks around the side of the house. As he reaches the back, he spots Mali standing out in the yard, soaked to the skin, crying. Hot tears burn his own eyes.

Mali looks up as Phillip draws near. Reaching her, he pulls her in his arms, pressing her face against his shoulder. The desperation of her embrace breaks his heart, and he aches to know what happened to cause her such pain. Drawing back, he presses a hand to her cheek. "Let's go inside," he whispers, wanting to get her out of the rain. She pulls away.

"What is it?" he asks. As she silently stares at him through pain-filled eyes, a feeling of desperation works its way to the surface. "Talk to me, Mali. Tell me what has happened."

Her bottom lip begins to tremble, her shoulders shaking from both emotion and the chill of the rain. "I can't marry you." Her voice cracks.

"What do you mean, you can't marry me?" He reaches out for her, but she pulls away. When he tries again and she repeats the action, his frustration grows. "Talk to me, Mali! Why can't you marry me?"

"Because I don't want to commit my heart and soul to you and have you leave me later on when you've grown tired of me!"

Her startling reply renders him speechless.

Where in the world did that come from?

He thought they were past this, having done everything he could to show her she could trust him. Closing his eyes, he takes a deep breath to calm himself, then he moves closer and gently takes her face in his hands.

"I know you have been hurt, Mali, and I wish I could take it all away. I wish I could say I understand what you are feeling, but I can't. You have been abandoned twice in your life and I know it hurt you tremendously both times. But I am not Jake, Mali. And I am not your father." He caresses her wet cheek. "I am a man who has loved you for almost half my life." His voice cracks with emotion. "And I'll never stop. Because my love for you is the forever kind. It's unconditional, Mali. Get that through your head once and for all. I will not abandon you. Never. You're going to have to trust me."

Her defenses weakening, Mali again allows his words to seep into her mind and reach into her heart. Her head is still tempted to fight with her heart, but when his warm mouth quickly presses against hers, all the fight leaves her. With his kiss, Jake's words fade from her mind. As Phillip's arms enfold her and his kiss deepens, she can literally feel emotion stirring in him, and she can no longer doubt his love. It had been there in everything he had said and done. She truly believes he has always loved her, and he always will. His love really is the forever kind.

After drying off, Mali tells Phillip about her earlier conversation with Jake. Phillip says he wishes he had been there. Mali is glad he hadn't been because she wound not have wanted anyone hurt, though if she were being truthful, seeing Phillip laying into Jake would have been rather liberating. Now she just wants to put it all behind her and begin her new life with Phillip. She is weary of doubting, and she just wants to trust. She vows silently that from this day forward, she will trust in him, trust in his love and their love for each other.

The two spend the rest of the afternoon talking, just enjoying their time together. Phillip informs Mali he is taking her out to dinner and she quickly changes and does her hair and makeup. On the way, they make a stop at Phillip's place so can change as well.

Phillip cherishes every moment he is in Mali's presence. After dreaming of being with her for so long, just being near her stirs his emotions, and his love for her grows with each passing second. He finds himself giving his arms a pinch every now and again, assuring himself that it isn't all a dream, that he is really with her and she really loves him. He knows deep down there are probably still a few doubts ingrained in her and it will take some time to put her fears to rest, but he is determined to do everything in his power to drive away her fears and help her to know with certainty that he will never desert her. He will show her what forever really means.

Having finished eating, Mali reaches across the table and takes Phillip's hand, squeezing it gently. "Do you think we will be as happy as your mom and dad?"

He smiles warmly. "Oh, at least as happy." He is thoughtful for a moment. "If ever there was a great love story, theirs is it. Mama shared it with me when I was ten, and I've never forgotten."

"What makes their story so great?"

Phillip laces his fingers between hers. "Well, to truly understand how amazing it is, I would have to start from the beginning."

"You remember that many details?" she asks incredulously.

"I remember every single thing she told me. It was truly incredible the way they came together."

As Mali observes his awe-filled expression, she longs to know the story that tugs at his heart so. "Start from the beginning."

He moves his chair closer to hers and takes her hand again. "Well, actually, it all started with my grandmother, my father's mother. Her husband died before Papa was born. She stayed in Venice and raised him alone. She worked hard all her life and managed to put some money away for Papa. After she died, Papa took the money she left him and moved to America. After moving around a bit, he finally settled in Salt Lake City and opened a restaurant here. It hadn't been open a year when an arsonist set fire to the place, burning it to the ground."

Mali's eyes widen. "How terrible!"

"I know. Papa moved back to Italy after that. He bought the home we now live in and opened *St. John's Place*."

"Where some the best Italian dishes in the world are created," Mali says with a smile.

He grins. "My father is an amazing chef," he agrees. "He always has been."

"And you take after him."

He looks down humbly. "I still have a lot to learn, but I try." When she leans over and kisses his lips, he smiles and clears his throat. "Anyway," he continues and she laughs as he attempts to get back on track. "A few months after the restaurant opened, my father met Ingo Kelly when he came in for lunch one day.

They soon became the best of friends. To Papa, Ingo was the brother he never had and they became very close.

"My mother was raised in North Carolina. Her childhood was painful, full of abuse and neglect . . ."

When he hesitates, Mali gives his hand a comforting squeeze, urging him to go on. She had never known much about Cisely's life and is anxious to hear more.

"Mama went through years of drug and alcohol addiction before becoming clean and sober."

Mali's eyes again widen. She would never have guessed Cisely had had so many struggles, and she cannot picture her ever living that kind of life. She turns her attention back to what he is saying.

"A little over a year after becoming sober, Mama met a woman named Jessica Kelly. She was visiting from Salt Lake. Jessica was Ingo's aunt."

"That's amazing."

"It is. Jessica and Mama became close in the week Jessica was there. A couple of months after she left, Mama received a letter from Jessica inviting her to come and stay with her in Utah for a while in the hope that she would grow to love it so much, she would want to stay permanently. So, Mama went because she wanted to start over. While she was living with Jessica, Ingo came to visit. His aunt introduced him to Mama, they fell in love and soon married."

"So, your brother was named after his biological father," Mali interjects.

"Yes, but it was actually a decision made by Mama and Papa." When Mali looks confused, he continues on quickly. "You see, not very long after they were married, Ingo was killed in a skiing accident."

"How awful!" Mali says, imagining the grief Cisely and Adagio must have felt.

"It was," he agrees. "But Mama and Papa were a comfort to each other and a bond formed between them. Then they slowly began to fall in love. They tried for a while to fight their feelings, and they both experienced guilt over the love they felt, but the time soon came when they could no longer deny what was between them. They both prayed a great deal and eventually came to the conclusion that what they felt was right and they were supposed to be together.

"After they confessed their love for each other, Papa asked Mama to marry him and she accepted. Before she had the baby, they decided together that his name should be Ingo Kelly St. John. They married a month after my brother was born and have been happy ever since."

"That's incredible!" Mali says, awed by the whole story. "They have an amazing marriage. It's like they were meant to be together."

"They were. I have never seen a couple more connected than they are."

Cupping his face, she leans over and kisses him and softly says, "That is the kind of love we will have."

He smiles. "We will."

Phillip takes Mali home and they stand on the front porch for a while, holding one another.

"I don't want the night to end," he whispers, tightening his embrace a little.

"Neither do I," she says, relishing the feel of his arms around her. She looks into his eyes. "I look forward to the day when we won't have to say goodbye to each other."

Pressing a kiss to her brow, he buries his face in her hair. "I do too," he murmurs, then sighs. "I love you so much."

"I love you, too. More than words can express."

"Soon the day will come when you will be totally mine. On that day there will be no more holding back, and I will be able to fully show you how much I love you."

Mali felt warmth spread through her. Pressing a kiss to his lips, she whispers, "I long for that day as well."

Ninety-nine

Three weeks later.

Surrounded by family and a few close friends, Phillip and Mali pledge their love to each other and are married on our veranda, continuing the family tradition. As Adagio and I witness our son's union, we are deeply grateful that another of our children has found happiness.

Looking over at Ingo and his wife, I feel a deep sense of contentment. They are doing well and seem very happy. Watching Ingo for a moment, I cannot help thinking of how much he looks like my first husband. He has his father's looks and mannerisms, and I can see why Erika immediately fell in love with him. They make a striking couple.

Isabelle's dreamy romantic expression warms my heart, and I know it is only a matter of time before it will be her turn to be the bride.

Ian's *"Let's get this over so we can eat"* expression causes me to choke back a snort. Some things never change.

I smile, glancing over at Sadie and Peter. They are so good together. Their adoration for one another is obvious, and I am grateful to have them in my life.

I feel the absence of Anna and her husband, Mario, and hope all is well with them. Mario underwent a complicated hip surgery last week and is still recuperating. We are all disappointed that they cannot be here, but they are in everyone's thoughts.

As my eyes move over to Wendy, I am saddened that she is still alone, and I hope she will one day find love again. I know Wendy still hopes for that as well, but she seems happier now than she has been in years, which makes me happy.

All the way around, life is good. I finally turn, meeting Adagio's loving gaze, and I sense his contentment in the life we share as well. He lifts my hand to his lips, silently conveying his love for me, and I reciprocate with my own adoring gaze before returning my attention to our son and his bride.

Phillip gazes into Mali's eyes as they are pronounced man and wife, and when he kisses her, those words penetrate his heart. He had longed for this day since he was twelve, and now that it is really here, it is everything he'd hoped for and so much more.

Mali sheds tears of joy as she contemplates that she is now Mrs. Adagio Phillip St. John the second. After everything that had happened in her life, she never thought she could be so happy or so blessed. She loves Phillip with all her heart and soul, and she is thankful that he never gave up on her.

At the conclusion of the ceremony, the two are showered with hugs from family and friends. Wendy and Mali share a long and emotional embrace. Finally releasing her, Wendy hugs Phillip.

"Thank you," she whispers tearfully. "Thank you for loving my daughter, and for helping her to realize how worthy she is of being loved."

He returns her embrace with fervor. "It is a privilege for me to love your daughter," he whispers back with emotion.

Adagio and I stand and wait until the last of the hugs are given. Then it is our turn. Adagio takes Phillip's face in his hands and presses a kiss to his forehead. Then looking into his eyes, he says, "I am so proud of you, son. You are a good man."

Tears quickly fill Phillip's eyes. "My goal has always been to be like you, Papa."

"You are a better man than me, son." Adagio then embraces Mali and says, "Welcome to the family, Mrs. St. John." He moves back, touching her face. "We have always considered you a member of our family. Now it is official and I could not be happier."

"Thank you," Mali says, smiling through the tears. "I feel the same."

Phillip reaches for me and I move into his embrace. Nothing is said between us, for no words are needed. He knows my heart just as I have always known his.

Drawing back, I press a hand to his face. "I love you so much."

"I love you too, Mama," he says, his voice thick with emotion.

"And I love you, my daughter," I tell Mali, hugging her.

"I love you too." She smiles. "I guess I can't call you Aunt Cisely anymore."

I grin. "Cisely will do just fine."

"How about Mama?"

Chuckling, I touch her cheek. "Even better."

After the wedding, we head over to the restaurant for a wedding brunch. Adagio had posted a flier two weeks ago informing customers that we would be closed today. He offered to pay the kitchen crew for working, but Sam and the rest of the employees insisted on doing the reception for free, offering their services as a wedding gift to Phillip and Mali.

The afternoon is filled with fun, laughter, good food, and warm conversation.

Phillip cannot keep his eyes off Mali, anticipating the time when he will have her all to himself. When the festivities finally wind down, he takes his bride's hand in his and announces, "We're grateful to all of you for being here to help celebrate our marriage, and we want to thank you for all you have done to help make this day so special." He grins slyly. "But now it is time for my wife and I to hit the road." After some laughter, he adds, "We will see you all next week." And with that, he picks up his grinning bride and carries her out of the restaurant, laughing as they move through the cheering crowd.

As they pass his parents, he hears his mother tell his father, "He is definitely your son."

Phillip smiles as his father laughs and pulls his mother close, saying back, "Exactly!"

The newlyweds change and ride the train into Venice to stay for the night before flying to Greece.

When they reach their suite, Phillip puts Mali down to unlock the door. As soon as they are inside, he pulls her into his arms and kisses her more passionately than he'd ever allowed himself to before. Mali clings to him and he feels both dizzy and deliriously in love.

Parting his lips from hers slightly, he whispers, "I love you so much."

"I love you too," she whispers back just before he picks her up and carries her into the bedroom. And when the door is closed, he teaches Mali what it means to be loved by Phillip St. John.

Adagio and I visit with our children and Wendy, and talk for the rest of the afternoon. As it grows late, we finally say goodnight and return to the main part of the house.

I change into a gown, replaying the events of the afternoon in my mind. It was a beautiful ceremony and I am so happy for Philip and Mali. The two have traveled a long hard road, but they made it, and I am sure their love will be stronger for it. I absently rub my leg for a moment just below the knee before picking up the brush to run it through my hair.

"Is it bothering you, *amore?*" Adagio asks, entering the bathroom at that moment.

"A little," I answer with a smile. "No more than normal."

He takes the brush from my hand and places it on the counter. Grabbing a bottle of lotion, he takes my hand. "Come," he says, leading me to the bed.

Leaning back against the pillows, I stretch out my leg. Adagio rubs some lotion between his hands and gently massages it into my leg. Closing my eyes, I sigh as he performs the ritual that he'd started years ago whenever my leg has given me any trouble.

"Thank you," I say softly.

"You are welcome." He looks into my eyes. "It is nothing compared to the sacrifice you made that day in the rain." He runs his fingers over the long scar below my knee.

"Not very pretty, is it?"

"No," he answers, leaning down and kissing it. "It is beautiful because it is a part of you." He continues to run his finger over the raised line of skin. "This scar will always remind me of how fragile life is, and it helps me remember to never take you for granted."

I press a hand into his hair and caress his face. "You never have."

Pouring more lotion into his hand, he continues to massage my leg. "It has been a wonderful day."

"It has been. And it has so good to see Ingo again. I will miss his little family when they go back to the states."

"So will I."

When Adagio is finished, I thank him again and we get in bed.

"Well," he says, turning off the light and pulling me close, "only two more weddings to go, Mrs. St. John."

I smile, snuggling deeper in his arms. "It won't be long at all."

"Time is passing by quickly." His voice is soft.

I hear the unspoken words in his somber tone. Cupping his cheek, I kiss his lips in the darkness. "I love you, Adagio."

"I love you," he murmurs back, deepening the kiss, and I silently relish his warmth as his touch transports me to another world—a world where our love roams free and we are untouched by time.

J. Adams

One hundred

We watch the growth and progression of our family with quiet contentment.

Phillip and Mali adjust to married life well. I am very happy they choose to live with us, and Adagio is pleased to have Phillip take over the position of head chef at the restaurant. He trusts Phillip implicitly and knows the kitchen crew is in good hands.

Three months after the wedding, we take a trip back to the states and spend a week with Ingo and his family. We treasure the time we are able to spend with our granddaughter and make the most of every opportunity to spoil her. We take her on a shopping trip to the toy store, a picnic in the park, walks through the neighborhood, and a day at a family fun center, all of which give Ingo and Erika a break and some alone time.

While we are in the states, we spend a few days in Salt Lake City. We relish being alone in the big house and again soak in the many memories we have made there through the years.

The following year, our family is abundantly blessed with more grandchildren. Ingo's wife gives birth to a son they name Patrick after his biological grandfather, and Phillip and Mali are blessed with triplet girls. They named one Marcella, after Adagio's mother, Geneva, after mine, and the third, Jessica. Needless to say, we are very touched by their name choices. The babies are small and have to remain in the hospital for a few weeks, but they are healthy and grow quickly.

We love our grandchildren beyond words and take every opportunity to spoil them as much as possible.

Within four years, we welcome three more grandchildren, including a son born to Mali and Phillip. There was no question as to what he would be named, and Adagio is thrilled to finally have a grandson carrying on his name.

Isabelle falls in love and marries a young chef working at the restaurant. Martino Battiato is a wonderful man from an affluent family who loves Isabelle with all his heart. The two were made for each other and are very happy.

Ian returns from college in California. The next year he marries Serena, an old friend, who also happens to be Martino's sister. We are pleased that both siblings are settled only twenty minutes away in Venice. We love having them so close, and we visit them often. Life is very good.

The Legacy

As I enter this new phase of my life, I find the purpose of life ever-present in my mind. The years are passing quickly, but time is also ringing more eternal. And my thoughts are permanently fixed on the important things.

Cisely St. John's journal

One hundred-one

The years come and go, and more grandchildren are born. Many holidays see the big house full of running and laughing children as we keep up our tradition of getting together every other year for Christmas.

And every evening, Adagio and I relax on the veranda and enjoy the sunset. We discuss our children and what is going on in their lives. They are all doing well and continually striving to live good lives. They have trials in life just like everyone else in the world, but they get through them and continue to endure. We cannot ask for more for them.

After decades of absence, the nightmares have started again. I try to pinpoint a trigger, but there is none, and though they are not as vivid or intense as they once were, they still cause me to awaken in a cold sweat. On these nights, Adagio holds me, giving me comfort. And when his arms are not enough, he makes love to me and helps me forget. His kisses and touches are like a healing balm, and I eagerly lose myself in his love.

I find myself passing many days in analytical thought and conversations with Adagio about the dreams, but nothing seems to bring me the clarity I seek.

So, I try to let it go.

With the passing of years, the sporadic nightmares continue, causing me to grow restless. I try to stay busy, doing charity work, traveling with Adagio, and anything else I can do to keep emotionally and physically active, but it still is not enough to calm the restlessness. It is almost like there is something I am supposed to be doing, only I don't know what it is. Adagio begins to feel it as well.

We finally sit down and discuss our feelings. After pondering on it a while, the answer to my dilemma comes.

And it is an answer that completely surprises us both.

A sense of melancholy fills me as I take in the familiar scenic beauty of North Carolina. It has been many years since we visited the state of my birth, and now here we are, back in Asheville.

And I have no idea why.

Pete and Donna have long since passed away, and Velma and her husband moved to New York years ago, so I don't know why I have felt such a strong need to return.

We have been in North Carolina for a while now, and though we miss the family, we've enjoyed ourselves immensely. However, each morning when I awaken, I carry the hope that I will finally discover what has drawn me back. For now, we will just tour the state and stop where it feels right.

We have been in Winston Salem for two months and plan to stay another month before going back to Italy. I've thoroughly enjoyed our time here, and though I still have no clue why we *are* here, there is still time to find out.

After spending the morning doing laundry, shopping for groceries, and writing letters to the family, we decide to grab some lunch at the mall food court. Adagio pulls into a parking spot, then comes around and opens the door for me. I thank him, giving him my hand.

Walking to the entrance, I glance over and find him staring at me. I smile. "What are you thinking about, my love?"

He smiles back slowly. "I was just thinking that no matter how old we are, you will always be the most beautiful thing in the world to me."

I squeeze his hand. "I feel the same way about you." At sixty-two, my hair is still thick and generously streaked with gray, which I still wear long, pulled back in a ponytail with wispy bangs. And at almost seventy-two, Adagio has aged like a fine wine as they say, his thick silver waves brushing his collar.

When we enter the mall, he whispers, "Okay, *amore*, don't look in any store windows until after we have eaten. Otherwise, I will starve waiting for you to shop."

I laugh. "Don't worry. I won't put you through that today. Besides, we already have plenty of souvenirs for everyone, so I'll probably only shop for things we will need until we leave for home." I chuckle as Adagio feigns relief.

We walk through the mall at a leisurely pace, observing people coming and going. The crowd is more teenagers than adults. Leaning over to Adagio, I whisper, "I suddenly feel very old."

He grins. "Well, if you are old, baby, I guess I am ancient."

I pat his hand. "Oh, you're not ancient, just very mature." He smirks and I laugh.

We pass a group of rowdy teenagers. The girls are immodestly dressed with various piercings in their ears and on their faces. The guys are equally disturbing, wearing baggy clothing and multiple piercings as well.

I remind myself not to be judgmental, and that I don't know anything about them or their home life. I am still pondering on the group when a young lady walks by pushing a cleaning cart. Looking at her, she cannot be more than eighteen or nineteen years old. She is curvy, her uniform is neatly pressed and fits her well. Her skin tone is slightly tan, and her wavy hair— which is pulled back in a ponytail—is the blackest black I have ever seen. Thin wisps of hair softly frame her face. Taking in her facial features, I muse that except for the hard look in her gray eyes, she is very pretty. She looks as if she is angry at the world and I sense a great deal of pain behind those eyes.

Taking Adagio by surprise, I stop and watch the girl as she stops to change the bag in a garbage can located next to the group of teenagers. One of the guys in the group points at her and they all start calling out hateful things. It is obvious the young woman is doing her best to ignore them. She finishes changing the garbage and tosses the full bag on top of the cart.

As she moves past the group, one of the guys bumps the cart, pushing it over. The garbage sack breaks and cleaning supplies scatter everywhere.

The girl swears softly, then stoops down and begins picking up the garbage that has fallen out of the bag. The teenagers laugh and walk off.

Adagio and I look at each other sadly. We approach and begin helping her pick everything up. Glancing at Adagio, I can tell he is a little annoyed that no one bothers to stop and help. People just step around the objects and continue on their way.

Anger flashes in the young woman's eyes. "You don't have to do that," she says harshly. "I can do it myself."

"We know you can," I say softly, smiling at her. "We just wanted to help."

Her eyes soften a little. She says nothing more as we collect all the things that have fallen. When Adagio puts the last rolls of paper towels on the cart, she looked at us and says, "Thanks." Her voice is a little softer this time.

"You are very welcome," Adagio says.

Glancing at us once more, she walks away.

"She is in a lot of pain," I say softly.

"I think so too," Adagio agrees, taking my hand.

Andrea walks slowly down the busy street, making her way home, a combination of anger and sadness creasing her brow as her thoughts rest on the incident at work. She thought she had become immune to cruel taunts and unkind treatment. After all, she has been cleaning up after loud mouthed teenaged patrons for a year now. She attempts to act tough, pretending she does not care, but it still hurts.

There have been so many times that she has asked God why she even exists. The world is rotten and she hates life, and she considers hers a total waste. There are no brothers or sisters, and no mother or father for that matter. Her father ran off before she was even born. Then her mother decided she really did not care for the title and left her with her grandmother so she could pursue her own dreams. Because of this, Andrea learned the meaning of rejection early in life. Her only achievement so far is graduating from high school. But what good did it do her? There is no money for college, and the little she makes pays the rent on her room and puts a little food on the table. She has nothing going for her and sees no reason to have aspirations. She doesn't have time for elusive dreams. She can only concentrate on surviving.

Andrea angrily brushes the tears away, determined not to give in to emotional weakness. She is stronger than this. At least she had been. Once upon a time she could handle any and everything the world dished out at her.

But now, as far as she is concerned, the sooner she can leave this world, the better. Since her life is worthless, living is just a waste of time as well. She will suffer through it just a little bit longer.

Maybe.

One hundred-two

Four days later . . .

We decide to catch an early movie and have dinner afterward.

As we pull away from the curb of the bed and breakfast we have lived in for the past couple of months, I put a hand over Adagio's and ask him to stop.

"What is it, *amore?*"

"Look," I say pointing to a girl entering a large house three doors down.

He follows my gaze. "That is the young woman from the mall," he states more than asks.

"It is," I say with a smile. "I have thought about her a lot this past week. There is just something that has kept her on my mind."

"With all the time we have stayed in this neighborhood, I can't believe we have not seen her before now," Adagio says.

"I can't either."

Squeezing my hand, he starts the car and moves forward a little, stopping in front of the large rooming house. He turns off the engine and we sit for a moment, staring up at the house. The place looks like another bed and breakfast. It is well kept and the yard is lovely.

"Let's go inside," I say.

"We will probably have to knock on a few doors to find the right room," Adagio says, opening the door for me. "And we don't even know her name."

"I do," I say, smiling.

His eyes widen in surprise. "How?"

"The day after the incident, I called the mall and asked about her. They couldn't give me any other information, but they did give me her first name."

Adagio smiles and squeezes my hand. "You are amazing, you know that?"

"No more than you, my love."

We enter the building and knock on several doors but get no answer. We walk up to the second floor. Two more doors are unanswered. I knock on the next door twice and am about to move on to another when I hear the clicking of the lock. The door is cracked open slightly and I quickly smile.

Andrea stares blankly at the two older people. "Yeah?" she says, wondering what they want.

"I don't know if you remember us, but we met you at the mall last week. Some teens were giving you a hard time while you were working, and my husband and I stopped to help you."

"Yeah, I do," she says warily. Suspicion fill her eyes. "How did you find out where I lived? You follow me home or something?"

Cisely again smiles, shaking her head. "It just so happens we have been staying at the bed and breakfast down the street from your building and saw you when you came home."

Andrea continues to stare at them, still wondering what they want.

"My name is Cisely St. John." She pulls Adagio within Andrea's view. "And this is my husband, Adagio. We live in Italy and have been visiting here for the past few months. We wanted to formally meet you and let you know we were thinking about you."

Andrea does not know what to say. This is something new for her. Even hearing the words, "we were thinking about you" is foreign. "I'm Andrea," she finally says.

"It is a pleasure to meet you, Andrea," Adagio says.

Andrea is again taken aback by their kindness, almost as much as she was the day that they stopped to help her. She leans her head against the door and sighs. "I can't tell you how many times stuff like that has happened." She looks into Cisely's eyes. "You were the first people who ever tried to help." She opens the door wider, her eyes softening. "You can come in if you want."

Adagio smiles, squeezing Cisely's hand. "We would like that."

Moving aside, she lets them enter. She clears some books from the small couch and places them on a table in the corner. Gesturing for them to sit down, Andrea pulls a chair from the desk and sits across from them, her eyes moving around the room. "I know it's not much, but it's home."

Cisely glances at their surroundings. "It's lovely, Andrea." A beautiful quilt covers the twin-size bed. The floral and check patterns are brightly-colored and it looks handmade. Cisely tells her how beautiful it is.

"Thanks. My grandmother made it. She died before she could finish the matching pillow covering."

"When did she pass away?" Cisely asks with compassion.

"Last year."

"I'm sorry."

"Yeah, well . . . me too."

"Do you have any other family here?" Adagio asks.

"No," she answers tonelessly. "My grandmother was it."

Adagio and I glance at one another, both of us curious about her parents but not daring to ask just yet. Instead, I casually pick up a thick book lying on the coffee table. "*Roots*," I murmur, opening the front cover. "I love this book." Glancing at Andrea, I notice a slight smile tugging at her lips. "The stories of Alex Haley's ancestors are incredible," I continue. "It's one of my favorite books."

"It's mine, too. I would like to do that one day."

"You mean, you would like to trace your roots?"

"Yeah." Her voice is somber, despite her efforts to sound tough. "I mean, since I have no relatives to speak of, or at least that I know of, it would be nice to find out about the dead ones. I'd like to know the kind of people I came from."

"I can empathize. Other than my immediate family and a couple of cousins, I have no other relatives. But you probably feel completely alone. It must be hard sometimes."

"It is," she agrees somberly.

"What about friends?" Adagio asks. "A great person like you must have many."

When she shakes her head, I smile. "Well, you do now."

Andrea knows nothing about these people, yet they are already working their way into her heart. They have a quiet way about them and she feels different just talking to them. And maybe knowing them will give her a reason to want to stick around in this life a bit longer. Yeah, that will be the test. She shakes her head slightly, unable to believe what she is about to say.

"I would like to be friends."

J. Adams

One hundred-three

I lay awake listening to the sound of Adagio's deep breathing, unable to turn my thoughts off enough to sleep. The whole evening keeps replaying itself over and over again in my mind. It had been one of the most amazing days we have had here so far.

Andrea Gaston was like a sponge, soaking in our every word. Each thing we shared about ourselves and our family was met with questions. And when we answered those, she bombarded us with even more questions. I have never seen such a desire, such a thirst for an emotional connection in anyone before. I could see her slowly internalizing everything just by looking at her face. By the end of the evening she did not look like the same girl. The anger that once permanently creased her brow had literally disappeared. And when she smiled, her face seemed to transform, making her absolutely beautiful. I know now what made her beautiful. It was the knowledge that someone truly cares about her, and the knowledge that she will never be alone in the world again.

Two hours later, we finally left, offering to take her to dinner tomorrow evening. Adagio and I talked about Andrea all the way home, neither of us able to believe all that happened. Not only did we make a new friend, we also managed to get her to open up more about herself. Andrea talked with us about growing up with her grandmother. She shared her feelings about her parents and the abandonment she still feels most of the time.

I brush a tear away as I remember Andrea's words to us before we left. She told us that we had literally saved her life, because she had seriously been contemplating suicide. She had been miserable for a long time and was basically done with this life. She said if we had not stopped to help her that day in the mall, she would not have given us the time of day, much less let us into her room. We tearfully embraced her and told her how special she is, and how glad we are to be her friends.

When I sniffle, Adagio turns to his side, facing me.

"Are you all right, *amore*?" he asks sleepily.

"I'm fine. Just thinking about tonight."

He opens his arms and I move into them. "It was pretty amazing, wasn't it?"

I nod, resting my head against his shoulder. "I think leaving the bed and breakfast at the same time Andrea was arriving home is one of those '*God moves in mysterious ways*' moments."

He pressed his face into my hair. "I think you are right. I am very grateful for those moments."

"So am I." I yawn. "I'm sorry I woke you up."

"It's all right."

Closing my eyes, I snuggle close, my final thought of the night being a prayer of gratitude to God for placing us in Andrea's life at the right time.

Andrea sniffles and wipes her eyes.

Getting into bed, she turns out the light and lay awake for a while, thinking about Cisely and Adagio and how special they made her feel. For the first time in her life, she feels important, like she is here for a reason and her life is not a complete waste. She cannot believe how much has changed, how *she* has changed. For the past year, there has been no hope. Now her heart is filled with it, and she wonders how it happened so quickly. How can she be so happy when just this morning she had been shrouded in despair?

She does not have an answer. But she loves the feeling and never wants it to go away.

Adagio and Cisely pick Andrea up and take her to dinner. The evening is full of warm conversation. She is again full of questions, which they happily answer. They drop her off that night with plans set to treat her to brunch in a few days.

Andrea gets up early on Saturday to get ready, wanting to look nice. After showering, she puts on a white blouse and the only dress slacks she owns. They are a pair of black slacks she'd purchased to wear to her grandmother's graveside service. She likes them because they make her look thinner. She pairs the pants with black dress pumps. She leaves her wavy hair down, falling just past her shoulders. Since she has never owned any makeup, she'd made a trip to the dollar store yesterday and purchased some blush, mascara, and lip gloss. Smiling, she applies the cosmetics with care.

When Andrea answers the door, Cisely immediately tells her how lovely she looks and Adagio echoes her sentiments. Andrea blushes deeply and thanks them, feeling beautiful for the first time in her life.

They enjoy a leisurely brunch at one of the nicest restaurants Andrea has even been in, and she does her best to take everything in, unable to believe she is really there. She smiles at Cisely and Adagio throughout the meal, feeling renewed gratitude to have them in her life.

One hundred-four

It has been two weeks since meeting Cisely and Adagio, and Andrea still marvels at the changes in her life. She has never known such peace. Before meeting them, she truly did not think she had much to live for. Now, not only does she have a life, she *loves* life. And she is being blessed beyond belief.

One of those blessings has been a new job. A man who recently moved into the apartment building next to her rooming house owns a small car dealership and had been in need of a receptionist. Andrea applied for the job, using Adagio and Cisely as references. Fortunately, they happen to be visiting Andrea when he stopped by to talk with her about the job and were able to meet him. The four were instantly taken with one another.

Andrea enjoys her new job and really likes working for Mr. Cole, or Jacob as he likes to be called. Getting to know the older black man, she finds she has a great deal in common with him. Jacob had been raised by a single mother who died five years ago at the age of eighty-three. He never knew his father because the man had been married when he had an affair with Jacob's mother. Jacob says he holds nothing against the father he never knew because he has made mistakes in his own life. A couple of times, Andrea, along with Cisely and Adagio, have dinner at Jacob's home. Since he lives alone and has no family, he enjoys having them over.

Cisely suspects Jacob is lonely a lot of the time. She and Adagio feel a great deal of empathy for him and stop by the car dealership to see him whenever they can. They also visit Andrea while there. Cisely is happy to see the bond forming between Andrea and Jacob. They have both been alone in the world, so the friendship is very important to them.

We spend our final week in Winston Salem visiting a few friends we have made during our time here and saying our goodbyes. While we will miss everyone, we will miss Andrea and Jacob most of all. They will always have a special place in our hearts.

Phillip calls us a couple of times during the week. We have missed him greatly and eagerly anticipate seeing him again. He fills us in on the rest of the family and how things are going at the restaurant. He tells us how well our grandson, young Adagio, is mastering his grandfather's recipes, and he is now cooking at the restaurant two days a week.

Adagio tells Phillip how proud he is of them both for running the place so well.

We long to see our family again and look forward to the day when we are reunited.

Two days before we are scheduled to leave for Italy, we stop by Andrea's place and catch her in the middle of doing some genealogy. She has been gathering all the information she can get her hands on during the past week. She has copies of birth and death certificates and is beginning to piece everything together. She is excited about some of her findings and has been anxious to share them with us.

"Oh, Cisely," she says as we sit around the table, "I can't tell you how good it feels to finally know something about my family."

I smile. "We're so happy for you."

"And proud," Adagio adds. "Okay, show us what you have so far."

"All right." Andrea unrolls the family tree chart.

Adagio takes his glasses from his pocket. He puts them on and bends a little closer as she points out all the names on the chart and tells us what she knows about them. We both notice the blank spot where her father should have been listed.

"Why do you not have your father's name written here?" Adagio asks.

Andrea looks up and sighs. "Because I don't know my biological father's name." When my puzzled expression joins Adagio's, Andrea says, "Darren Gaston was not really my father. My mother just picked his name to put on my birth certificate. My grandmother told me my mother was rather messed up. She didn't want me to one day go looking for my real father, so she used one of her many boyfriends' names." She pushes the hair back from her face. "Grandmother never knew my father. She only knew what my mother told her about him."

I squeeze her hand. "Well, not being a part of your life is his loss, isn't it? And your mother's as well."

Andrea doesn't respond. She smiles sadly and returns her attention to the chart. Her eyes move up to her grandmother's name, her expression turning melancholy. I can tell she still misses her. Her finger moves up to the name of her great-grandmother. "My grandmother wasn't too close to her mother."

"Do you know why?" I ask.

"Well, she said it was because she was a hateful woman who spent her whole life being judgmental of others and was just basically a miserable person." She pauses, becoming thoughtful. "My grandmother thought her mother was probably that way because of her own parents."

Adagio sighs. "If that is true, then how sad for them."

Andrea nods. "You know, my grandmother even mentioned something about her mother having a sister that the family had basically disowned. She never knew why."

Adagio and I shake our heads sadly. Looking into his eyes, I know he is thinking about my past trials with my own family. Life is just too short to hold onto grudges.

"Did your great-grandmother ever tell your grandmother what happened to her sister?" he asks.

"Not really. She just said she married some Hawaiian guy and moved away. I don't think anybody heard from her after that."

I study Andrea's features. Her look is subtly exotic. "Forgive me, but would you mind if I asked you what race you are?"

"No," Andrea answers. "I inherited my Cherokee blood from my mother. As for my father, I couldn't tell you what race he is. He had to have been dark though. Maybe black. Who knows?"

"God knows," Adagio says. "And as diligently as you are researching your family, I'm sure you will find out one day as well."

"I hope so, because deep down I have always wondered."

Adagio finally checks the time and decides we had better get going if we want to get over to Jacob's in time for dinner. As we stand, Adagio and I embrace Andrea and tell her how grateful we are to have her in our lives.

"I feel like you are my family now," Andrea says smiling through misty eyes. "I'm really going to miss you. Since meeting you, I haven't felt alone in the world."

"You never will be," I tell her. "We will always be thinking of you. Maybe you can even come and visit us one day soon. We will even foot the bill."

"I would like that," she says with a smile.

We have no idea, however, as we leave Andrea's that pieces are about to be connected, pieces which will complete a puzzle that will give new depth to our lives.

One hundred-five

We enjoy the delicious dinner Jacob prepared. He had informed us earlier that it is actually a going away dinner for us, and he told us how much we will be missed. We will miss him as well.

We repeatedly compliment Jacob on his cooking. Southern cooking is something neither of us have ever been able to quite master, even though I was born and raised here. Jacob tells us he learned everything he knows about cooking from his mother, and since he hasn't had anyone but himself to cook for since she died, he's had plenty of time to practice. He is happy to see us enjoying it so much.

We dine on breaded catfish, garlic potatoes, green beans flavored with bits of ham, and cornbread. Dessert is pecan pie and bread pudding. I can't help smiling as I watch my husband mentally taking notes of how everything is prepared, and I am sure he will be asking Jacob for his recipes before the night ends.

"I can't believe you've never been married," Andrea says, taking another bite of the fish. "You would make some lucky woman very happy."

Jacob smiles, his expression thoughtful. "I came close to being married once, but . . . it didn't work out. It turned out that we were more different than I'd realized, and we didn't want the same things–like me wanting to get married and her not wanting to be tied down."

"Well," Andrea says, "she didn't know how good she had it."

"Thank you," he says, smiling humbly.

"Have you lived here all your life?" I ask.

"No. My mother and I moved here when I was eight."

"Where did you move from?" Adagio asked.

"Charlotte."

"Really? I lived in Charlotte when I was young, too. I have never been back."

"I haven't, either. I've heard it has grown a lot though."

"I'm sure it has. Of course, I thought Charlotte was big when I was young."

Jacob chuckles. "Everything seems bigger at that age."

"This is true" I say, grinning. "What made your mother decide to move here?"

"Well, actually, she never would tell me. I mean, many years later she did, but during the time it was happening, she just said she wanted to start out fresh somewhere else. So, she moved us here."

"She must have been going through a rough time," Adagio says, spooning more potatoes onto his plate.

"She was. And I learned just how rough when she finally told me the real reason we left." Jacob pauses, again becoming thoughtful. "She found out that the man who fathered me was married and had a kid a little older than me. Mama knew someone who knew him and his wife. The person told her he was abusive. It was all a major shock. For years after that, Mama tried to move on in her life and forget about him, but she couldn't. Finally, she decided she couldn't stay there any longer."

I shake my head sadly. "So, you've never had any contact with him?"

"Naw," he drawls. "I never felt the desire to see him. Pretty sad, huh?"

"Yes, but it is also understandable. He was never a part of your life. You can't miss something you never had."

"I met him once before we moved. Even after seeing me, he didn't want anything to do with me. I guess that kind of stuck with me."

I nod, understanding. "It's sad how much we hurt others with our choices, especially when it comes to our children." Adagio takes my hand, squeezing it gently and I smile, knowing he is remembering just as I am. The years of sexual abuse I suffered at the hand of my father will never truly be forgotten, but I made my peace with him a long time ago.

"You know," Jacob continues, "his wife eventually died of a heart attack after years of alcoholism. He tried contacting Mama after that, but she would have nothing to do with him because it would've hurt too much to start things up with him again. Then years ago Mama heard he had died. I can't remember if it was from cancer or AIDS. I just remember mama crying." He shrugs his shoulders. "That's the way of it sometimes."

As he moves to another topic of conversation, for some reason my mind echoes over again the last thing he said. *"I can't remember if it was from cancer or AIDS." And the wife was an alcoholic and died of a heart attack?*

I lightly touch a hand to my hammering heart. I feel the squeeze of Adagio's hand and turn to find his expression mirroring mine. I chuckle inwardly, suddenly emotional. *You have got to be kidding me!*

It is Adagio who finally asks, "Jacob, do you by chance remember your father's name?" My grip on his hand tightens in anticipation of Jacob's answer.

"Yeah. His name was Alton Matthews."

We stare at him in silence. Only after the words have been spoken do I see it. Jacob has my father's eyes, and his smile. I cannot believe I didn't see it before!

"Cisely, Adagio," Andrea says, breaking the silence, "are you all right?" She glances over at Jacob, who also looks concerned.

I am suddenly so emotional, I can't speak. I press a hand to my mouth and the tears come. Adagio puts an arm around me, holding me close.

"It is all right, *cara mia,*" he whispers. Raising his teary eyes to Jacob, he says, "Forgive us. My wife felt that we needed to come back to North Carolina for some reason, but this is something we never saw coming." He chuckles emotionally. "You see, except for a couple of relatives, we thought all of Cisely's family had passed on, and now . . . we find out that you two have the same father."

I raise my eyes to Jacob, and I can tell it is taking a few seconds for his mind to process what Adagio just said. Then I watch his brown eyes grow large and teary. He looks over at me, his expression turning melancholy.

"So, you are the sister I never got the chance to know."

I swallow hard, tears falling down my face. "Not until now." With that, the two of us stand and move into each other's embrace. We hold onto one another and cry.

Over Jacob's shoulder, I watch Adagio and Andrea look at each other and smile, tears streaking their faces as well. I finally move back a little, pressing a hand to my brother's face. "This is a most unexpected blessing."

"For me too," he says, squeezing my hand.

We stay with Jacob until late, talking and sharing our lives. I cannot believe I actually have a brother! When I was a child, I wished for a sibling, then as I got older, I figured it had been for the best because of what the child would have been subjected to had it been a girl. And now to find out after all this time that I have a brother is more wonderful than I can possibly say. I know without a doubt that my prompting to come back to North Carolina was to bring our family together.

As Andrea listens to Adagio sharing how he and Cisely came to be together, she is amazed. They are two of the best people she has ever had the privilege of knowing.

"Yours sounds like a marriage made in heaven," Jacob says, taking of sip of hot chocolate.

Adagio looks into Cisely's eyes, pressing a kiss to her hand. "It is."

Jacob watches the two and smiles, a hint of sadness filling him. If things had gone the way he'd wanted in his life, he would be married with grown children of his own.

"Are you all right?" Cisely asks, covering his hand with hers.

"I'm fine. I just can't help wishing things would have worked out differently for me. I mean, don't get me wrong. I've had a good life. But it would have been nice to have a wife and kids."

Cisely squeezes his hand. "But as you said, you have lived a good life. You have accomplished a lot."

"I know," Jacob says with a smile. "I still can't help thinking about Brenda. She was a beautiful woman. I saw her a few times right after we broke up. After that, it was as if she'd disappeared from off the face of the earth. Sometimes I wonder how things would be now if she had married me." He chuckles. "I don't know, maybe we would have driven each other so crazy, our marriage would have fallen apart anyway. I was seventeen years older than she was. If we had gotten married, she would still be young while I'm now an old man."

"Hey," Cisely says, "I'm only a few years older than you. You're as old as you feel."

"Yes ma'am," Jacob says humbly and Adagio chuckles. "I won't make that mistake—"

"My mother's name was Brenda," Andrea interrupts softly. She looks at Jacob intently. "Brenda Anderson."

Jacob's expression changes, becoming unreadable. Except for Cisely's soft gasp and Adagio's whispered, *"Mama mia!"* there is silence.

"Andrea," Cisely finally says, "tell Jacob what you know about your parents."

Lifting a shaky hand, Andrea pushes her hair back from her face, then takes a deep breath, trying to steady her emotions. "Well, I only know what my grandmother told me. And she basically repeated what my mother told her, which was that my father left her pregnant and didn't want anything to do with me. That was a joke in itself considering that she dumped me off on my grandmother and took off to pursue her own dreams." She pauses, looking down at her shaking hands. "My grandmother told me she didn't really believe my mother and there had to be more to it, but I figured it was all true. I mean, why would she lie?"

Jacob closes his eyes and sighs, completely overwhelmed by the knowledge that lay before him. All this time, all these many years, he has had a daughter. He has lived in the same town with her for almost twenty years and had no clue. He opens his eyes, focusing his gaze on Andrea.

"Brenda told me she didn't want me, but she never told me she was pregnant."

"Well," Andrea says, looking at him tearfully, "she was such an unhappy person, maybe she wanted us to be unhappy too. Or, maybe she was so wrapped up in herself, she just didn't care."

"Maybe," he agrees, looking at her as if he is seeing her for the first time. He now recognizes Brenda's smile. And taking in her skin coloring, he has no doubt she is his daughter. He takes her hand, watching the tears spill down her cheeks. "Now that you know the truth, how do you feel about everything?"

Andrea smiles, moving into his open arms, and soaks in his embrace. Drawing back a little, she looks into his eyes, wiping at the tears trailing down his face. "Having had the opportunity to know you, I don't think I can ask for a better father." Hugging him again, she suddenly laughs. "This is incredible!"

Adagio and Cisely chuckle, drying their own tears.

"This whole day has been amazing," Cisely says. "We have discovered I have a brother and a niece! What a wonderful way to end a long vacation."

Adagio smiles at his wife, suddenly needing to be alone with her. "Jacob, would you mind giving your daughter a ride home?"

Jacob grins back, still reeling that Andrea is really is his daughter. "I don't mind at all."

Adagio and Cisely thank him again for dinner and the four of them share firm embraces, marveling at how wonderful the day has been for them all.

Adagio leans back against the pillows with me securely wrapped in his arms. To say the day has been a fulfilling one is an understatement. It is as if every event in my life has led me to this night, and everything has been laid out in the open before me.

"Oh, *amore*," Adagio whispers into my hair. "How fortunate I feel to be a part of something so incredible!"

I nod tearfully. "It's still so hard to believe. When I think of all the times I longed for a sibling as a child, it boggles my mind that . . . oh, if I had only known . . ."

He presses a gentle hand to my face. "All I can think is better late than never."

"True," I agree with a smile. "Thank you for sharing this experience with me," I say, pulling his head down to kiss him.

He smiles against my mouth. "By your side is the only place I will ever want to be."

J. Adams

One hundred-six

Many years later . . .

Adagio presses a light kiss to Cisely's hand as their children, grandchildren, and great grandchildren gather around them and sing the birthday song to him. Ninety-five is longer than he had ever expected to live, and he and Cisely are both grateful to have the whole family there to celebrate this special day.

He laughs as the great-grandchildren help him blow out the candles on the large cake Phillip had spent the whole morning preparing. Since he has had complete control of the restaurant for the past thirty years, he'd closed it for the family celebration. There is food galore covering a long row of tables. The rest of the tables are filled with Adagio and Cisely's posterity.

As Adagio takes in the various faces of his family members, he has to smile. The dream that had engraved itself in his heart when he was sixteen had come to pass. He has everything he could ever want. He cannot ask for more. He squeezes his wife's hand, noticing how tired her eyes look.

"Are you all right, *amore?*"

Cisely nods slightly. "I'm fine, but I wouldn't mind a cup of herbal tea." She slowly stands. "Would you like some?"

"No, thank you. Why don't you let one of the children get it for you?"

"It's all right," she assures him. "I need to stretch these old limbs anyway."

"You are only as old as you feel, angel," he says, grinning. "And you are still beautiful."

She smiles, leaning down and kissing him softly. "Thank you, my love."

Adagio watches her walk away, noticing the absence of the spring that usually accompanied her step. Even at eighty-five, she had always remained active and full of energy. This evening that energy is no longer there. The thought saddens him, so he tucks it away in the hidden recesses of his mind.

I am leaning against the metal counter stirring my tea when Phillip walks in. He smiles and I smile back, freshly amazed at how handsome he still is.

"You should have let me get that for you, Mama."

"I didn't mind."

He touches my face. "You look tired."

"I am a little tired."

"Too much partying," he says with a grin.

I chuckle. "Probably." Sobering, I look at him quietly for a moment as various thoughts flicker through my mind, but one particular thought stands out from the rest. Lifting a hand to his face, I swallow hard against the unexpected emotion. As his eyes meet mine, his face blurs through my tears.

"What is it, Mama?" he asks.

"I can't tell you how proud Papa and I are of you. You have brought us so much joy and happiness."

He touches my face. "You have been the best parents a person could ask for."

"We've tried."

"And you have succeeded."

"Thank you. Where is young Adagio?"

"As usual, he's out on the veranda indulging in one of his favorite past-times, looking through photos of you and Papa."

"Ah, I should have known. He always knows the way to my heart."

"I think you two are his favorite people in the world."

"We've definitely formed a bond." I pause, thinking of my grandson. "He's an amazing man. And I know his interests are different from yours, but give him time." I gaze around the kitchen. "This restaurant is in his blood. He will take over when it's time. Just be patient."

"I will, Mama. I think he knows Papa wants him to have it."

"He does. But even if he should choose another path for a while, it will be all right."

"I know," he says softly.

I nod, satisfied. "Now, I had better get back to your father before he comes looking for me."

Phillip waits as I take a couple of sips of the tea, then he takes my hand and we return to the dining area to be with the family.

As the evening grows late, I stand by the bedroom window, taking in the familiar view. I have come to know it so well, I can close my eyes and remember every single detail, like a snapshot embedded in my memory. Looking down into the backyard, I take in the amazing sight of our posterity as they play and wander about. I love each and every one of my family members intensely, and I've treasured every moment I have been blessed to spend with them. But I am afraid my time in this life is reaching its end.

I turn from the window at the sound of Adagio's soft voice. "Are you coming to bed, *amore?*"

"Yes." I walk over slowly and remove my robe. Sitting on the edge of the bed, I take a moment to shut my eyes against the blurred vision and breathe through the moment of dizziness, allowing the perpetual shakiness in my hands a few seconds to calm. When I am finally settled in bed, I turn to my side and face my husband. "It was a good day," I say with a sigh.

He smiles, pressing a hand to my cheek, letting his eyes roam over my face. "It *was* a good day," he agrees.

I then quietly study his face, taking in the lines around his beautiful eyes, the sign of years of laughter and living life to the fullest. I smile as my eyes move up to his full head of white hair and matching brows. Even with all the changes of old age, he is still the most handsome man in the world to me.

Fighting the light-headiness that is slowly descending upon me, I blink to clear my blurring vision and stare into his eyes again. "It has been a good life," I say softly.

Adagio reads in my expression and voice more than I have said. Continuing to caress my face, tears fill his eyes. Then he smiles. "It has been the best, *tesora mia.*"

Satisfied, I use the last of my strength to turn out the light and move into his frail arms. "I will be yours forever, my love," I whisper against his face, resting my hand against his heart.

"I know," he whispers back with emotion as his tears wet my cheek. "I know."

I'm yours forever, my love, my mind echoes once more as I slowly give in to the peaceful weightlessness—my spirit separating from the body in which I have experienced so much joy and happiness.

Epilogue

Hundreds of guests attend Cisely's funeral. The massive old church is filled with friends and acquaintances whose lives she had touched, as well as her large posterity. The day is not one of grief but joy as everyone remembers this remarkable woman and the wonderful life she lived. Cisely had made an impact on every single person she met with her kindness, generosity, warmth, and sincerity. Hers was truly a heart full of charity, and she lived her life striving to emulate Christ. She had been a potter's clay in the Master's hands, and He had taken a once-broken vessel and reshaped it into something beautiful and priceless. She will never be forgotten.

In attendance with Cisely's posterity are Sadie and Peter, and Andrea and Jacob. Jacob is now legally blind, but nothing would stop him from being at his sister's funeral, nor rob him of the chance to say goodbye to this sweet woman who he had known for too few years. He will never forget her and will always be grateful for the joy she brought to his life.

The next week, all of the children return to their homes, leaving just Phillip and his family. Though everyone is concerned about Adagio, it is Phillip and young Adagio who are most worried. They know more than anyone how desperately the father and grandfather loved his wife. Phillip is concerned, but he cannot help being amazed by the strength his father possesses. Instead of the family comforting him, he seems to comfort them.

Young Adagio spends as much time as he can by his grandfather's side, offering comfort and absorbing the love that has always been so tangible between them. He misses his grandmother terribly, and he knows he will lose his grandfather soon. It is only a matter of time.

So, he savors ever moment with the wise old man, gleaning bits and pieces of priceless knowledge from his *nono,* to record in his journal and look back on at a future time, when this loving man is no longer with them.

Phillip helps his father out to the veranda to watch the sunset. It has been a little over a week since the funeral, but the daily ritual his father once shared with his mother has not stopped. He imagines his mother there, unseen, taking her place in the chair next to her husband during these times.

Squatting down by his father's chair, Phillip asks him if he needs anything.

Adagio looks down at his son, studying his graying waves and the lines etched around his eyes. Pressing a hand to Phillip's face, he stares into his eyes intently. "I am fine, son," he finally answers.

Phillip holds his father's hand to his face, sharing his pain, yet admiring his courage and strength. "I love you, Papa."

His father smiles and slowly leans forward, pressing a kiss to his son's forehead. "I love you too. Never forget how much. You and your brothers and sister have all made me and your mother so proud."

Swallowing hard, Phillip stands to go back into the house. As he reaches the veranda doors, he hesitates. Overcome with fresh emotion, he moves back to his father. Leaning down, Phillip takes his face in his hands and kisses his cheek, saying with love and reverence, "I will always take care of things, Papa. Don't worry, all right?"

"I will not worry, son." Adagio's voice is soft. "But please be patient with young Adagio."

"I will, I promise."

Rising and moving to the door again, Phillip pauses a moment to look back at his father's tired and weary form sitting alone and taking in the sunset. He knows his father is desperately longing to be with his mother again. It is only a matter of time.

Adagio

Adagio focuses his gaze on the colored horizon, his thoughts with his wife. His life with Cisely had been more wonderful than he could put into words. She had given him everything, had *been* everything to him. How he misses her now. He has only been without her for a little over a week, but he misses her with a painful intensity that reaches deep inside and threatens to tear his heart apart.

He has done well at being strong for his family, but right now, again participating in this familiar ritual without the woman who had been a part of him for so long, the pain is magnified, becoming almost unbearable. His vision of the sunset blurs as warm tears filled his eyes. He blinks them onto his lined face.

"Oh, *amore*," he whispers, "I miss you so much." Closing his eyes, he raises his face towards the heavens. "Please come for me soon." He returns his gaze to the horizon as the sun slowly lowers. Looking down at his hands, he smiles as he pictures Cisely's light brown hand in his. He had never been able to resist touching her, and if he did not have her in his arms, her hand was usually in his. She had become such a part of him, he had felt incomplete whenever she was not with him. He feels that way now.

He closes his eyes as tears continue to fall down his face. *Please come for me soon.*

The familiar warmth that sweeps over Adagio is accompanied by a growing feeling of fatigue. He keeps his heavy eyelids closed, his body relaxing in the chair.

When Adagio finally opens his eyes, kneeling before him is his beloved, and he heaves an awe-filled sigh. Cisely looks the same as she did over sixty years ago, and her beauty takes his breath away.

She smiles up at him with eyes full of love, then reaches up and softly caresses his face.

"*Amore*," he whispers breathlessly, leaning forward.

Rising a little, Cisely presses a kiss to his lips and he closes his eyes, releasing a shaky breath. She stands, holding a slender hand out to him, her eyes roaming over his youthful, handsome features.

"Let's go home, my love."

Adagio smiles as her silky voice again washes over him. He places his hand in hers. Taking a few steps, he stops and looks back, allowing his gaze to momentarily rest on his tired old body in the chair. Turning back to his wife, he reverently touches her face before drawing her into his arms and kissing her fervently.

"Yes, my angel," he whispers against her lips, "let us go home."

The End . . . Of One Life
And the Beginning of Another

A Preview of

*T*hat *K*ind of *L*ove

The Legacy Saga

*A*ndrew is dead.

And the sigh that escapes me is one of relief and gratitude. My blind eyes can make out the shadows of medical personnel moving around the hospital room, but I can't see Andrew's still features. I don't need to. There is a new silence in the room now–the absence of irregular shallow breathing– for the next few moments. Then the soft sobs of his mother and mine dispel that silence.

With Andrew's death from undetected heart disease comes my freedom. The pressure of my parents to marry him has vanished and I feel as if a great weight has lifted, brightening my world like the sun coming out after a long, murky year of rain. I do not mean to be cold, but I never loved Andrew. I never even liked him. Nevertheless, my parents have been relentless in their desire to merge our family with Andrew Tanner's, to strategically combine two financial empires.

Andrew had been willing to put his own happiness aside, as well as mine, and go along for the ride. Had everything gone through, I would soon be trapped in a gilded prison I could not see, and would likely have died in. That death would have been a slow one, stealing my strength and my spirit a little each day until all of the things that have made me *me* disappeared, leaving an empty shell, my armor weakened, emotionally scarred and battered. Just like our parents, with Andrew, it had been all about the money. Love had nothing to do with it because, hey, let's face it. Who needs love?

"I do," I had told him. And he'd laughed. He actually laughed! It was never about our wants or desires. It was about our parents pimping us out, insuring the two companies went to bed together as soon as possible. *"After all,"* Andrew had said, *"the end justifies the means. Blind, deaf or lame, it makes no difference to me."*

I offer my condolences to the Tanners, and then extend my cane and turn to leave. I imagine the mouths of the men silently opening and closing, (sort of like I've been told that fish look lying on a shore in need of water,) and the women shooting invisible fire darts with their eyes. (That's imagined too, by the way.) Later on, I am sure my parents will dutifully harp about my cold and heartless exit, hoping to guilt me into showing the influential world the face of a grieving and heart-broken finacée.

But the days of me feeling guilty are long gone. If anything, I feel sympathy for the Tanner's loss. Andrew was their only son—their Golden Boy—the child they based their hopes and dreams on. His sisters are a different matter. Other than marrying rich men and breeding more sons to work in the family business, their two daughters are treated as if they are of no consequence.

And since I am an only child, my parents' dreams and ambitions for me are shot . . . unless a new financial opportunity emerges, an opportunity that will drive them to once again attempt to prostitute me for their gain. Of course, it figures since I am not the daughter of their blood. They adopted me during one of their philanthropic trips down south. Boy, did they ever rack up brownie points for adopting a token black baby, and a blind one at that!

Will I always be worth so little to them?

However, I have been given a healthy dose of strength, and I will no longer let my parents–Mr. And Mrs. What Can You Do for Me Patton–run my life. Thanks to the good Lord, I am in charge now, and I am open and ready to receive the kind of love, and the kind of life, He has in store for me. In God's eyes I am worth more. I don't know how much more, but definitely more than the value my parents place on my existence.

The trust fund I inherited four years ago on my twenty-first birthday has given me the financial freedom to live on my own in a downtown high-rise condominium that I own outright. And the money I earn giving violin and cello lessons takes care of my needs. I guess you could say I have it all.

Yes, you could say that . . . but you would be wrong. Until now, the thing I have desired most–what I have *needed* most–has eluded me.

I smile, sensing a coming change–a change that God has been preparing me for, and one I hope I am now ready to receive.

Treviso, Italy

Fixing his teary, emerald gaze on the large granite headstone bearing his grandparents' names, Adagio Phillip St. John the third removes his sunglasses and releases a deep sigh. It seems sunglasses have become a part of him, a shield and a mask.

It has been a month since he lost two of the dearest people in the world to him, and his heart still carries a fierce ache. How he misses them! They had always been an example to him of how he wants to live his life, and the love they shared was truly a thing to behold. His mother and father share a deep love as well, but what his grandmother and grandfather had between them was indescribable.

Adagio is thirty-four years old and has yet to marry. And he will never marry until he finds someone that he can share that kind of love with–the kind his grandparents shared. He refuses to settle. His sisters constantly tell him he is too picky, but his grandparents knew different. They truly understood him.

While he has always been called Dagio by the family to avoid confusion, his grandmother always called him "Young Adagio" because he is a mirror image of her husband in his thirties. Frequently, Adagio sat with his grandmother looking through photo albums, and each time they came to a picture of his grandfather, Adagio was amazed at how much he looked like him, even more so than his father, Phillip. It was uncanny.

Blinking tears onto his face, Adagio pulls a folded piece of paper from his back pocket. It is a letter he found inside his grandmother's journal along with two keys. She had given the book to him the day before she passed away. Tearfully opening the journal on the day of her funeral, Adagio had been surprised when the envelope fell from between the pages. It was addressed to him. A fresh tear stain appears on the paper as he unfolds it and again reads his dear *nonna's* final words to him.

My Dearest Young Adagio,

By now I am most likely gone from this earth, but I am never far away from you. I know you are hurting just as your grandfather is. I'm so sorry to cause you pain and would have spared you from it if I could. But the pain will one day fade and healing will come.

Since the day you were born, you have always been my light and my joy, and your grandfather's as well. And even though I will not be there to watch you find love and raise your own children, I will be watching from afar. You are probably thinking, "Yeah, right, Nonna. I'll never find anyone like you and will probably die a lonely old man." And don't try to deny it because I know you.

This part again draws a wide smile from him. She really did know him well.

Now, I know you recognize the keys and there is no need to tell you what they are for. When your grandfather and I pondered what to do with the old house in the states, the answer quickly came to us. No one understands the importance of the house and how much it means to us more than you. You and your grandfather share the same heart, which is why you could always read me so well.

So, this is what I would like you to do. Pack your things and move to Salt Lake. The move will be painful for your parents and they will miss you greatly, but you will not be gone long. This is a necessary step because your life won't truly start until you are where you belong. Remember what your grandfather told you about looking for love and finding it in God's time. Well, my dear boy, it looks like your life up to this point has mirrored his. And as surely as he found the love of his life, you will, too. I have a good feeling about this, and you know your nonna is never wrong, right? Shake your head.

Chuckling, Adagio shakes his head no.

Adagio, I love you more than I can say, and I always will. I am proud of the man you have become. Now, go live your life, and be happy. Remember, I will never be far away.

Love,

Nonna

P.S. Remember to take the ring. You remember where it is, right?

Yes, Nonna, I remember. He pulls her emerald engagement ring from the front pocket of his jeans, pondering the story behind it. It was given to his grandfather by his own mother to give to his future wife. His grandfather had taken it everywhere he went, never guessing he would eventually be placing it on the finger of the woman who had become his best friend.

And now it is my turn.

Refolding the letter, Adagio puts it back in his pocket and wipes his eyes. He looks at the headstone one last time. "I love you, *Nonna,* and you, *Nonno,*" he whispers. "And I will try to make you both proud." He smiles, then slips his sunglasses back on and walks away, charting a course toward his new life.

About the Author

Jewel Adams has written inspirational books in different genres and has over forty published works. She is a motivational speaker to both youth and adult audiences. In her spare time (when she has any) you can find her curled up with a good book and a healthy stash of orange Tic Tacs.

Jewel and her husband, Sean, and the parents of eight and are grandparents with an ever-growing posterity. She counts herself very blessed. She resides in Utah.

Email Jewel at jewela40@gmail.com

Website: thelegacysaga.weebly.com

Website: jeweladams.com

Blog: http://to-overcome-andbecome.blogspot.com

And be sure to check out her Amazon page.